Not Without Love

Not Without Love

MEMOIRS

Constance Webb

DARTMOUTH COLLEGE

Published by University Press of New England
Hanover and London

Dartmouth College

Published by University Press of New England, 37 Lafayette St., Lebanon, NH 03766

© 2003 by Constance Webb

Printed in the United States of America

5   4   3   2   1

Library of Congress Cataloging-in-Publication Data

Webb, Constance.
Not without love : memoirs / Constance Webb.
  p.   cm.
ISBN 1–58465–301–9 (cloth : alk. paper)
1.   Webb, Constance. 2.   James, C. L. R. (Cyril Lionel Robert),
1901—Marriage. 3.   Women biographers—United States—Diaries.
4.   Women political activists—United States—Diaries. 5.   Actresses—United
States—Diaries. 6.   Models (Persons)—United States—Diaries.
7.   Influence (Literary, artistic, etc.) 8.   United States—Intellectual
life—20th century.   I. Title.
CT275.W35214A3 2003
813'.52—dc22   2003016964

For

Edward W. Pearlstien

1928—2001

Acknowledgments

Thanks to Todd Crawshaw, Anna Grimshaw, and Leslie Zimmerman, who read the manuscript and cheered me on; to Hazel Rowley, who offered helpful advice; to Nils Nadeau, whose diligent copy editing and suggestions for additions and deletions improved the manuscript considerably; to Eric Bergman, Mary Bieber, Natalie Ely, and Janet Webb, whose loving concern helped me through the worst year of my life; and to Dorrie and Robert Barbagelata and my friends at The Alhambra, who were always there when I needed them. And special thanks to my editor, John W. Landrigan and his colleagues, for their enthusiasm, patience, and advice during the various stages of production.

Not Without Love

1

My father nearly killed my two older brothers; the youngest escaped his violence. He was only three and a half years old. I only witnessed one of the attacks. We were seated at the dining table ready to eat on a Saturday night. Father had been drinking because he did not have to work the next day. When he drank, he changed completely. It may have been an allergic reaction. Normally very white-skinned with blue veins showing in his wrists, he turned a red, almost purple color, and his face became swollen. When this happened all of us kept very quiet and tried to stay out of his sight. We were eating in the dinette attached to the kitchen since the dining room was reserved for Sunday dinners or when we had company. The room was long and narrow, with the appliances and sink at the far end. Mother was at the sink getting something ready and there had apparently been an argument we children had not heard. Mother was always hiding Father's liquor, but he managed to find it. Whatever the reason, Father spoke sharply to her and for the first time Mother replied instead of keeping quiet. Father got up and went to the end of the room and began to choke her. I cried or screamed, I don't remember which, and this startled my baby brother. Donald, my fifteen-year-old brother, jumped up, patted my shoulder, and said it's okay, I'll take care of it. He went over to pull Father away from Mother. Father reached behind him to the sink and grabbed an ice pick and raised it toward Donald's neck. Mother tore the pick from his hand and threw it across the room. The pick flew over our heads and clattered to a stop against the baseboard at the end of the kitchen. Then a fight began. Donald's side of the fight was to try to protect himself. He would not strike his Father. Father fought like a crazed person, which he was, filled with liquor. They fought through two rooms, ending up in the bathroom with my brother on the floor. He was turning blue because Father had tightened his necktie enough to strangle him. My sister, Decima, who lived next door, came running in, pushed my father out of the room, knelt on the floor, and undid the necktie. She massaged Donald's neck, sobbing all the while, and he began to breathe in choking gasps. Color returned to his face. I was hanging at the bathroom door watching, because although scared to death I still had to see everything. After a few minutes Donald was able to get up off the floor and my sister took him to her house. Years later I learned that almost every Saturday night she spent the early part of the evening in her bathroom, which was on the side next to our house, with her head out the window listening for any violent sounds. Her husband, Bill, complained that he rarely had a decent dinner on weekends because of her anxieties. He never came over during such fights because he said it was not his place to interfere in family business.

The second violent fight I did not see; Mother told me about it. This time it was between my oldest brother, George, and Father. The outcome was that George had an injured back that lasted the rest of his life. Mother said Father had bent him backward over the end of a brass bedstead until she thought his back would break. Both Donald and George left home at an early age—around fifteen years. We did not hear from Donald for over a year until he wrote from Hawaii. He had worked his way on a ship to get as far from home as he could. He never lived at home again, although he visited, always managing never to arrive on a Saturday night.

When I began this memoir I wanted to borrow a title from my friend, the late Chester Himes: *My Life of Absurdity.* But after nearing completion of a stage in my life, in which I was devoted to a radical group's ideology, I realized that the title did not encompass my experiences. The only absurd part is that for so many years I was a *know it all;* I had all the answers. I believed I knew what was right or best for everyone. And I was quite ready to force my circumscribed ideas on anyone. It's absurd, too, that I held such ideas for so many years. No one has the answers for anyone else. Only each person has answers for her- or himself and no one has the right to dictate to another. We must make our own decisions and live with the results. To reach this point of view is heroic. Not that I am a heroine, but I have waged a heroic struggle to reach where I am today. So where am I now? Some people might say I'm still a revolutionary, which isn't quite accurate. Of course, if people en masse—especially blacks—revolt against the way they are forced to live, then I am with them. But I am against all *isms;* they only cloud one's vision. Well, then, someone might ask: Do you support your government? Yes, I certainly do, when it concerns itself with education, welfare, medical care, affordable housing, an increase in the minimum wage, the protection of the environment—and everything else that benefits the average citizen. But I do not support actions by my government that harm human beings anywhere in the world.

There is the notion that when one grows older the past is what becomes important and sometimes obsessive. But since I am both an optimist and a worrier my mind dwells always on the future. That is where my worries reside. Another of Himes's titles might have been *The Quality of Hurt,* but I don't feel hurt by these early experiences. The feeling is more one of astonishment and, yes, that sense of absurdity. I am thinking now of more important pains, past, present, but I hope not into the future. These pains are the faces that some people are forced to wear just to survive. Someone once asked whether my associations and friendships with C. L. R. James, Richard Wright, Chester Himes, and Ralph Ellison were because they were luminaries. How little such questioners understand. In very few areas were these men recognized as anything but black. When Wright and I took our many walks he was a black man with a white woman. We had to don faces of indifference or pretend not to see the anger, the curiosity, and the hatred around us. C. L. R. James and I never touched each other when we were in all-white neighborhoods, especially when there were police in the vicinity who could arrest us just because we were together. Only in Harlem or parts of the Bronx was it safe for C. L. R. to say, Hook on and extend his arm for me to hold. One afternoon when I was visiting Wright, he was grumbling about having to take a trip to Brooklyn for a haircut. In my ignorance I asked, "Why don't you go down the street—there are several barber shops in the Village?" I've never forgotten the look on his face or his answer, "Yes, and get my throat cut? I just lay down in that white man's chair and he would put that razor across my throat and tell me, 'Nigger, get the hell out of here.'"

I was born into a puritanical household. My mother, Minerva Reynolds Webb, was a Calvinist by upbringing as well as inclination. She was extremely reserved, with a back as straight as an ironing board. Character is a word seldom used these days, but it is an important one. And that's what Mother had, character. She expected everyone else to have the same virtues and did not have much use for those who did not. Even though I was going with the son of a religious man, a Congregationalist minister, she did not approve. Norman Henderson and his brother, Wally, were radicals. Only misfits were thought to be radicals or even liberals in Fresno during the thirties. And I'm not sure there has been very much of a change in sixty-five years. The newsletters I receive from Fresno High School classmates indicate the thinking of right-wing conservatives.

My father, George Detwyler Webb, on the other hand, was of a passionate nature that was suppressed, probably because of mother's strictures. They did have six children, however, one of whom, Louis, died in infancy from the measles. The three remaining, born in Atlanta, Georgia, were Decima, George, and Donald. I was born in California, as was the youngest, my brother Roy. In physical appearance the eldest were very different from Roy and me. They were dark, while we were fair. Something must have happened to Father's genes in the transfer from the south to the north.

As soon as the family moved from Atlanta to Fresno, Father stopped going to church. We had a car, but his excuse was that his denomination was too far away for him to attend. He spent his Sundays either hunting or fishing, depending on the season. He was an expert in both sports and we regularly had venison, rabbit, quail, and other game birds, as well as every type of fish. He also played the piano and the mandolin, but late at night after Mother was in bed.

Mother did not nag; in fact she sometimes kept too quiet. It used to enrage Father because she would never argue or answer back. When he disagreed with her about anything, she listened until he stopped, exasperated, and then said a word or two, very softly. He would sweep his hand in the air as if trying to brush away a stinging insect. But worst of all, Mother would wear a slight smile and begin to whistle just under her breath, almost soundlessly. The whistling might go on for an hour or even for days, depending on how angry Father had been. He usually picked up a book and went out to sit in the garden. I think he knew that it was useless to discuss anything disagreeable with Mother. Poor lonely man. There was not a lot of joy or laughter in our home. Too much levity brought a frown or a shake of the head from Mother. As a result, for most of my life I felt guilty whenever I enjoyed myself.

There were good times, of course. These centered on occasional picnics when we would drive to a river and find a pleasant spot under the trees where Mother would spread out a blanket. The water in the rivers and even the irrigation ditches was so pure that it was almost crystalline. In the rivers one could see fish swimming way below the surface. We often swam in the ditches that were nearer our home. At the river, Father would take his fishing gear and go upstream while we children, well out of his way, would swim and splash about until we were called to have lunch. Lunch often consisted of deviled eggs, which we were not allowed to say—*stuffed eggs* was mother's preference—fried chicken, potato salad, crisp stalks of celery and cucumber, oranges, peaches, plums, and iced tea. We never had Cokes or other such drinks, they weren't considered healthy. Other good times included being read to by my parents and mother's patient instruction of Bible verses. I became so adept that I won a leatherbound Bible in Sunday school for reciting without error a long passage in the Old Testament. Mother was especially proud of this accomplishment.

My parents were not cruel or unusual. I grew up during the days when "spare the rod and spoil the child," was followed religiously and socially. It was preached from the pulpit and parents were admonished in articles and books to discipline their children by spanking and whipping. Even teachers in schools were permitted corporal punishment when children were unruly. A few times I had my hand whacked with a ruler by a teacher or the principal. Today, many parents are afraid to use any physical discipline lest they be accused of child abuse, and I'm not sure that children are better behaved; in fact when I see their rampant rudeness and lack of concern for others, I think a spanking might have helped in their education. My father would strike out in anger and something like outrage. He would grab anything handy, a board, a stick, the cord to the iron, and give me a couple of whacks on the bottom or legs. Mother was more deliberate. She took her time. Often I was sent out to the garden to pick my means of punishment from the peach tree. If the switches were smooth instead of knobby, Mother would send me back for better weapons. She then concentrated on striking my legs, sometimes until they bled. Donald, who was seven years older, was punished more often than I was. He usually yelled but sometimes he would bite his lower lip and not let out a sound. I did not feel much sympathy, because I knew from an early age that he detested me. He had been the baby of the family for seven years and then I came along. When I grew up Mother told me that when he had to wheel me in my carriage he always rolled me to face the sun. The sun, of course, made me close my eyes and soon I would be asleep. Once she caught him just as he was about to put an ammonia-saturated handkerchief over my face. When Donald was seventeen he forged the names of my parents on the application and joined the Navy. He worked his way up from ordinary seaman to full commander. During World War II, his ship was on the front lines, repairing planes that could be sent back into battle.

My older brother George was an engineer and worked on the great dams, the Boulder and the Grand Coulee. He was a favorite, possibly because he was gone from home before I was really old enough to know much about him. When he did visit he always made a big fuss over me and was demonstrative in showing his love.

My sister, Decima, married when I was about five years old. She married the manager of the Sun Maid Raisin Growers Association, headquartered in Fresno. She had been chosen queen of the Association's festival and he had fallen in love with this eighteen-year-old beauty. They were married quietly in our front parlor. The quiet wedding was probably due to the difference in their ages. She was only eighteen while he was in his thirties. A year and a half later they had a son, but a few years after that they divorced.

My very favorite in the family was my brother Roy, who was the youngest. Mother claimed that I was the one who raised him and she never needed to scold because he was so well behaved. She may have been right, because Father died when I was eleven and she was forced to go to work for the first time in her life, so we could survive. Roy became a Navy pilot, a lieutenant shot down during World War II. He was in the water for days and lost all but three of his crew. He was in bad shape, wounded in the leg and suffering exposure and dehydration, when he was finally picked up by a repair ship. When he reported to the commanding officer, to his astonishment it was our brother Donald. I believe he had a nervous breakdown while he was on the ship because later on Donald hinted, in a mysterious manner, that something terrible had happened to Roy during those days. Since my family believed that any type of nervousness or need for psychiatry was shameful the subject was never mentioned again. Donald told me, "You will have to ask Roy what happened. I will never reveal his secret." Roy, I know, would not go swimming after that wartime experience and would never discuss what had happened. He was a handsome, wonderful man, very family oriented. He was the only one in our family to have this trait. He married and had four daughters, Kristy, Julia, Nancy, and Janet, and one son, Kelly. When his young wife died of cancer he took over the care of their five children. He was fiercely protective of them and loved them without reservation. In fact, I always thought of him as a mother lion protecting cubs.

Roy and I were devoted to each other and after he had enlisted in the Navy he would come home on leave and want me to be his date. In those days, Hollywood Boulevard was a beautiful street, and that's where he always wanted us to go. Mother told me that Roy said everyone stared at me and this made him feel proud. My mother's reactions to anyone complimenting her on my appearance were "beauty is as beauty does," "beauty is only skin deep," and other such homilies. When someone asked her if she wasn't afraid that I'd be kidnapped, she'd say, "They will drop her at the first lamp post." This one is my favorites and seems to show that my mother was creative.

We lived at 326 College Avenue in Fresno in what might be called a bungalow. It had two bedrooms, a service porch, a dining room, a kitchen and a dinette. After years of living in New York I went back to Fresno and saw the house. I couldn't believe it was the same place, it was so small. It had seemed as vast as an empty gymnasium when I was a girl. The dining room had windows that took up an entire wall. Below the windows was a window seat divided into sections that could be opened up. It was in there that my brother and I kept our books and toys. That room was where the family spent its time. The front or living room was opened only when visitors came, which was not often. It was thoroughly cleaned every day nonetheless. The only other points of interest to me were that we had an upright mahogany piano and a record player with a handle that had to be wound before playing a new selection. At one end of the long, narrow kitchen was an oak icebox. The lid lifted up and beneath was a square metal lining in which ice was kept. Ice was delivered every day during the heat of summer and only a few times a week in winter. Underneath the icebox was a pan that had to be emptied every day or else the kitchen flooded. I don't know how the water got from the ice down to the pan without wetting the food. There must have been a tube or some type of drain mechanism. We had an ice pick, carefully kept out of our reach, with which Mother would chip off chunks of ice to put in iced tea. Vegetables that we did not grow in the backyard were purchased from a man with a horse-drawn cart who came past the house twice a week. Milk was also delivered from a cart pulled by a horse. It was in bottles, there were no such things as plastic or cardboard containers. The cream in the bottle was at the top and mother carefully poured it off into a glass to use in coffee or on our fresh fruit for breakfast. The only time mother purchased cream was when she made ice cream. It was the best ice cream one could ever eat, but it was a lot of work to prepare. It had eggs, cream, sugar, and fresh fruit, whatever was in season. There is nothing like the taste of apricots, peaches, or strawberries churned with cream, sugar, and eggs. I usually got to lick the dipper, the blade in the center of the metal container that whipped the mixture into ice cream. The metal container was placed inside something that looked like a small barrel, with metal staves girding its sides. Ice was packed around the container and coarse salt was poured over the ice. Then the mechanism for turning the blade was fastened on securely and buckled onto the sides of the little barrel. After that the labor began. A crank on one side of the contraption had to be turned for ages until the mixture froze into ice cream.

Roy and I used to play under the round oak table in the dining room while our parents sat to one side, both reading. On one side of the room was a glass-fronted bookcase filled with books. The bookcase had a key but it was never locked and we children were free to take any book out to read as long as we handled it carefully. The books that interested me very early were huge, blue-bound volumes depicting the southern way of life and the Civil War. I was delighted with the weight of the volumes and the roughness of the bindings. The paper was heavy, grained, and cream colored, with a trace of gold at the top. There was a second end sheet, then a glossy, stiff page containing a photograph of General Robert E. Lee in the gray uniform of the Confederacy, his semi-round, lined face self-assured, and a sheet of crinkly translucent paper to protect the photograph. There were also gold letters on the title page, which filled me with awe and admiration. The books were filled with photographs, which was probably another reason I liked them. The writer of the books, being a southerner, made heroes of the Ku Klux Klan, and there were many pictures of them riding on horses with the wind blowing their white garments while they stared through black holes in their pointed head and face masks. They were also shown lighting, or standing around, burning crosses. In one picture, a man was shown hanging from a tree with a sign fastened around his neck, but neither Mother nor Father would tell me what the sign said. The mysterious signs may have been one of the reasons that I learned to read at an early age. But I wasn't any wiser when I made out the word "rapist." Again my parents would not explain and it was quite a few years before I knew what it meant. I am not sure when my admiration for the Klan died, so completely that it was as if it had never existed. And it was not until I was years older that I remembered the lynching pictures. Before that, however, I met up with racism quite early, in my preschool days. There was an Armenian family living across the street from us and Marjorie Hagopian became my good friend. We played together every day, but always in our backyard. Mother would not let me go to Marjorie's house and I learned it was because she was *different,* she was an Armenian. Marjorie was different, I agreed—she had very dark brown hair and eyes and her skin was dark as well. But to me the difference did not mean anything and what did being *an Armenian* mean? At five years of age I was merely puzzled by mother's reaction to Marjorie. I did not know about prejudice and bigotry. But the oddness of the situation was filed away somewhere in my brain.

One Sunday there was a rare occasion: friends were coming for dinner. By choice my mother and father were not sociable; Mother had one friend, Aunt Lucy (no relation), and father had one friend, Mr. Valentine. Mr. Valentine was a Frenchman and he and father worked together and often went fishing. But the Valentines had never been invited home until that Sunday. After a mid-day dinner, Mrs. Valentine stayed indoors talking to mother while my father and Mr. Valentine went out to sit in the garden. I was much more interested in hearing what the men had to say and followed them outside. I took a book with me, my usual ploy when I wanted to eavesdrop and not be caught. I would seem to be intent on reading yet all the while I was listening to anything and everything around me. At first the two men talked about fishing methods and tactics and types of fish. Boring. But my ears pricked up when Mr. Valentine asked my father about coming north. What had been his first impressions? Father said he had not known about the Mason-Dixon line, but after he had crossed it a "big, black Nigra" had sat down beside him. Father immediately got up and knocked the man into the aisle. The conductor appeared and to my father's astonishment chided him. "And he was a white man!" father exclaimed. Valentine said, "Well, at least you taught the Nigra a lesson." Both men laughed as if some marvelous feat had been accomplished. It didn't seem funny to me. I knew that father fought with my brothers, but why would he knock down a stranger? And what did the Mason-Dixon line have to do with it? I imagined an actual line drawn in the soil but couldn't make any connection between it and Father's story. Something made me feel that I didn't want to listen to these men talk any more, and I went into the house. And something else drew me to the big blue books in the glassed-in bookcase, which I had not looked at for quite some time. Once again I turned the pages and studied the pictures. Suddenly everything came together— Marjorie, the black man my father attacked, the riders in the night in their white hoods, and the black man hanging from a tree. In some way, I think I grew up at that moment. Cold chills shook me and the tiny hairs on my arms stood on end. Those people riding in the night, with the wind flowing through their white robes, were not heroes, they were evil. The word *evil* was probably beyond my comprehension at such an age. The words I used were probably *bad, bad*. I was still too young to blame myself for ever believing the KKK men were romantic figures. I just knew that my life had changed—and that nothing would ever be quite the same.

No explanations about Marjorie were ever satisfactory and I kept nagging to play in her yard until mother relented. Before she let me go across the street she said I was not to eat anything or go into their house. I was more puzzled than ever and mother was uncomfortable, which I could sense, young as I was. We didn't serve Marjorie anything at our house and she never came inside, so why did food and going indoors seem so important? Later, when offered delightful and unusual bits by Mrs. Hagopian, I ate with gusto. It was there under Marjorie's grape arbor that I had my first taste of stuffed grape leaves, baklava, and a type of gelatin candy made from fruit with powdered sugar on the outside. Mother never knew, of course, and I didn't even feel guilty—because she didn't ask any questions. She assumed that I would be obedient.

2

I joined the Socialist Party when I was about fifteen. Actually, my inclination had been to join the Spartacus Youth, the Trotskyist forerunner of the Young People's Socialist League. However, members of the Trotskyists urged me to wait and join the Socialist Party, which they were soon going to enter. I waited impatiently for our first meeting with the Socialist Party, certain that life was beginning anew because we would be adding about fifteen people to our group of nine. Or, rather, we would be part of their larger group. I believed that we could work together to change the world into a more humane place for women, workers, blacks, Indians, Asians, Filipinos, Mexicans, and all the poor people on earth. And there were many of all of these categories in the beautiful San Joaquin Valley. There were, for example, people on "the wrong side of the tracks." The city was bisected by a railroad track, on one side of which lived the poor whites and other nationalities. Within that area there were careful divisions too, whites living with whites, blacks in one neighborhood, Mexicans in another. Originally there had been many Chinese people, descendants of those brought in to build the railroads, but they were driven out when their labor was no longer needed. Within the white area there were still other divisions: WASPS (white Anglo-Saxon protestants, but mostly of Baptist persuasion), Italians who were Catholics, and a few Armenians, as dark in skin sometimes as the blacks they spurned. My mother and father broke up the engagement of my oldest brother to a beautiful Italian girl from the wrong side of the tracks. I still remember her, but whether this is because of her beauty or her superb spaghetti sauce I can't say. We seldom had spaghetti and meatballs, since potatoes and rice were thought to be more nourishing. They also were more appropriate with the beef, lamb, pork roasts, trout, and game birds that were the mainstay of our diet.

A week before our meeting with the Socialists, the Trotskyists met at the home of Charles and Serena Cornell. Charles, the local leader, attended

Fresno State College, and Serena worked downtown in a doctor's office. Charles later became one of Leon Trotsky's guards in Cuernevaca, Mexico. Serena was probably about nineteen or twenty, but to me she seemed worldly and sophisticated. She had blonde hair, which at that time I did not realize was not her natural color, and she wore it long, pulled into a bun at the nape of her neck. She always wore earrings, which my mother would not allow on me. She had greenish eyes with yellow flecks in them, something like cats' eyes.

Lyle Moore, second in charge to Charles, our leader, and his wife, Dolly, also attended Fresno State College. Dolly was stretched out on a studio couch. When we entered the room, she didn't say anything to me but shifted her legs and patted a space at her side for me to sit. With the other hand, she continued to turn the pages of *Harper's Bazaar.* Both Dolly and Serena were addicted to *Vogue* and *Harper's Bazaar.*

Serena brought in coffee, which I did not drink, but I was too embarrassed to ask for milk instead. The door kept opening and closing as the other members arrived. When everyone was present Charles said, "The meeting will come to order." He and Lyle sat at the oak table while the rest of us crowded on the studio couch, two other chairs, and the floor. Lyle, as the Trotskyist organizer for the San Joaquin Valley, traveled often to San Francisco and Los Angeles, where the headquarters were located. He gave the first speech of the evening. The subject was Germany and its aggression against the smaller countries of Europe and how Hitler had smashed the German working class organizations. He also described the Trotskyist movement in Europe, spoke familiarly of the leaders, and reported that we had received newspapers from France and England published by our comrades in those countries.

Charles made the next speech, the subject of which was the strategy of the Trotskyists' national leadership. The strategy was that all of us were to join the Socialist Party. He said that an approach had already been made to the Socialists on the national level and that their local organization was expecting us. We were not to hold formal meetings of our own, such as the one that evening, but we would maintain a caucus. I had no idea then what the word "caucus" meant; I thought it was probably something Russian. The national leadership said we were to continue our work in the American Student Union on campus, in the migratory workers' area, and wherever else the Socialists decided we would be effective. Charles said that we were to work within the party and influence the younger, less revisionist members. The local Socialist Party's leadership was old, conservative, and would prove reactionary in a serious struggle against capitalism.

I'm not sure how I dared to ask a question, especially when the national office had sent out directives, but it was probably because I was new to the discipline of political organizations and thought I had every right to disagree or at least question a decision. At any rate I asked, "If we win over the progressive elements what do we do with them? Won't this destroy the Socialist Party? What will happen to those people who built up the party and kept it going all these years?"

Norman and Wallace (Wally) Henderson, were sons of the minister of the Congregationalist Church, Dr. Norman Braumage Henderson. Two hands shot up in the air, Wally's and Norman's, but Lyle answered: "The leaders of the Socialist Party are probably the only people who will not swing in our direction. The Socialists are parliamentary reformists and not revolutionaries. There is serious work confronting us. Fascism is growing in the world. In Fresno, both ideologically and practically, the Associated Farmers, who control the valley, represent Fascism. In this work, we need all the forces we can muster to fight their tyranny. We want to get rid of the Farmers Association. The Socialists wish to reform it. But as long as they are in existence and this association controls the means of production, the workers will be starved and tyrannized forever."

Wally could hardly restrain himself, and every time Charles came to the end of a sentence he raised his hand. When he finally got the nod, he jumped up and stood in front of the group but directed his answers to me. His tone was condescending and he rocked slightly on the balls of his feet. This movement made his thighs bulge. He was very proud of his legs and did a lot of exercise to keep them firm.

"You are a new member and you don't clearly understand all of the political factors involved so I want to add a few words to what Comrade Cornell had to say. Simply to pose such questions indicates concretely two things: one, you do not understand the full political implications of our move into the Socialists; and two, such questions could be interpreted as petty bourgeois deviationism."

I did not even know what "petty bourgeois deviation" meant. I think I thought that deviate had some sexual connotation. Whatever it was, I knew it wasn't a nice thing to be or to do in the Party.

Wally had not quite finished. "Of course, as a young and inexperienced comrade, we know that your questioning is innocent. I want to interject at this time, however, that a decision has been made by the Central Committee and the Political Committee that we enter the Socialist Party. Every Local in the country has discussed this decision. We are here tonight discussing *strategy*, not *disputing* national policy. There is no room in this meeting for such questions. All of us must follow Party discipline. If you had been with this organization in the past months, you would have been able to disagree or put forward other political ideas. However, now that a national vote has been taken, you must obey."

I felt embarrassed, but fortunately Lyle interrupted at this point and said he did not believe that I had any intention of disobeying Party discipline and that we should move on to discuss Good and Welfare for the last time as a separate Trotskyist group.

After the meeting Serena signaled to me to join her in the kitchen. From there she led me down the short hallway to the bedroom. Closing the door, she said she wanted to show me something. Serena made all of her own clothes and she was an expert; they were all beautifully designed and tailored. She bought materials with such passion that a large cedar chest in her bedroom was filled to the top with yardage of wool plaids and tweeds, silks, linens, cottons, taffetas, and voiles. Serena opened the chest and took out what appeared to be an entire bolt of white Irish linen. I asked her what she planned to do with so much material. Serena did not answer immediately. Occasionally, she enjoyed seeming mysterious. Taking the bolt of white linen, she unrolled about half a yard and held it under my chin. She brushed my hair back behind my shoulders, narrowed her eyes, and said: "I'll make one for you too." Surprised by this unusual generosity, I said, "One what?" Again, she did not answer, but turned away, tidily folding the white linen into its original creases and placing it back in one corner of the chest. "Wait," she said, "Look at these!" She took a huge box out of the closet, carefully untied the string around the brown wrapping, and removed the lid of the box, almost with reverence. "Aren't they beautiful?" she sighed, and ran her hand over the high polish of a new pair of brown English riding boots. After I admired the boots I asked her why she bought them. She did not ride horses. She very carefully repacked the boots, tied the package with string, and put the box well back in the closet. Then she took my hand, pulled me over to the bed and sat down close to my side. Ducking her head slightly, she whispered in a conspiratorial tone, "These things are for when the revolution comes! There will be rough days ahead for us and we will be so busy that there won't be much time for fussing with ourselves or our clothing. Also, if there's violence, I want to be dressed in pants, if I'm knocked down, for example. But I don't look very good in slacks." She patted her rounded hips.

"So, I'm going to make a really beautiful riding habit. Two of them, one white for summer, and the other gray or tan wool for winter. I may make an extra set, just in case something gets torn or bloody. Then the boots naturally have to go with the riding pants, and besides, they are very comfortable. We may be on our feet marching or fighting or standing for hours at a time. These boots will be easier on the feet than shoes. And besides, out in the agricultural areas the dust is so deep in summer and mud up to your knees in winter, these will be just the thing. Just think, they won't wear out as fast as shoes either."

Serena stopped to take a deep breath. I assumed that whispering for such a long time left her needing oxygen. She continued: "Then after the revolution, conditions may be unsettled for a long time and we won't have money, we'll all be working for Socialism and there may be destruction in the cities. Department stores may be wrecked. After all, if it starts in the camps, it will spread to the factories in the cities. I'll be able to sew my own clothes for years with the material I'm collecting."

$\textit{3}$

The following week, the night of the meeting with the Socialists finally arrived, but before I could leave home mother voiced her disapproval. She said she could not understand why my friends and I were joining the Socialist Party when we did not know the people and seemed not to approve of their ideas. She asked why we did not continue with our own group, if we had to have one. Mother nearly took the side of the Socialists, of whom she disapproved. "It is *their* party, after all, and they have kept it together here in Fresno since 1919. My word, dear, they must all be much too old for you to associate with. Are you going to destroy their party?" I didn't quite accept that it would happen, but that is exactly what was planned by the Trotskyist national leadership.

Norman and Wally picked me up in their tan Dodge sedan. Norman, my boyfriend, was eighteen, a freshman in college, and Wally was twenty-one, a senior at Fresno State College. I slid into the front seat between the boys, and Norman put his arm around my shoulder. Wally looked annoyed at any intimacy on such an important night and said, "Let's get going. Before we get there I want to give you a final political rundown." Although he was driving, he kept turning his head toward us, to be sure that we were listening intently.

"Comrade Max Shachtman has pointed out that the Socialist Party, after the 1936 split in Cleveland, is becoming more revolutionary, while the Communists are moving toward conciliation with President Franklin Roosevelt. The Communist Party's People's Front is a denial of the need for revolution and an independent struggle by the working class. They have let Hitler's and Mussolini's success in Europe frighten them into a toleration of the criminals Cardenas, Blum, Daladier, and eventually Roosevelt. The Communist Party now thinks the People's Front will be the means through which power can be achieved gradually and peacefully and handed over to the workers once the threat of Fascism is overcome . . ."

Wally was on a roll and couldn't be stopped, which was usually the case. "Constance is a very young comrade. If there were a Young People's Socialist League or Young Spartacus group in Fresno, that is what she should be joining. Not the Party itself. That's why these political points must be emphasized."

Fortunately we were at our destination, the home of the Grangers, president and secretary of the Socialist Party. Waiting on the pavement was the rest of our group. Among them were Charles and Serena Cornell and Lyle and Dolly Wood Moore. Dolly's brother, Sam, taught civics at Fresno High School. Hamilton (Ham) Tyler was also there, standing awkwardly to one side. He was the son of a doctor and went to Spain to fight against Franco, where he was almost killed. He came home so malnourished he had to be hospitalized. There were a few other people whose names I do not remember.

The Grangers' home was a white wood bungalow squatting far back on the lot among flowers and vines. The door was open, the entrance shielded by a new, silvery metal screen, and we heard voices as we approached. The house, with its open door to catch any breeze in this hot, dry summer, was ordinary. With my love of drama, I had hoped for something more clandestine. We entered a small hallway and just at the right was a front room filled with people. Charles, as leader of our group, entered the room first, reaching back to take my hand. I was the only one of the Trotskyists who had not met the Socialist members.

Centered in the room was a large armchair in which Mrs. Granger was sitting. Thin black hair grew along her upper lip and reddish black hair, masses of it, was wound in two braids twice around her head. She looked like a drawing composed of circles, with a powerful, rounded, tightly corseted body. Flesh pushed against the top and bottom of her corset, and rolls of fat were outlined by her thin summer dress. From her knees to her ankles her legs were slender and well shaped, and she was wearing stylish high-heeled shoes more suitable for a thin young woman. Just above the knee, her thighs burst forth. I wondered how tight her garters had to be to keep stockings, flesh, and corset from flying apart and scattering throughout the room. After Charles's introduction, Mrs. Granger simply nodded at me and said "Hello, Comrades," to the rest of our group. "Come in and sit down. We're having iced tea." As she spoke she looked back at me and seemed to force a smile. "So this is our *baby* Socialist," she said. Her words made me uncomfortable; I certainly did not consider myself a baby. But her stare was worse. *She hates me* was my immediate reaction. I tried to smile, but it wasn't easy because her eyes were going over my body as if they were hands. I thought that perhaps she didn't think slacks were the proper garb for meetings. My white ducks suddenly felt tight around my bottom and the T-shirt that I wore purposely loose seemed instead to emphasize the shape of my breasts. I wondered if she hated redheads or just young girls.

"And here are the Henderson boys. It's good to see you again." Mrs. Granger was all saccharine cordiality. She stuck out her hand with one thumb raised in the air. Both Norman and Wally reached for the hand, bumping into each other in their haste. I sat down by Dolly and Lyle on the floor and curled my legs under me.

"You got the once-over from the old cat," Dolly whispered. Dolly was a beauty, with dark brown hair and lashes so long that they shadowed her cheeks. She was always remotely kind, but what she loved best was saying things to shock me. When I reacted, it spurred her on. She was the first person I heard say *fuck*. She also called waste by its formal name. Pet expressions were *Frig you!* and Oh, *feces!* Dolly seemed to relish these words and her voice showed her love for them. Later in life, when I had more understanding about people, I realized that there was an easy, unaffected sensuality in all of her actions.

Mrs. Granger cleared her throat loudly. "I think we are ready to start the meeting. We will have roll call first." She stopped when a thin old man came into the room carrying a tray of glasses. "This is my husband, Gerald. He's made us some iced tea." Mrs. Granger sounded apologetic, but whether for her husband or for us I couldn't decide. Gerald did not take his eyes off the tray until he set it upon a side table and began handing out tea. He was a man of medium height with a slight stoop. His hair was dark blonde and clipped very short, similar to the Marine Corps haircuts. He had gray eyes, deeply set, a straight nose, though rather pronounced, and a wide mouth. When he finally looked around the room, there was something mischievous in his smile. "Good evening, Comrades," he said and then went to sit in a corner, very erect in a straight chair.

"This is a funny meeting," I whispered to Lyle, because a spirit of afternoon tea seemed to fill the room. It had heavy plush furniture and antimacassars on each armchair. Wooden folding chairs filled most of the space. Prints framed on the walls depicted landscapes and flowers. There was only one medium-size bookcase and among the volumes I did not see one pamphlet or a book marked Lenin or Marx. Serena, who had sat down next to me on the floor, widened her eyes when she saw me looking at the bookcase. Her comic expression stirred up a feeling of hysterical laughter that I had to force back. Everyone else was wearing business-meeting faces and I suddenly felt guilty and frivolous.

"The meeting will come to order!" Mrs. Granger barked. Bodies and legs shifted and everyone settled down in serious attention. "Now then, I will read the agenda, which is a short one tonight, and then we will see if anyone has anything to add." Her eyes examined all of our faces in a slow-motion swivel of her head.

"First is new business. We will have this on the agenda first tonight rather than last, so that we may formally welcome our new comrades. Then, old business: report by the Social Committee, report by the Literature Agent, finances, and Good and Welfare." She stopped for breath. "Any additions or corrections to the agenda?"

"Dear," Mr. Granger raised his hand. His wife scowled and he amended his words, "Dear Comrade. Inasmuch as this is the preliminary, or I should say first, meeting with our new comrades, I suggest that we dispense with the agenda and simply welcome them, ask whether they wish to speak, and then move into finances to take care of our dues. Then we can adjourn and get acquainted."

Some of the women, who looked like chaperones, rustled and moved about in their chairs like an inarticulate Greek chorus and looked toward Mrs. Granger. And she responded, "The agenda has been read and approved, therefore your comments are out of order and we will move on to the first order of business."

The Greek chorus settled back comfortably in the folding chairs. Just for a moment, it appeared that Mr. Granger would object, but instead he smiled slightly, not at all embarrassed, and reached down to pick up a cat that had come into the room. We all waited while the cat kneaded his leg, then turned around and lay down in his lap. Mrs. Granger frowned at the cat and her husband's stroking hand but turned back to look at her waiting audience.

"Well, then. To new business." Strangely, there was a change in Mrs. Granger's whole appearance. The irritated looks and saccharine smiles all disappeared. Even her face seemed to get thinner as she drew her neck out of her shoulders.

"We, the Socialist Party of the San Joaquin Valley, welcome you young militants into our fold. Our branch received its charter in 1919, and some of us here tonight were at the founding conference. In this traditionally Republican state, with the two-party system merely alternating between right-wing Republicans and progressive Republicans, it has at times been a difficult cause we have chosen. Since 1890, this division between the Republicans has remained fairly constant, emanating from the nineteenth-century fight between the railroad interests and the farming interests. The banks have long since forced these two together, under one umbrella, so to speak, but old hostilities remain, squabbles that erupt over the state vote. The only time the two groups of Republicans have combined is to defeat the Democratic Party, to support the Red Squad, and in labor frame-ups such as that of Tom Mooney."

Mrs. Granger stopped and took a sip of tea. What she had said changed my attitude toward her. She was a real politico. My enthusiasm made me see that she had lovely, luminous eyes. This was a serious woman, never mind what she looked like or how fat she was.

"But we have endured! And we shall prevail! The ideals of Socialism are invincible, and once we are fused with the rising American working class we will create a movement which will march irresistibly to victory, to freedom for all mankind. On the national level, the combining of forces between the Socialist Party and the young Trotskyists will enable us to move into ever more concrete action. Here in our state, supported by our joint press and national leadership, we plan the following work: free Tom Mooney by bringing his case before every citizen of this state and raising money to pay his lawyers. Committees have been working for years in San Diego, San Francisco, Berkeley, Los Angeles, and San Pedro. Our entering this arena will strengthen those groups who have worked so diligently to free this innocent man."

During a parade in San Francisco on July 22, 1916, a bomb exploded at the corner of Steuart and Market, killing ten people and injuring forty. Remnants of the bomb were never found and there was disagreement as to whether it had been sitting in a suitcase on the sidewalk or thrown from a building. The ineptness of the police destroyed any possible evidence. It was not maliciousness on their part, simply stupidity. Two union organizers, Tom Mooney and Warren Billings, were arrested and convicted of the crime. Billings received a life sentence, but Mooney was sentenced to death. This judgment was handed down even when the San Francisco district attorney had in his possession evidence that they were innocent but suppressed it. Government investigators' proof of their innocence, which exposed prejudicial treatment, was not admitted in the trial. President Woodrow Wilson saved Mooney from execution but he spent twenty-three years in San Quentin prison.

Mooney became a union organizer at a dangerous time for such work. When there were strikes, management hired thugs to beat the workers and, in some instances, the state would call out the National Guard. The Guard was not for the protection of the workers but to see that the scabs hired by the factories were escorted safely into the plants. The Guard was also known to attack the striking workers. Those men and women who risked their reputations and sometimes their lives were heroes. Today all of us benefit from their struggles. Unions brought in the five-day week, the eight-hour day, paid overtime, holidays, and vacations. And yet, many middle-class people are still hostile toward unions.

Mooney's involvement in unionization began when he started work at the Blake Pump Works, a foundry in East Cambridge, Massachusetts. The men in the foundry were earning $2.25 a day, after working nine hours. The women in another part of the plant were being paid only $1.10 for ten hours of work. Management decided to shift part of the work from the men over to the women, thus saving $1.15 an hour. Mooney believed that such actions were a threat to both groups in the foundry and organized a protest. He was promptly fired. He found work in other foundries in almost every state in the union. He was laid off for economic reasons, quit, or was fired. He was not well liked by owners or managers of factories because he complained about wage cuts and speed-ups and other inequities. His name soon began to appear on management's black lists. Mooney had to look for work throughout the United States. He said that he had seen all of America from the bumpers of freight trains, as he "rode the rods." He finally arrived in California, where he stayed.

For a brief time, Mooney was a member of the Socialist Party, but he found the actions of the Wobblies more to his liking. The Socialists, he realized, were more interested in politics and the future, while he wanted immediate direct action. Years later Mooney described himself as a militant unionist and a revolutionary Socialist. He was being held in San Quentin Prison at that point.

Mrs. Granger paused again to sip some tea while I waited, almost holding my breath in anticipation of the rest of her speech. "Next, we intend to educate the migratory workers and help them organize against the Associated Farmers here in the valley. We will work with the militant cadres among the workers at the Borden Milk Company and help them form a union.

"We will expose the Stalinists in their counter-revolutionary role here at home, and in their vicious trials in Moscow against the old Bolsheviks who made the Great Russian revolution. The Stalinists have betrayed the working class and they have betrayed our Socialist ideals. Part of our work, through educational meetings, will be to fight this monstrous bureaucratic organization, these betrayers of the cause of freedom."

Her forceful and passionate words made me imagine a devil, Stalin, stabbing workers and his comrades with a pitchfork. I had never met a Communist; in fact I did not know they were a threat in Fresno. It was good to find out how much I had to learn. But Mrs. Granger had not finished her lengthy speech.

"We will fight against the coming war whose prelude we have seen in Spain, Germany, and Italy. In Fresno, and throughout our beautiful valley, and in northern and southern California, we will build a vast pacifist movement. Our great work lies ahead, and the entry of you young people, bright-eyed with revolutionary spirit and fervor, is only the beginning. We do not agree with all of your ideas, but we are not sectarian and invite all Socialists to join our ranks with full rights, obligations, and privileges, including the right to defend their point of view. Together we shall create a common front against the Capitalist machine that is driving the world to war and Fascism."

Is a common front different from a popular front, I wondered? I would have to ask Lyle or Charlie after the meeting.

Mrs. Granger paused for a moment, cleared her throat, looked at our little group, those of us sitting on the floor, and then in a quiet voice said, "Now, Comrades, in the name of the Socialist Party of the San Joaquin Valley, I welcome you with a full heart and the pride of one who has spent her entire life fighting for justice and the cause of humanity."

Everyone was silent for a minute or two while all the Socialists looked at us. Then, suddenly, seemingly spontaneously, they clapped hands. All the faces were smiling. They were applauding us. My eyes filled with tears and I felt proud and humble at the same time.

"Oh, feces," Dolly whispered, and I felt Lyle's foot move behind me to touch his wife's leg in remonstrance.

During the collection of dues I handed over my weekly pledge of twenty-five cents, wishing it were a thousand dollars.

After the meeting, Mr. Granger came across the room.

"Well, my child," he smiled, and I did not feel anger at his use of the diminutive. After all, he seemed so old to me. "How did you enjoy the meeting?"

I told him it was wonderful and that his wife was inspiring and such a moving speaker. He didn't respond and in my own ears my enthusiasm sounded as if I were gushing. But I excused myself by thinking, what else can I say to an old revolutionary who must be as old as my father? At any rate Mr. Granger didn't respond to my enthusiastic outburst. Instead he said, "Do you like cats?"

I was surprised. "No, not more than others, that is, I like all animals, especially my horse, Rags, well, any horse, dogs, and cats. I've never thought about cats, we have dogs, collies—"my voice went on and on as if I could not shut myself up.

"Cats are remarkable animals," Mr. Granger said. "Much more intelligent than dogs. Stubborn, independent, curious, all signs of individuality."

For some stupid reason I began to blush, which happened to me quite often. I could feel the heat in my face. Later, I realized that I felt foolish talking about cats when my comrades were nearby. They would think I was feeble minded. Especially Wally, who would expect me to be talking about the speech and our future work. Most of the people whom I knew among the radicals did not seem to have a sense of humor. In fact, most levity was looked upon with grave suspicion. And Wally was the least humorous person I had met so far.

At my sudden blush, Mr. Granger simply looked at me sympathetically. Then he said, "Well, my dear, we will see you next week. We are, indeed, most happy to have you young people join us in the battle for freedom. And do not be misled, it is a battle and the bourgeois world will not let you alone now that you have joined against it."

Years later, I realized he was trying to prepare me for what did come next: a constant struggle against conservatives, reactionaries, and eventually my own comrades. At the moment I felt tenderness toward Mr. Granger. Even then I realized that it was foolish of me to think that a revolutionary could not discuss cats. Wally and Norman, who were very very serious, intimidated me. But that night, with the Socialist group, I was stirred by Mrs. Granger's speech, felt a little maudlin, and went away thinking that Mr. Granger was a man with strong feelings for humanity. Anyone who loved cats must love people and, ergo, be drawn to Socialism.

The meeting with the Socialists had me at cross-purposes. After all, we had held a meeting earlier in the month to discuss whether to enter the Socialist Party. There had been many informal meetings during study periods, lunchtimes, and after school, when Charles and Lyle came over to Fresno High School to see me. Under their tutelage I was reading *Das Kapital*, the *Communist Manifesto,* and Trotsky's *Permanent Revolution.*

I didn't tell them that I found these books pretty difficult to understand. Charles and Lyle said these were fundamental to an understanding of Trotskyist principles. But it had only been during our last meeting when we talked about joining the Socialists that I actually realized that we meant to *take away* their members. And I had liked what I heard during the meeting and felt they were sincere. Were we being sincere? Also nagging at me a bit was my mother's admonition that the Socialists had been together in Fresno since 1919.

After the meeting with members of the Socialist Party, and our introduction to the group, we decided to have coffee at the home of the Cornells. During the drive, everyone seemed to talk at once. Ham Tyler said, "That was some speech the old girl made tonight, wasn't it?" Norman agreed enthusiastically, but I noticed that Wally was hesitant. My mean thought was that he was saving up his answer for a larger audience. Ham's thin face, with its angular tight jaw and nose that was aquiline and seemed to twitch when he was excited, was alight. For the first time, I noticed what bright eyes he had behind the heavy lenses of his glasses. Usually, his thin face had an appearance of bewildered abstraction. Everyone in our group said he was a real brain.

The Cornells had a small one-bedroom house. A huge elm tree had branches that stretched over the roof and the front walk was covered part of the year with yellow and red droppings. One couldn't call them flowers; they may have been seeds in the shape of small caterpillars. The front room of the house, where we held most of our meetings, had an oak table that filled one whole corner. Whenever we arrived, the table held pads and pencils, neatly laid out and ready for note taking. Bookcases filled the entire back wall of the room. The other walls held prints of the paintings of Diego Rivera, Orozco, and Van Gogh's sunflowers. Most of the homes of Trotskyists had the same artists' prints. When we came in, Lyle and Charlie were in a corner of the room going over some papers. Lyle had a big head and his curly hair made it larger. He wore thick-lensed glasses with horn-rims. Because of the glasses and probably his solemn disposition I thought he was very intellectual.

When we got to the Cornells, a new member, Eugene, was sprawled on the floor. He was leaning back, with his spiky black hair resting against the couch. He was the son of a coal miner, and I thought he looked something like a young John L. Lewis, whom we all admired. Gene was going to Fresno State College on a partial scholarship while his father dug coal to pay for the rest of his tuition. His father was proud that his son was getting an education and would escape the deadly life in the pits. In our circle, Gene was unique and he, I think, flaunted his heritage. He wore Levi's when no one else was wearing such pants. He also wore a blue work shirt, never a tie, and combed his hair with his hands. His skin had little pits of blackheads but I thought he was romantic looking, a poet of the mines, and the only worker any of us knew.

He always teased me, and this evening he said, "Ho, ho, ho. Here's the firebrand. When we man the barricades, we'll pick you up and wave your hair at the Cossacks like a torch. They'll fall back in horror at the sight."

I liked him, not only because he was so different from anyone we knew, but also because he never treated me like an infant. My response to his salute was "Ho, ho, ho, yourself. Who's going to light the torch?"

Everyone laughed except Gene and, strangely, he blushed from his bushy hairline down his neck. Norman had a sickly smile on his face. I asked, "What's the matter? What did I say?" No one answered. Only Serena, passing around coffee, smirked. "You're not for real." Then she turned to the rest of the group and said, "Did you ever see such an innocent in your life? How old did you say you were?"

Charlie told her to leave me alone and for us to get on with our meeting. Charles lit a cigarette and looked at Lyle. "Do you want to begin?" Lyle told him to go ahead but then added, "One point I think we should discuss tonight, because it is too important to delay, is the question of revolutionary discipline." He looked at Dolly, his wife. Everyone was silent. I looked at Dolly too and remembered the snort she had made during the meeting at the Socialists' and Lyle tapping her leg.

"Suppose I take up the theoretical aspects as revealed by the meeting this evening, and then you deal concretely with Party discipline afterwards?" Charles suggested. Lyle nodded and Charles began to speak.

"An enormous historical responsibility has been placed upon our shoulders. With the march toward Fascism in all of Europe, the destruction of the Spanish Revolution, and the steady growth of monopoly Capitalism in the U.S., which is leading inevitably toward a second world war, it has fallen upon we Fourth Internationalists to build a strong, intransigent revolutionary party, forging a definite program, under a banner on an international scale to fight for the masses. The entire working class will not mature under Capitalism. Different layers of the mass mature by stages. We must educate the working class and, at the same time, represent them. I mean this dialectically, our own existence; our own painstaking maturation is a reflection of a stage of development of the American working class. The struggle for the maturation of the working class must begin with a minority, a vanguard. We are that revolutionary vanguard. Our central task at this stage is to penetrate the trade unions and work inside the Socialist Party. We are concentrating our forces on a definite program in order to penetrate the masses with united force."

Charles stopped for a moment and looked around the room. He hadn't finished. "The tactical problems that confront us are greater than they appear. Most of the Socialists we met tonight are centrist: petty-bourgeois revisionists whom we must either win over or, failing this, take over the Party. As a final resort, we may leave the Socialists and take with us those elements among the youth and the few revolutionists and form a separate organization. Fortunately, we have many contacts and it will be our role, in the next period, to persuade them to join the Socialist Party. This will, within a very short period, give us the majority. We will, or rather, our ideas will then prevail over the centrist sentimentality of the Grangers and their clique.

"If what has been said so far is clear to everyone, we can move on to a question and answer period. After that we will take up the question Lyle raised about Party discipline." Although I usually waited until others had asked questions, this time I raised my hand first.

"Comrade Cornell, the points made by Mrs. Granger on the work to be done—aren't these aims the same as ours? How are we different? Also, they all seem devoted and dedicated."

I stopped talking when I saw the stern expression on Charles's face. Also, Wally made an impatient move and then raised his hand. It seemed that every time I asked a question it was the wrong thing for a revolutionary to do. Wally took the floor and faced me.

"Centrists, especially during revolutionary periods, are always able to adopt in words the program of the revolution. But they are incapable of drawing tactical and organizational conclusions from its general conceptions."

Ham's hand went up. "To be more concrete, if I may, Comrade. The experience in Spain is a perfect case in point."

I think nearly everyone in the room held his breath. Ham, more than anyone, knew about Spain. He had volunteered, thin, bespectacled Ham, and fought in all the places we only read about. When he came back to Fresno, he was in the hospital for months, suffering from malnutrition and depression. All his unit had to live on, and fight on, were some jars of marmalade. Violent diarrhea alternated with shots at the Fascists. Guns sent them from Russia were obsolete and usually arrived without ammunition.

Ham could not talk about his experiences and had never mentioned Spain and the civil war against Franco and the Fascists in a meeting. We knew very little about the horrors he had faced. The betrayal and defeat of the Spanish people had dimmed a spirit that he still could not recall in himself.

"The heroism and personal honesty of many members of the POUM [Partido Obrero de Unificacion Marxista, or Workers Party of Marxist Unification] I can attest to. But by a pseudo-left position, the leadership of the POUM betrayed the revolution. They created an illusion that they were a revolutionary party, while at the same time they adapted themselves to every form of reformism. The leadership sought the line of least resistance and began a retrenchment in Catalonia, where anarchists held the leading positions among the workers. And in order not to become enemies of the anarchist workers they did not have a policy of penetration into the National Confederation of Labor, the CNT, and they refused to seriously fight the bourgeoisified leaders. The POUM fraternized with everybody, including the Stalinists and their United Front, instead of conducting its own intransigent revolutionary policy. If they had pursued a revolutionary policy then, at the May 1937 insurrection, they would have been carried on the shoulders of the masses to the forefront. The POUM, despite the heroism of individual members, was a centrist party raised by the wave of revolution. In the end, it stood as much in the way of victory as did the Stalinists and their supporters—the Russian counterrevolutionary bureaucrats."

Ham stopped talking quite abruptly. He looked exhausted. His tall, lanky body seemed caved in at the chest. A film of perspiration covered his forehead and limned his upper lip. His hand, when he lit a cigarette, was trembling.

No one said anything for a few minutes, and after our first look at Ham we all looked elsewhere, not wanting to embarrass him. Lyle then took over the meeting.

"Comrade Tyler has brought up vitally important points in the discussion this evening. We should, I believe, have an educational one night next week, prior to our next meeting with the Socialists. I am aware that henceforth we do not meet as a separate body, but if we simply have an educational without discussing business matters, it should be okay. I think the educational should be devoted to centrism. Then we can be concrete on specific issues and bring our relationship with the Socialist Party out of the realm of generalities and theory."

Lyle glanced around the room. "I don't think we need a formal proposal or vote on this, do you, Comrade Cornell?" Charles shook his head.

Lyle took a handkerchief out of his pocket and wiped his glasses. When he put them back on, he straightened in his chair and looked at each of us in turn. The usual abstracted look in his gray-blue eyes had disappeared. In its place was a keen yet dead opacity, similar to the steely gray that one sees in the eyes of many policemen. I felt a slight chill at the back of my neck and hoped that I hadn't committed some revolutionary sin.

"On the question of revolutionary discipline," Lyle cut each word sharply, "I will be brief. However, it is an extremely important political matter. We are a faction, a small faction, within the Socialist Party. It will take only a short time, I am confident, before we become the majority. But until this has been achieved, our role, our revolutionary duty, is to observe the utmost in self-discipline. Foolish though the Socialists may appear at times, we must control any desire to laugh at or ridicule their ideas. This is not to say that we cannot disagree with their political theory, but we must propose our own policies in such a manner as to win others to the correctness of our line. We will never gain the respect of the rank and file through mockery, only through political reason, self-dedication to revolutionary Socialism, the strict carrying out of party duties, and regular payment of dues. We have hard work ahead—work that we must accomplish within a relatively short period of time. Therefore, let there be no snickering, disgusted sighs, or remarks in meetings." When he finished speaking, Lyle stared straight at his wife, Dolly.

Dolly was looking down at the fingernails of one hand and held her head as if she were indifferent, even somewhat haughty. But her mouth gave her feelings away; there was a faint tremor that she quickly controlled. Poor Dolly. A part of me was hurting from the entreaty shown in her hurt mouth, but another part of me overcame the sympathy. Overcame any sense of human kindness. Obviously, I was becoming a true member of an organization. The organization is always right against the individual. My thoughts were that Lyle was correct. We must behave with impeccable revolutionary dignity. Discipline in a revolutionary organization is vital and Dolly had broken that discipline. An overwhelming sense of virtue filled me and I turned away from Dolly and took the side of the other members. Years later, her face and my betrayal would haunt me.

4

With my comrades I was serious, always trying to live up to their ideals and, naturally, to seem older than my years. But as senior prom night drew near it was hard to stifle my excitement. I had been to after-school dances in high school and to what the radicals call "socials." But the prom was different and very special. Mother had made a dress for the occasion using my design. It was white organdy with a wide ruffle around the shoulders, which were left slightly bare. The skirt was full and had two wide ruffles around the bottom, which made it bouffant. It was a beautiful evening gown, and Norman had sent a corsage of red roses. All in all, I thought I looked special. The day seemed to make only slight moves toward ending, seeming to falter endlessly, but night finally came. By the time Norman arrived, my stomach felt queasy. This was the senior prom, and I was the youngest senior.

Norman wore a white Palm Beach suit, which I had never seen. He looked handsome with his light brown hair and eyes only slightly darker. Although his Scandinavian heritage marked most of his features, his nose was shaped like some of the fine Italian noses, narrow at the bridge and nostrils, rather long and thin. He had long eyelashes that almost touched his cheekbones. That night he seemed like a perfect suitor, if only he hadn't been so serious. I wanted to laugh and dance, be admired, and forget politics just for once. Here I was dating a college freshman and going to my high school prom, so I made a decision not to have any serious discussions that evening.

At Fresno High School light sprayed from every side of the huge gymnasium, and we could hear the sounds of the orchestra members tuning instruments from a block away. There was a moon, of course, since it was June, and stars shining as they used to do before smog and gas pollution. In the gym we went down the receiving line, shaking hands with teachers who, it seemed, had put on new manners along with their party clothes.

The gymnasium was transformed. Twisted ropes of crepe paper streamed from the ceiling, balloons on strings bobbed with every opening of the door. There were huge pots of flowers all around the floor. The chaperones were lined up in a row, watching us as we danced. Most of them were rather plump. Now and then one woman leaned over to whisper to another at her side and the opening and closing mouth looked like a duck quacking. Norman said that our friends—Charles, Serena, Lyle, and Wally— would be there about eleven. Well, we at least had a few hours to enjoy ourselves. My joy didn't last very long, however. Norman said, "We'll meet them at the back entrance and then we'll take a ride to the river." A ride to the river meant we'd be talking politics again, over and over.

I didn't answer, which was just as well, because if I had shown any displeasure Norman would not have understood and probably would have been annoyed. In the middle of the dance we heard "Cut, please," and Bill Barieau smiled at me. Bill had been my first date when I started high school, and we were still good friends.

"How did you get in here?" Norman didn't smile. Bill was a college freshman, and unless college men had dates who were graduating from high school they were not allowed to attend prom night. Bill shrugged and put out his hand to me and Norman was forced to let me go. He wasn't pleased and stalked off the floor. I noticed that he sat down near the chaperones and kept his eyes on us.

Bill and I had gone steady briefly, before he went to Europe as a U.S. representative at a Boy Scout gathering. He was an Eagle Scout. I always thought of him as "before Socialism," when I was just a silly child, going horseback riding, skating, and swimming. Bill and I started to dance and he held me tighter than Norman ever did, but I presumed it was because he was French. He was a superb dancer and for a minute I was wistful, wishing he were a Socialist instead of a Capitalist. I immediately felt guilty. It seemed lately that I was always feeling guilt over something. But despite my devotion to Socialism, I didn't want to leave my senior prom and drive out to the river, much as I admired and respected my comrades.

Bill and I were doing the lindy and having a great time, but before we finished Norman cut in. We danced for awhile and then Norman said, "Let's have some punch," and pulled me off the dance floor. I think he was afraid that Bill would cut in again, because he wasn't dancing, just watching us from the sidelines. Norman poured a paper cup of punch for both of us and we walked to a corner that held clumps of flowers and gave us a little privacy. Norman put his hand on my neck and gently caressed it. He gazed into space while his fingers began to knead the back of my neck.

"You know what I read yesterday?" I was feeling romantic and ready to listen to what I thought would be about us, especially when he was rubbing my neck. Norman looked at me very lovingly before speaking. "Lenin had such a passion for Beethoven that he would not listen to any of his music. He felt that it weakened his revolutionary determination. You know, I can understand something like that, can't you?"

I agreed because I was devoted to Lenin and very taken by his face—the Tartar eyes, broad flat cheeks with small indentations, strong rounded chin, beautiful mouth molded like Greek sculpture. I even liked his name: Vladimir Illyich Lenin.

"Let's dance," I said to Norman when I was certain that he had said all he wanted to say about Lenin. But Norman decided that he had to go out and see if the comrades had arrived. I wanted to go with him, but he said no, he'd be right back. After he hurried away I felt abandoned and wondered if everyone dancing would think I couldn't get someone to dance with me. I hated being left alone in front of people. I thought of Bill again—he would never leave me alone. Even when we were at a drive-in and he leaned out of his convertible to talk to friends, some electricity, like a circuit that never disconnected, made me feel he was with me, that I was the first in his mind, in his life, in fact. Just as I was getting ready to follow Norman out the back way he came through the double doors and signaled by nodding his head. He had a very serious look on his face so I thought, of course, that something political was worrying him. At least his eyebrow was not raised as it was in anger; he just looked preoccupied. I decided not to ask him what he and the comrades had talked about; that would show him that I was self-disciplined, a good comrade. When I reached Norman he grabbed my hand like an owner reclaiming property.

"It's early yet and the comrades want to take a drive. They're waiting outside." Norman's hand felt a little clammy, and he held mine tight as if I were a horse that might run back to the stable.

Charles, Serena, and Wally were sitting in the front seat of a car just in front of the H-shaped building where I had taken zoology lessons. As we got into the back seat, Charles held his hand back over his head to shake my hand and started up the engine. Everyone looked so serious that I wondered what had happened. Only Serena was smiling and her eyes were shining like a cat's when one takes a picture with a flash. I felt very uneasy. We drove across Home Street, swung left around the center parkway, and headed out Van Ness Boulevard toward the Fig Gardens. Still no one spoke as we passed the rows of fig trees that lined the road. Only a few houses were lighted along the way. Norman kept crossing and uncrossing his legs, and Wally, who was sitting in front, tapped the back of the seat with one hand. At the very end of Van Ness was the river, overhung by bluffs.

Since no one was talking, I began to hum "When they Begin the Be-guine," but Wally drowned me out with his deep voice. "Norman said we had some important things to discuss," I said, hoping for an answer to rid me of the lonely feeling their manner gave me. Serena giggled, "*You, honey bun,*" I thought she said, but I couldn't be sure. Nevertheless, it worried me. I was to be the agenda? Maybe they didn't want me to be a member after all. Maybe they think I'm too young. Tears came to my eyes and I kept my face turned away, staring out into the trees, which lighted as our car passed by. Maybe the Socialist Party didn't want me and my friends were going to break the bad news?

We reached the river, turned right onto a rutted dirt road and bumped over gravel to the edge of the bluff. The moon was shining, lighting up the river ringed by trees. At night the river looked mysterious while in the day-time it was just a rather narrow greenish stream. The water was unpolluted and we often went swimming and fishing up and down its length. "Let's get out the blanket and sit on the grass," Serena suggested. Her voice had the tone of her husband's when he called a meeting to order.

"I'd better not get grass stains on my dress," I answered.

Charles said, "You look lovely." But Wallace kept quiet. I thought it was because he did not have a steady girlfriend. He always seemed disapprov-ing when anyone complimented me.

Norman lifted me over the gravel at the side of the car while Charles and Serena spread the blanket like a cloth for a sacrificial dinner. Serena sat down first, stretched out her legs, and pulled up a grass stalk to chew on. Charles told her to stop, that the grass was dirty. But Serena chewed on the stem and just smiled at her husband. The blue of the blanket was faded to white by the moon. There was a slight breeze stirring the trees, but the hair at the back of my neck was damp. A threadlike nausea came into my throat and slid down to my stomach.

After we were seated, Wally cleared his throat, but Charles spoke first. "This is by way of being an informal meeting. Nothing compels you, Con-stance (it was serious when he didn't call me *Connie,* which I hated any-way), to remain. If, for you, it appears out of order then you are free to leave and wait in the car."

Of course, nothing would make me leave. But I began to tremble, es-pecially my legs. What on earth?

"We are your comrades, both yours and Norman's, and we have only goodwill, as you know, toward both of you. The problem is, or rather, the one that arises, is that you are very inexperienced."

"But I can learn, I'm studying Marx's *Das Kapital* every night after my homework" was my breathless defense.

Charles held up his hand like a priest giving a blessing. "We do not question your revolutionary devotion, Constance."

I felt very strange. What was worse, I felt as if I were among strangers. The river-reflected moonlight shone on the trees, which ominously bushed around us like some creeping beasts. Charles seemed strange and the tone of his voice drove me into myself so that my thoughts resisted the sense of the phrases. With my anxiety increasing, I forced my mind to gather in his direction so that what he was saying would make sense. How long had he been talking? I had no idea; I had been out of it, maybe afraid of what he was going to say about our politics and how it concerned me in particular. ". . . that we have such confidence in you, such hope for and concern for your future development." Charles was praising me?

"Eventually, you and Norman may go through the legal formality of marriage. But that is merely a piece of paper forced upon us by a bankrupt society, by family, by employers, by the government, the church, and all the offices of bureaucracy. When a man and a woman love one another and live together they are married in the eyes of the Movement."

My legs started trembling again.

Wally had been quiet as long as he could bear it, and during a pause at the end of Charles's sentence, he leaped in, swinging his voice around us like some rattling circus toy. "This is the reality, Constance: you and Norman, and especially you, are too young to marry or live together. Both of you have years of college ahead. But to wait all those years because of some misplaced bourgeois conception about virginity in marriage would be fraudulent. It would be a form of dishonesty, as a matter of fact. Sex is a part of our lives and to close it out is harmful. We are working to become better all-rounded human beings as revolutionaries. Neither you nor he will be able to concentrate on the most important aspect of your lives—the creation of a Leninist-Trotskyist Party—if either of you is sexually deprived. Another point, it would actually be physically harmful for Norman . . ."

5

The meeting at the river on prom night was a shock. I knew nothing about sex; the subject had never been discussed in my home. My mother and father were not demonstrative and I never saw so much as a kiss on the cheek or an embrace between them. Roy and I were only kissed on the cheek, never on the mouth. Mother cautioned that kissing on the mouth spread germs.

My first reaction that night when I got home was anger; nothing in my life had prepared me for such an act, if it was to be done. All that I had been taught at home (which was very little), in church, in school, by friends, was that sex accompanied marriage. It did not come before. Girls, in the code among friends, were divided into categories. Nice girls, the good girls, necked. This meant kissing and fondling of the face and neck. Hugging or embracing was permitted, which brought one's body into contact with a boy's, but it could not be prolonged. Fast girls, some of whom overlapped into the category of nice girls because of wealth or position, allowed only their steadies to fondle their breasts. Bad girls allowed boys to touch them everywhere. I did not know any girls who belonged on the final list, those who *went all the way*. It was a realm that my upbringing and school associates had not, even in thought, allowed me to go near. Mothers, of course, disapproved of every category including the first. I did not need to wonder what my own mother would say if she knew my thoughts or the conflict that had been presented by my comrades. I would not tell her anyway, just as there were many of my thoughts and actions she knew nothing about. But this was different. This, in some way, would be a lie. Why and how? I could not find an answer.

My anger didn't last. After a few days I began to make excuses for my comrades. I couldn't stay angry with people whom I admired and had, so to speak, cast my lot with. I must have felt, though, that I had made sacrifices for what we called the movement. So I couldn't possibly continue to be angry. But my brain kept up a continuous chatter until finally I decided to forget what had happened.

I did, however, avoid seeing Norman the following week. He called every day suggesting that we go swimming or for rides in the country. I told him that I had to help my mother make strawberry jam. And, in fact, I did help a little, sitting with her at the kitchen table and carefully pulling off the stems and the tiny green scallops around the top. Mother's jam was delicious and a recipe of her own. Instead of boiling the berries, she put them in trays, all sugared, covered with cheese cloth, and let the sun cook them. The Fresno heat often reached 110 degrees, and when the sun shone on the berries a delicious scent filled the air. Most of the time, however, I spent reading or roller-skating.

Toward the end of the week, I had just completed one of my laps around the block, crossing College Avenue heading back from Van Ness, when I saw Mother on the front porch. Seeing an audience I began to show off, jumping in my skates and twirling. When I reached our walkway I braked my speed, turned and stopped about half an inch from the porch. "I am the best skater, boys or girls, in Fresno," I boasted. With one strap loosened I kicked my foot out of the metal toe clamp and the skate slid away down the path, then headed toward the lawn and stopped in the grass. Mother said, "You have company, Constance." She was wearing her agreeable company face, which meant that she did not like whomever was visiting. Before I could answer, the screen door opened and Serena stepped out onto the porch. Even in the heat of that summer day, she looked cool and mature. She was wearing a pale green linen dress and beige high-heeled sandals, and she posed in the doorway like a model.

There were grass stains on my white shorts and my face was probably perspired and my hands dirty from taking off the skates. I put up my hand and pulled off the rubber band holding the hair away from my face. My shirt was sticking to my back and my legs were damp.

"Serena and I have been having a little chat," mother said, sensing my discomfiture. To myself I said, "I'll bet!" Mother knew what I was thinking and looked away, across the street. Mother hated lies even for courteous reasons, and she hated for me to see her in a lie. Serena was not a person that mother would ever have a pleasant chat with. A list of obstacles to any sort of friendship was greater than an Olympic hurdle track. Serena had not finished high school. Serena had no family. Who were her grandparents? Probably second-generation Polish peasants. She worked instead of going to college. She was too old to want my friendship, and she was married. What does a woman her age want from a fifteen-year-old child?

Serena closed the screen door behind her and suggested that we go for a ride. When she glanced at mother, she smiled a false, bright, closed-mouth facsimile. She had apparently gotten mother's permission, because mother nodded. "Wonderful, I'll go in and change," I said, even though I didn't fancy going out with Serena alone even if she was a comrade. Serena said, "Oh, you look fine just as you are." What a lie. Mother intervened and for once I was grateful when she told me to put on a dress. There was Serena with her hair combed beautifully, in her immaculate linen, suggesting that I go for a ride, sweaty and stained. But that was Serena. She was always willing to look good to the disadvantage of anyone else.

In and out of the shower in five minutes, I brushed my hair while the terry cloth robe finished drying me off. Johnson's baby powder first, then panties, brassiere, and a white tennis dress. With a turquoise scarf, I tied back my hair and stuck my feet into white thong sandals. When I banged out of the house, Serena looked me over. "I wish I could dress so fast," she said and looked down at herself. I felt over-healthy, unformed in some way by her look and the tone of her voice.

Serena was a fairly good driver and she pulled the Ford neatly away from the curb and headed toward Fresno State College. College Avenue ran directly into the college at its end. Serena suggested that we drive out to the river, saying it should be nice and cool there. The last place I wanted to go was the river because of our meeting there on Saturday night. But I kept my mouth shut even though I knew suddenly that Serena was following "orders." Charles had suggested that Serena and I might want to talk. I did not want to talk to her. I had to force down my rising panic, or it might have been anxiety, they are not dissimilar. I made myself sit very quietly and made my face into a bland, agreeable mask.

On the bluff by the river, Serena stopped the car and I turned the handle of the door, ready to jump out. "Oh, let's sit in the car, shall we? It's cool enough and I don't want to mess up my new sandals. Like 'em?" Serena held up her leg as if preening herself. I felt spiteful. Her legs were too heavy for such thin straps. I told her they were very nice. Serena lit a cigarette, adjusted her head against the back of the seat and blew smoke out the window. One hand slid up and down the steering wheel, back and forth.

"Sex is terrific," she said, without looking at me. "Honest, when a man touches your breast, kisses the nipples, or even pinches a little bit, it gives you a warm tingle between the legs. It's hard to describe, it's a hot tingly feeling, and you get wet . . ."

Oh, God. My thoughts rebelled. I couldn't stand what she was saying or her slippery sounding voice. A creepy sensation moved over me and it made me feel dirty. I stared out the window in the other direction from Serena and took a deep breath. I felt asthmatic, with no air in my chest. I sighed and Serena giggled: "That's how you sigh when a man pushes his thing into your poonie."

Poonie! I couldn't look at her. What a word. Mother was right, she is common, even if she is a revolutionist. Why doesn't she say the real word if she has to talk at all? *Poonie,* and *thing!* I sighed again even while trying to stifle my reactions. She made sex sound like something awful. She pretended she was talking about herself, but I knew she meant Norman and me. I had to say something and not let her know how repulsive she seemed to me. "Oh, Serena, I'm too young, I couldn't. It frightens me. And what if I got pregnant?"

Serena said, "Listen, baby," and her emphasis on *baby* made the word sound like *idiot.* "Norman will wear something, a rubber." I think I became hysterical at that point because I had a mental image of Norman donning a rubber raincoat. "A *rubber?* A rubber what?" I started to laugh, gasping between spasms so that I wouldn't burst into tears.

"Hasn't your ma told you anything at all?" Serena was shocked.

No, mother never talked about such things. She was a lady. But I remembered a terrible day when I came home after riding my horse, Rags. I had found blood in the crotch of my white breeches and thought something had broken inside me. That's the only time mother talked about bodily functions until the day of my wedding a few years later.

"Well, silly, a rubber is something a man puts over his thing so you don't get sperm in you, so of course you don't get pregnant," Serena explained. I tried to veer away from these, to me, lurid details and asked whether she thought it was right and shouldn't we wait until we married to have sex.

"Charles and I didn't wait," Serena confided. "It is unhealthy for a man especially, when you're necking and all. It makes you nervous and it makes a man impossible. Edgy all the time. He can't think of anything else and, besides, he has to have it. If you don't do it, he might go to a prostitute, then you could get a disease and your children would be born blind. Or he might play with himself. That's very bad for a man. It can drive him out of his mind, even make him feeble-minded."

Serena's catalog of dangers sounded ridiculous. I had been reading medical books for years. I may not have known the reality, but I did know the medical terminology. The whole world would be full of feeble-minded people if masturbation caused brain damage. Since I had nothing else to say, Serena felt that I had been won over to the idea of sex with Norman. She started the car. "You'll see, you'll feel like a real woman after," she promised.

The week following Serena's visit seemed to be dedicated to get-Constance-into-bed-with-Norman. Wally and Norman came over every night, presumably to discuss politics and aid in my education but always ending up in a discussion of sex. Wally was so interested in our welfare that I was glad to be on the front porch. If there had been a bed nearby I began to feel that he would thrust us between the sheets and sit on the edge to explain each step. Years later, Wally became mayor of Fresno, and if he brought as much passion to that office as he did to my future sex life he must have been a success. I don't know because by then I was far away, living in New York, but that's a later story.

Sex began to be intricately related to politics and I was losing my way. One Fresno night instead of sitting in the porch swing at home we drove around in the Fig Gardens. Fresno skies at night were typical of the desert. No matter how hot it was in the daytime, at night it became cool and the stars sharpened and glittered. We talked and talked and talked politics, the three of us feeling connected to the entire universe. There was meaning in our lives and just like born-again Christians, or most radicals we were passionate about our faith. This night we were discussing crime, with Wally leading off as usual.

"We Marxists don't insist that all crimes are economic in nature."

"Is a broken home a cause of crime?" I asked.

"That's a good point," Norman said, "but a broken home is a manifestation of decay in capitalist culture. It is prevalent among those who live in ghettos, who can't find jobs . . ."

Then Wally interrupted, "If we look at crime objectively, from a historical perspective, then the increase in crime rates is a symbol of the breakdown of Capitalism, a precursor of rebellion."

"Remember Bernard Wolfe's article in the *New International?*" Norman was enthusiastic. "He pointed out something of extreme significance. And that is that there was a lot of public sympathy for John Dillinger. That means, he said, that most people don't see any real difference between the gangsters and the Rockefellers."

"Crime and revolution are part of the same turmoil and both, the increase of both, spells doom for this bureaucratic society." Wally's voice lowered and slowed on the word *society*. "That is still another reason for you and Norman to live freely, *now,* because as society further disintegrates and vigilantes rise as they have here in Fresno and the whole valley, we will be fighting for the revolutionary overthrow of the system. It will require all of our concentration. As part of the revolutionary vanguard we will be leading, teaching, working twelve hours a day, seven days a week. There will not be time for personal interests . . ." Wally's voice vibrated with a depth that I thought beautiful. For my part, I would do anything for the revolution and work days and nights if it were needed. The only part I didn't like in Wally's statement was, once again, the sex issue. But after he spoke we did feel bound together, our shoulders touching and a shared feeling of being useful and inevitably able to make a change for the better in the world, for everyone. Naïve, yes, but not selfish or preoccupied to the exclusion of others. Well, it was all about the Party, and we did exclude people whom we called the bourgeoisie.

Norman and Wally dropped me off exactly at my weeknight curfew hour, ten o'clock. Norman and I had arranged to go to a movie at the Kinema Theater on Saturday night and I wanted to be sure by being home on time that mother would not keep me in as punishment.

Saturday came too soon. I had an uneasy feeling that the reason Wally was not going to the theater with us was that he expected us to either talk about or have sex. In just these few weeks it seemed that life had become too complex. Politics seemed to be linked with sex. My comrades made me feel that it was my revolutionary duty to the Party and to Norman's wellbeing to lose my virginity. The paradox of comrade and boyfriend who was to become lover kept me from emotional detachment. Thinking back, the best word to describe what I felt then is anguished. I've always ended up debating between what I think life ought to be and what it actually is. And as always happens, each time is the worst time. I've always been a worrier. It does not matter how many times I speak sternly to myself and say STOP. I just go on worrying and this before anything ever happens.

We went to the Kinema Theater, which was in downtown Fresno, to see a double feature. Norman bought loge seats, which were arranged for privacy. The seats were in twos or fours, just above the level of the main audience. During the film Norman tickled the palm of my hand with his fingers. I hated it. Serena had explained that it was sexually stimulating. To me, it just felt itchy, but each time I pulled my hand away Norman would catch it again.

After the first film Norman, who sat on the outside, got to his feet and said, "Let's go." He went on ahead without waiting for me and I was forced to follow even though I wanted to see the next movie. Walking to the car, Norman looked up at the sky and said, "Look at that moon!" From his tone, a sort of pride in his voice, one would believe that he had invented it for the night. When we reached the car Norman pulled me into the middle of the seat and kissed me. When he put his hand on my throat, I pulled away, which angered him. He wanted to know what the matter was. He sounded so cross that I was near tears.

As we pulled away from the downtown area the streetlights were still shining. Norman turned toward Van Ness Boulevard but crossed Olive, where we usually had hamburgers and milkshakes at the Olive Inn. Norman didn't stop and I looked back to see if any friends were there. I really wanted to be in Bill's car, laughing, calling back and forth, and eating the inn's delicious hamburgers. But Norman had other ideas so we drove to the river and parked the car. A lot of other cars were already parked on the bluff, but they were somewhat distant from each other, for privacy. One car had music playing but appeared empty. I wasn't so dumb that I thought no one was in the car.

By this time I was trembling with nervousness. Norman told me to get in the back seat and was already climbing over the divider. When I didn't immediately respond Norman pulled at my arm so that I had to turn and slide into the back seat. My thoughts kept repeating, "what am I doing here?" I felt dumb, blind, deaf, and helpless. Norman lay across the back seat and pulled me toward him. One hand held the back of my head while he kissed me and fumbled for the zipper of my dress.

I was smothering. Tremors went from my throat to my feet and I stiffened, trying to move into a sitting position. Norman thrust his tongue against my clenched teeth. My mouth felt all wet and I couldn't breathe. All the while he was saying he loved me, that I drove him crazy, that he couldn't stand to be away from me . . . He sounded hysterical to me. I did not recognize his voice. He was suddenly a stranger, a complete stranger mauling me and I was trapped. I arched my back away from him but that brought our pelvises together. A hard-feeling mass hurt the bone of my pelvis. Norman and his hands seemed to be everywhere. He kissed me so hard again that I thought I would choke to death. Norman's face felt hot and I thought he was suddenly out of his mind. He pulled at the zipper of his pants and said, "See how much I want you?" Some giant thing was standing erect. I had never seen a penis before, except my baby brother's, which was a wee thing.

Norman jerked me forward onto the seat and was immediately on top of me. He kept thrusting at my clenched legs near the crotch of my panties. He was gasping and moving faster and faster, his penis striking my locked thighs. Finally, wet spurted all over my legs and trickled up to my stomach. An acrid odor filled the air and something slimy ran down my legs. Norman took out his handkerchief and daubed at me clumsily. Then he got out of the car, zipping his trousers. Without looking back at me, he said that we had better get going.

I groped my way to the front seat. On the drive home, Norman cleared his throat and coughed; several times he ran his hand through his hair. My mouth felt wet and bruised. To hide what I was doing I stared out the passenger window and rubbed my hand against my lips. Waves of disgust kept lapping at my throat and I swallowed hard to keep from vomiting. Norman told me to comb my hair, but I couldn't look at myself.

Norman put his hand on my knee. "Darling, it will be better next time, trust me. Have confidence. I needed you so much. It was too quick. We are married now in our own eyes, in the eyes of our comrades, and in the eyes of the Party." He sounded reverent when he said *Party*.

I shivered. If this was marriage and sex I didn't want it. A prison, it was slavery; an unending servitude to violence and wetness and smells, to back seats and beds. Something in me felt broken, although my hymen was still intact.

I've often wondered why many women cry at weddings. Perhaps it isn't joy at seeing two people unite. Maybe they are crying in anticipation of what a virgin bride will experience on her wedding night. Of course, these days, there are not many virgins around.

I entered Fresno State College when I was sixteen and found the new environment, only a few blocks from Fresno High School, much more to my liking. Sixteen made me the youngest in the class. I had skipped a grade in junior high school and another in high school. My precocity was partially attributable to a prodigious memory. I didn't study as much as my classmates, except just before a test. Then I crammed for hours and would usually receive A's or B's. Since I wanted to become a doctor my subjects were anatomy, psychology, advanced zoology, physiology, and chemistry. Lab work took four hours once a week. I had a passionate interest in such subjects, especially the lab work. One of my interests as a child had been drawing and painting, and lab work required detailed sketches of various microbes and bacteria. Entering college was satisfying in ways mother knew nothing about. At last I was spending the days in the same buildings as my comrades. We met between classes and often had lunch together. We did not see much of Charles and Serena since she worked downtown. But regularly Norman, Wally, Dolly, Lyle, and I sat on the grass and amid shouts, laughter, and Coke-drinking students the five of us plotted the strategy of the American revolution. We joined the American Student Union and soon dominated the small organization. We called most of the members revisionists, because we wanted to take over the administration and they wanted merely to reform it. The revisionists fought against us on specific issues while we pointed out incessantly that only by changing the entire structure of the college could anything real be accomplished. We blanketed the campus with leaflets every week, thus alienating the ground-cleaning crews to whom we paid no attention. Our membership tripled and our vitality drew the attention of the large Trotskyist groups in San Francisco and Los Angeles. We were soon visited regularly by leaders traveling between the two cities. Our meetings with these men were private;

members of the Socialist Party were not invited. In fact, we did not tell them of these visits.

In October I was elected secretary/treasurer by the Socialists. My vocabulary had grown glib and an instinctive comprehension of Marxism coupled with my youthful enthusiasm thrust me toward leadership. What I did not realize, of course, was the role Charles and Lyle had played, first in educating me (superficially), and then in quietly playing up my energies to the Socialist leaders. The Trotskyists from north and south approved because they thought I looked so innocent that people's fears about Reds and revolution would be assuaged.

With World War II approaching the subject in meetings began to revolve around our role. The U.S. was dominated by isolationist groups who wanted no part in a war in Europe. The Socialists, whose leader was Norman Thomas, were moving from a pacifist stance toward support of the U.S. against Germany if war should come. We Trotskyists were opposed to the war. News did not reach the U.S. about the death camps and the rounding up of Jews, Gypsies, the disabled, and the mentally disturbed until the early 1940s. Trotskyists declared that all wars are imperialist wars and as Socialists it was our duty to refuse to support any government, including our own. The Socialists argued that in a democracy we at least had certain freedoms, the most important one being that we could organize and attempt to change society.

Meetings gradually became a shambles. With such fierce debates it became clear that both sides were heading for a split. Glen Tremble, a Socialist Party leader from Oakland, came down to Fresno to support his compatriots. Glen was a thin, nervous, dark-haired man, who it was whispered had been a minister before joining the Socialists. He was a persuasive speaker and if I had not been so indoctrinated I might have been swayed by his arguments. As it was, I simply closed my ears and mind during parts of his speeches. I spent those intervals watching our recruits to see how they were reacting and at the same time sifted from Glen's rhetoric the parts against which we would argue.

The Trotskyists, not to be outdone, sent in one of their people from the Bay Area, Bill Gannon. Gannon had been a worker and a union organizer, somewhat of a rarity in the party except for a few seamen in San Pedro, whom we had never met. He was not as polished a speaker as Tremble but the logic of his arguments—particularly since we were in agreement— riveted us to our seats, almost holding our breath in fear that we would miss a word. After the meeting, Gannon went back to the Cornells' house, where he was staying, and we joined him. He informed us that James P. Cannon, the leader of all the Trotskyists, would be speaking in Oakland the following week and all of us should attend.

James Patrick Cannon was the son of Irish working-class parents who lived in Rosedale, Kansas. He joined the Socialist Party in 1908 when he was only eighteen and later joined the Industrial Workers of the World when he turned twenty-one. In the Socialist Party, Cannon was a member of the left wing and after the Russian Revolution he joined the Communist Party in 1919. Still a young man, he was elected to the Central Committee in 1920. He also served on the Presidium of the Communist International in Moscow and headed the International Labor Defense. At the Sixth World Congress of the Comintern in 1928 he was won over by Trotsky. Later that same year Cannon was expelled from the Communist Party and formed an anti-Stalinist organization, the Communist League of America. In 1938 he founded the Socialist Workers Party with Martin Abern and Max Shachtman and later that year participated in the birth of the Fourth International at a conference held in France. Also in France, Cannon was nominated and elected to the International Executive Committee. The formative years of the SWP were catastrophic times, with massive unemployment throughout the U.S. as a result of the Great Depression, which had begun ten years earlier.

Cannon believed in Marxism until the day he died. His entire life was devoted to attempting to create a better, more human and equal life for the working class and the poor. Although later I disagreed with him politically, I've always respected Cannon and his wife, Rose Karsner. They were people of substance and devotion to a dream for which they were ready to sacrifice their own wellbeing. On July 15, 1941, the federal grand jury indicted twenty-nine members of the SWP and of the Minneapolis Teamsters Local 544. Before the indictment, there had been FBI raids on the St. Paul and Minneapolis headquarters of the SWP. Acting Attorney Francis Biddle justified the raids by quoting from the antiwar sections of the Declaration of Principles adopted by the 1938 convention of the SWP. However, one of Franklin Roosevelt's strategists pointed out that with sentiment against the war so widespread, to persecute an antiwar party would gain the SWP sympathizers and probably support. Therefore the indictment was drawn up citing the party for urging, counseling, and persuading workers and farmers "that the Government of the United States was imperialistic." Cannon, in 1943, was sent to Sandstone penitentiary in Minnesota to serve eighteen months.

Our small group, now calling itself a *caucus,* did not inform the Socialist Party members about the trip to Oakland to hear Jim Cannon speak. Feeling somewhat like conspirators, we left Fresno early in the morning, while it was still dark. The drive was uneventful and since we were filled with excitement and anticipation the time went swiftly. We only slowed down going over the Grapevine, a mountainous and winding route rising past Bakersfield on the way to the Bay Area. Fortunately we arrived early enough to find seats, sitting together near the front of the auditorium. The place filled up rapidly with people coming from many parts of California and as far away as Seattle. Someone said that even Harry Bridges was in the audience but we did not see him.

When the meeting began, Cannon was sitting to one side and back from the podium. There was a milk bottle next to his chair, which we expected. He had been suffering from severe ulcer attacks off and on for several years. Party gossip had it that he liked his whiskey and was not about to give it up because of an ache in the belly. True or not, it made him seem more human. After the introduction Cannon rose and approached the podium. He was a big Irishman, tall and well filled out, with a ruddy face and wavy hair beginning to recede, leaving an expanse of forehead. His mouth was not very full, about medium, but it was wide. His ears were neatly shaped and about the right size for his head. His nose was straight except that it turned up slightly at the end. Under his chin the flesh had begun to sag and jowls revealed his age, along with the gray hair. All in all he looked like someone's genial father except for the firmness of his lips and the steadiness of his eyes behind rimless glasses.

Cannon began his speech by pointing out that in certain respects the situation at the onset of war in Europe had parallels with World War I. I don't remember the details or the parallels but the gist of the presentation was that ours was an international movement, we were for world revolution, and it fell on our shoulders to build a Leninist revolutionary party that would fight against the destructive status quo that was convincing workers to support the war. Members of the party who were in trade unions needed to fight to protect the unions, defend the right to strike, and convince workers that the coming war did not give the Capitalists the right to roll back the gains made by the workers during their union recruitment and drives in the 1930s. Cannon also spoke about the members' position

45

in regard to the draft. Pacifists were refusing to serve, but he said that such a position would keep us from contact with young workers who were recruited or joined of their own accord. Cannon pointed out that within the army Party members could struggle for workers' control over the armed forces. Being part of the army would also provide an opportunity to educate the worker soldiers and lead them into the Party.

Back in Fresno we settled down to our individual routines. I was busy with politics but spent a lot of time studying as well. I was taking all the science courses offered at Fresno State College. It was a heavy load. A certain amount of time had to be spent with the American Student Union, the most liberal organization on campus. Most important were weekly meetings of the Socialist Party. Then in between we had educationals. At one of our meetings, the situation in the migratory workers' camps was the topic for discussion.

Fresno was almost centered in the fertile San Joaquin Valley, the heart of a great agricultural empire. Ranches were as large as small counties. Someone described them as being marked off by horizons rather than fence posts. In 1936, the California Packing Corporation, which employed about 35,000 men and women migratory workers, saw its preferred and common stock estimated at $2,059,256. Such a sum does not seem so large today, when government bandies about billions and trillions of dollars. But in the 1930s it was a small fortune. Of course the migratory workers did not reap any benefits, although it was their labor that produced such a number. Their wages were estimated at a top sum of $375 a year. Malnutrition, rickets in the children, and scurvy were common among the workers and their families.

There had been very heavy rain most of the winter and the camps were flooded. Many people were stranded, locked behind barbed wire by the grape growers and unable to get food or medical supplies. The shacks in which the people lived had dirt floors and very often there were not any closures on doors or windows. It was decided that we, the Socialists, must get into the camps and take food and give whatever nursing care we could. After some lengthy discussions I was assigned the task. At first I felt proud, feeling that my comrades had confidence in me, a fairly new member of the organization. However, I asked Charlie and Lyle after the meeting, "Why me?" Charlie explained that since I was a premed student and knew a lot about sterilization and the human body, it was an ideal assignment. He also added that I looked bourgeois and the Associated Farmers might be lulled into inactivity by my appearance.

Lyle's approach was different. He said, "In addition, you will bring back reports on conditions in the camps to help us organize the workers. You are hypersensitive to people and, in this case, that makes you a perfect choice for the job. Neither Charles nor I can go because the Associated Farmers have a dossier on both of us. They would not let us get anywhere near the camps."

After these explanations, both men looked at me and, of course, I said that I would accept the assignment. How could I refuse, even if I had wanted to do so? What "Party discipline" meant had begun to sink into my head.

Charlie then gave me a history of the valley and the role of the Associated Farmers. In the fall of 1933 more than 15,000 cotton pickers went on strike in the San Joaquin Valley, followed a few months later by migratory workers' strikes in the Imperial Valley south of Fresno. Farm workers began forming groups in an attempt to better their conditions in other parts of the valley. Wages for pickers and migratory workers ranged from twelve cents an hour to seventy-five cents a day. Other changes happening in California that gave encouragement to the farm workers included the formation by Harry Bridges of a strong union of the longshoremen; Oklahoma ranchers who were used to independence flooding the state after fleeing from the seared and wind-blown dust bowl; and radical movements such as the campaign of the author and idealist Upton Sinclair, who was running for governor. There was also the Townsend Plan, proposed by Dr. Townsend, a physician in Long Beach, that would have given older people a pension of $200 a month.

It was in this atmosphere of change that the Associated Farmers was incorporated in 1934. The chairman was S. Parker Frisselle of Fresno, a director of the California Chamber of Commerce. Frisselle had been the manager of a 5,000-acre ranch near Fresno, an active leader in the Agricultural Labor Bureau of the San Joaquin Valley, and a director of Kern Sunset Oil Company. The executive secretary was Guernsey Fraser, an American Legion official who was known for attacking anything or anyone liberal by calling them Communists. Also a leader in the initiation of the organization was R. N. Wilson, also a member of the State Chamber of Commerce. These men were the controlling members of the Associated Farmers, through which they organized vigilante groups in the valley. The organization consisted of a group of vineyard owners who pledged to help one another in cases of emergency. Emergency, of course, meant any attempt by the migratory workers to organize. Although the leadership gave

lip service to the welfare of farmers, its main goal was to resist unionization, which they said was fomented in the farming areas by Communists as
a definite part of Moscow's program to change the form of government in
California. The financial contributors to the Associated Farmers were the
Southern Pacific, Santa Fe, and Union Pacific railroads, the Bank of America, and the Pacific Gas and Electric Company. It was also supported whole-
heartedly by the State Chamber of Commerce, which announced that farm
laborers who demanded more pay and a union such as that of the longshoremen had to be countered through aggressive action if business was
to survive.

The idea was that Associated Farmers was to be a so-called voluntary organization and offer special deputy services to the local sheriffs if a strike
should occur. Both Frisselle and Wilson, as members of the State Farm Bureau and the State Chamber of Commerce, used their political positions
and money to appoint a representative to go from county to county presumably to explain the organization's purposes but really to recruit members. In only one year, over thirty counties formed affiliated farmer groups
and a convention was held in Fresno for the purpose of creating a statewide
organization.

The organizational set up was that each farmer paid one dollar per year
as dues, and one dollar for each thousand dollars he spent in wages. Since
many members were big land owners, the amount garnered for their trea-
sury was considerable. And every member, large and small, pledged that in
the event of trouble—that is, a strike—he would appear at the local sheriff's
office and be deputized. Frisselle and Wilson made up the rules. Each man
was to be armed alike. They would carry a pick handle at least twenty
inches or more in length. Some of the farmers preferred to carry guns, but
initially this was discouraged. As the organization grew, an office was established in San Francisco and files were kept on migratory workers who
showed any independence or were suspected of sympathy toward joining
or organizing a union. Photographs were taken of such men and a card file
was set up. In some cases, the farmers sent around shabbily dressed photographers who were ostensibly earning a living by taking pictures. These
photographers took front face and profile pictures, like prisoners in jails.

Strikes continued throughout the valley but one of the largest was in
1936 in Salinas, where most of the country's lettuce is grown. Colonel Walter E. Garrison, then the Associated Farmers' president, organized against
the workers. Peace officers in and around Salinas were advised by promi-
nent Associated Farmers who took rooms in a downtown hotel. They in

turn mobilized the men in town to defend law and order. Associated Farmers were named special deputies. Vigilantes marched against the Central Labor Council.

The Associated Farmers had (and have) so much influence with the governor, the mayors, and the rest of the corrupt state apparatus that at one time the State Bureau of Criminal Investigation loaned its own investigators to ferret out troublemakers in the camps. The association put out a regular bulletin, the *California Reaper,* and one member visited Germany during the Nazis' rise and then wrote an article for the paper. Hitler, he claimed in the article, had done more for democracy than any man in history.

The people in this organization were not only antistrike and antiunion but the worst kind of racists. Frances Perkins, the secretary of labor, issued a statement repudiating a throw-away leaflet that the Associated Farmers distributed in which they called her a Jew.

The organization also sponsored and organized meetings for Reverend Martin Luther Thomas, who was the Los Angeles head of the Christian American Crusade. He was notorious for his frenzies against Jews, Negroes, and Socialists.

The Associated Farmers movement became so strong it managed to force through antipicketing legislation in every rural county. Some of its members bragged about what they called its "greatest coup": during the earthquake in southern California in March 1938, Associated Farmers pushed through emergency disaster ordinances that enabled it to take over the valley during any time of crisis. With this ordinance on the state books, the leaders of the organization instructed the County Counsel in Los Angeles to draft legislation that would permit counties to spend funds erecting concentration camps for use during major disasters. Thus they had a governmental apparatus for a constitutional Fascism.

Several camps were built, one near Salinas, another near Fowler, complete with barbed wire and a substantial fence with corner towers for armed guards. The Associated Farmers group was able to mobilize approximately 1,500 men for deputy duty within only six hours during the Salinas migratory workers' strike.

One of the landowners then decided that he wanted his own private concentration camp. He built one with a huge moat around one of his orchards and had armed guards in towers at the corners holding machine guns on mountings. All roads leading to the ranch were blocked with wire and surrounded by dikes of water.

During the strike, some of the hotheads in the Associated Farmers burned crosses outside the workers' camps. Their slogan was "We'll teach these workers to work, or else!" And during the Sonoma strike, members of the organization included the main banker, the mayor, the head of the welfare bureau, several motor police, a member of the state legislature, several hundred American Legionnaires, and the president of the local chamber of commerce. They grabbed two American Federation of Labor organizers, dragged them through the streets, forced them to kiss the American flag, then kicked, beat, and tarred and feathered them. Other supporters drove around shooting indiscriminately through the shacks of the migratory workers. This behavior was not punished, instead receiving open public support. Only the *United Press* questioned it, in an article claiming that the vigilante terror in the valley was frightening away workers so that there were not enough pickers to save the crops.

The Party decided that two Mexican-American sympathizers (anyone who showed interest in Socialist ideals was called either a sympathizer or a contact) would accompany me on daily trips to the camps around Fresno. One man, Florencio, was to act as guide, and the other, Manuel, would drive the ten-ton truck in which we would carry food, medical supplies, and clothing. We had unexpected help from Norman's father, Dr. Henderson, as well as from Dr. Peabody, president of Fresno State College, and A. G. Robinson, head of a chain of California department stores. These three men had recently formed a committee to investigate the conditions in the camps and had won the support of other ministers, educators, and a few businessmen throughout the state. Charles, Lyle, and I met with this committee to ask for their support. A rare, heavy rainstorm had brought flash floods down the valley and it was on the basis of the suffering people that we approached the committee. No mention was made of Socialism or of our affiliation with the Party, although Dr. Henderson was aware of our wider aims. If Dr. Peabody or A. G. Robinson suspected political affiliation, they ignored it. The crisis in the camps was extreme, and we were asking for very little. We persuaded the committee to bring its influence to bear on the mayor of Fresno to deputize me as a nurse who would take food, clothing, and medical supplies out to the migratory workers. The committee was successful in its efforts, and I was put on the city payroll with wages of $1 per year and given city authority to visit all of the camps in the valley. Dr. Henderson's committee paid a minimum salary to Florencio and Manuel. The committee also helped us collect additional supplies.

7

On a Saturday before my first trip to the camps, after meeting with Florencio and Manuel to supervise the loading of a ten-ton truck, I drove to the Cornells' home. My sister had loaned me her convertible, and I felt very dashing driving with the top down. I couldn't compete with my sister, of course; she used to drive about wearing a chiffon scarf that blew back over her shoulder. People used to stare when she passed, because there was a sense of the dramatic in everything she did. It wasn't only that she was stunning to look at; Decima had a type of magnetism. She simply attracted people wherever she went.

The reason for my trip to the Cornells' that day was to take lessons from Serena on how to use a hypodermic needle. In the camps I would probably have to give injections against various illnesses. Serena, as a doctor's assistant, was skilled in what might be called this medical art. She was also able to get medical equipment for us at a discount through her doctor's suppliers.

Charles came dashing out of the house just as I pulled into the driveway, and as soon as the car stopped he whispered: "Minna is here! The Communists have gotten wind of our plans. Don't say anything. Let me do the talking and give you the lead. Okay? Be careful. She's in a state!"

Minna, Charles's sister, was a slender woman with high cheekbones and a small pointed chin. Her eyes were so large they made her appear gaunt. She was pacing the floor when we came through the front door. She didn't wait for an introduction but snapped at us, "What were you doing out there? Caucusing, hmm?"

"Now, Minna," Charles was patient, "let's discuss your views and ours rationally. Okay? But first, let's have some fresh coffee. Connie, will you go help Serena with the coffee? Thanks."

I hated to leave the room because I didn't want to miss a single word, but Charles had spoken and he was our leader so I had to obey.

Minna was awesome, a legend in the valley before she was thirty years old. At eighteen, small and vividly beautiful, she had been part of the first drive by the American Federation of Labor (AFL) to organize unions among agricultural workers in the valley. The drive failed because of dissension in the AFL. The leadership was hostile to the idea of spending energy and money to organize workers whose work demanded a continual shifting from place to place. A union leader from San Francisco and spokesman for the state issued a release to the newspapers claiming that only fanatics or nuts were willing to live in shacks and tents and get their heads broken in the interest of migratory workers. "They never appreciate anything anyway" was the spokesman's classic statement.

Minna, who considered herself one of those fanatics ready to live with the workers, was bitter in her disillusionment with the AFL. But she was not disillusioned about doing work to save the women, children, and men who followed the crops, season after season. She joined the Communist Party, and in San Francisco she met with the organizers of the Trade Union Unity League, which was preparing a drive to consolidate the migratory workers into an industrial union. In the Imperial Valley, she worked to establish the Agricultural Workers Industrial League (AWIL) and set up an office in Brawley. Her efforts and dreams began to be realized as hundreds of workers joined the AWIL. Never before had farm workers been organized on such a scale. "They are men," Minna said, "and now they know they are men and not animals."

Because of Minna's activities and the response of the workers, a gigantic rage and some fear pushed the Associated Farmers into action. They formed vigilante committees, picked up their pickaxe handles, and smashed the AWIL office, killing one organizer and beating others. Hundreds of workers were arrested and held in jail, with bond fixed at $40,000 each. The organizers who were arrested were sent to prison, charged with a violation of California's Criminal Syndicalism law. Minna escaped to San Francisco hidden under a pile of lettuce. The Associated Farmers had wanted Minna in particular, saying she was "a nigger-lover, a Mex and Okie lover, and Red." But the migratory workers were determined to save Minna, and they did. When the Associated Farmers found that she had escaped the valley, they thought they had won. But Minna announced, "We've only begun. The effect of the attack was to cripple the union, but the workers have gained a sense of solidarity and some experience in organization. We will win next time."

Two years later, the Communist Party opened a drive to form the Cannery and Agricultural Workers Industrial Union (CAWIU), because Minna had convinced the leadership that there would be greater strength in the inclusion of cannery workers, who were an integral part of processing crops. A small group of organizers came into the valley with Minna at their head. Party strategy was to follow the spontaneous strikes that had begun to occur and form unions. Every worker was to be included in the organization: men, women, and children. Children were included because many who worked the crops were under fifteen. The objectives posted by the union were 75 cents an hour for skilled labor, an eight-hour day with time-and-a-half for overtime, equal pay for women, the abolition of child labor, and decent homes with sanitary conditions. The growers had been paying an average daily wage of 56 cents, and entire families of ten, all working, were averaging less than $5.00 a day at the peak of the season.

Strikes erupted with such rapidity and over such a wide area that it was obvious they could not have been started by Minna or the still-small CAWIU. But the Associated Farmers were convinced that Minna and her friends were responsible and should be gotten rid of by whatever means necessary.

A general strike of pea pickers was followed by cherry pickers in Mountain View and Sunnyvale and over one thousand people stopped work. Minna was chosen by the pickers to present their demands to the growers. At the ranch where the negotiating committee was to meet, the Associated Farmers groups prepared to greet her. When Minna arrived, men hidden in the trees jumped down on her and beat her until she was unconscious. All her ribs were smashed and her nose was broken, and a concussion of the brain kept her hospitalized for many months. The attack against Minna, and its particular brutality, enraged the pickers, who continued their strike until they forced the price per thirty-pound hamper of peas up from ten cents to seventeen cents.

When the grapes were ready for harvest, over six thousand pickers went on strike in Fresno, followed by workers in Lodi, a few miles distant. A frothing madness, similar to a mad dog's obliviousness, infected the growers there; led by the Associated Farmers, night-riding vigilantes gathered under the leadership of Colonel Walter Garrison. The workers in the valley called Garrison "the Fuhrer." Masked men in cars indiscriminately kidnapped pickers and, together with the thousands who were arrested, they were penned into large, open-air fields surrounded by barbed wire and guarded by the vigilantes and German police dogs. Just when the Associated Farmers believed that Garrison had the valley under control, the strike spread again and more than twenty thousand pickers stopped work. The entire San Joaquin Valley was affected and the union set up patrols for protection and picketing. Picketing extended across the valley for 116 miles. I don't believe that even Caesar Chavez, with all his accomplishments, received so much support.

Minna, out of the hospital, her scalp showing striations of scar tissue when the wind parted her hair, set up a camp community on the outskirts of Cocoran with the only other organizers, three men. Streets were laid out, guards were established at the entrances, and a committee of workers was set up to govern. Particular attention was paid to sanitary conditions so that city authorities could not close it based on medical grounds. Workers in other parts of the valley set up other offices. It appeared that at last the migratory workers would be victorious in establishing a union, but the power of the growers was too great. They chose twelve noon in Pixley to ambush workers meeting in their union hall. As the workers left the building it was riddled by bullets, and the workers were all shot down. The Associated Farmers struck at the same hour in Arvin, a nearby community, and most of the strike leaders were murdered. But the strike continued. Finally, the National Guard was called in at Hanford and Visalia and together with the local police and vigilantes rounded up the strikers. Over three thousand men, women, and children were herded into a ten-acre field, which lay barren in the intense valley sun. Raids continued throughout the valley until the American Civil Liberties Union (ACLU) intervened and obtained an injunction in the U.S. District Court at San Diego to prevent interference with the workers or their meetings. Immediately after the ACLU lawyer had won the injunction, he was kidnapped from his hotel in El Centro, driven into the desert, and left there without food or water. Then, the combined forces of police, sheriffs, state highway patrolmen, and vigilantes working under the guidance of the Associated Farmers, systematically raided workers' camps throughout the valley. They burned the camps to the ground and drove women, men, and children before them.

Minna was injured again when she ran into a burning tent to rescue a baby. When they pulled her out, her hair and clothing were in flames and the baby in her arms had been asphyxiated. Minna was eventually arrested in Sacramento, where she had gone to recover, and with eighteen other workers was sentenced to prison for criminal syndicalism.

The day I met her at the Cornells', she had been back in the valley for some time, organizing relief for the workers whose tents and shacks had been flooded, along with the crops upon which their wages, and lives, depended. I was not happy helping Serena make coffee in the kitchen when such a famous person was talking in the other room. I stood as near to the kitchen doorway as I could and eavesdropped. Minna was angry and arguing with her brother.

"What the hell do the Trotskyites expect to gain by sending that infant into the jaws of the Associated Farmers? You, at least, should know they mean business. Look at me, Charles! Dammit, I said look at me!" A spasm of coughing interrupted Minna's tirade. Charles had said that her smashed ribs had damaged her lungs permanently. When the coughing stopped, Minna began the attack again. "Charles, you are not so much younger than I am not to remember that once people thought me pretty." There wasn't any self-pity in her voice that I could detect. "That child will come back to your damn traitorous party smashed up. And for what?"

"Listen a sec, Minna," Charles sounded as if had become his sister's baby brother again.

"I'm not going to listen, and furthermore, what the damn hell are you doing with that rotten bunch of Norman Thomas finks? You think you're going to *vote* in the revolution? Reformists—they're getting ready to support the war. Get out in the field instead of sticking your nose in a book all the time and you'll find out what revolution and class struggle mean.

"*The* Party," Minna continued, and from my spot in the kitchen I could tell that she meant the Communists, "has been mobilizing relief units from its San Francisco headquarters. Ours will be a long-term campaign, which'll help the workers get on their feet, keep up their morale, and unify them while there is no work. They'll go back more militant when the floods are over. Even in their worst times, the Party will give them a sense of cooperation, give them an organizational as well as an ideological base from which to work. They'll go back even stronger, and there'll be no stopping them this time." Minna stopped abruptly, but she wasn't finished and began talking again, this time raising her voice still higher.

"Charles, all you and those milksop SPers and counterrevolutionary Fascist Trotskyites will do is disorient and demoralize the workers. You're going to give them charity. Charity! For God's sake! And the Trotskyites will sow dissension as they always do, just to gain a few new members."

I followed behind Serena, carrying cups while she carried the tray with coffee. Minna looked at me and ignored Serena. They hated each other. Serena detested Minna because she was jealous of the close brother and sister ties, and her husband's intense admiration for her despite their political differences.

When Minna stopped looking at me and shifted her attention to her brother, I studied her face. She was still a beautiful woman as she sat with her legs crossed, smoking intensely and tapping one foot on the floor. Her hair curled around her head like a Caravaggio urchin's—an urchin whose curly tendrils did not cover the scars on her forehead.

I couldn't help thinking that it was too bad she was a Communist, because she would be such a help in our organization. Minna turned to look at me again, almost as if she had been reading my mind. Then she stood, pushed her hands through her curly hair and tapped Charles on the arm. "Come on outside," she ordered. Turning to Serena, she said, "Thanks for the coffee."

Charles sat for a moment looking at Serena's sulky face, but then he stood and in a gesture similar to his sister's ran one hand through his own tight black curls. When he reached the door he told Serena that she should get started teaching me how to use the hypodermic because I was to go out to the camps the next day.

$\approx$ *8* $\approx$

On a Sunday, close to 4 A.M., we headed out. Norman picked me up, started the engine, and as quietly as he could pulled away from my house on College Avenue. The night was cold; a desert chill penetrated the valley even in the hottest summers. I shivered, but whether it was from the cold or my excitement about the trip to the camps, I can't say. We drove across town in the dark, down Blackstone to the railroad tracks, crossed over and headed onto Stanislaus, made a left and then a right turn, passed the Edison Technical School, and finally pulled into a lot next to a wooden gray shack. I was now on the wrong side of the tracks, the area of Mexicans, Indians, Negroes, Armenians, Filipinos, and poor whites. A delicious sense of adventure hit me suddenly as I looked over this forbidden territory. Around the shack scraggly grass grew on three sides of a solitary tree standing in the front yard. The tree was so spindly that it could hardly give any shade during the hot summer days. Somewhere I heard some chickens clucking and their fetid scent was all around us.

A short, fat woman in a nightdress down to her ankles came out to welcome us. "Buenos dias," she said softly. A thick, single black braid hung down her back, and when she smiled her teeth were like small white squares against her reddish brown skin. The screen door, which sagged and creaked when it opened, moved outward, and Florencio and Manuel came to greet us. Both were wearing denim jackets, frayed at the cuffs.

The men greeted us in Mexican Spanish, and I realized that my school studies in Castilian would not be appropriate. I'd have to learn Mexican Spanish, but that didn't worry me. It was another welcome chore, part of the excitement of being a Socialist and doing important things that helped others. Norman was looking around him, his eyebrows lifted in the way that he had when checking things out. I was never certain whether he disapproved or approved of a situation because of those reddish brown eyebrows and how they went up and down.

"Entonces," Manual said. He led the way to our ten-ton truck and opened the cab door. "Señorita," he said, and held out his hand to help me up the step and into the front seat. Florencio climbed in after me, sitting on the outside, while Manuel sprang lightly into the driver's seat.

Manuel was a good-looking man with something of a swagger, not caused by conceit but by confidence in his own body and mind, rather like a highly trained athlete. He was wearing a straw hat slightly tilted over his thin brown face. We drove out to the city limits and onto the highway without talking. Manuel's face was impassive, but his eyes squinted against the smoke from the cigarette between his lips.

He knew that I was looking at him, but the muscles in his face didn't adjust or change as some people's do when one stares at them. I had a sudden intuitive feeling about Manuel's character. He was still reserved toward me, but I didn't think he had yet come to any conclusions about my character. I also felt that he would not be harsh in judgment if I showed fear, or cowardice, or even vanity. I also did not know whether his reserve came from an assessment of me personally or from my connections with the Socialists. I thought then that as long as there was no rot at the core, I'd be accepted. This turned out to be true. As far as fear or cowardice, I immediately reassured myself. My devotion to Socialist ideals prevented fear and cowardice. But vanity? Was I vain? No way. Then why had I worn my white riding breeches, black shiny boots, and short, red suede vest, instead of brown jodhpurs and boots? Well, jodhpur boots only came above the ankles and we were going into flooded terrain. But conscience nagged enough to keep me quiet for several miles into the countryside.

Florencio was different from Manuel physically and in personality. He was round and short, with rosy cheeks, while Manuel was tall and thin and had a grayish tan complexion. Florencio smiled a lot and was slightly flirtatious and very jolly. He chattered, whereas Manuel was silent. Manuel was not forthcoming about our trip, but Florencio explained where we were going on this Sunday.

"Señorita, we do not tackle the big ones today. Much later. They have needs as great, those peoples, but it is good for you to get your first taste where there is not so much danger. You will see some things I don't think maybe you have seen before."

Manuel glanced at us and I thought he was going to speak, but he just removed the cigarette from his lips and tossed it out his window.

As was my way, unfortunately, I interrupted Florencio to say that we had discussed the needs of the pickers in our meetings. I told him we Socialists knew how bad it was in the camps, that people were hungry and had had no help—

Neither man responded. Finally, Florencio said, "They starve." After that, he closed his full lips and turned to gaze out the window.

In some way I felt chastised. I was failing already with these two contacts. We rode in silence, watching the white line in the road streak toward the truck faster and faster until it disappeared under our wheels, then we would lift our eyes to where it began again at the horizon. At least that is what Florencio and I did; Manuel kept his eyes on the road. On either side stretched sodden cotton vines. The pods had not fully opened before the flash flood. Many of the vines lay under water, and where the road dipped, the truck fled through muddy rivulets that threw spray to either side. Sometimes we drove miles without seeing houses. The land holdings were so vast that the big houses of the growers and overseers were miles from the highway. All feudal estates.

We hit the first camp around 8 A.M., after driving off the highway for about twenty miles. Manuel slowed the truck as the mud rose up around the wheels, sucking at the tires. Everywhere I looked there was water and mud. If there had been any green shoots, the land could have been a rice paddy, except for the crazy box shacks clustered in a slight hollow. The shacks had dirt floors but were now filled with water and mud. I asked Florencio, "Why didn't they build on the higher ground just ahead? Everybody knows that it floods here every few years. How can people live in water?"

"Señorita," Florencio's smiles and animation were gone, "ahead is better land. This is good enough for crop pickers."

Our truck had been heard in the hollow and people began coming toward us, trying to run but in slow motion, having to pull their feet out of the sticky mud. At first, everyone looked alike—men, women, and children were all gray, faces and clothes, muddy and dirty. One child was carrying another child who had scabs all over its head. "Impetigo," I thought, and I shuddered. "Well, let's get out the medical kit and the box of literature," I said.

Manuel's response was immediate, "First, we will take out the food." He then turned toward the crowding people and a change came over his face. It appeared to open up, like a tight rosebud suddenly flaring open, and even his skin color changed as a faint blush suffused his skin. He smiled with such warmth that I was amazed. From the crowd a shout sounded, "It's Man-well, Man-well!" Another voice queried, "Que tal? Ole, Man-well." The crop pickers changed too, from gray to faces with color. Even their clothing seemed lighter, less muddy. Everyone was laughing and excited and they surrounded Manuel, pulling him out into the center of the crowd. People got as close to him as they could and children hung onto the sleeves of his jacket or caught hold of his Levi's. He picked up a dirty little baby from the arms of an Okie and hoisted it to his shoulder. People from Oklahoma had been fleeing the dust bowl of that state and coming into California. At one time, state authorities refused to let them cross the borders of California, turning them away after they had driven many miles. However, some Oklahomans had managed to elude the border patrol. They joined the crop pickers because it was the only work they could find. Also, the growers did not ask questions about where one came from. As long as people would work and live under their terms they were accepted. Growers usually sent around advertisements, one-page flyers promising work to Mexicans. And they sent trucks to the border to pick up everyone who responded to the ads.

Manuel announced, "Well, amigos, we bring food. And we bring you a nurse." Everyone cheered. The noise startled the baby Manuel was holding and it began to cry. He rubbed its head softly. Raising his voice he told everyone to bring boxes or sacks, if they had them, so they could carry the provisions. "You will eat well, I think, at least for once."

A few people standing nearest to Manuel spoke to him and I saw him nod. I couldn't hear what they were saying. I wondered why people weren't leaving to get the boxes and bags for food. Manuel handed the baby to its mother and returned to the truck door.

"Señorita, they wish to meet you and to offer you hospitality. They say you must have coffee after driving so much distance and they will wait until you have finished to get their food." I made another gaffe. "Well, that's very nice of them," I whispered, "but do we have time? We have to visit several other camps today, you know."

I felt as if a cold pocket of air had dropped around Manuel's shoulders. Florencio was looking down at his feet and sloshing the mud back and forth with one foot.

"It is their cortesia, Señorita." I didn't know what Manuel was trying to tell me. "We have time," he said when I just looked at him. People had come up to the truck where we were standing, and Manuel turned to them again. "These are all my friends," he told me, "and this is Señorita Constancia, who brings food for your babies, and medicine."

I was surrounded then and we all moved toward the shacks in the hollow. I looked down at my boots, already spoiled by the mud. We came to a shack that looked the same as all the others: mean, dirty, and ugly. A wet gunnysack hung at the entrance and served as the door. The mud was not quite as thick inside the shack because the floor had been worn and swept to hardness. The smell of grease, slime, and unclean bodies assaulted my nose. This is what poverty smells like, I thought. Against one wall of the one-room hovel was an iron bed. The lumpy gray mattress was covered with an army blanket. There was an oil drum on which was spread some newspapers. Two smaller drums were used as chairs at the makeshift table. There were cafeteria mugs set out on top of the newspapers. I whispered to Florencio, "How did they know we were coming?"

Florencio joked that they had grapevines, not just the ones they pick, but like a telephone. He said that the moment we turned off the highway they knew we were coming. "The boss, he knows you are on his property too. He has his own grapevines."

Just a few people had come into the shack; it was too small to hold any type of gathering. I saw only three cups on the table and asked Manuel if the host and hostess weren't going to join us. He shook his head and I could see he didn't want me to say anything else. I thanked the woman who handed me the steaming cup of black coffee. It smelled so strong that automatically I looked around for some milk. I almost asked for milk before catching myself. They had no food. Then each of us was handed one thin tortilla, grey with tiny brown spots, wrinkled at the edge. I thought to myself, I'll probably get trench mouth or something worse. I thanked the woman and somehow forced down mouthfuls of the cold tortilla with the vile coffee.

Outside again, I filled my lungs with clean air. People had lined up near the truck with bags and old sacks. For a second they reminded me of Christmas, waiting expectantly for their presents. Manuel and Florencio began filling each dirty bag or sack or in some cases an old oil tin. No one crowded or grabbed and no one looked to see if he had received as much as his neighbor. It seemed very strange to me, not to see pushing and grabbing. "Workers are wonderful" was what my Socialist ideology made me feel at that moment though I admit that I added "even if they smell bad."

I climbed up into the truck and took out the medical kit. "Manuel," I called down to him, "I want to go through the camp and check for typhoid and smallpox or whatever problems there may be."

Manuel paused in handing out the food and signaled to two women, who came up to the truck to get me. We went back to the same shack where coffee had been served and the women covered the bed with newspapers. On top, I put a clean white sheet, which I had carried in the medical bag Charles and Serena had given me. Then I took out my sterno heater, put a little pan on the flame, and boiled up a syringe and about a dozen needles. I was ready. Typhoid had been discovered in the next county so everyone lined up for his shot. The alcohol swab left rings on gray, white, brown, and black skin. Injecting the serum into babies was torture. Their arms and legs were spindly from lack of food and even their buttocks seemed too small for a needle. Their wailing was almost deafening but didn't seem to disturb their mothers, who held them still while I jabbed and jabbed.

I don't remember how many shots I gave, but when we finished my hand was numb and my shirt and riding breeches stuck to my body from perspiration. At one point, the room tilted and I felt a nauseous reflux, tasting of coffee and tortilla. All the bodies heated the mud-encased shack and made me dizzy. I sat down on the bed, trying to hide how I felt. I lectured myself that I could not let them see that I was tired or felt sick. How happy they all were. They smiled and smiled when I jabbed the needles into their arms. I wondered how on earth they could smile and live this way. Why live at all, if this was life? I hated the growers even more than when I had heard about their history in our meetings. I vowed to spend my life fighting them.

Manuel came to the doorway and pushed back the gunnysack with one long arm. He looked at me thoughtfully, sitting on the bed, but didn't speak for a moment. Then he said, "Ready to move on?"

Outside people lined our way clear to the truck door. Everyone was smiling, and as we walked through the lane they made for us, they cried out, "Gracias, gracias, thank you!" A tiny child took hold of my breeches, now pretty dirty, and then let go of the cloth and waved her small hand. "We will come back," I promised.

On the drive to the next camp, the three of us were silent. I leaned my head against the seat and closed my eyes. There was too much misery, much too much. What stopped me from thinking about the terrible conditions was a sense of failure. "Oh, Lord," I sat up straight. "We forgot to hand out the literature."

"You gave them much more," Florencio said.

"Why did we have to drink that vile coffee and eat that wad of dough?" I felt that I had let the Party down and took out my anger against Manuel.

Neither man spoke, but I heard Florencio sigh. "Well," I insisted, "why did we have to?"

Manuel shifted his hands on the steering wheel and slowed the truck slightly. Then he glanced at me and back onto the road. He did not look angry and he answered me patiently. Manuel, who spoke unaccented English, spoke this time with a Spanish accent on certain words. It was startling.

"The coffee and meal for three tortillas was the last they had in the camp. They saved it, all the people getting together and sharing that little bit. When they heard we were coming they put it together for us. They could not let us visit and have nothing with which to welcome us. It is necessary for even poor people, who starve, to give to a visitor."

My cheeks felt hot and red, and I could feel my heart pounding. Shame and self-hatred filled me as we drove in silence along the ribbon of road. The only sound was the rattling of the truck. I kept thinking, what a horrid, stupid fool I am. How can I be a Socialist and know so little about human beings? What did I mean when I talked about humanity, universality, and Socialism? I do not even know what they are. Although I hadn't shown my feelings to those people, I almost hated them when they gave me the dirty looking food and bad coffee. My conscience, ever ready to pounce, insisted *you felt superior to those people.*

All the rest of that day and the following week we visited camps. They gradually took on the same coloration, gray, gray misery. In one camp there had been nothing at all to eat except boiled dandelion greens. The greenish liquid was being fed to babies to stop their cries of hunger.

In another camp a baby lay as if it were dead. Its eyes bulged and its stomach was bloated. It looked almost like a brown spider. It was very difficult to find enough flesh for the needle, but I managed to give the baby typhoid and vitamin B shots. Then we opened a tin of canned milk and mixed it with warm water, which I heated on the Sterno heater. There wasn't a baby bottle to be found and as I watched the baby seemed to be collapsing. I filled one of the syringes with the milk and fed a few drops into the baby's shriveled mouth. At the first taste, its tiny clawlike hands moved, and when it finished the small amount in the syringe and I took it to refill, the baby's mouth made a slight sucking sound, wanting more. The infant drank three syringes full of milk, and I was afraid to give it any more. The mother and I watched closely, hoping that the infant would not throw up. But it went to sleep and its color seemed to have changed, losing the bluish tinge under the skin.

The baby's mother followed me out to the truck, and as I turned to climb into the cab, she put out a hand but was afraid to touch my arm. I took her hand and she clutched it and then put it to her lips. She turned to leave very quickly but I saw her tears.

A week in June, all of July, and part of August we went out early in the morning, five or six days a week. Some weeks I had to be home to go to church and Sunday school or mother would not let me go out to the camps. I felt so ignorant that I began to carry medical books and read while we were driving, looking up symptoms and treatments and then trying to find out more about different medicines.

Back at home I read everything I could find on the history of California, trying to understand how we could have such feudal estates, which held as serfs an army of Filipinos, Mexicans, Negroes, Chinese, Indians, and poor whites. I quickly dropped the word "Okie" from my vocabulary, which so many people used to describe the farmers from Oklahoma.

My own city of Fresno had a shocking history in its treatment of immigrants. Chinese laborers were brought into the valley to help build the railroads. Then in 1892 the Geary Act demanded the registration of all Chinese. Upstanding citizens—businessmen—had personally raided their camps, set fire to the shacks, and shot people who tried to escape. This valley exported a billion dollars in produce a year while its laborers hovered over the land, following the crops, without homes or enough to eat. Manuel told me that during that summer's flooding more than 77,000 migratory workers had been stranded. And this valley, with soil as rich as that of the Nile Valley, would not share a grain with the workers.

When I had time, but secretly, I read *Grapes of Wrath, In Dubious Battle, The Octopus, It Can't Happen Here*. I felt guilty reading novels instead of the Marxist books and literature that had been assigned. And I was reading from novels to Manuel and Florencio while we drove from camp to camp. I was supposed to be reading Party literature and/or talking to them about Socialism. That was part of my assignment. I was supposed to educate these contacts and get them to join the Party. I certainly couldn't explain to my comrades that they were educating me.

In August we began to enter the territory of the growers whom Florencio called the "hard hombres." We visited some of the 20,000 acres belonging to Thomas Fowler in Kern County and Tulare without incident. But at Di Giorgio's main holdings near Delano, armed guards met us. I showed my Fresno City authorization, but it didn't have any affect. Two of the men leveled their rifles at us and demanded that we leave our load at the entrance to the property. One of the men said, "We all'll see that it gits to the pickers." We did not unload because we knew the guards would probably take everything for themselves.

The comrades were very pleased with what we accomplished during the summer months. I regularly made out reports for them, giving names, dates, places, and conditions in the camps. The reports were brief: thirty shacks near Visalia unfit for habitation; twenty families near Compton living under a bridge; twenty Oklahomans living in one shack; Camp Weed Patch, fifty babies with flu, typhoid, skin diseases. Two children dead last visit to Tulare. No doctors or health authorities will visit the camps in Firebaugh, Kearn, or Selma. Members of the Party then took these notes, wrote their speeches around them, and spoke before civic and religious groups. Many people were sympathetic and ready to help. Dr. Henderson and the field secretary for the Gospel Army denounced the growers from their pulpits. We were flooded with food, clothing, and medical supplies. But the conditions in the camps were hardly improved.

I did not mention it to my comrades, but Minna's diatribe against her brother stayed in my mind, nagging away. If I had not spent the summer visiting and trying to help the pickers it would never have occurred to me that anything a Communist said would have any effect on me. They were supposed to be the enemy. Minna had raged against the idea of charity. Charity: that's what we had been involved in, and how much good had we done? The lives of the pickers were still as bleak and futureless as before.

❧ 9 ❧

Norman and Wally enrolled in the University of California at Berkeley. It had been my dream to study premed at that university as well. However, my father had died when I was eleven and mother went to work outside the home for the first time in her life. There wasn't any money for tuition. So I chose the second best career and was accepted at the Highland School of Nursing in the Alameda County General Hospital. Toward the end of my first year I had a ruptured appendix and missed a month of training, so I would have had to repeat all of the subjects from the beginning, something I was not willing to do. Norman urged me to leave as well, because he and Wally were returning to Fresno because their mother died, which left their father alone in the rectory provided by the church. Norman had for years assumed we would marry, and although I had not made up my mind we were more or less engaged and I did not know how to avoid our union.

When mother heard that we planned to marry, she visited Dr. Henderson and asked him to intervene. She was adamantly against the marriage, particularly since I was not quite eighteen. To her dismay and horror, he not only wanted us to marry but warned mother that *something might happen* if we did not. Mother knew quite well what he meant, and the idea that her daughter would have sex before marriage was an insult. She never recovered from that conversation with Dr. Henderson and although she remained civil when they met, she detested him. His remark, to her, was blasphemy.

Norman and I were married in the First Congregationalist Church a few days after my eighteenth birthday in June. Dr. Henderson, of course, officiated. There were approximately five hundred people in attendance at this formal wedding. I was dressed in a white peau de soie gown and my train was a veil held by a cap of seed pearls. Mother and my sister, Decima, told me the facts of life while helping me to dress. Without being very specific they said that lovemaking was just something that I had to put up with, that it was painful, embarrassing, and humiliating. I started to cry. They did not know that I had already been through such an experience. Mother wiped away my tears while my sister put on the cap of pearls and fluffed out my hair.

The reception was held at the rectory and nearly the entire congregation attended. My mouth and cheeks began to ache from smiling so much and I could hardly wait to see the day end. But finally the last guest departed and since Norman and I were exhausted we went to the Kinema Theater to see a movie. Afterward we stopped at the Olive Inn for hamburgers because we had not been able to eat at the reception. There were classmates at the inn and they were amazed to see us on our wedding night. We took a lot of teasing, some of it good natured and some malicious. By the time we got back to the rectory Dr. Henderson and Wally were asleep. There were four or five bedrooms on the second floor and I had already taken one in which to put my things. Norman quite naturally believed he would share the room but I went in while he was downstairs and locked myself inside. When he came upstairs and tried the door he whispered for me to let him in. I told him no, that I was too tired and was going right to sleep. He rattled the knob but did not dare make any noise because his father's room was just across the hallway. He and Wally were to attend summer school at Shaver Lake and were leaving the next day about five in the morning. This suited me perfectly, since it would forestall any intimacy for at least two weeks, when it was planned that I would spend a weekend at the lake.

I had gotten a job in a doctor's office and would stay in Fresno, working and playing hostess for Dr. Henderson during the visits of members of his congregation. There were also visitors from New York who came to give lectures. Dr. Henderson was a liberal and was very pleased when Max Eastman accepted his invitation. I was enthralled with Eastman. He spoke about the importance of laughter in one's life and was not only persuasively articulate but handsome as well. He stayed overnight in the rectory so we had a chance to see and be with him offstage, as it were. Since joining the Party, I had not laughed very often, and Eastman's topic and his own personal ambience, serious but lighthearted, filled me with joy.

Mother used to say that I was a changeling. Obviously, she did not know the meaning of the word. I was not a turncoat, a child secretly exchanged for another in infancy, or an imbecile. What she meant was that when I mastered a subject, understood an environment, or experienced something, I was ready to move on. I cannot stand monotony, the same thing day after day. I am a lover of change. So it was not strange that early in life I wanted to escape from this small valley town. I'd had enough of Fresno and was impatient for the next steps: Los Angeles, New York, and, if I was lucky, Europe.

When summer school ended at Lake Shaver, Wally, Norman, and I moved to Eaglerock, outside Los Angeles, so the boys could attend Occidental College. I don't know why they did not return to UC Berkeley, but I was delighted to leave Fresno. I drove our V8 Ford convertible to Los Angeles ahead of Norman and Wally because I had to find work and a place for the three of us to live. Dr. Henderson was going to pay college tuition for his two sons, while I was to pay for our living expenses. At the time this did not seem unreasonable. I don't know why. Be that as it may, I found a job in a doctor's office once again and in Eaglerock a bungalow in a court. As far as I can remember, there weren't dwellings such as courts in Fresno. At least I had never seen such a living arrangement. The court in Eaglerock consisted of small, individual houses arranged in a U shape around a small grassy plot, with cement walkways leading to each bungalow. There were front and back doors and, although they were close together, only a few feet between each house, there was more privacy than in an apartment. Also, as the sun shifted there was light on all sides of the tiny house. It was furnished in what was called Monterey style, which meant that the couch and one armchair had wooden arms. There were two bedrooms, a living room, and a kitchen with a small nook at one side for dining. I did not particularly like eating all our meals in the kitchen, but there wasn't space for a table in the front room.

Eaglerock was between Los Angeles and Pasadena, which allowed us to attend branch meetings in either of the two cities. We were still firm believers in Trotskyism and its concept of world revolution. We had broken with—had actually been expelled from—the Socialist Party and were now in Cannon's Socialist Workers Party. I drove to my job in downtown Los Angeles early each morning and arrived home around six in the evening. Norman and Wally did the cooking, which was a big help, since I was tired from having been on my feet most of the day. I always went to bed early, before either of the boys, and was able to avoid sex at least during the week.

In Los Angeles there were three or four meeting places rented by the Party, called branches or branch offices. We found the Los Angeles branch livelier than the one in Pasadena and went there more often. When the comrades learned that we had been active in aiding the agricultural workers in Fresno they assigned us to the West Side Branch. I learned later that their reasoning was that since I had been closely associated with the Mexicans Manuel and Florencio, the West Side would give us the opportunity to become friendly with Mexican and black people who lived in the area, and then we could bring them into the Party. After settling in with new comrades, we began to hand out leaflets and party literature in the neighborhood and made some acquaintances. The members of the Socialist Workers Party were entirely different from people we had known in Fresno. Most of them were older than we were and they assigned us to the Young People's Socialist League. We attended classes on *Wage, Labor, and Capital,* the *Communist Manifesto,* and other works of Marx, Lenin, and Trotsky.

After our small group in Fresno it was exciting to be part of an organization that had branch offices in many parts of the city. We felt part of a large current that swept around the world. Our activities were wider as well; instead of distributing leaflets to students, we distributed the *Militant* to dock workers in San Pedro. We drove out in two cars once every week, four or five of us to a car. We put the papers in the trunk of the car "in case the police stop us." Then we carefully followed or were followed by the other car carrying the other members. We gave away thousands of papers. The dock workers were neither friendly nor unfriendly, though very few refused to take the paper, and some would stop for a few minutes and talk to us about the conditions of their work. But essentially our reassurance came from each other. The trips were somewhat like a surreptitious picnic. After handing out papers we had coffee and compared experiences, then discussed Hegel's dialectics or argued about one aspect or shading of meaning in something Lenin or Trotsky had written. We discussed religion, art, music, and writing, and we reviewed all the latest books.

Sometimes there was flirtation, but we were serious and idealistic. We worked hard at our Party work. No one told us we had to study hard, attend meetings once or twice a week, and sell or distribute the Party paper. We disciplined ourselves because we felt that everything should be given up to see that Marxism succeeded. None of us felt like martyrs; we were living an exciting life. There was nothing humdrum about it and the world awaited us. We associated with people whom we might never have met outside radical circles, particularly those of us from a small town. In this group we met people from Europe and Asia and knew that there were members who worked in many countries for the Party. We were international; we were fervently democratic; we felt that mankind had a future and that we could end want and pain and unite mankind in a giant human brotherhood. Among us were sensitive, self-sacrificing, and, often, very intelligent young people. If we gave away twenty thousand papers that did not result in a subscription or money it did not dishearten us because we believed people were becoming educated through our press. With such an education then the revolution would naturally take place. It did not matter that we were only a few hundred in Los Angeles; we knew there would be a revolution eventually, perhaps within ten years. We were passionate in our desire for the world to change, for segregation to end, for bureaucracy to collapse, for an end to the fear of atomic warfare. We were happy and active and felt anything was possible, that we held the truth in our hands and were eager to share it with everyone. We held socials, and people we met in the neighborhood came very willingly to dance, eat, and drink beer and nonalcoholic beverages. Many of these contacts began to attend meetings and we were confident that soon our branch on the West Side would recruit black members.

During our second summer in Eaglerock, the main Los Angeles branch invited all members and sympathizers to a picnic in Griffith Park. Our group from the West Side, with our contacts and sympathizers, mostly black men, were late in arriving at the picnic site. As we came over the hill above the picnickers, a cry went up from the comrades, "The West Side Branch brings 'em back alive!" My face burned and I turned to look at our friends, wondering whether they would turn around and leave. Their faces were impassive. I was shocked and angry at the bigotry expressed by, of all people, my comrades. What were they calling our friends? Animals from the jungle? Was that what my comrades really felt? Although occasionally I had sensed a patronizing air toward minorities by the comrades, I had stifled my criticism because they were so vocal and firm in pursuing what they called the "Negro question" and freedom for black people.

That picnic marked the beginning of my wariness toward my comrades and the Party itself. Either I had been blinded by revolutionary fervor or had brushed aside as unimportant these telltale signs of bigotry. White comrades were not comfortable in the presence of blacks despite the sacrifices they would make to end segregation. Unease was shown variously: conversation became stilted; they were overfriendly; they considered all black people heroic; and the only disagreements were on a particular political subject, as long as it had nothing to do with race. Less sophisticated comrades were sometimes embarrassing when they volunteered in conversations with a black contact, "We hate prejudice. We're for equality. It's criminal the way you are treated and the life you have to live." White comrades said no one should write or speak in a derogatory way about a black person. It might prejudice people against all blacks and make integration impossible. Blacks were stereotypes, either martyrs or heroes. Gabriel, Vesey, Attucks—the great Negro leaders were idealized and every black a comrade met was a potential Vesey or Gabriel or a defenseless creature who had been beaten and lynched. All blacks, because they suffered, were automatically "good" and would behave admirably in a crisis. They would naturally be "on the barricades" with the Trotskyists, fighting for justice and freedom, and the Party would make the world a safe place for blacks to live in. The Party would help black people; no one recognized that they were quite capable of helping themselves.

During the spring, we learned that all branch members were to attend a service in a Negro church, where a comrade visiting from London was to speak. We drove into Los Angeles fairly early, but when we reached the church it was almost filled. Most of the comrades were sitting in a group near the back of the church, but motioning to Norman I went up nearer the front to sit with some of our contacts. The church soon filled up completely, with people standing in the back and along the sides. There was an air of expectancy, but I sensed some skepticism in the black audience and wondered whether it was the presence of so many white radicals. The black minister made an introduction and then from the wings strode a six-foot-three-inch-tall, brown-skinned handsome man. His back was ramrod straight, his neck rather long, and he held his head slightly back, with chin lifted. There was an elegance and grace in his stance, and he looked like a prince or a king. He was carrying books and an untidy sheaf of papers that he placed on the podium and never looked at again. The man was C. L. R. James, the author of numerous books, among them *The Black Jacobins,* a study of the revolution in Haiti, and *World Revolution,* an attack against the Stalinist regime in Russia. He was the ghost writer of the great cricket player Leary Constantine's biography *Cricket and I.* He had also written numerous short stories and a novel, *Minty Alley.* We had read reviews of the first two of his books in *Time* Magazine and the *New York Times.* Norman whispered, "This should be good."

James looked out into the audience and then at his wristwatch. He said, "It is now II A.M., and I shall speak for exactly forty-five minutes." He then began. I had already heard speeches by two great orators, Winston Churchill and Franklin Delano Roosevelt. Now I was hearing a third. The three men were masters of the English language, a skill that gave them extraordinary power. Their voices were in absolute control, with at times startlingly original sentence structure. They also had *presence,* what Hollywood calls *animal magnetism.* It is an irresistible power of attraction, just as iron filings cling to a magnet. For a few minutes, it was difficult to concentrate on James's words because of the beauty of his voice. It was rhythmic, the cadence lilting, and his British accent had shadings of the music of the Caribbean. However, I heard some whispers from the black audience about what a man from such a background could possibly tell them about life among Negroes in the United States. The topic of the lecture had been advertised as the "Negro question" and C. L. R.'s main point was that Negroes, from their position in society, will be in the forefront of any change in the United States and, in fact, the world. He said American Negroes touch on one side the American proletariat, on whom so much depends in the present period; on the other side, they and *not* the British or French proletariat are the link with the African revolution; also, they could form a link with the millions of Indians and Negroes and half-castes who form so much of the population of Spanish-America. And not only before but also after the revolution. The American Negro would have to do most of the actual contact between Western civilization and the millions of Africans.

Before many words were spoken the audience became so quiet that the faint twitter of the birds outside the church seemed loud. There wasn't a cough or any shifting in seats, simply a dead silence. It was as if everyone was holding his breath. James did speak for exactly forty-five minutes. The audience was won over completely and eager to ask questions. As far as my reactions to James's speech, I was enthralled. At last! I felt that someone was saying exactly what I had been feeling and his speech assuaged the anger I had felt toward my comrades at our recent picnic. I was reunited emotionally with the Party and my comrades.

A few nights later, after I had gone to bed, I heard voices in the front room and one sounded like C. L. R.'s. I pulled on a red woolen robe, brushed back my hair, and went to investigate. Carlo, a cartoonist, and one of our comrades, who had moved to Los Angeles from New York, had driven C. L. R. to where he spoke at a meeting in Pasadena and stopped at our place afterward. Off the stage and at close view James was even more handsome, and he moved with ease despite his height. Everything about him was in perfect proportion. James, who was a British comrade, was a member of the International Executive Committee, a world organization of special Trotskyist leaders from each country. He was on a speaking tour of the United States and after speaking in California was to meet with Leon

Trotsky, who was in exile in Coyoacan, Mexico. That evening, James appeared to be reserved and extremely self-controlled. He sat listening quietly, smoking his pipe, smiling at me off and on, and let Carlo do most of the talking.

I was so sleepy that even though I was impressed by the visit of such a well-known comrade in our tiny house, I went back to bed after half an hour. The next day, Norman and Wally took me to task for what they called my rude behavior. But my job and the daily commute to downtown L.A. were wearing me out, even though I was young and healthy. I think now that what was wearing me out was not the commute and the job but the demands and criticisms of my husband and his brother. Perhaps I was beginning to resent their outstretched hands for my weekly paycheck on Fridays. However, until a minister friend of Dr. Henderson's visited us, I was not aware of the feelings building in me, not only about money but other problems. Dr. Henderson's friend came to dinner on a Friday night and witnessed Wally and Norman's immediate request for my paycheck. The expression on his face showed surprise and distaste, and he became very quiet. I knew what he was thinking.

Soon after the visit by James and Carlo one of our sympathizers, Sol Babitz, called me at work to say that someone wanted to speak to me. It was James. He said he was leaving for Mexico in two days and wondered whether I could take an afternoon off from work to meet him at Sol's house for "a small conference." When I asked him whether I should see if Norman and Wally could get out of classes, James said that it was not necessary, that he simply wanted to talk to me alone. As I recall, I was not impressed one way or another, but perhaps slightly curious. Whether this indicates conceit I have no way of knowing. I do know that I was eager to have a chance to tell James about the prejudice I'd found among the L.A. comrades. But without thinking much about it, I did not mention the call to Norman or Wally.

The next day I left work about noon and drove to Sol's house, which was perched on the side of a hill near downtown Los Angeles. Sol had made sandwiches for our lunch but did not join us. He was a serious musician, a talented violinist, and went back to practice. James and I took our sandwiches outdoors and settled in the November sunshine on stone steps that led up to the road above. It was not very warm but still pleasant, with a breeze ruffling the leaves of the trees around us, especially the eucalyptus with its pointed, silvery leaves, moving like ballerina dancers when the wind hit them. James listened intently to my complaints about the comrades. We also talked about the speech he had made in the church and his views on the question of race. He was impressed by my passionate concern about race relations in the U.S. James asked a few questions and I suddenly found myself telling him everything I'd been feeling. James, I learned, had this effect on everyone he met. In one case a young Italian girl, Filomena Daddario, just out of high school and poorly educated, confessed to him that she liked poetry, especially Emily Dickinson and Shakespeare. James suggested that she immerse herself in the work of Dickinson, reading all of her poems and any available biographies. Filomena was so encouraged that she became quite an expert on Dickinson's work. Another example was a young, uneducated factory worker, Phil Singer (Paul Romano), who talked to James about his daily work. He had never written a line of prose but James suggested that he write down his experiences—the work itself, what it entailed, management's relation to the workers, the workers' feelings or attitudes. Singer's essay described the conditions in a General Motors plant. In describing the assembly line and its dirt and oil he revealed its effect on the workers—pimples, rashes, and boils on their legs and arms. No one had dealt with such details of factory life before. The pamphlet, *The American Worker*, was published by the Johnson-Forest group and widely distributed.

My outpourings were essentially complaints about the Trotskyist Party. There did not seem to be any particular interest in the condition and treatment of blacks. And there were only one or two black men; they might come to our socials but not to meetings, and they did not join. As far as the leaders, they seemed to feel that blacks were accounted for by white workers who would, with the Party leading, initiate a revolution. Blacks would simply follow. The Party slogan *Black and White Unite and Fight* certainly did not stir anyone with whom we came into contact. Blacks knew too well, working alongside white workers, what their attitude was toward them. They were used to hostility, derogatory remarks, and at times violence. So how does one unite with one's enemies? I wondered.

James turned the questions inside out. He did not believe that a revolution could or should be led by a vanguard party. A revolution would be spurred on by black people because of the circumstances of their lives as outsiders. White workers and the poor would then follow. Leaders would spring up from within the masses of people. James proposed to try to educate Party members and sympathizers and perhaps draw blacks into the Party as a result. He explained that the subject was at the top of his list to discuss with Trotsky, and he planned to suggest that a bureau devoted to

"Negro Affairs" be set up within the Party. One of James's intentions was to write weekly and biweekly articles in the *Socialist Appeal* and the *New International,* Trotskyist newspapers. He had prepared a paper on the history of the black struggle that included self-determination; the relationship between the black struggle for basic democratic rights and the Socialist movement; the organization and recruitment of black members; and a program for educating Party members about the race question. He needed to get Trotsky's backing, because the Party was averse to concentration on the issue. Later the Party would frown on interracial marriages or liaisons because, the leaders said, white workers would be antagonistic and not want to belong to an organization that promoted such relations.

James told me he had gained organizational experience when he worked with George Padmore in England for the International African Service Bureau. He seemed to feel there wouldn't be any problems as a black man either within the Party or as a member of American society. I wondered, but I kept it to myself, if he knew what he was facing in the U.S. Neither the Caribbean nor Britain had the virulent and overt racism that existed in our country. James was very inexperienced when it came to understanding the complexity of race relations, not only between black and white but among Jews, Mexicans, Asians, Italians—all of this so-called *melting pot* of America, which is not a melting pot at all. Eventually, he was told "you are not a black man at all." What they meant was that they could not fit James into their conceptions of what a black man should do or be.

James said that if I wanted to help with such a program, the first thing to do was educate myself. "First you must understand the Civil War itself: Beard, *History of American Civilization.* In Woodson's *History of the Negro in America* there are many chapters on the Negro. This should be looked through. Aptheker has a small volume for ten cents, *The Negro in the Civil War.*" I was surprised that he suggested reading Aptheker, because he was a member of our enemy, the Communist Party. Jameas also told me to subscribe to the *Pittsburgh Courier* and read George Schuyler's columns. He also warned that I must not try to form a Negro organization. "It is not Party policy," he said. "But you can form a small discussion group and investigate the conditions of Negroes here in California. Then, eventually you can write a pamphlet." James said he would help in every way and send clippings and books as they turned up.

A week or two later, in April, I received a letter from James telling me that Trotsky had agreed with his position on the Negro question. On self-determination, in particular, there was no difficulty.

At the end of August 1939 I was in turmoil about our politics, as were all of my comrades and the Party itself. The main issue was the signing of the nonaggression pact between Stalin and Hitler, which freed Hitler for the invasion of Europe. As a group and individually we were hostile to the Communists, but we had still supported the remnants of the Russian Revolution. It had been absolutely unthinkable among people on the Left that such a political alliance could be agreed upon. Unless one was involved in politics one cannot imagine the horror we felt toward Stalin taking the bloody hand of the murderer Adolph Hitler. Germany had dismembered Czechoslovakia, and then Hitler had turned his attention to Poland. The signing of the nonaggression pact meant war between Germany and the other European powers. And very quickly England and France did declare war. In the U.S., the principal question was how to stay out of the conflict. Hitler seemed to have paralyzed the democratic nations by his aggression. And in the U.S., for the first time, isolationism versus limited intervention became a hot national issue. Herbert Hoover, the former president, advised the U.S. not to enter into alliances with openly antifascist European democracies because such a course might lead to war. The Communist Party lost members as well as a majority of its "fellow travelers." (We used the term *sympathizers;* the Communists' term was *fellow travelers.*)

Added to my political concerns was a personal upset when I ended my marriage to Norman Henderson. It felt more like ending a marriage to two men. When I think about Gertrude Stein's remark "There is no there, there," I'm reminded that Wally was always *there.* And because he was older and had joined the Party before we had, he always acted like the elder statesman, always teaching us, whether invited to or not. He more or less dictated the way we lived, where and how, so except for there being no physical relationship it was like having two husbands, both telling me what to do. By nature, particularly at that age, I could be persuaded quite easily through subtle influence, but I did not like to be governed or regulated. The reason that persuasion worked was that I had not learned to understand or live with the almost violent swings in my temperament, from elation to despair, and I was uncertain of myself.

Norman said he was in the depths of despair, could not live without me, felt his life was over, and refused to drive me to my friend Marian Ornstein's home, where I was to stay. The first evening, sitting over dinner with my friend, I felt euphoric, swept by such jubilation in my sudden freedom that I felt like laughing and crying simultaneously. Norman did not call for a few days and then phoned and asked to see me. Feeling guilt at the sound of his voice I agreed reluctantly. My poor about to be ex-husband looked as if he had not slept in a year and I felt a sharp stab of pain. But when he tried to put his arms around me, I pulled back. At first he pleaded with me to return and promised everything he could think of to persuade me. I felt so sorry for him my eyes teared. He then reached into his pocket and took out a sheet of typing paper. In Norman's neat handwriting, notes covered both sides of the sheet. He began to read to me a list of what *I* had to do when we reunited. In other words, the conditions of my surrender. I can't remember every point, but one was that I was to quit my job and find another because he thought my employer, a surgeon, was in love with me. I was also to end my friendship with Marian, because she was not a member of the Party and could have a bad influence on me. Norman got halfway through the list before I opened the car door and said goodbye. A few weeks later he called again and said that he was taking all of our sterling silver wedding presents and wanted my engagement and wedding rings. The conversation ended by my agreeing that he could have all our wedding gifts and the engagement ring. Out of petty pique, but alone on the Santa Monica Pier, I threw my wedding ring into the sea.

Norman deserved the wedding presents and the engagement ring. He had earned them. He wanted love and I was prudish and cold. I met his youthful, passionate love with repulsion. There were no marriage counselors in those days or he might have suggested seeing one. Instead he did all he could to win my affection. On the surface I appeared to outsiders, and even in our home, to be sexy and outgoing. In reality, I was icily reserved and kept my emotions under control. We didn't discuss sex—that was beyond me. That I was young and inexperienced wasn't a satisfactory excuse for frigidity. I seemed to view myself and the people around me as separate entities, unconnected. We had few disagreements, but when we did I withdrew and became silent, sometimes for days. Without knowing it, I was emulating my mother in her relations with my father. I didn't whistle, as did mother, only because I didn't know how and never learned. The silence was the same and was a refusal to engage myself. Norman had loved me from the first time we met and felt ours was an ideal marriage. We were passionately involved in the same dreams, to change the world for the better and do away with injustice to the poor and to minorities. Neither of us was religious, although both of us had attended church regularly.

Since his father was a minister and liberal, he was a staunch believer and Norman had to conform. His disappointment and grief at the dissolution of our marriage was unmistakable. Why shouldn't he have the poor substitutes, wedding presents and engagement ring? If he was being spiteful, why not, since he was the one wounded?

❧ 10 ❧

In October, we learned that a citywide meeting had been held by the Party in New York to discuss the Stalin-Hitler pact, which was called the "Russian Question." Lines were being drawn with Cannon's majority facing a formidable opposition including Max Shachtman, James Burnham, and Martin Abern. Many members of the youth group were also part of the opposition. Trotsky intervened in support of Cannon, but many of the youth stood firm against Cannon. The majority argued that support for the unconditional defense of the Soviet Union was in no way incompatible with the struggle for the overthrow of the Stalin bureaucracy. The minority position posed by Max Shachtman was that we should refuse to defend a degenerated workers' state. His theoretical position developed into something called "bureaucratic collectivism." The debate was creating a fracture within the Party to the point that Cannon hoped the minority would simply disappear. But in the beginning the minority was determined to stay in the Party, fight for its position, and win over as many members as possible.

Intense debates began around the two positions at all of the branches and at the headquarters in Los Angeles. There were some very staunch Cannonites in the organization, particularly Charles Curtiss and Murry Weiss, who were in the leadership. I was on the side of the minority together with most of the group in the West Side Branch. Norman and Wally, I was pleased to hear, had also taken the minority position. They attended either the main office or the branch in Pasadena, probably to avoid seeing me. It was just as well, because at one of our socials I met Edward Keller, a close sympathizer. He introduced me to many of his friends and took me home to meet his family. I fell in love with his mother and father as well as his two sisters, Lillian (Lily) and Alice. Lily suffered from agoraphobia and never left the house. She was, however, a delightful person, warm, intelligent, tender-hearted, and interested in everything. Mrs. Keller was a small roundish woman whom Edward called "Little Mouse." Although she was not religious, she was raised not to eat pork, but her children loved bacon and ham so she cooked it for them regularly. Despite the delicious aroma from frying bacon she would never take a bite. Alice, the youngest in the family, was considered an *intellectual,* along with Edward. She was moody but always friendly toward me. She once left her job and spent a year cloistered in her room reading mystery stories. Mr. Keller was a quiet and reserved man, with a generous spirit and a dry sense of humor. Shortly after I met the family he noticed that my coat was not very warm. It was a cold winter that year and the next time we visited he gave me a package marked Sak's Fifth Avenue. Inside the tissue wrappings was a beautiful camel's hair coat, a classic style that fit me perfectly.

Edward had completed his thesis for a Ph.D. in philosophy and received a letter of commendation from John Dewey. Before taking his orals he decided that he did not want to be a professor and quit to take a job as a sign painter at Paramount Studios, where his brother worked as a grip. When we met, Edward seemed worldly and sophisticated. Although not classically handsome, he was attractive and had the biggest, deepest blue eyes I had ever seen. They made me think of Thomas Hardy's novel *A Pair of Blue Eyes.* It is a blue that never alters, a pure, clear color that is startling to see. When he was talking to you, it seemed you were the only person in the world. He was also charming, intelligent, and sensitive. When we became closer than friends, he told me that in his teens he realized he was not and never would be handsome. So he made up his mind to make the best of what he had. He spent many hours standing in front of the bathroom mirror practicing different expressions with his eyes and mouth. He mastered a very faint smile and at the same time, through his eyes, registered in turn deep interest, humor, skepticism, disagreement, superiority, and passion. Coming from Fresno and only having known Norman and Wally, both of whom were intelligent but lacking in worldly charm, I was intrigued. I was also impressed by how quickly Edward seemed to fall in love with me. And it was not just *seemed;* he was completely devoted. It did not take him long to propose marriage. I did not accept, having so recently gained freedom from male domination, but his persistence was flattering and I enjoyed being with him. His support of the minority position and the support of his friends were added attractions. Edward attended meetings regularly and was an excellent speaker, which added to our group's ability to counter the arguments of the Cannonites.

Toward the end of 1939, the Los Angeles members, led by Charles Curtiss and Murry Weiss, who took their cue from the Political Committee in New York, became aggressive. Instead of listening to our point of view they began calling us names. We were petty-bourgeois revisionists, calamity howlers, literary panic mongers, deviationists, pessimists, quitters, and betrayers of the proletarian revolution. One or two members of the New York majority came to Los Angeles during the six months of discussion, and we listened politely. However, when James came to Los Angeles the majority members tried to prevent him from speaking. Fortunately, we persuaded a few majority members to join us in protesting such undemocratic behavior and he was allowed to hold a meeting. It was my first experience in a factional fight, but not my last. It was, I think, one of the worst. The leaders of the minority, Burnham, Shachtman, and Abern, seeking to keep the Party together, requested permission to publish a newspaper that would argue its views. The request was refused. Cannon wrote later that such an offer was merely "to make a split in the hypocritical guise of unity; to attack the party in the name of the party—[and] was rejected out of hand by the majority of the convention. The minority was confronted with a clear alternative: either to accept the decision of the majority under the rules of democratic centralism or go their own way and unfurl their own banner."

Initially, James had been disgusted with the fight among the Trotskyist leaders, minority and majority. Although he clearly would not and did not support the Soviet Union, he disliked the infighting. In September, he wrote in a personal letter:

> I am not going into the rights and wrongs of the case but under such circumstances it is pathetic to see each side laying all the blame on the other. It seems this quarrel has a long history . . . I am a member of the I.E.C. [International Executive Committee] and am waiting to intervene when the question comes, as it must, before the international. But to-date the majority says of the minority "irresponsible, jittery and unprincipled, subject to social-patriotic pressure." The minority says of the majority "Stalinist, bureaucratic and unable to lead the party." A split on such issues would show the utmost irresponsibility on both sides.

James said he felt that the rank and file of the party should listen to both sides and *impose* a decision. According to him, they should say, "If you leaders cannot agree, then we shall examine the questions at issue and say 'Do this or do that.'" In another letter to me in September of 1939, James wrote that World War II was on and that everything should be subordinate to that: "Our party is reacting very badly (strictly between us). As a matter of fact, it isn't reacting at all. But some effort is being made to pull the centre together. It is no longer a question of Hitler-Stalin and the politically minded. It is a question of mass appeals and mass demonstrations."

At the SWP convention held in New York on April 5–8, 1940, the minority lost its struggle. Prior to the split the majority offered the minority a continuation of the political disagreement in the internal bulletin but limited all articles in the *New International* to theoretical material only. At the same time the resolution decreed that all discussion about the differences around the Russian Question in every branch of the party must cease. Gagging the mouths of the membership was unacceptable and the minority voted the resolution down. There was no choice for the minority but to leave the SWP.

Shachtman, Burnham, and Abern led the minority out of the SWP to form a new organization, the Workers Party. James followed. The split reduced the SWP from a thousand members to six hundred and almost the entire youth group joined the minority. Shachtman and Abern had been friends as well as comrades of Cannon's for many years, so it must have been a painful time for Cannon.

James, who had been writing me regularly since leaving California, indicated in a letter, marked as usual *Special Delivery,* that there were fundamental problems within the party that the fight over the Russian Question simply exacerbated. Trotsky as a symbol in the struggle against Stalinism was more important to him than his commitment to Trotskyism as such. When he visited Trotsky in Mexico, they had agreed on the Negro question but had sharply disagreed on James's thesis in his book *World Revolution.* There James attempted to show how Stalin had seized power after Lenin's death and subverted his revolutionary principles. James did not believe that the Soviet Union was a workers' state and took a revolutionary position utterly opposed to the Stalinism there. Trotsky firmly believed that the Soviet Union was a workers' state, albeit degenerate, and that it had to be defended. In one of his letters, with *Strictly Confidential* written at the top, James wrote that he admired Trotsky's sharp insights on the Negro question but was not confident of his approach to history. During their discussions in Mexico, James had pointed out that when Stalin abandoned the position of world revolution and declared "socialism in one country" in 1924 it severed Russia from the international movement. What followed was the barbarous suppression of all opposition within Russia that set it against popular movements elsewhere in the world. James was already moving toward a view of the Soviet Union's tyrannical administration as "State Capitalism."

In Los Angeles, the new Workers Party rented headquarters and met regularly. In April 1940, at a conference attended by approximately eight hundred people, we became official. Our goals were to build a small mass party in opposition to the Stalinist's Communist Party; to oppose the coming war; and to go to work in mass production industries—shipyards, steel mills, coal mines, auto plants, and airplane factories. This we called *proletarianization*. We believed that working side by side with people in such areas would provide opportunities for publicizing our ideas and winning new members. Authors who had been sympathetic to the Trotskyists—James T. Farrell, Saul Bellow, Hal Draper, Irving Howe, and Dwight MacDonald—and the well-known art critic Meyer Schapiro began to attend our meetings.

We were most concerned with the war in Europe and the preparations for eventual entry by the U.S. During our internal fight with the majority in the SWP, Hitler's Nazi legions had invaded Norway and Denmark by sea. In May, German Panzer divisions swept into the Low Countries and outflanked the Maginot Line of the French. And by June, France had fallen and Marshal Petain became head of a German satellite regime at Vichy. Closer to us, and a great shock and sadness to both the members of the SWP and our new party was the murder of Leon Trotsky on August 21, 1940. An assassin sent by Stalin drove a pickaxe into the old man's brain when he turned his back to find something the murderer had asked to see. We held memorial services in Los Angeles and a large one was held in New York by the SWP. Both groups mourned the death of this brilliant man and put aside political differences, if only briefly, to speak out against Stalin's murderous act of assassination.

Our new publication was named *Labor Action* and we took with us the *New International*. The SWP renamed its newspaper the *Fourth International*. The WP leaders also sent internal bulletins and letters to guide local activities. I never fully understood bureaucratic collectivism; it was supposed to be a regime of a new type, antidemocratic but neither Capitalist nor Socialist. For some reason both groups felt it vitally important to have the correct position on this question of Russia. I kept my mouth shut with all sides, not only because I didn't really know what they were talking about but because I failed to see why it was of primary concern in our struggle as revolutionaries. My special interest at the time was to learn all I could about the history and lives of black Americans. Richard Wright's

Native Son had just been published, and it illuminated areas that I had never imagined. There hadn't been anything written or distributed in the U.S. on a national scale in fiction that did not reflect either the church attitude toward blacks or those of the philanthropically oriented ideas of the subsidized black leaders. The novel showed that the personalities of blacks living in slums bore the effects of that life—and it was *news! Native Son* was critical of philanthropy, Negro leadership, Communism, and the role of black preachers. It did not try to solve any problems; it simply stated the racial problem in America in terms of its tragic enormity. This was a book that was going into the homes and schools and libraries of white Americans. As soon as I had read and understood Wright's novel, I wrote to James and urged him to read it, telling him what I thought and felt. My belief and hope was that Wright's book would awaken the general populace to an understanding that we must change the way we live—that is, a revolution was necessary. I had also watched reports on the election. Roosevelt was reelected, but to me the important aspect of the outcome was that Norman Thomas got way over 100,000 votes, more than double the number for the Communist candidate, Earl Browder. This translated for me into an awakening of Americans to a need for social change. I felt euphoric. As a gung-ho, seventh-generation American, what cared I about Russia? But I kept my lips sealed, even in letters to James.

In California, we were surprised to learn that James Burnham was leaving the group with a hostile farewell: "I cannot wish success to the Workers Party." As soon as we heard about Burnham leaving I wrote a note to James, asking his opinion. Because his visa had expired, he had gone into hiding in December of 1939 and great care had to be taken in writing. One time I had to write to him as someone named Petersen and enclose the letter in another envelope marked Goldberg. My instructions changed often enough that I always had to find a previous letter and follow its directions carefully. James wrote back in a letter that I could share with my comrades. I read it during a meeting, omitting the words "dear, and my precious," and it alleviated some of the worry about Burnham's quitting our group. There hadn't been a statement from Shachtman, and since he was the leader of our party we had expected him to reply. (When Communists tell me that they do not take orders or direction from the Kremlin I always have to smile. Our own little group did not feel we were ordered, but we certainly accepted whatever line the political committee handed down.) James wrote:

ot Without Love*

About M'sieu Burnham. My dear, nothing to be disturbed about. Nothing. Did you know that his passing never stirred the movement more than a ripple? For a man of such great ability and one who had played such an outstanding role in the party and during the faction fight his defection should have caused a storm. *Cannon & Co. were counting on that.* Those idiots didn't understand what was happening under their noses. The party was seeking a way out. Burnham and *Max were being borne by a current.* They were not leading a split. They were pushed into a position by the development of events. I have traced it in "The Roots of the Party Crisis." But all movements need leaders. Max responded splendidly. When the thing had started, Burnham *drew back.* He shrank from the responsibility of leading the split, because though he had managed to dodge responsibility before, the new party would need him. He now had to face the question—are you coming in full-time or not? He could dodge it no longer. And we could see him bend and finally break under it. Nothing became him less than the manner of his going. He stayed away for weeks immediately after the split—just didn't even come around or phone. Then he turned up with the most god-awful document you ever saw. He didn't believe in Marxian economics, he didn't believe in the Marxist theory of history, he didn't believe in the party, he didn't believe in Socialism, he disavowed everything he had preached for five years: Reasons? None. None at all. Theories he had taught for five years he dismissed in three lines. Now, my precious, I know Mr. James B. very well. He is an intellectual of intellectuals—professor of logic and philosophy, advocate of scientific method, a man of reason to the point of arrogance. Very good. But now at a moment of crisis in a movement of the highest intellectual traditions, Burnham comes to the conclusion that he must leave. That is his privilege. But to write the rubbish that he did. Thereby he proves that *he did not leave on intellectual grounds at all.* Had he genuinely developed differences with us, he being who he is, would have set them down as clearly as anyone I know, except L.T. [Trotsky] That he didn't, that he wrote so badly is proof that it was a miserable rationalisation of his wish to get out. He was tied strongly to bourgeois society—wife, children, job, *social life,* easy living. Marxism never completely enveloped him. He wouldn't let it. Hence the pitiable figure he presents today. A man of remarkable intellect and great strength of character—has crawled out of the revolutionary movement by the back door; today stands nowhere; tomorrow will have to stand with the bourgeoisie, for our society offers you no third choice in this crisis. Either Wall Street's war—or Fifth Columnist.

He was correct in his predictions. Burnham joined with other evangelistic renegades from the Trotskyist and Communist parties, such as Max Shachtman, Whittaker Chambers, Frank Meyer, and many more. Burnham was admired by President Reagan, who said, "I owe him a personal debt." The *Washington Post* reported, "According to Burnham, a choice confronted America in the Cold War—either 'appeasement or liberation.' By posing the question so starkly, he helped set the whole litmus-test tone for the conservative movement."

11

Time and again, my political enthusiasm flagged. I felt played out. But underneath the feeling of exhaustion, a new sensation or a reassertion of my natural self—rebellious—was growing. Although I had been studying Negro history and was eager to start a study group, fear held me back from taking such a step. The only people who might be interested were some of our contacts on the South Side, and they didn't need a study group to know they were mistreated and had been throughout history. They could teach me more than I could ever teach them about race relations. Also, I was fearful not only of the leadership but of rank and file members who were diligent in carrying out the Party line. I did not like fetters on my brain. James's attitude was that "corsets were for the body, not the mind." Presumably such a freedom was possible for him, but not for a lowly rank and filer like me. I could not see any way out of my dilemma. Where else would I find people devoted to ridding the world of injustice? The Socialist Party wanted accommodation, I wanted change. The Communist Party, in my mind, was akin to Fascism. The Republican and Democratic parties did not seem very different from each other, and they certainly did not want a new society. There wasn't anywhere to go; I was stuck. But the growing friction and petty factional disputes in the Party seemed pointless. There was very little articulation or circulation of differing positions. When members got fed up, they simply left, although some would present their differing political ideas. Being naive, my feelings were that we all agreed on our goals, so why couldn't we get along with each other and everyone speak his mind? I knew from letters James wrote that there were serious political differences among the leaders of the Party. But in Los Angeles only the views of the current leadership were discussed, and differences among them were withheld from the membership. There were no time limits set on speakers to discourage monopolization of discussion by long-winded individuals. The leaders did not provide time for all those who wanted to speak. We were constantly bombarded by members who tended to go on and on. What happened was that most people not used to speaking felt intimidated and discouraged. Occasionally one of the leaders would ask point blank for our opinions about something he or she had proposed. When I refused to take sides, proponents would become hostile. The reason I couldn't choose one point of view over another was ignorance; I was confused and sometimes didn't understand all of the political jargon. I began to stay away from some of the meetings, which made everything worse. A comrade told me that some members said they didn't expect much from me because I was a petty bourgeois. My mind was like a see-saw, swinging up and down from guilt at not attending meetings and anger at the leaders for not being more forthright with we lowly members about their differences.

My job with Dr. Fishler was enervating, six days a week, sometimes ten hours a day. Dr. Fishler was a close sympathizer of the Party. He was generous in his contributions, ready to give money to publish our papers and help comrades in need. He was also a workaholic, dedicated to his patients. Dr. Fishler was a good surgeon who specialized in tonsillectomies. He paid me sixteen dollars a week, a good salary in those days. He also taught me to give anesthetics, and that is what I did every day. The patients were generally very young, but often there were a few teenagers. Giving anesthetics then was called "pouring ether." Ether was not literally poured or there would have been bodies lying around. Ether came in metal cans, not flat on top but having an opening similar to a bottle. One removed the metal cap and replaced it with cork. On one side of a cork the size of the opening, a small opening was cut into the shape of a V. A sliver of cotton was placed in the slit and the cork was placed in the can of ether. When upended, the ether dripped either a drop at a time or more if the can was tilted. A wire cone, similar to a small basket, covered on the inside by two layers of gauze was placed over the patient's nose and mouth, and the ether was dripped slowly onto the mask. The anesthetist wearing a mask did not inhale as much as the patient, of course, but still left the operating room reeking of ether.

In the stage just before losing consciousness patients struggled against the straps that held them on the operating table. The struggles of small children were easy to control, but teenagers thrashed side to side and up and down with vigor. I sat on a stool at the head of the operating table with one hand under the patient's chin and the other holding the can of ether. Teenager struggles used to lift me from the stool, they were so violent. At the end of the day my neck, back, and arms ached and my hair and breath smelled of ether. No matter how tired I was, I washed my hair every night, but sometimes I wondered why I bothered. The smell would return the next morning after the first anesthetic poured.

Sometimes there were bleeders, people who began to bleed hours after surgery. Dr. Fishler had a large, ward-like recovery room—he had from five to ten patients a day—and they were kept there for several hours, until he was sure there wouldn't be any problems. However, there were many nights when he would be called to the home of someone bleeding. When this happened he called me to accompany him, in case he needed assistance. Or, I thought, maybe he just wanted my company.

Our Workers Party meetings were held on Friday night, and on those days Dr. Fishler arranged half-day surgery so that I could attend and not fall asleep during discussions. I never told him that many times I did not go to a meeting but went out with Edward Keller instead. Dr. Fishler usually attended most of our open meetings but not the Friday night business meetings. Fortunately, we did not very often have a bleeder from Friday morning surgery. As a matter of fact, bleeders seemed to occur more often on the weekend, or perhaps that was my imagination.

Edward Keller was still more than attentive and by now I called him Eddie because he preferred it to his formal name. It had been a year since I left Norman and our divorce was almost final. We had decided on that old saw, *incompatibility,* as the reason for our separation. Eddie proposed almost every time we met, but I was reluctant to marry again. Most of the time I blamed myself for my failed marriage. What did I do wrong? Was there something wrong with me that I couldn't stay married? There were times when depression or dark moods settled on me like a flock of ravens— a sense of futility and worthlessness, a feeling of what's the point of it all swept me into a black pit. Fortunately, these periods lasted only a few days, but while in such a state I felt that the depression would never end. During this time I did not want to see anyone or talk to anyone, I just wanted to wallow in misery. Marian Ornstein, with whom I was still living, was not perturbed by my moods. She was a reserved, quiet person and never tried to talk me out of whatever was bothering me. We never had a fight, only arguments about left-wing politics. It had nothing personal about it. We remained friends. Marian was a member of the League Against War and Fascism and, of course, I felt that she should join the Workers Party, my group. She resisted joining and as it turned out she was right and I was wrong. The FBI often followed us, but we did not feel intimidated. *They* could do as they like, was our attitude. This was a free country, wasn't it?

Marian and I moved from Adams Street to Echo Park, which was nearer downtown Los Angeles and closer to where we both worked. Echo Park was beautiful, a small hillside of houses overlooking a clean pond on which ducks used to gather. Trees and grasses surrounded the pond and the area was secluded enough to create the feeling of being out in the country. Yet just a block or two away, traffic and buses rumbled past. We had just settled into our studio apartment with its wall bed when I awoke one morning unable to take more than a few steps. I was in excruciating pain with every movement. Marian called my physician, Dr. Louis Gogol, who was a sympathizer of the Workers Party. His wife, Bessie, was a member and the sister of Raya Dunayevskaya. Gogol was a well-known surgeon and later became the Los Angeles Chief Coroner. Doctors made house calls in those days and Gogol arrived within an hour. He diagnosed my malady as diverticulitis and said that I would have to stay in bed until the pains subsided. If they did not, surgery was in the offing. A diverticulum is a small pocket on the side of the colon that fills with stagnant fecal matter and becomes inflamed. It is associated with acute pain and, in some cases, bleeding. I was in bed for almost a month and grew very sick of being an invalid, especially since the bed, when pulled down from the wall, took up most of our living space. But Marian looked after me before and after work without complaint. Eddie came several times a week, bringing potted plants, flowers, and food. We ate very well, Chinese and Mexican food of all kinds, and from a Jewish delicatessen on Fairfax wonderful corned beef, pastrami, lox and bagel, coleslaw, and matzo ball soup. One of my favorites was half-sour kosher dill pickles, but they were forbidden until the inflammation subsided. Dr. Gogol visited every other day and sometimes joined us for dinner without telling his wife. Bessie was a domineering woman, outspoken as well as loud-spoken, who in meetings was always interrupting. She was very tall and thin, with short, dark brown hair. She was also ungainly and hunched her shoulders when she walked, swinging her arms, which made her look something like a bat from a distance. Bessie had to know where her husband was every minute of the day. Even on the one afternoon during the week when he did not have office hours, Bessie arranged some or another outing or picnic that she insisted he share. He only wanted to be alone, desperately desiring peace and quiet, but he had to acquiesce in her plans to avoid arguments.

I was eventually able to return to work and was very happy to do so, in spite of its strenuous demands. Dr. Fishler was pleased to see me again and, in fact, after a few days showed signs of having deeper interests in my well-being. One weekend he invited me out to dinner and afterward became amorous, but I had become experienced in fending off undesired advances from men. Most women know exactly how this is done, but there are some men who never "get the message." Harry was one. I hate to be touched unless I initiate a move. And Harry found it difficult to restrain himself. Even at work I began to feel that I had to keep the operating table between us. One evening I told Eddie about these maneuvers, ending by saying I thought I'd have to buy some track shoes. Eddie thought the situation was hilarious and couldn't stop laughing. I was annoyed, always taking myself too seriously. When he stopped laughing, he said, "Marry me and you'll be safe." I told him I had only been divorced a short time and didn't want to make another mistake. Eddie proposed then that we live together first and when I was ready we would marry. "What will your folks say?" was my response. There wasn't a problem with my mother, she still lived in Fresno and I would not tell her. Eddie said, "My parents love you almost as much as they do me. In their hearts you are one of their own." He also told me not to be a fuddy duddy, that people were living together without license everywhere. This was certainly true among radicals, and they justified it by saying that legal marriage was imposed on us by bourgeois society. That night I told Eddie that I'd really think about what he proposed but that he must promise that if I agreed he would not pressure me to marry until I was ready. I was not sure that living intimately might not persuade me to marry. Sometimes I thought that I did not know my own mind, especially when depression hit me. Aside from the matter of Harry Fishler, who would cease pursuit, Marian was now seriously dating Healy Alzofon, a man whom she would eventually marry. A one-room apartment made it impossible for privacy, and although she had not indicated any discomfort with our living arrangement I knew that she would be too polite and kind to suggest any change.

But those were not the only reasons for my acceding to Eddie's proposal. He had won me over, particularly during my long, boring weeks in bed. There was no doubt in my mind that he loved me and I needed always to be loved. I think the primary reason was that being by nature reserved and apart from others, I needed grounding like an electrical outlet for a computer. The swings of my emotions might be controlled; I'd be less vulnerable, less hurt by the harsh world. Maybe grounding myself with Eddie could control these emotional ups and downs.

While I was at work Eddie found a furnished apartment midway between Hollywood and downtown Los Angeles. It was a studio with a large front room, kitchenette, breakfast area, and two steps that led up to an alcove that held a closet and a built-in chest of drawers. It was decorated in a pseudo-luxurious manner, but without good taste. The entire place was carpeted in a crimson red. The chairs were black wrought iron covered by velveteen cushions. There was a pull-down wall bed. Fortunately, there was a drop leaf table in the front room on which we could eat dinner. Neither of us liked eating in the kitchen area except for breakfast. There were windows only on one side of the apartment and we placed the table there, so we could have a view, though limited. Both of us were amused by the gaudiness of the place and determined that we would find something more suitable later on. I have never been in a whorehouse, but that apartment fits my imaginary picture of what one looks like. The compelling reason to move in quickly was so that I could let Harry Fishler know that we were living together so he would stop his antics. Antics is unfair as a description of his behavior because he was a serious man who was attracted to me and saw no reason to hide his feelings.

Sex: I told Eddie before we moved in together about my only experiences with lovemaking, including the first frightening and frightful backseat experience with Norman. He was not a novice and soon discovered how he could arouse me. His technique was to talk me into bed. Talking did not include anything salacious; it was about ideas and theories. Eddie had a breadth of reference, wit, and incisiveness, and he sometimes spoke in classic prose. He was an organizer of ideas with a gift for assembling the particulars that made a theme glow. Eddie's discussions encompassed opinion, memoir, rant, criticism, humor, analysis, and experience. He was fascinated by the interplay of opposites, science and art, fact and fantasy, disciplined work and brilliant intuition. His wide-ranging ideas may have been based on philosophical training, but also a kind of personal genius. At any rate after half an hour of listening, and sometimes questioning, I was in a passionate state. He also taught me French kissing, which had only been described to me by someone else. I had shuddered at the thought, absolutely turned off at the idea of someone sticking a tongue in my mouth. Eddie did not thrust his tongue in my mouth; instead, as a first stage, and of course not talking about it, he gently tickled my lips with his tongue when we were kissing. After a few such encounters, after he had talked me into the mood, such kissing became more intense and I began to take part tentatively at first and then more boldly.

I was still pouring ether for Dr. Fishler and coming home tired and smelly. Eddie never complained about the ether aroma and when I asked if it bothered him he said no. Did it bother me that he came home smelling of paint and turpentine? What began to bother him was that I was always too tired. My day began at 7:30 A.M. and usually ended at 5 P.M. Under such circumstances we did not do much cooking and bought prepared food to eat in or went to his parents' home to eat. Both Mr. and Mrs. Keller urged me to quit my job and offered to help us financially if it were needed. Neither Eddie nor I would accept their offer.

After two months we found an apartment on a hill above Echo Park Lake. It seemed spacious to us since it had a bedroom as well as a dinette. It was unfurnished, so Eddie's folks gave us some furniture and we bought the rest. We had a clear view of the lake from our front room and there was a balcony along the front that ran clear around to the back door. Soon after moving in, we married. In a sense it was a forced marriage. It appeared that the U.S. would enter the war and all the leftist parties were opposed. That is, all were opposed until Russia became involved and then the Communists, following the party line, became avid supporters. Cannon's party, the SWP, opposed the war ideologically but proposed that its members be drafted or enlist. If the workers had to go, then Cannon said the party's place was to fight alongside them. This experience was supposed to lead to the revolution with Trotskyists in the leadership, having thus won the confidence of the workers. The Workers Party opposed the war and told its members to refuse to go. No one whom I knew had heard anything about the concentration camps and the murders being committed by Hitler and his henchmen.

Eddie was determined not to be drafted and he certainly was not going to enlist. He began trying to persuade me to get pregnant. Marriage and my pregnancy, he said, would ensure his safety. I had no desire to become pregnant and resisted. We had fierce arguments that were wearing me down. Some evenings when Eddie kept nagging I walked out and strolled along the lakefront or visited Marian. Ultimately, he would find me and be contrite, but the next day he would begin pressuring me once again. I became extremely nervous and at work my hand holding the can of ether would sometimes shake. One Saturday morning Eddie and I were having breakfast. We had as part of our set of dishes consommé cups that we sometimes used for serving coffee. I was feeling very tired and shaky and when Eddie began again on the pregnancy scheme I looked up and saw the cup's handle on the left side. Thinking the cup was somehow floating in air I grabbed at the handle and spilled part of the coffee all over the table. "What the hell is the matter with you?" Eddie shouted. I burst into tears and sobbingly explained that I had forgotten we were using consommé cups that had two handles. While I mopped up the mess, Eddie laughed so hard he spilled his own coffee, but it didn't seem funny to me. I thought I was losing my mind. Eventually, because I cannot stand arguments, I gave in and became pregnant. The draft board marked Eddie for nonservice and two months later I had an abortion. He had not wanted a child at that point any more than had I. Although on the surface there was harmony, the marriage had been ruined irrevocably. Eddie was extra loving and solicitous but something froze in me. It was difficult to respond and once again sex became a nightmare.

At Dr. Fishler's surgery it was usually the mothers who brought their children for an operation, but one day a man brought his teenage son. He sat rather uncomfortably among all the women until I felt sorry for him. After finishing the morning surgery I offered him coffee, which we kept in a small alcove off the reception room. He was pleased to accept, but while drinking the coffee he kept staring at me until I felt I must have looked untidy and wondered whether the mask had smeared my lipstick or the surgical cap had messed up my hair. I was about to leave to check on my appearance when he stopped me and asked, "Have you ever done any modeling?" I thought at first this was some type of come-on, not too original but probably useful in some instances. I smiled, shook my head, and moved toward the archway. He put his hand in his pocket and handed me a card, explaining that he was a fashion photographer.

That evening I showed the card to Eddie and he said he had seen some of the man's work in a magazine. He urged me to follow up and call for an appointment. If the man had work for me, then it would be possible to leave the surgery. I have forgotten the name of the photographer who started me in the new position, but after my picture appeared in a newspaper advertisement and then in a magazine, I was encouraged to "make the rounds." I prepared a portfolio of photographs that the first photographer shot and gave to me at a discount, and I made a list of commercial studios of photography. Eventually, I worked for Tom Kelley, who was famous for taking early pictures of Marilyn Monroe before she became a star, and then Paul Hesse, one of the first photographers in the area to use color film. There were many other photographers whose names I've forgotten, as well as a famous illustrator, John La Gatta, who originally did magazine covers and was then painting women modeling lingerie. Thus my new career began, and I had more free time to resume studying the "Negro question."

We had moved to a house in Laurel Canyon. Since I needed the car I drove Eddie to the studio in San Fernando Valley every morning and picked him up in the evening. At first Eddie seemed proud of my new occupation, but gradually he became possessive. He didn't want me out of his sight. He also became dependent and showed the first signs of neuroses. I began to feel like a bird in a cage, very well fed, housed, and clothed, but without any freedom at all. Eddie also began to worry about money and was always pushing me to ask for pay immediately when each job was completed. Since this was not the way either studios or illustrators worked—they had to receive payment from clients and models had to wait their turn—this put pressure on me. We soon tired of the house in Laurel Canyon; it was old and run down and difficult to keep clean. Another reason to move was that we loaned the house one evening to a couple of comrades. When we returned we found they had been playful. There were bare feet marks throughout the house, ending in our bed. With my attitude about sex I was outraged and didn't want to stay in a house that had witnessed such hijinks. We found another, more modern house, also in Laurel Canyon, and thought we'd settle down at last. The house was small but the design was original and it was well constructed. A short stairway led from the living room to a bedroom and bath upstairs. A wood-burning fireplace took up almost one whole wall in the living room. And the house had a small back garden, behind which was a hill that went straight up. At the top it was covered with trees. The garage was under the house, since it was built on a hill. We had just settled in, and I had a new pet kitten that I had taken outside. Eddie came bursting through the door, calling me to come inside. Pearl Harbor had been attacked by the Japanese. I think everyone must remember exactly where he was when something momentous happens. Today I can see the house and garden as it was in 1941. Pearl Harbor and Laurel Canyon are indelible imprints that have never left my mind.

A few months after the war began Eddie decided that Laurel Canyon was too isolated and it would be closer to his work if we moved to Beverly Hills. The move to Doheny Drive would be the last Eddie and I shared. We lived down the hill from Ronald Reagan and Jane Wyatt in a much less posh area, though it was nice enough. Next door to us lived Bess and Neil Reagan (nicknamed Moon), Ronald's brother.

Mother and my brother Roy moved from Fresno and stayed with us for a few weeks while searching for their own place. Roy planned to enlist in the Navy air corps, but in the meantime he found a job as a welder in the shipyards. He was given the swing shift and came home late at night after we were asleep. Because of the nature of his work he was covered by oil and particles and had to shower before going to bed. Eddie began to complain that he could not stand being awakened every night. He was polite but cold toward my mother every morning but said nothing about what was bothering him. Mother did not complain but I could tell she was puzzled by his attitude. And I was angry that he was behaving like a rude child.

We began to have fierce arguments, and one time I threw a cup of coffee at him. He ducked but it left a mark on the wallpaper in the dining room. Fortunately, mother had gone downstairs before this episode. She had made friends with Bess Reagan, who found a cottage for mother and Roy in the complex where she lived, in a court. The court was right next door to our apartment building and they moved in immediately.

On the surface our marriage appeared to be a happy one. Eddie was demonstrative, often in public, giving me hugs or a quick kiss, holding my hand, and calling me pet names. Even his family, the Kellers, did not know that things were not what they seemed. We had many friends, among them Jack and Marie Cooper. Jack was the chief publicity man for Warner Bros. motion picture studios. Among other publicity stunts he named Anne Sheridan the "oomph girl." Every Saturday night we went to the Coopers' home near Beverly Hills. And each Saturday we listened to music for a few hours. Television had not been invented but the Coopers had a very good phonograph and a large collection of symphonic and operatic records. After listening to a particular record we discussed the quality of the musicians, the singers, and the ideas of the operas, and I learned a lot from listening to Jack and Eddie's analyses. We would then go into the kitchen, where at one end there was a nook with padded seats. Marie had laid the table and set out a buffet. Everything one could imagine was there for our gluttonous delight: chopped liver or herring; salami, pastrami, corned beef; potato and coleslaw salads; rye bread and rolls; lox, cream cheese, and bagels; dill pickles; and all topped off by a chocolate cake Marie had baked in the afternoon.

Another couple with whom we spent weekday evenings was Ida and Ben Perry. They lived only a block away from us on Robertson, so we walked over often. Ben was a gag writer for movie comics and Ida worked as an assistant to Marlene Dietrich. Another of their friends whom we often saw was Romey Greenson, whose name was actually Romeo. His sister was named Juliet and played the cello in the Los Angeles Symphony Orchestra. Ida was an excellent cook and I often sat on a stool in her kitchen drawing pictures in her cookbooks while she prepared dinner. The reason I spent so much time with Ida in the kitchen was because when

Greenson came to visit the three men talked about things I didn't care to hear. Romey was a psychiatrist and had a number of motion picture actresses as patients. The three men loved to discuss bodily functions. One of their favorite topics was how to deal with the odor in a bathroom after a bowel movement. Ben opted for smoking a cigarette. Eddie chose to burn wooden matches, saying the sulfur took care of the problem. Romey chose to close the lid and flush the toilet three times. I felt such a subject should not be thought of, much less discussed. Romey eventually became Marilyn Monroe's psychiatrist, and I wonder whether they had such intimate discussions.

Ida was the first to sense that my marriage was not working out. However, she did not ask questions or intrude in any way, which is probably why I felt like confiding in her. Having her as an outlet probably kept the marriage together longer than it would have otherwise lasted. One evening I told her that Jack Cooper had called to ask if I wanted to be Salvador Dali's model for a few months. He was coming out to California to work on some designs for Hitchcock and Jack Warner. Ida urged me to accept.

Dali was staying in a suite at the Beverly Hills hotel not far from where we lived. I drove over to meet him alone, because Jack couldn't get away from the studio. Somewhat intimidated, I knocked at the door of his room. A voice called enter, in French, but I simply stood there, frozen. The door swung open precipitously and there was Dali. He was dressed in formal black trousers with a pinstripe, a starched ruffled shirt, and a velvet jacket. In those days, men did not wear ruffled shirts. He had a gardenia in his buttonhole, but his little brown feet were bare. Dali ushered me in, bowing and gesturing for me to sit on the sofa. He hopped up onto the arm of the sofa and looked me over. He said I had the face of a cherub, an angel, and the soul of a devil. He raved about my bone structure until I was overcome. It was difficult to follow his expostulations because he spoke in both French and Spanish. I could understand the Spanish but had trouble with the French. It was obvious I had the job. We arranged for my arrival at 4 P.M. the next day. Before leaving, Dali told me to wait, he had something for me. With great solemnity, as if presenting me with diamonds, he gave me a large naval orange, and then he rushed over to the sideboard to take up a dimestore mouse trap, those little wooden ones with a lethal wire to break the little animal's neck. Again, very solemnly, he pinned the trap on the lapel of my suit.

Dali's work method was to lie in bed half asleep until late in the day. He called those hours "dreaming." Later I realized that he was actually working out visually what he would put on canvas or a drawing board. He then breakfasted, laid out the charcoal and oil paints, and lighted two floor lamps to shine on the model. We worked every day except the weekends until 6 or 7 P.M., depending on whether he was satisfied with the day's work. Every time I arrived, there would be a fresh order of large gardenias and the entire suite smelled of their perfume. He usually draped one of the flowers behind his left ear. On his easel his drawing board was so large that nothing could be seen of him except his small brown feet. Every once in a while he would suddenly poke his head around the side of the board and stare intently. His dark brown eyes reflected the light and glittered until they looked almost black. His mustache quivered at the curled-up ends. He looked so ludicrous that I wanted to laugh. Sometimes I did smile, but he was so intent it never distracted him. Dali when painting or drawing was almost as flamboyant as when posing for publicity shots, except that he was utterly concentrated on the work and not on an audience.

After I had posed for him for several weeks he began showing me collages, created during the night, where as a base he used color pages of illustrations from magazines and then drew designs or painted over the originals. I don't know what happened to these; no one seems to have found them and they are never mentioned in reports of his work. One morning Dali invited me into his bedroom to see some more artwork. He walked over to a low, long chest of drawers in his bedroom and pointed dramatically at the drawings. There were about a dozen, all of penises. Dali's mastery of his craft enabled him to make a drop of water look so real that one wanted to touch it to see if it was wet. The penises, carefully drawn in ink, represented every stage of activity from flaccid to vigorously erect. And they were as realistic as the drops of water he painted. Because I knew he was watching closely for a reaction, I pretended I had seen such sights every day of my life. I don't know whether this spoiled the fun for him or whether it gave him a different idea about his model who "looked like an angel." At any rate, he did not comment, simply saying, "Well, we must work."

When we finished at night he took me most times to Chasen's restaurant in Beverly Hills. There one could eat a hamburger that cost around five dollars during a time when a hamburger at many cafes cost ten or twenty cents. The first night we ate at Chasen's Dali chose our dinner. To start, he ordered snails and bone marrow. I was terribly eager to appear sophisticated to this worldly genius of a painter so I controlled my shudder at the thought of such food. I didn't want him to know that I had never eaten a snail and had known only those that crawled in our garden, leaving a silvery trail behind. I sat like a person condemned to death, trying not to shiver. The marrow was served first and I thought it was the snails. It had a creamy exterior with what looked like tiny blue veins running through it. Several pieces were laid out on white toast. We were to share this delight. I had to persevere so I took up the fork and cut off a small piece, meanwhile holding my napkin, ready to receive it from my lips. Dali was eating away with gusto while I felt sick to my stomach. He kept gesturing to me to have more but I managed to avoid another taste. When Dali finished eating, the waiter approached bearing silver dishes from which there rose a marvelous aroma. My mouth watered; I was really hungry. The waiter placed the silver dish in front of me and there in tiny indentations were beautiful little shells surrounded by drawn butter and giving off the heavenly scent of garlic. All my fright disappeared. I had mistaken the marrow for snails, so the horror was left behind. These delicate and pretty shells invited me to take a taste. I finished the entire dish, even dipping a bit of French bread into the buttery garlic sauce.

While I worked and dined with Dali, Eddie had dinner at home with his parents or with Ida and Ben. He did not object to my long days because Warner Bros. was paying me seven dollars an hour. For photographic modeling I had been earning only five dollars an hour, which was considered good pay. I had worked an entire week for Dr. Fishler for sixteen dollars. Since Eddie made about thirty dollars a week my extra money gave us some financial freedom.

Toward the end of my assignment with Dali on a day little different from any other he showed me some of the sketches he had made of me. These were to be sylph-like in the backgrounds of other paintings. We then worked for about an hour and I took my usual break, lying back on the sofa. I wasn't paying much attention to Dali, who usually studied his work or sharpened pencils or went out of the room. Suddenly he leaped onto the couch, penis erect, and after a few quick motions ejaculated all over my breasts. Then to my shock, disgust, and horror he proceeded to lick off the sperm. I couldn't wait to get to the bathroom, where I showered and tried to control my shaking body. Although married twice, I'd only known the "missionary position" as the sexual act. When I came out, Dali darted into the bathroom and I heard the sound of the shower; I dressed as fast as I could and ran out of the suite.

Eddie couldn't understand why I stopped working for Dali, and I made the excuse that we had finished the work he had planned. Fortunately, I had other modeling assignments so he was satisfied that money would still be coming in. One evening Jack Cooper suggested that I study acting and recommended a place called the Actor's Lab. It was, he said, an offshoot of the Actor's Studio in New York. He knew many of the actors and actresses who were connected with the lab, including John Garfield, Shelley Winters, Lee J. Cobb, Edward G. Robinson, and many others. He said that the lab produced very good work, using a method based on that of Konstantin Stanislavsky, the Russian actor, director, and producer. I'd never heard of this famous man, but I went out the next day to buy his book. He created a system of instruction based on emotional, spiritual, and physical reactions. I fell in love with what was called "the method." As an aid in acting one should recall a traumatic experience from one's own past and try to recapture the moment. The engendered emotion, of course, had to relate to the script and character one was portraying. Another on-stage technique, helpful to actors, was to bring one's concentration to bear on a cup or saucer, a cigarette, or some other prop, and try to actually see and feel the object.

During an interview with the lab's administrator, a short, dark-haired woman, I knew immediately she was either a member of the Communist Party or a close sympathizer. Many of her questions had to do with social issues. And I had been around in political circles long enough to smell the leftist aroma. This revelation posed a problem, because I was vigorously anti-Communist. But when offered a scholarship, I decided to attend classes and see what developed. I was a little worried about being discovered as an enemy, a Trotskyist. But I reassured myself by thinking that after all our goals were similar and our language much the same, so no one would know. Within a few days, and after they sometimes broached leftist opinions and heard my radical response, I was warmly embraced and eventually singled out as a star pupil. The Actors Lab, although a Communist front, was equally serious about perfecting the art of drama. The teachers were well-known actors and actresses who gave their time freely to teaching students who were serious. If they eventually joined the Party, there was rejoicing, but I was not aware of any serious coercion. And there were many well-known people associated with the lab who were not members. Many were interested in the same goals, of course. Those were exciting days, coupled always with a feeling that I was being dishonest. But because of what I was learning and the comfort of knowing that most of the people associated with the lab were sincerely interested in trying to improve society for the benefit of all people, I learned to dismiss my conscience, at least for a time.

We performed a lot of Clifford Odets' plays, which pleased me because he was a writer of proletarian drama. One of my first roles was in his impressionistic play about a taxicab strike, *Waiting for Lefty*. He also wrote *Golden Boy* with a member of our group in mind, John Garfield. At the time, I did not know that Odets was one of the founders of the Group Theater in New York. Orson Welles came to lecture fairly often and he inspired everyone with his brilliant analyses. His talks covered a wide range of subjects, from his experiences as an actor in the company of Katherine Cornell, actor/director in the WPA, to the formation of his own company with John Houseman, the Mercury Theater, to certain film techniques he was perfecting. Welles claimed that when they produced H. G. Wells's *The War of the Worlds*, which frightened people into believing aliens had landed in New Jersey, he and Houseman had not anticipated such a reaction. "It was just a damn good show," he said. He stayed quite late unless he had other appointments and patiently answered all our questions. I worked hard at mastering some of Stanislavsky's techniques and in a few months was cast as the ingenue in *Arsenic and Old Lace*. I was also chosen to emcee another show that was performed for the naval recruits stationed on Catalina Island, twenty-two miles offshore from Los Angeles. Navy personnel met us at the dock in San Pedro and we boarded an LST (landing ship tank). A member of the crew told us that LSTs conveyed tanks or other rolling stock that could exit right into shallow water, which was why they sat so low in the water. When we neared the island we had to wait until the chains were lifted. Because of the war, there were underwater chains as guards against submarine attacks. The boat rocked back and forth and I got very seasick. One of the sailors, feeling sorry for me, fed me dry white bread, saying it would settle my stomach. We performed at the Avalon Casino ballroom, a massive, white, Moorish-design rotunda with a red tile roof. I was a terrible emcee, much too nervous and still too sick to fill the bill. I was good, however, in plays with other actors, taking to the method style of acting as if it were born in me. My work in Clifford Odets' plays won me praise from teachers.

After a few months I tried out for and got a part in a play starring Nancy Carroll, who was attempting a come-back. The only stipulation was that I had to bleach my hair blonde, because Nancy did not want another redhead in the cast, particularly one so much younger than she. We were to open in San Francisco within six weeks. Eddie did not object outright to my acting in the play but as the time neared when we were to leave he said he would be deathly ill the whole time I was gone. In the next minute he would say, "Baby, I really want you to go. It's a good opportunity for you. But I'll miss you so much that I'm sick to my stomach just thinking about it." I tried to make him laugh, "You're saying, 'I want you to go, but I'll be throwing up in the toilet the whole time you are gone'?" Eddie was not amused.

We went into rehearsal and after some weeks of intensive work opened at the Strand Theater in San Francisco. Fortunately, my old friend Marian was living in the area and I was able to stay with her. The show closed after one week because of poor attendance. In that short time I contracted poliomyelitis. Back home the doctors began following the Kenny Method, a new treatment consisting essentially of bedrest and the application of steaming hot, wet compresses to the legs. The treatment was successful and after a couple of months I was well, left with some weakness in the back but otherwise almost normal. During my illness, Eddie was impossible. He had never shown jealousy before but while I was ill he kept asking with whom I had been sleeping in San Francisco. He said I must have caught polio from someone. The nurse had to ask him to leave the room because I was so weak I'd tremble and cry, which was certainly not conducive to getting well.

I was glad to return to the Actor's Lab and begin studies once more. Eddie and I were quarreling most of the time. He nagged about everything. I was not very kind to him, either. I told him he was mentally ill and should see a psychiatrist. When he wanted to make up after a fight I pushed him away. He didn't seem to realize that the way he acted didn't lead to sex. Foreplay is more than stroking, kissing, and touching sensitive spots, it encompasses daily kindness, gestures, loving looks, and a feeling that one is respected as well as sexually desirable.

Eddie and I had stopped attending Party meetings and socials and I occasionally had stabbing guilt feelings, but James's letters and enthusiasm for my new career made me feel I was not wrong in the choice. In September, he wrote:

> I am thrilled beyond belief and proud as if I have done something. You write "I read every book I could find on acting" and again "I was monomaniac about acting." Sister, that is life and living and finding yourself. Stick to it and squeeze it dry. The feelings that surge and must be expressed are the

pulsation of a life within you more powerful than in the average person. All people have it, capitalism stifles it. But with some it is so powerful that it breaks through. You achieve or you don't achieve. But the thing that matters is to live your life, to express yourself as long as it is not ignoble or mean or actuated by cheap motives such as getting a lot of money. You seem uncertain about my understanding what you are doing and why. Some pseudo-Marxist has been getting at you, telling you that what you should do is to join a party and work in a factory? Just tell them to go to hell, that's all. I worked at literature for years and made my own way to where I am. I made my own way. Not a soul contacted me. Nobody taught me. And, thank Heaven, I find that I am still making my own way while so many others are floundering around, repeating.

Now you are a creative person and express yourself to society in a certain way. Sweetheart, no revolutionary of any sanity or experience would dream of your doing anything else—*as long as you did something about it, which you are doing.* The wishy-washy, who sit around and *talk,* they are detestable. You are serious about it. To be serious about an art is a contribution to society. You are young. Very young. In two or three years you will know more clearly what you are doing and what you are expressing and what are your prospects. Perhaps longer. Meanwhile, sweetheart, your chief backer, supporter, press agent, inspiration, and rooter is just me. And particularly with those who say that you should join a party, pass them over to me. I'll destroy them or give you the weapons to blow them to bits. That is, if you need them.

Sometimes after class the actor/teacher or the woman in charge of the place would take us to a nightclub where their friends were performing. One evening we went to the Macombo to see an actor, Jack Gilford, a comedian who had been brought to Hollywood for a film and was also starring in a stage revue. He was one of the funniest men I had ever seen or heard. He could imitate anything, the MGM lion or a golf ball. He was the first person to use the line "Pay attention, I'm going to ask questions later on." When Jack finished performing he joined us at our table, but there were no empty chairs. He made a helpless gesture to me and I immediately stood up and gave him my seat. He then held out his hand and pulled me onto his lap. People around us at other tables were whispering and staring, trying to identify others in the group who might be famous. My head was turned, I felt important. Jack looked at me and said he ought to have my name since we were so intimate. I told him, "You were wonderful!" with all the gush of a schoolgirl. From the way his face lighted up I knew at once he was a man who desperately needed praise. It was true. Years later an interview with one of Jack's children demonstrated his father's lack of confidence. The boy said that when their father became very depressed they took him out for a walk. As soon as someone recognized him as the actor and made it obvious his whole attitude changed. He became cheerful and happy and the blues vanished.

The following week we were in rehearsal fairly late in the evening when Jack walked in and sat in the front row. Afterward he asked if I would have a sandwich with him. We went to the Player's Club on Sunset Boulevard and sat upstairs on a balcony overlooking the street. He talked and I listened. I talked and he listened. When we finished eating we dawdled over espresso, both hating the evening to end. On our way out people looked at us and whispered Jack's name. I loved the attention and felt a reflected glow of celebrity. For the next few weeks Jack came whenever he could to meet me and we continued to go to the Player's Club for late night snacks. One night he kissed me with great fervor and invited me to his apartment for brunch the next morning. Around 10:30 A.M., after driving Eddie to the studio, I parked the car at home and rode my bicycle to Jack's place. Jack was still in a robe but the table was set and he was getting ready to scramble some eggs. Freshly squeezed orange juice in stemmed glasses was waiting at each place setting. We had a wonderful time over breakfast, laughing until our sides ached. Together we cleared the table and I started for the door, ready to get home. Jack caught me to him and kissed me, but I pulled away. When he looked disappointed I explained I could not make love to him until I had separated from my husband. After we became lovers Jack confessed that my attitude, shown in such a statement, made him love me even more. If I had gone to bed with him then still married, he would never have trusted me—I might have been unfaithful to him at some later date.

That night I told Eddie I wanted a divorce. At first he was shocked, but he quickly became angry and marshaled all the reasons we should stay together. This was my second marriage, he said, and that being the case, it was an indication there was something seriously wrong with me. He was now the one to say I needed a psychiatrist. Eddie then said that he could not possibly live without me; he might as well be dead. I hardly listened to his plea. All I could think of were my own desires and I persisted, saying I wanted him to move out by the weekend. He could stay with his parents until he found his own place. Nothing he said changed my mind, not even his tears. Deep inside I was frightened, wondering whether there was something sick about me, that here I was ending a second marriage.

When Jack showed up at our next rehearsal I told him that until everything was settled with my husband I did not want to see him. Eddie moved out, saddened and crushed. I learned from Lilly, his sister, that he subsequently sought out a psychiatrist. She gave me his name and I called to ask if there was anything I could do to help. The doctor was curt—"You have done enough already, it's too late,"—and banged down the phone. I felt chastened, which added to my pangs of guilt. Nevertheless Jack and I began a passionate love affair. It was not long before we slept together, which we didn't actually do, because I went home at night to sleep alone. But I still cannot use the word for what we were actually doing. Jack was a marvel as a lover, skilled and tender. He made me feel that no one like me had ever been born, that I was more beautiful than a movie star and more intelligent. With him, after two marriages, I had my first orgasm. It was a most marvelous feeling, and I wondered why it hadn't happened before.

Here was a man almost unredeemably ugly who was at the same time irresistible. Jack had a pear-shaped face, narrow at the top, and with tiny eyes bisected by a large nose. His skin was reddish and lumpy, as if he had had a severe case of acne as a child. In repose there was nothing in his face to admire. But when he smiled and spoke or was acting he appeared handsome. The ugly individual features were forgotten. We screwed every moment we could; after one of his performances we could hardly wait to reach his apartment. Sometimes just inside the doorway, with Jack kicking the door shut with the back of his foot, we'd fall onto the carpet, not waiting to reach the bedroom. He gave me a huge bouquet of roses one evening and so great was our haste we ended up lying on the rose petals scattered on the floor. When he had an orgasm he whispered my name three times, "Constance, Constance, Constance." I bought him a silver identity bracelet with the words inscribed and we smiled when people thought I was staking out ownership. We had only one disagreement and that was my persistence in aiming to go to New York. During these times Jack wondered aloud whether he was not too old for me, the fifteen years' difference becoming a concern. He did not think I had fully matured, and I probably had not. My going to New York for an acting career was his problem. My particular problem was my difficulty reading and discussing the Communist newspaper, the *Daily Worker*. My stomach seemed to curdle when I read their half-truths and the agitprop in every report. Since Jack was a

member of the Party, I was careful not to let him know of my political be-
liefs and background. Keeping silent increased my feelings of guilt. I was
being dishonest with someone who loved me. One night we attended a
Party celebration in honor of Stalin's birthday and his climb to power. A
film was shown that was so filled with lies I could hardly watch it. The history of the Soviet Union, the role of Trotsky, who was portrayed as a traitor, and the adulation of Lenin's presumed favorite, Josef Stalin—all the
lies made me feel sick. I felt like a traitor to my friends, and worse, to my
own integrity.

In Hollywood we attended the actors' cell meetings. The Communists
had created various small groups, each devoted to a professional affiliation.
There were cells for songwriters, directors, actors, scriptwriters—everyone
was represented. The idea was that no one in one group would be able to
identify members of another, in case of FBI infiltration. Outside of Party
meetings, people in all the industry met freely in each other's homes. Jack
was friendly with many who were either members or sympathizers, among
them E. Y. (Yip) Harberg and his wife, Harold Arlen, Walter Houston,
Lena Horne, Cab Calloway, Larry Parks, Judy Holiday, Lee J. Cobb, and
many others. Although Danny Kaye's wife was a sympathizer, I never met
him because of Jack's attitude. He disliked Kaye intensely, claiming the
reason he became such a celebrity was because he had had his nose fixed.
Jack thought the plastic surgery was to hide Kaye's being Jewish.

All the time we were together and despite Jack's proposal of marriage
and my acceptance, I was saving money for my move to New York. I did
not hide from Jack my intentions to try for an acting career on Broadway.
This bothered him so much that he broke off our engagement and said he
would not see me again. We went through a two-week separation that was
painful. I had developed a zest for sex and was fooled into believing it was
love. I longed for Jack and finally went one night to see him perform in the
revue. Afterwards I went backstage and he said he knew I had been in the
audience, that my laughter was unmistakable. We became lovers again that
same night and Jack grudgingly accepted my plans for New York. The film
he was in had been completed and there were only a few weeks more of
the revue booked. He said he would join me in New York as soon as he
was free of engagements. Jack still complained about my acting, saying
we'd be separated when a part required shooting on location. That was not
good for marriage, he warned. Wives seldom accompanied their actor husbands, I argued, so what was the difference? Despite Jack's Communist
ideals about equality he declined to answer my question.

People at the Actor's Lab were enthusiastic about my trip to New York and gave me letters of introduction to the head of the American Theater Guild. They assured me that she would help me get started. They also gave me letters to John Garfield (whom I had met at the Actor's Lab) and Clifford Odets. They arranged for an actor who was a Party member to meet me at Grand Central Station. The day arrived and I boarded the Chief with a first stop and change of trains in Chicago. There wasn't any possibility of my taking the other, very luxurious train, the Super Chief on which the stars traveled. But the Chief was new and nice enough. I had managed to save one hundred dollars and Jack gave me twenty dollars in change for tipping purposes. He also made sure I had the latest issue of the *Daily Worker*.

⚜ 12 ⚜

The train from Chicago to New York was a letdown. The seats were covered in dusty, old, red-plush material and the windows were grimy. The Chief, because it was new, had been sparkling clean and even though I had traveled by coach it was comfortable, with space enough to stretch one's legs. This was not the case with the battered old train in Chicago. But the train could not dim the excitement I felt en route to the magic city of New York.

At last the train pulled into Grand Central Station. The station's grandeur was overwhelming, and the people rushing back and forth with such speed were bewildering. I thought about Dickens's essay on New York, but only part of it seemed accurate. He wrote about people "all travelling to and fro; and never idle . . . These restless Insects, confused heaps of buildings . . ." Nothing seemed confused about New York—I was the one confused but at the same time filled with intense excitement and already falling in love with everything around me. Later in the week I was taken to the New York Public Library at Forty-second Street and Fifth Avenue. The immense marble steps leading up to it, watched over by two giant-sized carved lions, its grand Corinthian columns, and its foyer with its swooping archways and glittering chandeliers had me gaping. Upstairs the rooms were wood-paneled and very large. I looked forward to sitting in one of the wooden chairs at one of the long tables and studying. The room was so quiet that I felt I should be on tiptoe. There was no sound of the traffic outside, just utter stillness in the reading rooms. My first ride during rush hour on the subway was literally breathtaking. It was difficult to breathe because of the crush of people; books or newspapers were pressed against bodies; arms and legs couldn't be moved; and the aroma rising from some people was unbearable. I wrote Mother that there were attendants whose job it was to stand on the platform and shove people onto the trains so the doors would close. She couldn't believe it. If one wanted to stay near the door so as to get off at the first stop it wasn't possible. Fortunately, on the express a lot of people usually got off at every stop, leaving space for a few seconds until another crowd got on. People leaving the train faced those entering and there were shouts of "Let us off before you get on!" There weren't any fights, not because people were sanguine but because there simply wasn't any room to raise a fist or hand.

I had reserved a room at the Barbizon for Women near Central Park. It had been Jack's recommendation, principally I think because it was a women-only hotel. No men were allowed anywhere except in the reception room on the first floor. It suited me just fine; I had no intention of seeing anyone, being still enamoured of Jack. My room was small, just large enough for one chair, a narrow bed, and a desk. It was immaculately clean and I settled in happily. The first night I was there I tore up all the letters of introduction and the *Daily Worker*. For too long I had lived a lie, not being myself, working with people whose vision of the future was so antithetical to my own. I would face New York on my own, without the assistance of the Communists, no matter how influential they might be. I'm afraid I did not blame myself for having worked with them at the Lab, using them, in fact, and letting them think I was someone they might recruit. I had lived a lie and probably my detestation of all they stood for was partly hatred of myself for being dishonest. I was not a novice politically, having been a member of three different left-wing parties. So there was no excuse, but at that stage of my life I just wanted to be free and blamed them for a feeling of oppression. Not myself.

Afraid that someone might piece together the bits of newsprint, I put them in my purse to throw away the next day outside the hotel. Next I called C. L. R. James, and he was ecstatic about my arrival. He asked for my telephone number and address and asked how soon he could see me. I hedged a bit and said I had to get settled and see to a job, but I would call him later in the week. James had written me a disturbing letter early in the year, in January. It read: "Now about my love for you. Darling that is my problem at present, not yours. You have mighty problems of your own. I can guess at them. There are many aspects of life that are to me very mysterious. One of them is the electric spark, something in the blood, that flares when two people meet. It did for me with you."

I looked upon James as a close friend and nearly a father figure, perhaps because my own father had died when I was still young. Whatever the reason, I was not ready for a more intimate relationship, much as I valued him as someone I could talk to about my dreams and aspirations. He always cheered me on and I needed that kind of approval, especially when step-ping into the unknown, such as New York of all places, that city of cities. New York excited me but I had to find a way to make a living before my hundred dollars was exhausted. I had rented the apartment in Beverly Hills, leaving the furniture in the place, but it only brought in sixty-five dollars a month, and rent wasn't due for several more weeks.

The following day I received a special delivery letter from James and a huge sheaf of gladioli, probably the only flower that I dislike. But the girls in rooms on either side of me were more than happy to accept the flowers and it meant for me new acquaintances in this unfamiliar city. I was already in love with New York—had always been through articles, photographs, and film—but at the same time the actuality was intimidating to a small-town girl. And I hoped that I would not be seeing members of the Com-munist Party. For some reason, I had forgotten or put out of my mind Jack's devotion to the *cause*.

Early the next day I took my album of photographic work from Cali-fornia and made my way to the Harry Conover agency on Vanderbilt, near Grand Central Station. I had considered the two leading agencies, Conover's and Robert Powers, which were competitors, the only two major agencies at that time in New York. Both agencies were devoted to photographic modeling, although they accepted jobs for major fashion shows as well. Powers's models were called "Long-stemmed roses," "American beau-ties," or "Long-stemmed beauties," I've forgotten which, but the phrase denoted tall, long-legged women. Conover was known for his "cover girls," models who appeared most often on the covers of magazines and on signboards or in advertisements for beer, wine, cigarettes, toothpaste, soap, small airplanes, and automobiles, all in leading magazines such as *Vogue, Harper's Bazaar, Glamour, House Beautiful,* and newspapers. Powers's models worked mostly for *Vogue* and *Harper's* and were reed-thin, glamorous creatures who appeared extremely sophisticated. I was the healthy, outdoor type and didn't feel that Powers's agency would ac-cept me.

If I had been nervous at the coming interview at Conover's, I became almost paralyzed when entering his offices. I had never seen so many beau-tiful women all in one place in my entire life. Some were talking quietly with each other while others were leafing through fashion magazines. Ap-parently they were waiting to be interviewed and I wondered how long I would have to wait. With knees trembling, I approached the receptionist; before I could speak she asked if I had any experience and photographs.

Too intimidated to answer, I simply thrust my album at her and she rapidly scanned a few pages. To my surprise she got up, said "Just a minute," and left me standing at her desk. I felt embarrassed because all of the women in the room were watching me. I think they wondered why I was getting special treatment and not being asked to sit down and wait. The receptionist returned and motioned to me to go with her through a door nearby. She introduced me to Lee, Mr. Conover's administrative assistant, a woman seated in a private office. Lee was an attractive blonde woman with a round face, a pleasant, rather ingenuous smile, and a mature figure. She wasn't fat; simply, in contrast to the models, fuller in figure. She appeared to be about thirty, which at my age appeared old. Little did I know that one day I'd feel that someone of thirty would seem like a child. After only a few questions and a review of the photographs in my album, Lee went into an inner office marked "Harry Conover." She came out in a few minutes and took me in to see Conover. Conover was not handsome but rather a good-looking man, with brown hair and eyes, tall and heavy set, a little too much weight but still within reason, not fat. He looked at me from my toes to the top of my head, and I could tell by something in his eyes that he was either attracted to me or he responded in such a manner toward all women. At any rate, he had me sign a contract and said to return the next day. He had, he said, "to think about me and how I was to be launched." When he said *launched* I laughed, actually without meaning to, but a vision of a ship being sent to sea for the first time and my general nervousness overcame me. Instead of asking why I was laughing, Conover's brown eyes became almost luminous, and he put his hand on the top of the photo album. "That's it!" he said. "I've got it! You are a friendly, typical California girl and we don't have many in New York. I'm going to name you 'Frosty,' that's it, 'Frosty Webb.'"

Lee explained later that Conover renamed all of his top models. There were Choo Choo Johnson, Candy Jones, Chili Pepper, and others. That Conover had chosen a name for me made me feel that he thought I would become a good model—that is, make money for his agency. The names were chosen because photographers would ask questions as to why a person had such a name. This offered an opportunity to talk to them and thus fix oneself in their minds. When a job came up that needed someone of a certain type, photographers would remember the previous discussion. Hundreds and hundreds of young women were constantly visiting photographers and few would be remembered or called for an assignment. Strange names, particularly unsuited to the person, kept one from being a cipher; it was a type of imprinting. The ploy seemed to work for the Conover models; they were kept very busy posing for various advertisements or strutting on runways in posh hotels—the Plaza, Waldorf Astoria, Ritz Carlton.

My first assignment was to sit for new photographs and order a hundred copies. The cost was ten dollars and I wondered how soon money would be coming in rather than going out. I was highly cheered, however, when Lee told me that my fee would be five dollars an hour less a 10 percent commission to Conover. Location jobs would pay fifty dollars a day, and lunch was included. This sum meant riches; really good jobs paid only thirty-five dollars a week. At the time, one could eat a hamburger at the White Castle for five cents and a two-pound lobster from Maine was less than a dollar for lunch in many variety stores or drugstores that had lunch counters. I wanted to sing and dance; in one day, eight hours, I would earn forty dollars! Added up quickly in my mind was a sum of two hundred dollars each week. Why, my father never earned much more than that for a month of work! In Los Angeles, working for Dr. Fishler only paid sixteen dollars a week. It had not been so long ago, in 1938, that the Wage and Hours Act, signed by President Franklin Roosevelt, raised the minimum wage for workers engaged in interstate commerce from twenty-five cents to forty cents an hour. Of course I assumed I would be working eight hours a day, five days a week. I was ecstatic. I could send money home to my widowed mother, put some in the bank, and still have enough left to feel secure for years to come. What an innocent I was. Little did I realize that there were almost no modeling jobs that lasted eight hours, except for the occasional location shoots, and there would be weeks without any work at all.

When the photographs were ready, we had to stamp Conover's name on the back, which included a form. Our name was imprinted at the top of the form. The form requested color of eyes and hair, height and weight, sizes of bust, waist, hips, dress, glove, stocking, and shoes. When I saw the name *Frosty* at the top of the form, I shook my head but signed away, taking comfort in having been chosen for the name change.

Next, the selected new models were shown how to put on makeup for camera—Max Factor Pancake was used—and we had to demonstrate different ways of styling our hair. At that time, models did not have makeup and hair stylists furnished by a client. We were also instructed on how to dress when looking for work. We always had to have shiny shoes and were told that every morning we were to take black liquid shoe polish and darken the rim around the edge of the shoe. White wrist-length gloves were to be worn and almost always a hat. They advised us to wear one pair of white gloves and keep an extra pair in our hatboxes, because New York was filled with oily dust. We had to be immaculate and, if possible, slightly dramatic, but ladylike. Those tasks finished, we had to spend the rest of the week studying in a recreation room at the agency. Studying consisted of looking at the photographs, observing the poses of models and their makeup, hairstyle, and expressions in *Vogue, Harper's Bazaar, Glamour,* and *Charm* magazines. Teenage models were to study *Seventeen,* but they could look at the adult assignments after completing their course, which consisted of stacks of magazines. We were presented with—that is, we paid five dollars for—a large, round, shiny, black hatbox. The hatbox was the trademark that denoted "model" in this supposedly glamorous business. It drew the attention of everyone, and it was plain shiny black with no advertisement to spoil its contours. The hatbox and the large leather photo album were our stock in trade and they became pretty heavy to carry around. We had to carry the hatbox every day, whether filled or not. When filled it was even heavier and held makeup, comb and brush, curlers, extra shoes, and, depending on the assignment, hats, dresses, aprons, jackets, fur pieces, and scarves. Unless the photo op was for advertisers of clothing we had to furnish our own wardrobe. It was not unusual for a photographer to request three dresses or five hats or a fur coat, or even housedresses and aprons for ads in *Good Housekeeping.* Models had to make friends with each other pretty quickly so they could lend and borrow items on the spur of the moment. There were of course a few models who had money and extensive wardrobes, but most of us lived from job to job.

The day finally arrived when I was given a list of photographers and their addresses and sent out on my own. Fortunately, many photographers had studios in the same area but there were many off the beaten path. We walked and walked and climbed many stairs—up and down, round and round we went, hour after hour. New York has hard pavements and we had been told to wear high-heeled shoes. In 1943 there were not many places in New York where one could sit down and rest. A year or two later the city began to establish little oases where people could ease their aching feet and backs. One such place not far from the agency had a fake waterfall at the back of a cement square between buildings. Whoever designed the area was inspired—the water falling unceasingly from the back wall was soothing, almost soporific. Greenery was furnished by trees and bushes planted around the perimeter, and tables, benches, and chairs offered a welcome retreat. If the chairs and benches were filled, one could sit on a cement parapet that rimmed the area.

When I was modeling, the only place to rest was the Vanderbilt Hotel near Grand Central Station. The hotel's desk people did not mind our sitting in the lobby; in fact, the management thought beautiful models might increase business. We could always return to Conover's, but we didn't want to give the impression that we were not hard at work. In Los Angeles I had always driven to assignments and when looking for work, but here in my beloved city of New York it was walk, walk, walk. The first few days were almost unbearable and by the end my feet were swollen; my neck, shoulders, and back ached; and I felt as if I could not carry the hatbox and photo album another step. I had tried putting the album inside the hatbox but it was awkward when being interviewed. If one was lucky enough to be seen by the photographer, rather than an assistant, he was always in a hurry. He would grow impatient if a model wasted his valuable time fumbling with zippers and pulling out and opening an album. It was not good policy to leave a poor impression on these nervous, intense artistes. Some of the photographers were cruel. They found fault with a model's figure or facial structure or some other permanent feature that couldn't be altered. Dorian Leigh, who became famous, particularly in France, was once told by a photographer that her eyebrows were all wrong and that she would have to either shave them and pencil some in or pluck them into a different shape. Dorian refused and went on to win approval from many other photographers.

However, on a shoot photographers' personalities changed from Satanic to angelic. Generally, when modeling, even head shots, one had to move, slowly changing angles and positions. Photographers would then say, "Just a little to the right, ahhh, beautiful, you look lovely, now turn your head slowly, slowly, and look to the left. Wonderful, you're gorgeous, hold it!" Then after a moment: "Let's see that beautiful smile, yes! Just right!"

After visiting several photographers in one day and not getting an assignment, I usually crept home feeling hopeless and disillusioned, afraid for the future, and wondering what to do. Until I became friendly with other models I thought something was terribly wrong with me, and I was a fool trying to be a New York model. I attributed my ease in modeling in Los Angeles to it being a provincial place after all and now I was facing the real thing, big city New York. Modeling is a destructive experience—that's the nature of it. There is also an extreme loss of privacy. We were stared at wherever we went. When we walked into a room everything seemed to come to a standstill, with people gawking. Many times some women would give us dirty looks and hate us without our having said a word. Almost all of the models with whom I worked found it hard to bear. To protect ourselves we walked the streets as if wearing blinkers, seeing no one, looking straight ahead. There were always one or two models who preened themselves the more they were watched, but they were the exceptions.

Another thing I learned was that most of the sought-after models were not what one would call classic beauties. What was important was bone structure—makeup did the rest. The camera required good and/or unusual bone formation, because the lights and shadows that were picked up then made the face glamorous. There were exceptions. Models required mostly for teenage or out-of-doors advertisements where they worked outside, on location, did not need superior bone structure. The shots were generally smiling, lighted by the sun with sometimes a windblown look. Even when shooting outdoors, however, reflectors were used by the photographers to focus the light exactly where it showed a model or clothing to best advantage.

Models today appear to be strange creatures. Most of them appear belligerent or angry. They stare straight into the camera lens as if ready to hit someone—or as if a pout or glare makes them desirable. The only exceptions seem to be the catalog models, who still face the camera with smiling faces. But they, too, have changed. Lingerie catalog models in the 1940s had to be innocent in appearance, something like slim, milk- or cornfed girls. They were to appear romantic, offering love, not lust. No attitudinal *come on* was allowed. Today there are the Victoria's Secret models—most of them with spread legs, as if needing to air their vaginas. When I was a model there were distinct categories. High-fashion models were not permitted to pose in lingerie catalogs, even though that area provided almost half of the modeling assignments. And I, as a model for major products, was also forbidden such shoots. There is an ungainly ugliness rampant in the profession today. Bodies are contorted, there is the shot hip, way out to the side, toes pointed inwards, knees and arms akimbo—never the grace of the famous models of sixty years ago. When I was modeling no cameraman would allow his subject to look ugly, unless the photograph was for a story in a magazine with specific instructions as to facial expressions and positions. Neither the models nor the photographers are to blame for these phenomena today, except cursorily—they do have to earn a living. Models, after all, are used to sell products, and they become products themselves. Thus a manufacturer who wishes to sell diet foods and drinks hires a giant advertising firm to glamorize his offerings and needs models who appear anorexic. In the 1980s there seemed to be a wave of stick-thin models who looked as if they vomited after each meal and/or were taking dope. In fact, this was the case among some models during that period. Photographers had to shoot faster than usual to snap a picture before the model either fell asleep or passed out. Then during the 1990s a glut of overt sex began, the real works, in films and on television. Language, too, dropped to the gutter when the words *fuck* and *shit* peppered every sentence. It appears today that the American public is virtually desensitized to sluttiness in behavior and in speech. And the models reflect this society, with their sense of entitlement, surgically enhanced with silicon breast and lip injections. Again they are simply responding to what the advertisers believe the public wants and will buy.

When I was modeling a war was raging, touted as the war to end all wars, and most Americans believed in it—two monstrous, murderous men, Hitler and Mussolini, had to be defeated so democracy could flourish. Boys were fighting overseas, men were working overtime in factories to produce armaments, and women—probably for the first time—were being urged by the government to join in the war, at home and in Europe. I posed for a poster in a navy uniform—with only a faint smile, this was serious business—looking straight into the camera and wearing an honest, open-eyed, but determined expression. And then there was my counterpart, Rosie the Riveter. Because of the war, we had to look somewhat like a glamorized girl next door, someone for the soldiers to fight for, waiting virtuously for them to come home and marry us. We, in a sense, epitomized the ideals of a democratic society fighting the barbarism rampant in Germany, Italy, and Russia.

All models had to be careful of their diets. The camera added pounds and that was anathema to the agency because photographers would not use a model who was overweight unless they were showing larger-sized clothing. Some of the outfits we modeled were a little loose but an assistant to the cameraman would take clothespins and clip the surplus at the back. To show skirts to their best advantage, unless they were very fitted, tissue paper would be pushed up the sides to fill them out. There were many such tricks that I watched with interest. For beer advertisements, after the beer had been poured and just before the shoot, salt or sugar would be added to make a frothier top. In paper towel ads contrasting two brands, the one being touted would be sprayed with some type of fixative.

Then when water or liquid was poured into both, the fixed one would be firm and the other would collapse. Models posing for hand ads were told to put their arms above their heads just before the shoot so the veins would shrink as the blood ran out of them and the hands would appear flawless. Indoor shots that required a small pond were created with a mirror surrounded by foliage from a florist. The resulting advertisement looked as if a model was on the edge of a stream, reflection and all. Despite dieting, most models loved demonstrations for cookbooks. Models were perpetually hungry and after a shoot everyone was invited to eat the remains. When we had a chance we ate so much that observers would ask how we could stay so thin. They didn't know that we did not eat very much or very often, not only because of the demands of our jobs but also because most of us were pretty poor.

I made the rounds to studios day after day for almost six weeks without getting a single job. In July Harry Conover asked me out; we were to go to the Stork Club. When I hesitated about accepting, he reassured me by saying that Lee would be going with us. Well, with a chaperone I saw no reason not to go out with the boss. I was dying to see the Stork Club. What to wear was my chief concern—I didn't have an extensive wardrobe. Fortunately, full skirts were in style, worn with what were called "peasant blouses." Mine was all white cotton with a ruffle around the neck and short sleeves. With it I wore a black faille skirt. Around my neck I put a thin black ribbon that held a small locket. The ribbon was similar to a choker necklace. Harry Conover and Lee picked me up in a cab and we drove to the fifties, on the east side of New York to the famous, exclusive club. Harry was greeted by Billingsley, the owner of the Stork Club, quite familiarly, so I knew he must be a frequent visitor. When we walked in, we passed Walter Winchell's table and he called out, "Harry, how're you?" To my astonishment Winchell waved to the chairs at his table and the three of us sat down. I was in such awe at meeting someone whose columns I had read in Los Angeles that I couldn't find my voice and only nodded when Conover introduced us. Winchell had a sharp nose and an intense stare, as if he missed nothing. Every so often he would focus on the room around us as if boring holes in the place and everyone in it.

We ordered dinner; Lee and Conover had salads but didn't look askance when I had much more. I started with a prawn cocktail served in a wide-mouth stemmed glass, with the shrimp hanging all around the rim. Then I had a rare filet mignon, baked potato with sour cream and chives, a mixed green salad, white asparagus, and for dessert a meringue filled with chocolate ice cream. Winchell watched me eat but I was too hungry to care. For almost a week I had subsisted on a boiled egg, a banana, and a five-cent bag of peanuts for dinner. My money would not stretch to anything more. Winchell at last made the usual remark, "How do you models do it? Stay so thin and eat so much?" That was his first remark since acknowledging the introduction. He appeared all gray, with his thin, somewhat hawklike face and bristly hair. Staring at me quite openly then, he shifted his gaze to Conover and said, "This's your latest, Harry?" There was something in his tone that made me uneasy, but I reassured myself that Winchell must have meant *latest model,* nothing more. The way I had been protecting myself in New York was through a pretense that I was an inexperienced virgin. No one knew or even guessed that there were two marriages and a love affair behind me. So far, this subterfuge had worked; men didn't make passes at me so readily. If they did, I pretended even more through a seeming lack of understanding about what they had in mind. Most men gave up and were content just to be seen out with a Conover model. Except for one man—he worked on the *Sun* newspaper and had been interesting to listen to when he talked about his work and the history of the paper from the time it was first published in 1833. But he seemed to think that buying me dinner was a fair exchange for sex. When we arrived at my boarding place, I defeated him by closing the door in his face while he paid the taxi. He was so angry that he hammered on the glass until I thought it would shatter, but by that time I was safely up the stairs and out of his sight.

Another night the three of us went to Sardi's for sandwiches, and it was a warmer, seemingly friendlier place than the austere Stork Club. There were pictures all around the walls of famous actors and actresses of stage and film. There eventually arrived an evening when Conover and I were to go out to El Morocco but he didn't mention that Lee would accompany us, but when I said, with wide eyes, "What about Lee? I want her to go with us," he gave in. At El Morocco we danced. Conover wore a double-breasted suit that I hadn't seen before. Lee told me he wore that suit because he planned to dance with me and had to hide an erection: "He gets a hard-on when he dances with you."

I continued to be taken out by Conover and Lee and he never made a pass at me. Finally, however, there arrived a night when we went to the Co-pacabana to see the floor show with the very tall, beautiful chorus girls. Conover said Lee would be joining us later in the evening and I, quite innocently, believed that this would be so. Conover had not made any suggestive remarks or told any dirty jokes as some men do, hoping to entice a woman into bed. We had been at the Copa for about an hour when Conover looked at his watch and wondered aloud, "Wonder where Lee's got to?" He excused himself to go to the phone and came back saying she was not feeling well and couldn't join us. After watching two shows, the chorus, and a comedian, Conover suggested we stop at Café Society, saying it was in the Village and on my way home. He wanted to see Jimmy Savo, who was famous for the song "One Meat Ball." I loved Café Society partly because I had heard about it from Jack, who had appeared there. About 1 A.M. we got in a cab bound for my place. As we drove downtown through Central Park, I leaned forward to look at the trees and foliage. Conover bent forward, seemingly to see what I was looking at, but in so doing he put his arm around me. I drew away and was able to escape his embrace. When we reached the Barbizon, Conover saw me to the door and rather forcibly put his arms around me and bent his head to give me a kiss. I pulled sharply away, turning my face aside, and disengaged his arms. He gave a great sigh and muttered, "Okay, Webb, you little virgin, you win." I pretended ignorance. That was the last time he invited me out and he was soon involved with another newcomer, also a model, whom he named Candy.

13

Jack called every other day but after telling him about visiting the Stork Club I hadn't mentioned the many times I had gone out with Conover. He did not take kindly to such adventures despite my assurance that this was all for publicity and my stressing the meeting with Winchell. I also kept it a secret that I was running out of money. Jack had not wanted me to go to New York and I wouldn't give him the satisfaction of hearing me complain about anything. One night when he called, however, he brought up the question of the expense of the Barbizon. He said that his mother was going out to Hollywood to visit and that I could stay in their apartment in Flatbush, Brooklyn, while she was away. I don't know whether he felt that I'd be supervised, staying there where his older brother also lived, but I was grateful to know that for some weeks I would not be paying rent. There had been a few modeling jobs, but not nearly enough to support myself.

I packed my trunk and shipped it off to Flatbush, then took a subway and arrived at Jack's home after work on a Friday. Murray Gellman, Jack's brother, greeted me rather formally but was not unfriendly. Gellman had been Jack's name until he changed it to Gilford. The name Gilford sounded less Jewish than Gellman and there was prejudice even in the theater. In Los Angeles there had been areas where the for-rent signs specified "No Jews or Dogs Allowed." The changed name got Jack through the doors of producers and he was such a talented person that he was able to show his skills and being Jewish was forgotten, or at least put aside. The apartment was large, airy, and immaculate, but instead of a carpet it had flowered linoleum in the front room. I was given Jack's room, in which I spent my few free hours writing poetry and sleeping. I never saw the rest of the apartment except once the living room and the kitchen, where there was a breakfast nook on one side. Murray, it seemed, did not work, because he was always at home, reading, listening to the radio, going to the bakery every morning. His visits to the bakery suited me because he always bought freshly baked Kaiser rolls, crispy on the outside, soft in the middle, and still warm.

I left Flatbush via subway every morning about 8 A.M. but didn't begin making the rounds to studios until 10. During the day I also tried to fit in visits to producers and casting offices, hoping to land a part in a Broadway play. Many producers would not interview a newcomer at all and I wondered how they expected to find fresh talent. Most dispiriting was when a call came out for auditions where there would be, perhaps, fifty applicants. Many of these actresses were more experienced than I; at least that was my impression. My first audition was a nightmare. I was handed a script, told to walk to center stage, stand under the lights, and act. In the wings other actresses were watching, waiting for their turns to come. The empty theater stretched unendingly because lights were on only on stage. There were a few men sitting in the front two rows whom I assumed were directors and producers. When I walked to center stage they were not even looking at me but seemingly consulting each other about something else. I waited for a few minutes, but when no one said anything I began to read from the script. The emptiness of the theater echoed back my voice. Since there were so many people auditioning, I was not given time to exercise my favorite medium, the method of Stanislavsky. Very soon a voice came from the pit below: "Next." Only pride made it possible for me to walk off the stage with my head up, not drooping.

Diligence eventually paid off, but it was through the Conover agency, not the casting offices, that an acting opportunity came. I landed a part as co-mistress of ceremonies with another model for the first musical being made for television, a new art form. Rehearsals and final production took almost a week and we were paid fifty dollars a day plus lunch and a light breakfast. Then another good assignment came my way and when it was finished I was thrilled to see a half-page photo of myself in *Life* magazine. It was an advertisement for Folgers coffee. After that appeared I was asked to take part in a fundraising affair in support of the war. Marlene Dietrich was the star, urging the audience to buy war bonds. She was pleasant to work with and felt not a bit competitive with the models in the show. I was surprised to see that up close she had a poor complexion. My friend at Warner Bros., Jack Cooper, had told me that she was always filmed through silk—that is, a sheer silk stocking was put over the lights. This had been initiated by a grip calling out, "Put a silk on that broad." The *broad* was a light, not the actress.

Between assignments I still had to walk the streets from studio to studio and office to office. The heat in New York almost did me in. I had experienced 110-degree heat in Fresno but at night it was always cool desert weather. In New York hot was hot, day and night, and the humidity made it worse. Sometimes I showered in the middle of the night and lay on my bed still glistening with water. As the water evaporated it cooled my skin, and it was the only way I could get to sleep.

My longtime friend C. L. R. James—or Nello, as he now asked me to call him, a childhood name shortened from Lionel, his middle name, and coined by his mother—wrote almost every day and called often. We had dinner together every few weeks, usually at Connie's on MacDougall Street just above Washington Square in Greenwich Village. Connie, the owner of the restaurant, was a remarkable woman from the West Indies. She had, I believe, the first integrated restaurant in New York. She welcomed blacks with blacks, whites with blacks, whites with whites—everyone was welcome except bigots. If Connie noticed someone who seemed hostile to white women dining with black men or black women dining with white men, she marched up to the table and invited the person to leave. She was a well-built, rather husky woman and could be a formidable opponent. Only once did I see Connie escort someone to the door, and the man looked intimidated. She had caught him glaring at me, seated at the next table with Nello. When he began to turn red and mutter under his breath, with his eyes still on us, Connie took action. After a few visits she took me under her wing and greeted me with a joyful smile and a bear hug. "Where've you been keeping, child?" she always said when I walked through the door.

Connie was a superb cook and I learned to enjoy West Indian food. According to Nello she made the best callaloo that he had tasted. It was a dish of crabmeat and some sort of greens that I couldn't identify. They tasted something like spinach but without the slightly bitter iron flavor. Another dish that I began to appreciate was couscous, made of okra, loads of butter, and fine cornmeal. Connie taught me how to make it because it was one of Nello's favorites to accompany salt cod, or baccalau as he called it. I think Connie was probably matchmaking by giving me the recipe. At the time I thought she was completely out of her mind. Be that as it may, the recipe was simple. Okra was cooked separately from the cornmeal. After both were done a cube of butter was dumped into the cornmeal and then the okra was added. Salt and pepper were sprinkled in and then the tiresome part began. The mixture had to be beaten until thoroughly blended. The okra simply melted into the melange and didn't even change the yellow color of the meal. When the dish was ready it was about the consistency of softly mashed potatoes and its bland flavor went well with spicy dishes. It seemed that no matter when we arrived Connie would have anticipated whatever Nello was likely to order. It was as if they were on the same wavelength when it came to food. He loved fish, especially red snapper, kingfish, porgies, and cod. He was also fond of clams, shrimp, and lobster. Sometimes he wanted rice and beans cooked with pork or ham. One time I made the mistake of saying beans and rice and he admonished me. "My dear child," he said, "it is *always* rice and beans, not the other way around."

Richard (Dick) Wright joined us sometimes when he lived in Brooklyn, and more often after he and his wife, Ellen, moved to Charles Street on the west side of the Village. He loved to eat and made Connie happy by the way he approached her cooking with gusto. Dick always seemed bursting with enthusiasm when he met Nello and listening to them talk about literature, art, music, and politics was not only a great pleasure but also an education.

One evening Dick voiced concern that Nello's visa had expired and that he might be deported. The entry visa had been good for only six months and was extended for another six months when he collapsed from a perforated ulcer and had emergency surgery. But he knew that neither the Immigration Department nor the FBI would forget him for long. For a time, he stayed with various friends or in a room in Harlem and seemed to disappear. In the Workers Party he changed his name to the pseudonym J. R. Johnson. Under that name he wrote regularly for the two publications of the Party, *Labor Action* and the *New International*. Gradually, Nello became the leader of a small group of devotees within the Workers Party drawn together in a study of Marxism paying particular attention to Marx's theory of the degeneration of the revolution under Stalin. I had called myself a follower of Nello's from the time he gave his position on the Negro question in Los Angeles years before. The first person in New York who joined Nello, not on the Negro question with which she agreed but on his analysis of the Soviet Union, was a Russian-Jewish emigrant who as a child had lived through the raids of Cossacks in her village. In Russia her given name was Raya Dunayevskaya. Her party name was Freddie Forest and before meeting Nello she had been working toward the same analysis he had, that Stalinist Russia was a form of state Capitalism. Raya's field was political science. She had worked as Trotsky's secretary in Mexico and been in the SWP for many years. Her affiliation had not been a happy one. A major grievance was that the leadership, all male, treated women as their handmaidens, leaving it to them to do all the mimeographing, the serving and cleaning up after making coffee, and sometimes the sweeping of the offices. Raya had rebelled and was not very well liked by many of the women. There were a few, however, who respected her intelligence. Nello welcomed her and was especially pleased that she could read and translate Russian and German. They worked closely together and because she contributed many ideas and interpretations he eventually suggested they join their names, politically. Raya was married, so for many years I did not realize that she and Nello had sometimes been joined in more ways than politics. They called themselves the "Johnson-Forest Tendency." When Nello told me the name I couldn't help laughing and blurted out, "Tendency! What does that mean, for goodness sake?"

Quite a bit later a Chinese woman, Grace Lee, came from Chicago and was recruited by Raya to join this "tendency." Already close friends and political allies of Nello's were Lyman Paine and his wife, Freddy. They were a rather unusual combination. Freddy prided herself on her working-class background, orphan status, and self-taught education. Lyman was a direct descendant of Robert Treat Paine, one of the signers of the Declaration of Independence. He had graduated from Harvard and been a well-known architect, winning a prize at the World's Fair in New York for one of his designs. Lyman came from a Cambridge, Massachusetts, family not only of prestige but of considerable wealth. His father owned a twenty-room house in Cambridge as well as half of Sutton Island in Maine, across from the Rockefeller estates. As a child, he and the Rockefeller boys played together and went sailing during the long holidays. Lyman's first wife, with whom he had two sons, was descended from Ralph Waldo Emerson. One of their sons, Michael, married Ruth Hyde, who took in Marina and Lee Harvey Oswald prior to the Kennedy assassination. One of the guest houses on Sutton Island, in which Nello and I stayed one summer, was right on the sea, a two-story white-wood construction with four bedrooms. Other houses, equally large or larger, included the main house, a school house, and two cottages. Lyman more or less subsidized Nello, giving him seventy-five dollars a month on which to live. Freddy and Lyman had a summerhouse in Northport, Long Island, where Nello could sometimes hide away, not simply from the authorities but also to do some uninterrupted writing away from everyone he knew.

Jack's show closed in Hollywood and he and his mother arrived by the Super Chief on a Friday. The following week he was to appear as a solo comedian in the Adirondacks, on Lake George, and he had arranged for me to accompany him. As soon as Jack introduced me to his mother and I had thanked her for letting me stay in their apartment, she said: "We're happy to have you. Jack will sleep on the couch in the living room." Jack didn't look at me, nor did I look at him. That afternoon he called two friends and made plans for us to visit right away. As soon as we arrived the man and woman excused themselves, saying they had to leave to take care of some errands. Jack could hardly wait for the front door to close before he pulled me into the bedroom. Although I was as eager as he was to hop into bed, everything was happening too fast. Here was a strange apartment and someone else's bed. On top of that, I had not seen Jack for months and never in such a frantic mood. So it was a poor beginning, too fast, and I had to pretend that it was enjoyable because if I hadn't Jack's feelings would be hurt. He would blame me, not the atmosphere or his lack of any sort of preliminaries. I wanted at the least a little talk first, just some words that showed that he loved me, thought I was wonderful, had missed me, very simple desires. It wasn't altogether his fault, of course; I was nervous and worried that the couple who had loaned us their apartment would be back any minute. All these things considered I was let down but had to appear fulfilled and happy.

Saturday night Jack took me to a club on the Hudson River, close to Grant's Tomb. It was a night that poets would describe as romantic. There were shining stars in the clear sky and a crescent moon was reflected in the water of the river. Although we had dinner I can't remember what we ate, which is not usual. I can remember every dinner that was outstanding in flavor, going back for years. I can usually visualize such meals and I see the restaurant, the people serving, the dinnerware, the silver, and the food upon the plates. It is the poor dinners that I cannot remember. We danced and looked at the windows, which reflected the swaying bodies. Jack held me close, kissed my neck, nuzzled my ear, and whispered that he loved me.

We left the club around midnight and walked over to Grant's Tomb. There the fairy tale ended. Jack began to discuss articles he had read in the *Daily Worker.* He expected me to comment, which I couldn't do since I had not even glanced at the paper while in New York. After receiving noncommittal remarks for some minutes, Jack asked me if I had taken out a subscription and followed the reports. Welling up inside was a desire to tell him exactly what I thought about Stalin and his bloody regime, but what I took for love made me compromise. Foolishly I had believed that we could agree on an abstract plane, both hoping for and working toward the same ends, albeit guided by different theories. We were both Marxists, were we not? Trying to have everything, I was confused and neither honest nor dishonest, a sad state to be in. Stubbornly, I did claim that I was not convinced that the Communists were correct, but I never gave a hint that I had chosen the side of Trotsky and now Johnson-Forest. At first Jack was shocked and then irate, almost speechless. We rode the subway to Flatbush in complete silence and there was no goodnight kiss when he left me inside the front door and went to sleep on the living room sofa.

No, I did not cry myself to sleep. For the most part I was angry for not having been completely honest. A real hatred had grown in me toward the Stalinists with their murders, first of Trotsky, and then the trials of all the old Bolsheviks. The next morning we had breakfast with Mrs. Gellman and Murray, and Jack and I put on pleasant faces. We were to leave that afternoon, presumably, for Lake George, where Jack was to perform. That was what he told his mother. But Jack actually had reserved rooms for us to spend one night at the Beekman Hotel on the Upper East Side. It was a place he had always wanted to stay in, feeling it was romantic, perched on a hill with a view of the East River. One could walk up the street to a parapet and see from one end to the other where the river stretched.

It was a terrible night. Jack got drunk right after dinner and threw up a few times. He kept me running for sips of ice water and to put ice on a washcloth to bathe his face. In between vomiting episodes he almost wailed about my betrayal in not reading the *Daily Worker* and casting doubt upon the Soviet Union and its leadership. Of course there was no intimacy that night and the next morning Jack's headache and hangover were so great that we showered separately and dressed without talking. We took a bus to Lake George and were given a small cabin near the lake. While I unpacked and changed into shorts and a halter top, Jack went up the hill to the office to see when and how often his performances would be held.

When he came back he said that he was scheduled to be on stage that same night and would need to rest until dinner time. Mistaking the word "rest" for both of us having a siesta, I started to untie my halter. Jack immediately made it clear that he wanted to be alone, that he needed to think about which lines and impersonations he would use at the first show. Somewhat reluctantly I left the cabin and wandered down to the lake. Lake George was beautiful, a deep blue green, and surrounded by trees. Some of the trees growing close to the shore dragged their branches into the water. It was a large lake and people in canoes were dotted about, some rowing, others simply drifting in isolation. It was romantic and I envisioned hours of pleasure floating about in a canoe. Surely such scenery and time to be together after so many months apart would heal the rift caused by my dereliction of duty—not reading the *Daily Worker.*

We had an early dinner, Jack eating very lightly, nibbling on a salad. He never ate very much before a performance, but afterward he was always hungry. There have been articles about the resorts in the Adirondacks, and most have mentioned the quality and amount of food offered. That evening I stuffed myself, like everyone around me. Everything I ordered was delicious and fresh. My problem was that Jack, who was eating so lightly, finished long before I had been satisfied. Dieting was out the window for this week and I was going to make up for the times I'd gone to bed hungry.

Jack's performance was, as usual, a great success, and he had many encores. I rather basked in the reflected glory when people nearby whispered to each other that sitting in the next row was his girlfriend. After the show admirers surrounded Jack and I stayed in the background. First, I do not like crowds—they give me a feeling of claustrophobia—and second, I might quietly enjoy people linking me with Jack, but I cannot abide riding on someone else's coattails. He was the artist, not I, and he had earned the right to undivided attention.

Later on Jack introduced me to other actors and actresses who would also be performing during the week and, rather than try to be alone with me, he suggested that we all have sandwiches together. Around midnight we found our way down the path to our cabin using flashlights. Jack went into the bathroom to remove his makeup and shower while I undressed and put on a diaphanous nightgown, shivering in anticipation. When Jack came out of the bathroom I was surprised to see that he was wearing pajamas. He went immediately to the bed, took the inside position, turned his back, and said not a word. So much for my frilly nightgown. He hadn't even so much as glanced at me. I didn't give up immediately but turned out the light, slipped into bed next to him, and put my hand on his shoulder. He promptly shrugged it off and pulled the covers tightly around himself.

I tried to be philosophical about his behavior, making the excuse to myself that he was probably wound up and tired from the show, that things would be different on the morrow. Always the optimist. Nothing changed, everything got worse. When we went out in a canoe Jack took along a book called the *History of the Communist Party of the United Soviet Union* and read to me while I did the paddling. When he was not reading he explained what he had read as if I was a moron. That's how I must have appeared, anyway, because I did not respond either to what he read or to when he emphasized what he had read by telling me about it. About mid-week Jack became exasperated and railed at me, "I don't understand you. You seemed as fervent about the revolution as I did. Are you just a fellow traveler? I've never trusted them, they are bourgeois." Later a member of the Johnson-Forest group told me I had *bourgeois tendencies,* probably because I was an actress and a model and had experienced a world they hadn't been in. During Jack's forced readings, or rather, my forced hearings, I was glad that I had to paddle the canoe. It gave me something to do while listening to a rewritten history by some Russian Stalinist. I had to be a little careful and not let my eyes glaze over or my face show any distaste. Even then, my obdurate silence annoyed Jack.

He also withheld sex in the same manner that women are accused of doing when displeased with their husbands. But at least such women claim headaches; Jack said nothing at all, just set his mouth and turned his face the other way. There were no kisses, hugs, or of course sex for the entire week. The only time we communicated was when he was with other people and kept up a pretense that we were intimate. Otherwise it was reading and lecturing; I don't know if he ever looked at the beauty around us. There was once a motion picture called the *Lost Weekend*. This was a lost week. At first I was terribly hurt, then angry, then sorrowful, then optimistic again—things would certainly change when we got back to New York.

We returned to Flatbush on a Sunday afternoon. On the way back on the bus Jack told me that we had to stop seeing each other. "I will not, cannot marry anyone who does not agree with my political ideals. I am sorry as can be; of course you will have to move out of my house. You've dashed all my dreams, but me and my friends are serious politicos, we want to change this world for a better one, for all people, blacks, Hispanics, the poor, the workers. I need a wife who will share my dreams and work alongside me. I thought you were too young for me from the beginning. And now you've broken my heart."

It was fortunate that we were on a bus, in public, because I wanted to cry—actually, to wail. At that time, I thought I loved him, but I know now that it was a strong sexual attraction, something so new to me that I did not know whether I could live without him. As soon as we reached his apartment, I called a model friend who lived in Tudor City on the East River. When I asked if I could stay with her for a few weeks she was delighted. She was going to be away for a month and was trying to find someone to stay in her apartment and look after her cat. That night I packed my trunk so Jack could send it on later, a suitcase, and my shiny black Conover model's bag. While I was packing, Mrs. Gellman popped in every so often, presumably to ask if she could help. I could not help noticing a small gleam of satisfaction in her eyes and her manner. Her son was not going to marry a shiksa after all. The next day Jack took me in a taxi into New York. I had dressed very carefully, probably hoping he would change his mind. My suit was a pale yellow, almost a cream colored, wool and with it I wore violets in my hair. In the cab, Jack stared silently out the window and I saw a tear run down his cheek. He brushed it away angrily but not before I saw it. But he was as stern and rigid as ever when he carried my bags upstairs to the apartment. He dropped the bags just inside the door, glanced out the window, which looked out onto the East River, and said goodbye. Not even a handshake and certainly not an embrace or kiss on the cheek.

His footsteps echoed down the corridor and I heard the elevator door close. I was alone and for the first time not happy about it. The cat, a tortoise-shell color, was my only companion, and I think he comforted me in my misery. He would climb into my lap and knead my thigh until I'd put my hand under his paws, and then he would turn around and lie down in my lap and purr. What was this resistance in me, when I really felt that all the joy in my life was ending? Why couldn't or wouldn't I pretend to accept his politics if that meant keeping him? What stubbornness was so ingrained that I could not live such a lie? After all, I was not *that* active in politics, hadn't been for a few years—what would it have mattered? But I could not, no matter how much I tried to argue with myself. Such a sense of loathing came over me at the thought of the Stalinists, and then at myself to think that I could even entertain the slightest hint of subjugation—to give in to something that was corrupt. Impossible, my conscience warned. Voices in my head chattered, for and against compromise. *Against* won, as it usually did.

In my pain, in the feeling of a torn ripped place in the heart—and that is what the anguish felt like—I turned to my longtime friend Nello. Instead of commiserating with me, he was jubilant. He promptly invited me to dinner at Connie's at the end of the week. The very next day I received a special delivery letter in which he tried to bolster my feelings. The letter did not mention Jack but considerable space was given to discussing and dissecting the poetry I had been writing for a long time. Although I had been writing most of my life, on the train from California there had been an outpouring of verse, as if something had been pent up for a long time. I sent the poems to Nello and he thought they showed talent. Of course,

I think that almost anything I did at that time would have influenced him in my favor, but I am not entirely sure, because he could be very critical at times.

On Friday my eyes were puffy from lack of sleep and crying so I used a little makeup. Unless I was working I didn't wear makeup, just tinted moisturizer to protect my skin from the sun. And although I didn't particularly want to go out for dinner I dressed with care, choosing a black, silk Balanciaga that I had modeled and then purchased with a hefty discount. The dress was classically simple, with a round jewel neckline, long fitted sleeves, a nipped-in waist but a straight, rather narrow skirt. It came to mid-calf, the length that was fashionable at that time. With the dress I wore a pearl choker and small pearl earrings. Black high-heeled pumps, a small black purse, and wrist-length white leather gloves completed "The Look," as Conover called it. He liked his models to look elegant, wearing simple, well-designed grey, black, beige, or white classics so that people would pay attention to their faces, since they were his Cover Girls. His livelihood. His competition with the John Powers agency, whose models were the soignée *Vogue* and *Harper's Bazaar* types also may have influenced Conover. One day he became almost apoplectic when a model came in wearing a flower-patterned dress and open-toed shoes. When we were on a shoot it was a different matter, that was business and we wore whatever the client demanded. As far as vanity, the moment I felt properly dressed and was half-satisfied with the reflection in the mirror, I forgot all about myself and the way I looked, being more interested in new or strange ideas, whether I agreed with them or not. In fact, sometimes when I felt strong disagreement my mind became more active.

From Tudor City I walked down as far as the New York Public Library on Fifth Avenue and caught a bus going downtown. At Eighth Street I got off the bus because I wanted to walk through Washington Square, first passing the only Mews that I had seen anywhere in New York. Closed at one end of University Place, it had cobbled streets and small two-story houses that used to be stables. Now there were window boxes flowing with flowers, bright polished doorknockers, and an air of European charm. My love for New York had increased because of all the unusual and rare areas. It wasn't a melting pot so much as a city divided into ethnic sections, each one fascinating and distinctive. On my days without work I explored all the neighborhoods. Along Third Street there was an elevated train, stretching high overhead and creating dim shadows below. There were small stores selling almost anything one could want—and very inexpensively. Uptown along the Hudson River was an area stretching for miles filled with bushes, trees, grass, and benches to sit on. It was like being in the country except that one could watch the ships coming in and look across to the Jersey shore. Downtown, called the Lower East Side, especially along Orchard Street, there were pushcarts and peddlers, mostly Jewish. Some of the men had paises (long sideburns) and wore wide-brimmed hats and long black coats, very formal looking. Women wore babushkas, scarves tied under the chin, as if they were still in Russia or Eastern Europe. The carts overflowed with different items—shoes, blouses, skirts, coats, underwear, scarves, and toys, a cornucopia of goods. There were also shops selling fresh fish that one would not want to pass during the heat of the summer. Best of all were the cafes, some small, others large, where one could sit and listen to arguments over ideas.

Then there were the two giants, the Hudson and the East Rivers. Flowing on either side of Manhattan, they made one feel as if she were on a gigantic ship. At Tudor City I found comfort in walking a half block, crossing the highway, and sitting beside the East River. Tugboats chugged by, going about their business as escorts to liners and freighters; something was comforting about the sight. For two weeks after Jack's rejection, I went every day, until eventually some of the tugboat captains began to wave. There were a few who tied up alongside the wharf and we'd exchange a few words, hello, how are you, nice day. I think watching the current with its steady motion helped get me through a painful time. Since there were not many modeling assignments, which would have taken my mind off of myself, the river was a good substitute.

❧ 14 ❧

When I reached the restaurant, Connie met me at the doorway with arms stretched. She then took my hand and led me toward the back of the room, where I saw Nello and Richard Wright rising to their feet. In those days, men always stood when a woman entered a room and both men and women stood for an older person. Some people, who were raised when courtesy and manners were thought to make it possible for people to live together in harmony, still observe these customs. Nello had taken me to meet Wright shortly after my arrival in New York. He was living temporarily in a sublet apartment just on the west side of Washington Square, between the square and Sixth Avenue (renamed Avenue of the Americas, though no New Yorker ever calls it that). *Native Son* had been published and was selling up to a million copies. I had read the book in California and was surprised it had sold so widely. As far as I knew, there had never been a novel written like *Native Son*. The book was critical of Negro leadership, religion, philanthropy, and communism. It did not pose solutions; it simply stated the racial problem in America in terms of its tragic enormity. It was a moral indictment of the U.S. Wright and I became friends almost immediately after our first meeting. Both of us were passionately interested in the nuances of racial prejudice. We spent hours examining its various forms and the incidents we experienced or observed. During such discussions Nello sat quietly by, listening intently. Later he said he was astonished both at our preoccupation with the subject and at our closeness—after all, he said, "You are white, Dick is black, and I am black. But I am out of it entirely when the two of you get together." He went on to explain that in Trinidad he had never been particularly aware of being black and as a result the subject had not interested him. In London, Amy Ashwood Garvey, the first wife of Marcus Garvey, told him: "You are not a Negro." She, of course, had the experience of the U.S. as a reference. And although Nello began to experience what it was like living in the U.S. in a different color skin, it never preoccupied him. When he went to Missouri to organize black sharecroppers, he was so clueless he almost provoked a white taxi driver to run him down. He had made the mistake of signaling the man as he did taxis in New York. Only the quick action of another black man saved him; he pulled Nelo out of the way and asked, "Man, what's wrong with you? That white man felt you insulted him, thinking he'd pick up a nigger!"

After the three of us finished dinner we walked Dick home and then Nello and I took a taxi to drop me off at Tudor City. Nello then went to Forty-second Street, where he spent many nights watching two and sometimes three movies. He said he had trouble sleeping if he went home early and was also addicted to American films. Another reason he went to see films so often was to keep his brain quiet after hours of writing. He was always mentally composing unless there was external distraction. At first he despised Hollywood movies, but then he began to learn from them, even the poorest ones. "The rubbish I look at would astonish you," he wrote me in 1943. He especially enjoyed discussing the personalities of the actors. Unlike most Trotskyists, he did not believe that motion picture subjects and stars were foisted on the public. He said that people paid their dimes to see what they wanted to see. Probably because I had studied acting, I was always asking him to analyze the personalities of actors and actresses and explain why they were so popular. First, Nello would ask me to name the stars that interested me the most. I began with the women rather than the men—Greta Garbo, Marlene Dietrich, Ingrid Bergman, Bette Davis. Nello added Greer Garson to the list. He said that Garbo and Dietrich were the exotic charmers, but he believed that the three women at the head of the profession were Bette Davis, Ingrid Bergman, and Greer Garson, claiming they were a wonderful study in types. Bergman, a Scandinavian, was a typical representative of one of the finest examples of European bourgeois civilization. The Scandinavian countries and Denmark, acting as food producers or agents for the great imperialist powers, had all the advantages and none of the responsibilities (great armies, navies, colonial oppression, excessive political corruption, etc.) of imperialism. Hence they produced some of the finest people in a bankrupt Europe. He then compared Greer Garson to Ronald Coleman, although she was in his opinion a better craftsman than he. Then he talked about the American actresses. Surprisingly, he believed that Bette Davis surpassed anyone from Europe. He said, "This *American* woman has something that neither of these representatives of the older civilizations have—a tremendous vitality. She is not so fine a person as Bergman, you can feel it, and Garbo achieves some extraordinary effects with the greatest economy of means, but Davis is simply terrific at her best. She sweeps on like a battleship."

"When I become a star, if I do, what would you say about me?" I asked. Nello smiled indulgently, as if he were about to chuck me under the chin. "You, my precious, are *the* typical American." I was disappointed—*typical,* of all things. Nello laughed at me and said that I obviously did not understand what it meant to be typical of a society. He said it was to be symbolic or representative of something, in this case American women, and that to be typical meant one was beyond the average—something more. I wasn't too sure of Nello's description, but my vanity urged me to accept his definition.

Nello was different from all the radicals I had known. He claimed to be a Marxist until the day he died, but he was more than that. In public Nello was reserved in demeanor, always very self-controlled and in charge of any situation that arose. Privately, and I think only with me, he was playful and tried out many roles, as if donning different costumes. First of all, he was seldom gloomy. He had an almost elfish sense of humor and he loved to tease. One time he found a cheap ring, the type given away in Crackerjack boxes—gold-colored, glass faking a diamond, a very ornate affair. He promptly put it on his little finger, where it shone against his dark skin and appeared even cheaper. And on a man's finger it looked ridiculous. When he saw I disliked it, he kept wearing it for days, admiring it openly and remarking on its beauty whenever I was around. In cooking a meal he would exaggerate every movement, sometimes acting as a great chef with varying moods—offended by a customer, annoyed by his helpers, ecstatic over the aroma of garlic, and regal if approached for an autograph. Nello told preposterous original jokes, read cartoons, admired Americans enormously, and had a restless mind that ranged widely—literature, poetry, art, music, opera, and sports. Nello's moods were stimulating, but something we shared from our first meeting was equally important: we could be quiet together, not talking for hours but utterly content. Sometimes we sat on a bench behind the New York Public Library and simply watched the people passing by. Nello would exclaim, "See how Americans walk! The ease, the swing of their legs, straight backs—and the women! The self-confidence in their movements. You can tell that these are people who have never been weighed down or oppressed by their past as in Europe."

When my model friend returned to her apartment in Tudor City I found a room on Thirty-sixth Street around the corner from Lexington

Avenue. The room was on the third floor of a brownstone owned by a couple of retired actors, a man and wife. They were English, and I was invited to tea when I rented the room. The rent was ten dollars a week, a little steep but the neighborhood was lovely and safe at all hours. The bathroom was down the hall but shared by only one other person. It was also immaculate. My room had an alcove in which there was a marble basin with a wide surround where I could plug in my single-burner hot plate. My landlords said I could make tea but not cook meals. Even if I had wanted to, there wasn't money enough to buy groceries to cook. I received sixty-five dollars rent a month from my tenants in Beverly Hills. The twenty-five dollars that remained after I paid my rent had to pay for bus and subway fares, laundry and cleaning, shoe repairs, and sundries. Fortunately, makeup for work was not a problem. To advertise their products, many cosmetic companies gave us samples when we went on a shoot.

After I had spent several weeks making the rounds to photographers' studios, the agency began to receive calls for my services. Some of the jobs were coveted by most models. Edelbrew Beer signed me to a one-year contract. The contract entailed a thousand-dollar signing agreement and payment of ten dollars an hour when we were shooting. The beer company was running a big campaign consisting of magazine and newspaper advertisements, billboard posters across the country, and cardboard cutouts. I was free to work for other companies with the stipulation that I would not work for any firm advertising beer, wine, or liquor. I also did a shoot for Coca-Cola, a one-time break just before signing with Edelbrew. Since I was getting paid pretty regularly for the beer ads, I sent the thousand dollars home to mother. I wanted her to spend it on whatever she needed, after doing without so many things after my father died. But she put the money in a joint account with me and didn't say what she had done for many years. She still made skirts and suits that were as beautifully designed as any that I wore in fashion shows. Before Dior's new look was introduced in Paris, she made me a cocoa brown wool suit in his exact style.

Through a male model, Stu Hoover, I was introduced to Gus Schirmer, who owned a store that sold sheet music. He was also the producer of a stock company that played every summer in Stamford, Connecticut. Stu had been signed and hoped that I too would get this chance to act in a prestigious company. I don't think Gus was enthusiastic about me—he seemed not to like models—but he gave me a chance. Stu and I were the workers. We painted scenery, helped set it up, prepared publicity announcements, did clean-up chores, and ran errands. In return we were given small parts in each of the plays. The visiting actors were well known, usually from their film roles—Joel McCrae, Frances Dee, Celeste Holmes, Sam Levine, Bramwell Fletcher, Victor Jory, Joyce Carpenter (then married to Milton Berle), Alan Baxter, and others I can't remember. Stu and I had one day off a week, but never the same day and only when the theater was dark. My friends from New York, Francesca and Eugene (Gene) Raskin, kept their boat at Stamford and I'd spend whatever time I had with them. The boat was a fifty-five-foot ketch that slept about eight people. Gene and Francesca were Socialists, voting every year for Norman Thomas. They were also musicians, who sang and played guitars. During the winter Gene taught architecture at Columbia University, while Francesca looked after their two sons. The evenings when I could spend all night we'd sail off to some other port, moor the boat, and go ashore for dinner. Sometimes before taking the dinghy ashore we would swim in the pure, clear water. Those were idyllic times for me—although they were only a few years older than I, they treated me as if I were one of their cosseted children. I had been having anxiety attacks after my break-up with Jack, although I did not know what they were. The only way I could escape was to keep active, almost to the point of frenzy. But on the Raskin's boat, with their kind, live-and-let-live philosophic approach to life, I was comforted. They let me be myself. I didn't have to pretend that life was a rosy dream and my fate was to appear to be serene and eternally smiling, living behind a mask.

Toward the end of our two-month service Gus relented and gave me a lead part in *Three Men on a Horse* with Sam Levine and Alan Baxter. I played Baxter's wife. I was not very good in the role. There was no transition. The script called for a happy-go-lucky housewife, slightly brainless, whose husband is kidnapped by Levine and his cohorts. Up until the kidnapping I was fine. However, instead of being changed through my fear for my husband's life, when he was returned safely I was still the same as in the first act.

I met Al Capp, the cartoonist of *Lil' Abner,* while working in a studio shoot. He was a friend of the photographer and came in without knocking or speaking. He took a seat to one side and back of the cameraman so that he could watch the action of the models. When the session was finished, the photographer introudced us and then sent out for sandwiches and beer for the men and Coca Cola for the other model and me. She was impressed at meeting Capp and, aside from some flirting, had nothing to say. I had been following Capp's comic strip for years and liked all his characters, especially Daisy Mae. When I told Capp about my preference he asked, "Why, Daisy Mae?" My answer was that she was obviously an independent woman. "How so?" Capp probed. "Well, she wears a very short ragged skirt that shows her thighs. [This was years before the introduction of mini skirts.] And she plays as strong a role as Lil' Abner." I don't know whether Capp was interested in me because of these comments or that he just liked models. At any rate, he called a few days later and took me out to dinner. We saw each other off and on, platonically, usually talking about how Capp approached his work. Unlike many cartoonists, who had an associate to supply the words and setting for the artist, Capp at that time was working alone.

Capp came to Stamford to see the play. Afterward he told me how good I was, which was clearly a lie. Since Al had been trying to get me into bed for some time, his compliments had no effect. We had an ugly encounter after the curtain fell. He asked me to go out with him for a bite to eat, but when we were driving through a wooded area he pulled the car over and became passionate. When I resisted, he grabbed my hand and tried to force it on top of his penis. I managed to pull away and get out of the car. Since Capp had a wooden leg, he did not chase me, just drove alongside trying to get me back into the car. That night was the last time I saw the creator of *Lil' Abner*. Nello also came up from New York to see the play twice, and he wrote me later. He was honest and severe and told me flat out what was wrong with my interpretation of the role. Many years later someone asked me whether I wasn't angry or hurt by his honesty. No, I wasn't—he merely reinforced what I had known—and there was no way to make up for the failure because each play ran only a few showings, depending on the schedules of the Broadway and Hollywood actors.

When the season ended, Stu and I, having earned some money, decided to take a trip to Los Angeles, he to visit his family and I to stay with my mother. The journey out by train was torturous; every car was jammed with soldiers, many sitting and sleeping on the floor. There wasn't room in the dining car for so many people and we subsisted on stale sandwiches, Coca-Colas, and an occasional orange or banana. Mother had moved from Doheny to Palm Drive, also in Beverly Hills. She was surprised that the first thing I did after our hug and kiss on the cheek was to ask for food. The next day I called an old friend, Larry Parks, and we went to Santa Monica to swim and sit on the beach. Larry and I met through Jack Gilford and dated briefly during weeks when Jack and I had been estranged. Larry was a good actor, but more important as far as I was concerned was that he was a gentle person. I was very sorry to hear later that he had crumpled before the House Un-American Activities Committee (HUAC). He was probably frightened, but bravery is doing the right thing even when one is scared to death.

When I returned to New York, a friend and fellow Conover model, Madeline Patterson, asked me to live with her in Scarsdale. She did not want any money, just companionship. Madeline was recently divorced and had a small son. She also had a lover, a man twice her age who was married with grown children: Sandy Calder was CEO and owner of one of the largest paper bag companies in the country. He had a house in New Jersey and a suite at the Waldorf Astoria in the Towers. After I moved in, Sandy asked Madeline to bring me with her when they met for dinner at the suite and he would introduce me to his son. Sandy greeted us at the doorway of an immense living room, with a view of the city on three sides. He was fairly handsome, if one admires the WASP type. He probably had blonde hair as a young man but it was now white. He played a lot of golf and was tanned and very fit. Sandy's son, Stanley, stood up as we walked in. He was in the uniform of a West Point cadet. Sandy asked whether we wanted to order dinner in or go to the restaurant downstairs. He clearly wanted us to choose the restaurant and Madeline, who knew him well, vetoed dining in his suite. I think Sandy liked to be seen with Madeline, a beautiful woman, and now he had two Conover models to escort. Madeline had recently been shown in *Vogue,* a full-page photograph advertising pearl jewelry. And my Edelbrew ads had attracted attention as well. So Sandy rather preened himself in the eyes of the other diners. Everyone in the restaurant stared when we walked into the room, and Sandy's chest seemed to expand, something like a pigeon's when it is sexually aroused. Stanley was rather quiet and seemed eager to please his father, but at the same time he paid a lot of attention to me.

After dinner Sandy suggested that Stanley and I go off together—it was obvious that he had plans for Madeline. This evening, unlike most others, she would not be staying overnight because she felt I needed company on the train back to Scarsdale. Stanley and I went walking in Central Park. After about an hour he asked me out the following weekend. I think his father planned to spend that time in New Jersey with his wife and other children. He and Madeline always met during weeknights. I wasn't sure that I wanted to go out with this young West Point man so I invited him to Scarsdale, knowing that Madeline would not object. To make a long story short, Stanley became seriously attached and invited me to New Jersey to meet his mother and the rest of the family. It was one of the dreariest weekends I ever spent. Mrs. Calder, it was obvious, disapproved of models. This was not surprising—my mother and father also thought actors, models, waitresses, and such like were beneath associating with, below their station in life. Mrs. Calder's disapproval was strengthened by a fear that her son was in love and might do something rash like marry this most unsuitable girl. She need not have worried; this was not a family that I wanted to be part of. I was fond of Stanley, but there was in him too much prejudice and a complete acceptance of the status quo. He humored me when I talked about politics by listening quietly, but I knew he would be shocked if I introduced him to Nello or Wright. Since I had promised to attend as his date when he graduated from West Point, we continued to go out for a while after my visit to his home in New Jersey. There's no point in a detailed description of the graduation dance at West Point. The dancing was fun and I wore an ice blue crepe gown that everyone admired—not a total loss for my ego. But the people—these were girl-friends and relatives of men being trained to kill, all in the name of God and country. I had very little if any tolerance in those days for such people. They are not people whom I could ever agree with or become close to, but I don't dislike them now as much as I did then. I find excuses for such people, putting their narrow vision down to their environment and general ignorance. I comforted and excused myself while at West Point by thinking about armies that crossed over to the people during certain revolutions.

Madeline was so in love with Sandy that she accepted many indignities. He bought her two expensive hostess gowns and lingerie from Bonwit Teller, but she was not allowed to take them home. They had to remain locked in his closet in the Waldorf Towers. He was afraid she might wear them when entertaining someone else. She, on the other hand, had no thoughts for anyone except Sandy and was not the kind of woman to sleep with two men at the same time.

Every so often my feelings of anxiety returned. What was frightening was that they seemed out of my control—like some stranger that I could not dismiss. One of my friends was a ballet dancer in the New York Ballet Company, and he came to Scarsdale whenever he wasn't rehearsing. He was gay, which made possible a friendship that I could not have with other men; they had other ideas. We used to put on leotards and walk over to a park, a rather untamed wild park, and leap and run. This physical activity often held my anxiety in check for several days. Anxiety is difficult to understand. The feeling is similar to the adrenaline rush one experiences when in danger, but it doesn't let up, as if something has one by the throat. Sometimes I dug my fingernails into the palms of my hands, hoping that the pain would counteract these frightening emotions.

Nello and I met a few times a month, sometimes for dinner but more often between 11 A.M. and 1 P.M. when I had finished my rounds to pho-tographers' studios. He would come down from Sutton Place, where he usually worked with Raya and Grace, and sit on a bench under the trees. If I didn't turn up, he would go to the library and do some writing or research. If he didn't turn up, I would pick up a sandwich and walk back to the Conover agency, a few blocks from the library. Nello was like a lifeline; he always wanted to know everything I was doing, how I was feeling, and what progress I was making toward getting a part on Broadway. He helped ease the pain when I broke up with Jack—or when Jack broke up with me. Nello wrote almost every day. He put my personal experience in social terms and claimed I had made the break, not Jack. He believed I would have capitu-lated had I really wanted to maintain the relationship. Nello was the only person I could talk to without reservation and he admired me, a great boost to my often-battered ego. Think of constantly going on interviews for jobs—the need to look one's best, to adapt one's personality to that of the interviewers', the constant turndowns. And the interviewers were not in-terested in one's intelligence; they looked at a model from head to foot—many times with a cold and critical eye. And I, who preferred being invisi-ble, who suffered from agoraphobia and the stares of the public when I was alone, found my discomfort tripled when I was accompanied by Nello. I felt that my bleeding nerves lay on the outside of the skin, not under it. Alone there was curiosity; with Nello there was hostiliy from the public.

I built up self-confidence in other ways besides the meetings with Nello, by dating every weekend. The work of a model takes her into a variety of circles, so she never has difficulty finding presentable men, many of whom were well known or had money. Then there were people we'd meet in the theater, actors and would-be actors. Despite the war there were plenty of men to choose from. In dating, I eventually fell into a weird pattern. I would not get into bed with a man unless he was in love with me and we were engaged. These "engagements" would last three to six months, but as soon as the man began pressing for marriage I'd break up with him. My friend Francesca Raskin eventually scolded me. She said that I was going about hurting men, that it was cruel behavior. But, much as I loved her, what she had to say did not make me change my ways. I don't know whether I fooled myself into thinking I was in love with each victim; I think I did. But marriage! There had been two such ventures in my past, both of which combined boredom with a feeling of strangulation.

Marriage made me feel helpless in part because I tried to be whatever the current husband wanted me to be, or at least my interpretation of what he seemed to want in a wife. I felt as if I was living a lie in an unreal world. I was also somewhat frightened. Both husbands had used my feelings of insecurity in an attempt to preserve the marriage. They had little understanding of why I felt as I did; they simply sensed an underlying frailty. My feelings of inadequacy were because I was never as good as I thought I should be and I wanted to be. I never seemed to live up to my own expectations—to be perfect in every way. This feeling had nothing to do with physical appearance—that was a matter of genes over which I had no control, and although I was glad that it could be used to earn money, or make life easier, it meant very little. But there was an eternal commotion in my brain that I call chattering. When the words sorted themselves out they were always condemning my actions, letting me know that in some attitude or deed I had fallen short. Norman's technique was to make it appear that leaving him meant being less serious about social causes. Edward had it easier, following upon my divorce from Norman. His approach was to say, "Something is seriously wrong with someone who has been married twice—and breaks it up." Everyone was influenced by the work of Freud, who was popular at that time. Most radicals rejected his theories, claiming that only environment molded human behavior, not the subconscious. But there were others who embraced his theories, and Edward and I were among those who did. Many of our friends were using phrases such as, "Psychologically, I feel great today," and talking incessantly about the meaning of dreams, the id, and the ego. As a result, when Edward said there was something wrong with me, the influence of Freud's writing combined with my own insecurity and feelings of guilt kept me in the marriage longer than I otherwise would have stayed. It is curious that until another man was in the offing and professing love, Edward in the case of Norman, Jack in the case of Edward, I did not make the break. A man, therefore, must represent a point of stability, something I need if I am to feel secure. Fortunately, many years later I found a man who made me feel secure but let me be myself.

In addition to the Conover Agency I was also able to find an agent who handled theater and motion pictures. Bramwell Fletcher, an English actor married at that time to Diana Barrymore, introduced me to him while we were in Stamford, Connecticut. The agent had attended a number of the productions and, despite my poor showing in *Three Men on a Horse*, he decided to represent me. We discussed the Stanislavsky method that I had learned while studying at the Actors' Lab in Hollywood. It was his belief that the screen would be a better genre than the stage for me because it would pick up the subtleties of the method, which I had been good at when working at the lab. Eventually he got me a screen test at Warner Bros. studio. They would pay my way by train, on the Super Chief, out of Chicago. Nello was both delighted and saddened when he heard the news. He said that my being in New York where he could see me and watch my progress was his major happiness. During all the months in New York I had been writing—essays, criticisms, poetry—at night after the days of modeling and looking for work were over. I had recently begun to make notes and do research for an article on Richard Wright's *Native Son* and *Black Boy*. So it was with some unease that I faced a screen test. Was this what I really wanted? On one level I was excited about the prospect of acting in films, on another I was fearful that my whole life would change. And then, though not formally affiliated with a revolutionary group, I considered myself a good Marxist and agreed with Nello's political ideals. How would all these parts of my life, so necessary to me, fit together?

Despite my foreboding I went to Hollywood for the test. The studio told me to arrive at 6 A.M. and report to the makeup department. After passing through the guarded gate I found my way in and was immediately handed over to two men, one who would do my makeup and another who would do my hair. Next I was sent to the wardrobe department and didn't much like what the mistress decided I should wear. By now, though, I was somewhat numb and did not protest, just let them move me around like a mannequin. Finally, on the sound stage I was introduced to a young man who was to play opposite me, given a short script consisting of only a few lines, and told to be ready in half an hour. So much for Stanislavsky's method, was my reaction. My hands were cold and my knees trembling. Somehow I got through the test but barely paid attention to what I was doing. Afterward they dismissed me without giving me a clue as to whether they thought the test was good or bad. I had been used to the photographers with whom I worked always letting us know if the shoot had been successful. In fact, they were always successful, because we would do a pose over and over until they were satisfied. When I reached Mother's apartment I called my agent, but he had no news. He assured me it would be some time before they made a decision about whether to offer a contract.

Mother was hoping that a contract would be offered; she didn't trust New York, that awesome city. I don't know whether it was her daughter she didn't trust or the big city. She felt that I had made two mistakes in marrying Norman and Eddie—she had approved of neither—and she hoped that I had learned my lesson. Fortunately she rarely put her disapproval into words, but I knew my mother. At least she didn't stop speaking to me or go about whistling under her breath as she had with my father.

After a restless week and no word from the studio or my agent I returned to New York. Once again I was thrilled and overcome by Grand Central Station. The interior of the depot is sheer drama; the main concourse ceiling soars to 125 feet and is painted blue, so that when one looks up it appears that the sky is overhead. The approach outside is equally impressive. Approaching from Park Avenue one uses an entrance boasting mighty statues of Minerva, Mercury, and Hercules surrounding a clock thirteen feet in diameter. Before leaving for California, I had found an apartment facing the Hudson River. It was actually a huge room in a brownstone building. A closet had been transformed into a kitchen that was too small to hold more than one person, and the bathroom was down the hall. I hated sharing a bathroom but the view of the river more than compensated. One side of the room was mostly glass, with window seats along the sides. From there I could watch the ships coming and going and see waves kicking up during storms. My passion for watching water, first the ocean in Santa Monica and now this river that stretched from New York across to New Jersey, was at last satisfied. Surely there wouldn't be any anxiety attacks; water always soothed me, made me less restless.

Nello introduced me to Ralph Ellison and I met Chester Himes at Wright's home. Ralph was serving as a cook in the Merchant Marines and we saw him when he was back in New York. He joined the Merchant Marines because although he was willing to fight in the war he refused to be part of a Jim Crow army. Ralph tried to enlist in the Navy Band in 1942 but enlistment was temporarily suspended, at least for trumpet players who would serve in Negro bands. During a trip onshore Ralph received induction papers from the Army despite his Merchant Marine affiliation. He called Wright and went to see him. He told Wright that if the Jim Crow Army tried to get him he would get a ship and go to sea before they could grab him. Wright suggested he see a psychiatrist friend, Dr. Fredric Wertham, and see if he could get an excuse. Ralph did visit Wertham, but all he did was send him in for a complete physical examination. Ralph told me he never needed psychiatric care, had never been in analysis, and that "Old Man Bailey," whom I never met, just told him to take off and go back to sea without answering the Army's notice. Within a month or so Ralph sailed again on a Merchant Marine ship and when he returned in a short while he was released from service. He received a Rosenwald Fellow-ship during the winter and left for Vermont, where he began work on *Invisible Man.*

While Ellison was at sea, Wright received a phone call and then a visit from a man in the War Department Military Intelligence. Wright told me, with his usual gleeful look that was almost a trademark, that when the man arrived it had been snowing and the wind was howling outside. He said the man was rubbing his hands to warm them and for a moment Dick thought he should offer him hot coffee. He would have done so for anyone else who was so cold, but to himself he said, "No, let the sonofabitch freeze; he is a cop—worse than a cop, he is a spy. Snooping in people's lives." The agent asked Wright if he knew Ralph Waldo Emerson Ellison and his relationship to the Communist Party. There was nothing to hide. Ellison was not, and never had been, a member of the Party. Ellison wrote for the *New Masses* but never joined the organization. He told me he wasn't "on the make in that sense. I wrote what I felt and wasn't in awe of functionaries and published where I could. I only wanted to be a writer, not a leader of anything or a politician."

On one occasion, Ralph said he had been interested in sculpture, but only for about a year. His first love was music, which he had been playing since he was eight years old. He played in bands and orchestras during grade school, high school, and college, and in high school he was the student conductor of the band, held first chair in the trumpet section of the orchestra, and was also student conductor for awhile with Wallingford Reigger at the Downtown Music School in New York. He was rather proud, and with good reason, of having mastered the difficult study, *The Harmophonic Forms of Musical Composition*. He also said that when he first started writing short stories, something was wrong: "They just didn't work." He felt that they were too unformed and his musical study helped him recognize that they were incomplete and lacked resonance.

I wasn't very tactful one time when we were talking about Langston Hughes. I never met Hughes but talked to him several times, once for an hour, on the telephone. He was a wonderfully gracious man. I called to ask him questions about a history of black struggle I was studying. During one of our conversations he told me that Ralph had written to him from Tuskegee, where he was attending the institute, asking for the address of Richard Wright. Ralph had read some of Wright's poetry and was impressed enough to want to meet him. He was around nineteen years old when he met Wright in Harlem. My tactlessness was that I asked Ralph if Wright had been his mentor, or was still his mentor. The reason I asked, I think, was that from time to time I noticed that Ralph seemed perhaps only faintly—but it was there—jealous at the attention Dick always received.

Ralph was visibly annoyed at my question. He said he had been playing with words in the form of verse since the eleventh grade. Everyone at Tuskegee Institute knew of his interest in literature, especially poetry and its techniques. When Ralph was annoyed, he seemed to freeze, and he began to speak pedantically. His manner was chilling to experience, but I deserved it for asking such a question. I suppose no one wants to believe he has been guided or led or shepherded by someone else—but I don't know why. Most people are followers of some ideal, whether in a person, a great drama, literature, or music. They learn a technique and then infuse it with their own unique creativity. Many beginners in painting go to museums and copy from the great masters. Ralph would not admit that Dick influenced him in any fashion. But Dick told me the first short story Ralph had written was almost a duplicate of one he had done, and he had scolded Ralph. In fact, Ralph said Dick exploded, telling him he had copied his ideas, his words, and his sentence structure. He told Ralph to find his own symbols and dig the content out of his unconscious and use it instead of duplicating someone else. Ralph claimed he was not vain about his writing because he wanted to be a musician, so he didn't answer back, just accepted what Dick had to say and tried to follow his advice.

There must have been some inner conflict in Ralph, between admiring someone and believing the person intellectually inferior. Wright, after all, had not attended college and had been born in the Deep South, whereas Ellison was from Oklahoma and had been in better circumstances financially. What he failed to recognize was that Wright's mother and an aunt were schoolteachers and books were an early part of his life; he read voraciously—novels, criticisms, essays such as H. L. Mencken, *A Book of Prefaces* and *Prejudices,* philosophy—and was a self-taught intellectual, equal in every way to Ellison. But Ralph's idiosyncrasies mattered very little to Wright—he helped him as he did everyone who came his way.

Chester Himes was a friend who fascinated Wright. He whispered to me that Himes was a violent man, that he had killed someone and spent years in prison. Himes, of course, had not killed anyone. He was in prison for armed robbery. I don't know why Wright told me such a lie; perhaps because he wanted to frighten me—he was a terrible tease. One night I finally met Himes, who visited Wright on some urgent business. The urgent business, Wright told me later, was to borrow some money. Himes was completing *If He Hollers* and living in Los Angeles. He was handsome, lighter in complexion than Wright, with large eyes that were rather round until he laughed, when they took on a slight slant. He had a neat mustache, and dimples showed in his cheeks when he smiled. There was elegance about him, not simply in attire—he was very put together—but in movement. There was grace when he walked or sat, or in the way he moved his hands when illustrating a point.

But there was in his stillness at times a feeling that he could be dangerous. Himes is usually depicted in biographies as an explosive, violent man who beat up women. In all the years I knew him I only saw him lose his temper one time and he did not become violent. We were living in an apartment in the Albert Hotel on Tenth Street just above Washington Square. Chester and his wife, Lesley, were visiting. They had been out shopping for groceries and other things that they couldn't purchase in Spain, where they lived. Chester was carrying a huge bag of oranges and when he entered our kitchen the bag suddenly split. He was outraged as oranges scattered all over the linoleum-clad floor. He began yelling at Lesley, blaming her for the breaking bag. After a second or two we all began to pick up oranges and the whole scene was over. Chester was in a good humor once more, laughing and joking. Among the many qualities I liked in Chester was that there was nothing pretentious about him, nothing of the famous writer, nothing of the solipsist. People who didn't know him loved to dwell on how violent a man he was and gossiped about his rages over slights, describing him as an angry person, as if that was his only characteristic. Sometimes Chester played up to such a reputation by writing that he didn't care who he hurt, that he was a detestable person. On the contrary, based on my experiences with Chester he was generally thoughtful of people and kind more than he liked to admit. Part of the pleasure of spending time with him was his storytelling. He was a marvelous raconteur and an evening with him was thoroughly enjoyable.

When Himes moved to New York he and Wright became close friends. Himes was also friends with Ralph Ellison and they had more things in common—formal schooling, middle-class behavior or decorum, greater sophistication—but it was Wright with whom Himes felt close. It may have been Wright's wide-eyed enthusiasms or extraordinary energy. Whatever the bond, their friendship lasted until Wright's death. Chester said Ellen Wright attempted to come between them. Her side of the story was that Himes was a bad influence; his whoring and drinking would influence Dick. Chester said it was only after he rebuffed Ellen's advances that she turned against him. I have no idea which side to believe, except that when Ellen talked about Chester and women, he had settled down with Lesley Packard, an elegant, blonde English lady whose father was a gentleman farmer.

From time to time Chester talked about parts of his past life. He had attended Ohio State University, enrolling as an arts and science major. He was expelled in his second term for having taken some students to a combination speakeasy and whorehouse to drink bootleg beer and dance to phonograph records. He was only nineteen years old when he was sentenced to twenty-five years in the Ohio State Penitentiary. He was paroled after eight years. Chester seldom talked about his experiences in prison, never mentioning the terrible fire in 1930 when more than 330 inmates were burned to death. He had been transferred to another area of the prison shortly before the fire engulfed the part where the prisoners locked in their cells were burned alive. They died because the keys to the cells were in another area. Chester talked about work in the shipyards, and then in the Works Projects Administration (initially the Works Progress Administration or WPA) Writers Project, which gave him time to write, and where he felt that black and white were forced into one human family by their struggle for bread. Wright, also, had enjoyed working for the Writers Project in the WPA. Chester's cousin was Henry Lee Moon, a journalist who worked as a federal housing official in Washington, D.C., during the late 1930s. Moon's wife, Mollie Lewis Moon, was portrayed as the sexy hostess in *Pink Toes*. Chester said Wendell Wilkie often visited her in the Moons' luxurious apartment in the West Sixties. Moon and his wife went out of their way to introduce Chester to people who might help him get ahead. They also loaned or gave him money from time to time, so he could continue to write.

Money was always a big problem, although Chester did all types of work from washing dishes to digging ditches. Only later in life after the success of his Harlem detective series was he free from constant worry about paying rent or even being able to eat a good meal. Chester's Harlem books are the most original and powerful in American literature. He broke with the protest novel and above all demonstrated the resilience of people in Harlem, who created their own world when they were excluded from the larger white one. When Chester began writing the series he said he never knew what was going to happen. He just typed away. He enjoyed letting the stories unfold as he wrote and sometimes laughed out loud while writing a sequence.

Nello had a closer relationship with Wright than with either Ellison or Himes. Himes was seldom in New York and Ellison tended to lock himself away when working. Wright began work before dawn and generally finished around noon, when he would be ready for distractions. Nello had read and admired *Native Son* in 1940, and he felt Wright had enormous potential. He was concerned, however, that Wright was a Stalinist, and he said that in its "evil garden nothing creative flourishes." Wright might cease being an artist, Nello feared, because of the Party's corrupting influence. But about a year after the two men met Wright told Nello he was thinking of making a break. He could not stand the smothering, dictatorial policies of the Communist leadership. Wright left the party in 1942, and after announcing his decision to Ellen I think the next person to whom he gave the news was Nello. Whenever he could find the time, Nello enjoyed sharing ideas with Wright. Their views on the concept of human freedom were the same, a belief in the importance of the individual—his personality development, rights, freedom, and dignity. In creating his novels Wright was always struggling with the concept of individual freedom—a life free of illusions, ideologies, and hatreds. He did not have many close friends, from choice, not for any other reason, and many people came to him for money as loans or gifts. He was generous.

In 1944, Wright talked to Nello about a book he was planning to do for Harper, his publisher. He had already received approval. The book was tentatively entitled *The Meaning of Negro Experience in America*. It would consist of essays: "The American Negro Looks at History," "History Looks at the American Negro," "America with the Negro," "America without the Negro," "What the Negro Pays to Live in America," "The Folklore of American Race Relations." Wright planned to write the title essay, and Nello would write "History Looks at the American Negro." The book would be written entirely by black scholars and, in a sense, was a response to Gunnar Myrdal's *An American Dilemma*. Wright believed if a white man from Sweden could write such a book, he and his friends could produce a more serious and better one. The essays were not to protest mistreatment or discrimination against blacks. They would be concerned with valuations and interpretations about the Negro people and their place and meaning in America. The scholars Wright had in mind were Horace Cayton, a sociologist; Ralph Ellison; Elmer Carter, a Harvard-educated writer and sociologist; Lawrence D. Reddick, a historian and curator of the Schomburg Collection of the New York Public Library; St. Clair Drake, a sociology professor; and C. L. R. James.

The first and only meeting to discuss the book was held at Wright's apartment. Nello had gone along with Wright's suggestions and said he would write one of the essays. At the same time he did not think the scholars involved would form a harmonious working group. He did not tell

Wright what he thought, not wanting to discourage him or, maybe, letting him find out for himself. The meeting was a shambles. St. Clair Drake came out with idiotic remarks; he was obviously opposed to the entire project without actually admitting it. Instead he disputed everything Wright had to say. He began with an attack on Nello, saying he wanted to be re-assured that Nello would not put a Marxian interpretation on the Negro question. Nello did not respond, simply leaned back in his chair and smoked his pipe. Wright looked at him for help, but it wasn't given. Drake then said he was against any general statements about *the* Negro. Wright said that one could say in general that the English were a naval, seafaring people. Drake said one could not make such a supposition for the simple reason that not all Englishmen went to sea. Wright countered that Americans had a genius for production. Drake didn't reply, instead going back to ask if there were actually any Englishmen, and what is an Englishman? Drake did not believe that whites in general actively kept Negroes in their place. They did not actively hate Negroes. Wright was disgusted. He said whites did not have to actively hate black men; whites did not even have to think of Negroes at all unless they tried to get out of their *place,* and then they used violence against them. The meeting ended at last when Wright asked Drake, "Why are Negroes in a subordinate position in the United States?" Drake's answer was, "There are poor people everywhere and other factors were involved such as disliking someone with blue eyes or red hair." Wright closed his part of the discussion by saying, "I've never heard of a white man being lynched because his hair was red." Reddick and Cayton took up the argument but were unable to change Drake's attitude. The meeting became heated and Reddick gave up in disgust, calling Drake "infantile."

A few days later Wright called and asked me to go with him to see Nello. He met me at the subway stop nearest my apartment and we rode up to the Bronx and walked up the hill to Nello's apartment. It had snowed during the night and the streets were slippery with ice. Even so, and in a mixed neighborhood, we couldn't hold on to each other for protection; too many white policemen were around. When we reached the building on the corner of Chisholm and Freemont we climbed the four flights of stairs, shivering in every limb. Nello made coffee and, after serving us, handed out yellow lined pads on which to make notes. Nello and Dick decided that instead of the book of essays they would produce a magazine. It would be a popular publication that would appeal to the white middle class in an effort to clarify the personalities and cultural problems of minorities, using the Negro as an abstract yet substantive frame of reference. The magazine would contain articles, feature stories, fiction, poetry, cartoons, profiles of people who lived the *American way,* such as Frank Sinatra, Gene Krupa, and Bette Davis, and studies of crimes and criminals, both black and white. There would be no preaching or blatant ideological remedies proposed. The assumption of the publication would be that the Negro problem was the problem of all minorities, and that the problems of antisocial individuals were but phases of one overall national cultural problem, a lag in consciousness, a primitive expression of personalities caught in an industrial society whose demands were far beyond the emotional capacities of the people to contain or resolve them.

Both Richard and Nello agreed that black self-discovery, the facts of black life, constituted a great body of important facts about Americans in general. The Negro people were exaggerated Americans containing in embryo the emotional prefigurations of how a majority of white Americans would act under stress. My notes for articles they discussed included a national collection of jokes that Negroes made concerning their plight; their views of whites and reactions to the world scene; simple, illiterate letters from whites, Negroes, or others revealing their bafflement about the American scene; interviews with foreigners and their reaction to first visiting America; portraits of prizefighters and what actually happened when they first met in the ring—what was said, epithets or boasts, for example; what sexual illusions were held by whites about Negroes and by Negroes about whites; fads, crazes; articles on the KKK, Father Divine, Marcus Garvey. Both men were certain that their friends James T. Farrell, Nelson Algren, Ralph Ellison, Allison Davis, and Jack Conroy would write for the magazine. The publication would be called *American Pages* and subtitled "A magazine reflecting a minority mood and point of view. Nonpartisan, nonpolitical, espousing no current creed, ideology or organization." The magazine remained in the dream stage because Dick became involved in buying a house and then made a trip to France and Nello was busy writing articles for the Trotskyist paper and magazine. I couldn't have known it at the time, but the ideas and topics were similar to those proposed years later for the Johnsonite paper *Correspondence.*

15

Nello and his weekly, sometimes daily letters were bedrocks for me through all the problems I faced. He worried about my health and once when we had a siege of rainy weather he sent me ten dollars with the understanding that I was to buy what he called "overshoes" to keep my feet dry. Nello could always come up with an extra few dollars and I didn't know how he managed to do so until later in our friendship. When he needed extra money, he simply said to someone: "Let me have ten dollars." Nello never said *borrow*, always *let me have*. The money was never returned nor did anyone expect that it would or should be. As for my health, he urged me to eat an egg for breakfast and hamburger for lunch to keep up my strength. When I had ulcer pains he sent me letters on what I had to do to quiet them. He had an ulcer, so he became quite expert about the condition and how symptoms could be allayed. During our meetings we talked about everything, not simply my interests. Nello had a mind that ranged widely despite his devotion to Marx and Marxism. He knew English, French, Russian, Spanish, and some Italian literature. He could quote long passages from memory from Shakespeare, Shelley, Keats, Byron, Thackeray, Tolstoy, and Dostoevesky. He was especially fond of *Vanity Fair*. One of the lines that moved him deeply was, "Darkness came down on the field and the city; and Amelia was praying for George, who was lying on his face, dead, with a bullet through his heart." It is a beautifully constructed sentence, but I wanted to know whether it was simply the syntax that created such feelings, so I spent a lot of time thinking about it. When I posed my solution to Nello, he was as pleased as a father seeing his child take its first tottering steps. My explanation for the emotional impact Thackeray's sentence had on him (and on me) was not so profound. It seemed obvious when given a little thought. George Osborne had been portrayed by Thackeray as a shallow man, egotistical, ungrateful, one who believed himself both brilliant and gallant. In his relations with Amelia he was selfish and unfaithful. Some French cynics say that in love affairs there is always the one who loves and the one who allows herself or himself to be loved. Osborne had condescended to be loved by the tender, gentle Amelia, who was pregnant when he went gaily off to war, expecting to be a hero with his name in the newspaper. Therefore such a beautifully simple sentence, the pathos it inspired in a reader for this unworthy man, was a stroke of genius.

Nello also loved music. He was passionately fond of Bach, Mozart, and Beethoven. He also liked Chopin, especially the ballades. We would listen for an entire day to Beethoven's last quartets, changing the records over and over on our tiny machine. At one time he began to write a book about Michelangelo. He preferred baseball to football, saying the latter was too brutal. The baseball players in their graceful movements and strength reminded him somewhat of cricket athletes. Cricket was his favorite sport and one he knew everything about. And he loved opera, theater, and motion pictures. He could talk at length about actors and actresses. There didn't seem to be any subject of consequence that missed his study and/or attention. Whenever he talked, people would sit spellbound at his feet, forming a half circle around him, both men and women. One of the minor leaders in the SWP, a man whose party name was David Coolidge, tried to mimic him. He wrapped a scarf around his head, sat on the floor with his hands in a position as if salaaming, and tried to imitate an English accent. Coolidge was an American black so he must have thought that West Indians wore turbans. Followers of Shachtman, hostile to the Johnson-Forest group, made a circle around Coolidge and adopted prayerful attitudes. It was so ludicrous a scene and so poorly executed that most of the Johnsonites merely laughed about it, although some younger members became indignant. The only accuracy in the slapstick portrayal was the mimicking of the worshipful audience. Most of the Johnsonites were slavishly devoted to Nello. Two young women in the group began to speak with English and Trinidadian accents, but not at all in his melodic cadence. One woman was Italian, born and raised in Queens, and the other was Jewish from Brooklyn. Both of them sounded absurd because underlying the assumed notes were traces of their own natural pronunciation of words.

Probably from the very first in 1938 Nello was writing me love letters. Whether I realized it or not or disregarded their intent, I can't say. He was my friend, which was all I had in mind. My first two husbands read the letters and did not object or show any jealousy so it may be that I was thus able to turn a blind eye to the romantic parts. There was, finally, after many years, a time that I did awaken to the fact that he was professing love and hopes of a more intimate relationship with me. When that happened I wrote him to please stop calling me *sweetheart, miracle, darling, sugar pie,* and *precious* and explained that he was like a father to me. My attitude amused him and in a few of his letters, if one of these endearments appeared, he made elaborate apologies. I stopped protesting essentially because I was self-preoccupied and in too much conflict between acting and writing. My friendship with Wright had led to my devouring his *Uncle Tom's Children* and *Native Son* and, best of all, here was the author himself with whom I could talk. This led to my desire to write about his work and I wrote an outline for a biography. Wright read it and was enthusiastic about the approach—said that he had not looked at certain of his writings in the same way. And when he read what I described he felt it was true. He urged me to write the book. The problem, hence the conflict, was that I wanted to be on the stage acting. I also had to earn a living, which took a lot of time. And one other factor was that I was not ready to live in a garret. At fifteen the idea of being a starving artist had appealed to me, but the short time I had to go without food—the peanuts, banana, and egg days—destroyed the romanticism. I also was and am disturbed by my surroundings. A picture hanging crooked bothers me; space is important, as are flowers and good paintings, even if the art is a reproduction. It's not a need for luxury, but surroundings do need beauty and harmony. Ugliness is physically painful. I also enjoy food and what I like is not inexpensive— good rare steaks, prime rib, lobster, caviar, crab, prawns, frog legs, snails in garlic butter, Stilton cheese, French Brie. Perhaps when I was fifteen and thought of a garret it had a small balcony with plants, probably overlooking the Seine or the Hudson. And I have lived in worse than a garret, but that is later in this story.

To add to my confusion, Nello always told me, "you must find one thing to which you dedicate your life." Somehow I knew that instinctively, and that was the basis of my shilly-shallying between acting and writing. One afternoon Dick and I took a walk in the Village after he had finished his morning's writing. He began very early, sometimes at five A.M. I asked him when he knew that the only thing he wanted to do in his life was to write. How old was he? He said it started, he thought, when he was eight and a young schoolteacher who was boarding with his grandmother told him the story of "Bluebeard and His Seven Wives." The story opened the door to a magical world. His grandmother, an extremely religious Seventh Day Adventist, thought novels were the work of the devil. But after hearing that first story he used to sneak into the schoolteacher's room and borrow her novels. He would then hide behind the barn and try to decipher the words. When he was twelve or thirteen he tried to write poetry from passages in the Bible. But he grew bored and thought up a story about Indians. He had been reading a volume of Indian history and the story was about a beautiful Indian girl who sat alone beside a stream of water surrounded by old trees. He couldn't think of how to end the drama and solved the problem by killing off the heroine. The next story that had an impact on him was a newspaper serialization of *Riders of the Purple Sage* by Zane Grey. And then at sixteen, Wright wrote his first short story, "The Voodoo of Hell's Half-Acre." It took him three days to write and ran to 3,000 words. It was published in three installments in the Jackson, Mississippi, *Southern Register* in 1924. Seeing his story in print was thrilling, he told me, but it didn't compare with how he felt right after he had finished writing it. It was a sense of elation, as if he were among clouds, as if the air was rarified—he had a feeling of fullness and completion. He thought it was then, when he was sixteen, that he knew he had to write, wanted to be a writer, in fact, *had* to be—there was no other choice.

When I went back to my studio room after talking to Dick, I made a cup of tea, put some Mozart on the record player, and sat on the window bench to watch the ships moving on the Hudson River. I kept thinking about Dick's remark that there was not a choice. Ever since learning the alphabet and starting to write, I had spent hours reading, then writing—initially poetry, as most young people do. We think it easy, but it is one of the most difficult disciplines. At that early age there wasn't a conflict between writing and painting, which I was also immersed in. When I left Los Angeles for New York, poetry began filling my head, starting while I was on the train. I have poems scribbled on the Chief's monogrammed stationary. Every night after looking for work and after getting modeling assignments or having dinner with Conover I would get into bed with a pad on my knee and scribble away for at least an hour or two—forgetting sometimes to get enough sleep not to have circles or other lines that would be picked up by the cameras. While politically active I stopped writing and painting, but the idea of New York and then living in New York broke open something in me like water flooding over a dam. Sometimes I couldn't write fast enough and during the day my head was filled with images and phrases. Everything around me was a stimulant, something to fashion into metrical writing. I knew very little about the science of poetry. Nello had to tell me that an *iamb* is one short syllable followed by one long syllable. All I was attempting to do was concentrate my imaginative experience in language arranged to satisfy my emotions through sound and rhythm. Not for others, but to satisfy myself. Usually a poem arose from an imagined first line or phrase and then other lines followed to the end as if they had a will of their own.

Every day I mailed the work of the night before to Nello, the only person I showed the poems to with the exception of one that I sent to Jack. He surprised me by not being overly interested in poetry, even as an actor, or maybe it was just my poem that turned him off. Nello marked up the poems in pencil and sent them back—he didn't edit the poems, he simply commented on the rhythms or cadence or imagery. He pointed out poor or trite lines and praised me mightily when they were good. I needed educating and he began the task. He wrote:

> Here is a list of what distinguishes "modern" poetry–"imagery patterned increasingly on everyday speech, absence of inversions, stilted apostrophes, conventional end-rhymes, poetic language generally, except where used deliberately for incantatory effect," "freedom from the ordinary logic of sequence, jumping from one image to the next by association rather than by the usual cause-effect method, emphasis on the ordinary, in reaction against the traditional poetic emphasis on the cosmic," "concern with naked consciousness and the newly identified unconscious as against the soul," "concern with the common man, almost to the exclusion of the 'hero' or extraordinary man," "concern with the social order as against 'heaven' and 'nature.'"

So when I talked to Dick about writing I knew that his description of the emotions he felt after finishing his first short story was accurate. This was how I felt after completing a group of poems. Not that I was satisfied—they were never exactly what I wanted them to be—but then I'd start again and try to interpret ideas or sensations. I was always left feeling that they were not up to what I was imagining. Nevertheless I had to write, no matter what, and felt useless and restless when I did not. I contrasted that feeling of rapture or wholeness with how I felt about acting. About writing—many times I had to force myself to sit at the typewriter or pick up a pen. I would do everything I could to avoid facing that blank page. So it wasn't all fun and games. Sometimes it was torture, sitting in front of a white sheet of paper with nothing in my head with which to begin. But if I sat long enough, words began to well up and gather in front of me on that white sheet. About acting—it was something similar to how I felt about horseback riding—scared to death until I rode a few paces. In acting, until I said that first line onstage I was so sick and frightened I didn't want to go on. Marlene Dietrich's daughter, Maria Riva, told me her mother had similar feelings. She would sit in the wings and very meticulously apply nail polish. The concentration on such a chore calmed her nerves sufficiently to enable her walk on stage, where she would then be completely at ease.

And after a performance? If there was applause, and I felt that the part had been dealt with skillfully, and my fellow actors were pleased, there was a glow of self-satisfaction. But it was nothing at all like the emotion I had after writing. I don't know how other actors feel, probably the great ones like Alec Guinness experienced these emotions. I was only good in two roles and that was probably because I didn't have much to say and could fall back on my internalization a la Stanislavsky's. One role was with Victor Jory and Mary Welch in *The Spider*. Mary and I were Jory's assistants; he was a magician. We wore black lace stockings and short bouffant sexy costumes cut low enough to show the V between our breasts. One at a time we would follow Jory's bidding, handing him props, smiling constantly, and sort of prancing about like two beauty queens. The other role was with Bramwell Fletcher in *Berkley Square*. Our costumes were nineteenth century and we were demure maidens, radically different from playing in *The Spider*.

Maybe my preference for writing was because on stage I was interpreting someone else's work instead of forcing words and ideas from my own head. Writing is the hardest art form of all. Why choose that lonely work over acting? No one claps or shouts *Bravo* over a well-turned phrase or beautiful syntax. And there is something very exciting about receiving approval from an audience. A wave of warmth rushes to an actor from receptive audiences. It happens sometimes after only one sentence is spoken. To make the transference more mysterious, an actor cannot see the audience because of the lights on stage. But there is this tangible connection that occurs. Of course, if an audience does not like the play or player, it can be horrible. And an actor's ego is actually quite fragile, so if everyone does not like him, he is devastated.

Weighing everything while sitting in my window that day, I came to the conclusion that if I had to choose, it would be to write. In the meantime, though, despite my decision, I'd still make the rounds trying for parts, since in future I'd need some way to support myself after my modeling

C.W.'s father, George Detwyler Webb.   C.W.'s mother, Minerva Reynolds Webb.

C. L. R. James's family in Trinidad;
from left, Olive (sister), Robert (father),
Judith (aunt), and Bessie (mother).

C.W. at the time when she first met C.L.R. (Nello) in California, 1938.

Nello, about 1946.

Conovor Cover Girls (C.W. on right).

C.W. as Conovor model, about 1943.

Coffee advertisement from *Life Magazine*, featuring C.W. as model.

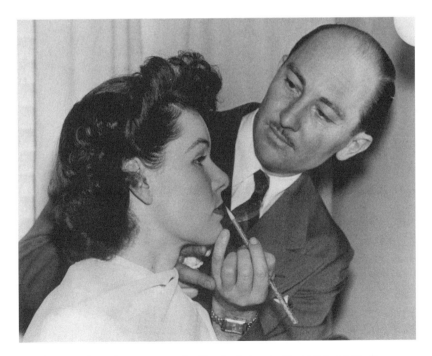

C.W. being made up for a screen test by Maurice Lolvotsky, David Selznick Studios.

Richard Wright. Photograph by Bernard Cole.

Richard Wright in costume as Bigger Thomas for film version of *Native Son*.

C.W. and Ellen (Mrs. Richard) Wright in Paris.

Lyman and Freddy Paine, C.W., and Nello, Northport, Long Island.

Nobbie at three weeks, April 1949, with
C.W. and Nello.

Nello and Nobbie, Northport, Long
Island, 1949.

C.W., Nello, and Nobbie, Northport, Long Island, 1949.

Nello and Nobbie in 1949, on the roof of their apartment building in the Bronx.

Nobbie at Martin Luther King, Jr.'s, March on Washington.

days were over. I had matured enough to know that writing would not pay the rent or buy the food.

Nello called the next day to say that Ellen and Dick had invited us to dinner, especially to see their first child, Julia, who was about a month old. We took the subway to Brooklyn and made our way to 11 Revere Place, where the Wrights lived at that time. Their apartment was across the street from City College and was spacious although it only had three rooms and a kitchenette. Dick had given cooking lessons to Ellen, as well as a gift of Fannie Farmer's *Boston Cooking-School Cook Book,* because she didn't know how to cook when they married. And Dick loved to eat. He was a good cook and told me he had taken it up because after writing for five or six hours he was overexcited, too stimulated to sit still, and he needed another though less creative medium that would take his mind off his work.

Ellen was petite, with brown hair and eyes on the hazel side, attractive but without a trace of glamour. She appeared fragile, with a slightly wistful air, but that was a façade. In reality she was tough as nails. She had gone against the wishes of her parents and married a black man. When they refused to meet Dick she stopped seeing them altogether. She had been an organizer for the Communist Party, not a role for anyone of weak will. We became friends, but even then I knew that Ellen, as with most people who embrace causes, whether right, left, or center, thought in formulas. Her particular passion, Marxist Communism, was temporarily in abeyance because Dick had broken with the Party and been much maligned. And Ellen was absolutely and completely in love with her husband. She was almost like a teenager having her first love affair. Dick on the other hand never thought in formulas; his mind was always free ranging and that got him into trouble with the Communists and others as well. As far as marrying Ellen he had no doubts; it was his second marriage to a white woman and he knew what to expect from a prejudiced white and black world. Dick said, "Ours is a mixed marriage, yet I and Ellen never think of it as such until we're reminded that it is. There're no problems in people of different races marrying and living together; the only problems that may arise come from those who look on, and those who look on are usually the ignorant."

Ellen told me that when her mother, Mrs. Poplar, learned she was pregnant her attitude changed somewhat—after all, the baby was half-Jewish. But she and her son-in-law remained aloof. She was never able to speak to him frankly and directly, and he, on the other hand, treated her with excessive courtesy as if she were a stranger. Ellen was not torn between her parents and Dick, not at all. Early in her marriage and before, she worshipped him and thought he was the most gifted and handsome man in the world. She told me, "he is a magnificent creature."

That evening when we were ushered into baby Julia's room by Dick it was as if it were holy ground. She was a pretty baby, lying on her tummy with her hands slightly above her head. Dick explained that she had the sniffles and pointed to the bricks he had put under the legs at the top of the crib. He informed us, as if he were a physician, that raising the infant's head aided her breathing. Ellen said that when people visited he stood at the doorway of Julia's room like a sentinel on duty. He also insisted that anyone who came within six feet of the crib had to cover his mouth with a handkerchief. I guess we were favored—we didn't have to cover our mouths and we were allowed to stand next to the crib.

After our short visit to see Julia, Ellen served drinks and we sat for a while in the front room while Ellen completed dinner. She wouldn't let me help, saying everything was practically ready. We ate in a fairly large dining room on an oblong table covered with a white linen cloth, and we were served a delicious lamb ragout with steamed rice. The dish was one of Dick's favorites; he could eat it every night, or so he said. And it was the best I'd eaten as well. Nello and Dick were agreed on rice; they could eat it three times a day. Dick said rice calmed his nervous stomach and Nello, who had an ulcer, agreed that it was soothing in such cases.

After that evening, we didn't see much of Ellen for a while. The Wrights moved from Revere Place to the parlor floor and basement in a building rented by Carson McCullers and other artists. The huge Victorian building was in Brooklyn Heights just under the bridge. We continued to see Dick, who didn't seem completely happy about the new living arrangements. The house became well-known. Anais Nin named it "February House," because so many who lived there were born in that month. Over the years outstanding artists in their fields came to live or visit: W. H. Auden, Louis MacNeice, Christopher Isherwood, Paul Bowles, Aaron Copeland, Virgil Thomson, Leonard Bernstein, and many others. Dick complained that there was interminable talk, talk, talk drifting down from upstairs when he was trying to write; this distracted him. He was a man with overwhelming curiosity, so I know it wasn't only his inability to concentrate on his work, it was that he couldn't clearly hear what they were saying. What finally made him decide to move was that Carson McCullers was drinking heavily and he worried about such an atmosphere and its effect on Julia. The Wrights then moved to a large apartment on Lefferts Place, also in Brooklyn.

Nello and I met as usual in the park behind the New York Public Library and I told him I had made a choice between acting and writing. He was pleased, showing his feelings openly and abandoning his public face, a normally reserved, almost solemn demeanor. He smiled all over his face, an expression he sometimes used, and his enthusiasm was contagious. I was drawn to him and yet there were half-conscious feelings of resistance involved. Arising from what? My previous marriage failures? My own stubborn personality, which required detachment? Whatever the cause, it kept me from becoming one of his worshippers. On his part, Nello said I was the only person in his life who did not treat him like a leader or someone special. To me, he was just a man, and he welcomed the attitude, as if it gave him breathing space. I did agree with him for the most part about politics—so much of what he believed, particularly about black/white relations, I had felt before we met. We also shared an admiration and belief in the uniqueness of individual personalities, which were being stifled by the society in which we lived. My experience with Socialists and Trotskyists had been that they lost sight of the individual in their analyses and their support of the masses. And no one whom I knew in the leftist organizations had the same appreciation of the arts as the two of us did. But there was the combination of fascination and, at the same time, an inner aversion toward getting involved as more than friends. At that time I did not know that there was much more to my reluctance than I had yet faced.

My first step in my new direction was to write an essay on Wright's *Native Son*. Soon after I began writing it, Nello introduced me to L. D. Reddick, curator at the New York Public Library's Schomburg Collection and the editor of *Phylon* magazine. He showed interest in the article and asked to see it when finished. If it was good, he'd publish it in his magazine. Nello had arranged our meeting and introduced the topic of an article about Wright. Since Reddick was an admirer of James, he was always willing to listen to what he had to say, so here was my chance. Actually, although I was a little frightened by my temerity in choosing to write about *Native Son* when so many famous critics had praised and attacked the book, I felt confident in knowing that both Nello and Dick would read and comment before Reddick would see the essay. My two good friends would not let me fall on my face—they would tell me whether it was good, bad, or indifferent. Then I'd make up my own mind about what to do. I finished the article and named it "What Next for Richard Wright?" and it was published in the 1946 issue of *Phylon*. Reading it today I find that it had a Marxist slant, but at least my instinct in contrasting Wright's disillusionment with the American working class with Chester Himes's confidence in it is meaningful. Wright had little if any experience with masses of workers and/or unions, whereas Himes had worked in the shipyards during the war and was stirred by the energy and desire for change he saw in the people around him. Most important for me at that time was reading something in print; it spurred me on and made me feel that my choice of writing over acting had been the right one.

Nello was traveling a lot, making speeches in various parts of the country, so I was again receiving letters every day. I found I was beginning to miss seeing him, that the letters were a good substitute but not enough. In addition to letters, he always sent articles he had written, as well as Party resolutions and speeches. Often he said, "You must criticize the resolution freely, say what you think. I leave it entirely to your own good judgment and regard for me to know how to speak your mind." But now Nello began to write more intimately, about himself. He was a reserved man and in the past he wrote and talked about me and my future, politics, art, literature, music, plays, and movies. In one letter, after asking for criticism about a political document, he enclosed a letter about his feelings.

He said that for the first time in his life he was "taken out of" himself, not by things but by me. He believed that he was beginning to find himself, something he could not do alone. He went on to say that I helped him break down barriers and get rid of defenses. He had sometimes wondered if his personality was so mobilized in a particular way for a particular purpose that he might suffer if he tampered with it. But that attitude, he said, was defeatist. Why should anyone be afraid of knowledge? Why should anyone be afraid of life? As with everything in his life, the personal was always a reflection of the social. He claimed that I was a peculiar combination of personal individuality and social manifestation, something he marveled at as a miracle. He also explained that his time in the U.S. was uncertain and he didn't know when he would be told to get out, to be deported. Such a fear kept him in a state of personal insecurity that somehow, somewhere, ate into him. His answer to these fears was to tell me everything, to let down barriers and, in so doing, to be free.

After so many years of correspondence I was used to Nello's excessive admiration of my appearance and intellect. I did not feel flattered so much as accepting, so great was my ego in some ways. What was becoming disturbing was the personal revelations he was making about his own fears. These aroused a terrible feeling of responsibility alongside my worry that I might fail him, that one day I would have to break off our friendship because of his love for me. He was also, obviously, pressing in some letters for a greater degree of intimacy. Greater degree! We had never touched except to shake hands.

In one letter Nello suggested that we go somewhere and spend a week together. He promised not to get too near, just to be with me, to say good night but know he'd see me in the morning, to have the time to talk about everything we enjoyed—art, music, and poetry—away from his political group. He confessed to feeling worn out and complained that one morning Marty Glaberman, an organizer of the Johnsonites in Detroit, had dropped in using the excuse that he thought they had an appointment that day instead of the next. Then he said a stream of people followed. At any rate, I did not go away with Nello and for a short time decided that we had better stop seeing each other. Losing him as a friend would leave a terrible vacuum. Who would understand me as he did? No one whom I knew, and I was tired of getting engaged and then breaking it off just to satisfy emotional needs. And in the circle of models, clients, photographers, and actors there was no one with whom I could really talk with any depth. In fact, I was leading a double life. I couldn't let the people with whom I worked know about Nello, and the people in his group didn't accept me—even my mother chose not to recognize our friendship, much less anything of a more serious nature. Then there was my writing. Who would be so honest about it and provide constructive criticism? Dick, I felt sure, would still be my friend, but he was beginning to think about moving either to the country or out of the U.S. altogether. Besides, I loved Nello as I would my father or younger brother. It would be impossible to end such a feeling that was also partially dependence or a feeling of safety. He knew me so well and yet loved me despite my mistakes and often foolish behavior. I began to feel I was taking advantage of him. Was I leading him on, when I had no intention of forming an intimate relationship? Naturally, I turned to him and explained that I was plagued with doubts about our friendship, that perhaps I was using him unfairly, and I explained that we should stop seeing each other. Absurd, but there you are: I needed his approval, even in such a contemplated move. He answered by sending me violets and a letter marked, as usual, *Special Delivery:*

Talk to me again and again. Now to me and you. First me. Look at me. I am 45.

I am not a healthy person.

My hands shake.

My beard is terribly gray. I can very often look my age.

I don't know when I will be yanked up from here and told to get out with no possibility of ever coming back again.

I am a Negro, which means that an association with me will be tough for anyone.

My life with women in the past has not been good for me. I am just beginning to learn.

That is me. Not all of me, the best of me you know. I'll come to that later. But that list is a formidable one, and there is no need to exaggerate them for someone with your outlook and possibilities. Furthermore talking and writing are one thing. An intimate life is another. The two are connected. To-day I believe that they are closer than I thought—formerly I was merely in love with you—now you are a well of inspiration and an embodiment of some of my deepest ideas and longings.

The conclusion I draw *to-day* is this. If in a year's time you should say "I have seen someone. I am in love," the only thing for me to say is "I have had every opportunity to win you, to make you feel that your life will only be complete with me—that you will never find recognising arms but mine. Yet I didn't make it. The differences, the obstacles were too much. You have fought and overcome many barriers. But this is your intimate personal life. You have decided. So be it."

What, my precious, could I ever have to reproach you with? You are unjust. For the last two years, have I lost anything? Have you taken and not given? You think if it were to end tomorrow, I would regret anything? As usual you underestimate yourself. You underestimate what you mean to me, actually and symbolically. Can two people live their own lives and have so much respect for each other, given so much, have so much respect for the *developing* personality as not to wish to limit, to constrict, to hamper, to bind the other? . . . I believe that your personality is such that you will search far before you will find anyone with whom you could so completely express yourself as with me. . . . I have lived dissatisfied for 25 years. I have chosen. I have decided. But I could not find it in me anywhere to reproach you if you decide not to choose me. I am not trading with you my interest and attention and friendship in return for your surrender, and then if you don't, to feel that I have not got my share, I have been cheated.

Listen. If you made love to me, gave me all you could, and then left me I wouldn't, I wouldn't reproach you. Isn't that what I marvel at in the others? They had their chance and lost—the fools. If you gave me only a part of yourself, then it is my business to make you come further. I can't see it any other way. This is a matter not of our future—it is a matter of *now*. That is and must be the correct relationship between us. Dig into yourself and see what barriers and constrictions are created, how wrong it is, for you to carry in your mind, to have carried, the conception that you had to be on guard lest you deceive me. Sure I know you had cause. I know you were fighting instincts and doubts and fears—Oh! Yes fears too. (Don't you think I have them too?) But at an rate those must go.

These were strong words, and here was a man who worshipped me, who insisted I was one in a million, "the most wonderful woman in the world." These were the words and emotions of an extremely handsome, graceful, brilliant man. He was at forty-five still physically fit except for his ulcer and shaky hands and had played cricket well into his thirties. He was experienced in relations with women in Trinidad, England, France, and the U.S. Women—to use a trite phrase—threw themselves at his head, or rather, into his bed. And still I resisted. Why? That was a mystery I needed to solve.

16

Madeline Patterson and I were on a shoot, modeling sable, ermine, and beaver coats in Central Park during a hot summer day. Time and again the client's assistant wiped our faces, or patted them gingerly so as not to spoil the makeup. In between sessions we were fed hot tea, which made us feel cooler but was not the best thing as an antiperspirant. A crowd had gathered, which was not unusual, but its presence seemed to add to the stifling atmosphere. Fortunately, the people did not get too close because a beat cop took pity on us and kept them away. To add to our misery the photographer's assistant used reflector boards to light the furs or our faces. In the studio he would have used lights. These boards are covered with a material like tinfoil and when shone on our faces they increased the heat another ten degrees. When the shoot was completed Madeline and I went to the Tavern on the Green, in Central Park, in those days a rustic place rather like a pub. We wanted to have iced tea to try to cool off. I wasn't very talkative, but then I never was, especially with Madeline, who was vivacious most of the time and talked for both of us. But this day she was quietly observant and in the middle of our tea drinking asked me if I was still seeing Mr. James. She always called him *Mr.* James. She did not approve of my friendship with a black man, but at the same time she, a southerner, used the "Mr." out of respect for me. Yes, of course, I told her. Madeline didn't comment, just looked into her tea and stirred the ice with one manicured nail tip. Then she looked at me and said, "Why?" Whether I was being rebellious or answering without thought I have no idea, but I said: "Because I love him." To my absolute astonishment, Madeline said, "Well, it's all right then." I don't know whether she empathized because of her love for Sandy Calder and the hopelessness of a future with him or the romantic notion that love is all. Her response jolted me and once again I realized how often I prejudged people or situations, based I think on viewing everything through political ideas. I did not like this trait and again determined to wait, watch, and try to see things as they really were and as I defined them by formulas or dogma. Sometimes I felt as if I was in school with myself, always having to act as pupil and teacher—not leaving out scolding and feelings of guilt.

Madeline asked me to go home with her to Scarsdale but I told her that I'd rather be alone. I could always be honest with her; she didn't need excuses or evasions. When I reached my aerie above the Hudson River the first thing I did was shower and put on the coolest, most loose-fitting garment in my closet. On the way home, I had picked up a small bottle of rum; not a usual habit, but I needed something that might quiet the activity in my brain—the stream of consciousness was today more like a clatter than monkeys chattering. The heat exhausted me. Fresno had been hot but not humid. New York was hot and muggy, day and night.

All day I had been going back and forth, thinking about Nello's recent argument. I was especially wondering about his letter saying, "dig into yourself and see what barriers and constrictions exist." With my drink of rum and bitters over cracked ice, a lovely pale pink, I took up my favorite spot, the window seat overlooking the trees below and the moving river. Well, he commanded, so I would try to obey. It appeared an easy task at first. Naturally, I told myself, I would be leery of marriage after messing up two earlier ones. Most likely, I just wasn't someone who could stay in a relationship for any length of time. Another voice argued, but you were ready to marry Gilford? If you were afraid of marriage, how did that happen? Well, that was probably sex. It was the first time you realized it could be enjoyable? Could that be the reason for your readiness to marry him? You mean you were ready to compromise everything you believe in for some thrilling interludes? No, that argument didn't wash. What then? I didn't seem to be getting anywhere digging for reasons not to marry James. I decided to take a different approach, something more positive— contemplate marriage with him. As soon as I opened the door to such a possibility the reaction was so violent it sent off what seemed like electric shock waves in my brain and body. And very soon, much like the light bulbs used by cartoonists to indicate bright ideas, there was the answer. At first I denied the revelation; it could not possibly be true. But something persisted until I had to acknowledge that my reluctance toward marrying James was because he was black. The shock was profound, like a nightmare, and I did not want to own such an emotion—hadn't I always fought for minority groups, especially black? Didn't I become furious at the Los Angeles comrades who treated our black sympathizers as if they were from the jungle? Wasn't Wright my closest friend after Nello? Hadn't I been studying the history of slavery and everything else I could find about the struggle for equality and freedom? Hadn't I been in demonstrations and protest marches? There was no escape, no way out—I was prejudiced; it was this keeping me from even touching Nello, except to shake his hand. A *bigot* is what I called myself that terrible evening. Part of me simply wished I had not gone beneath the surface to find such a truth. At the same time, I don't think I could have lived with myself if I had hidden such a feeling—something would have nagged at me—there'd be no way I could believe I was a moral human being, or worthwhile at all.

Nello called as soon as his train from Philadelphia arrived in New York. He was in high spirits, filled with enthusiasm about the group of John-sonites in that city, all splendid people, he said. When he asked when he could see me I put him off for a few days, saying I had to work, which I did, though I could have managed a few hours in between. But self-revelation held a grip on my emotions which were trying to deny any prejudice. I knew I had to tell Nello just what "digging deep," as he had suggested, brought into view. I had an impulse to laugh, wondering what grave-diggers felt like on their days off. When working, of course, they simply had to concentrate on getting their jobs done and since there were usually two or more there wasn't time for introspection. Remembering that work is the best way to escape problems, I called in to the agency to get the next day's bookings. Fortunately, there were several. After a restless night, not good for a model's appearance but remedied by old Max Factor's Pancake, I gathered the items needed, packed my black plastic modeling case, and set off. The day finally ended and there was a letter waiting for me from Nello. Shortly after I got home, some violets were delivered. I called to thank him and we arranged to meet Friday evening for dinner at Connie's in the Village. This was one time I did not look forward to seeing Nello or even eating Connie's cuisine.

Friday arrived, Nello talked, I listened, and we had a good dinner. Despite the trepidation I felt about telling about my monstrous discovery, I ate everything in sight. However, at the end of the meal, over cognac and espresso, Nello covered my hand with his and said: "What's the matter, precious? You're not your bright self tonight. Is something troubling you?" Unconsciously, I almost jerked my hand away. His solicitude made me feel like bursting into tears—how I was going to hurt him when he knew my awful secret! I told him I was fine, nothing was the matter, I was just tired from a week of work. I was not going to confess in public. We left the restaurant and walked slowly through Washington Square and still I couldn't tell him about my dreadful discovery. We were nearly out of the park when I forced myself to turn back and ask that we sit down for a while on one of the benches. Nello was more than happy to delay saying good-night and we found a bench without people sitting too near us. Taking a deep breath, I told him what I had discovered, that I was resisting him because he was black. It took so much strength just to get the words out I thought I would choke. When I finished my story, Nello began to laugh. I must have shown pain and hurt because, forgetting his reserve, Nello put one arm around me, but he withdrew it quickly when he felt me stiffen. He then took hold of one of my hands. "Listen, sugar pie, do you think I didn't know how you felt? It certainly isn't a surprise. All white people in America, and many other countries, are prejudiced. Everyone! You are not special. I've known what was troubling you all along, but you needed to find this out for yourself. Now, precious, listen to me. The only way to overcome such feelings is to recognize prejudice and then every time a sign of it appears, fight it down. That way you can tear it out of yourself." We sat quietly for a few minutes, and then Nello took up the subject of prejudice. He said when the revolution occurred it would be the southerners who would make the greatest strides toward accepting blacks as equals. Southerners know they are prejudiced, so when they change they go through a personal revolution. Northerners don't believe they are prejudiced, and unless one recognizes that such is the case he cannot change. There is an expression that a southerner does not care how close a Negro gets, he doesn't want him to achieve status. A northerner doesn't mind a Negro gaining status, he just doesn't want him to get close.

During the next few months I gradually became less frightened of forming a more intimate relationship with Nello. He did not make any overtures except through letters and I, in turn, worked out my fears in poems. One of the poems, which Nello enjoyed, was about a bird being fed grains by a man. The bird approaches him, hopping forward and back, steps seeming to retreat more than advance, head faintly turned to one side to catch any movement so it can fly away. The bird darts up fast to take one grain and rushes back across a wide circle. But a breath, a tremor on the part of the man, and the bird flies into the air because it knows the man is a lover of minced bird tongues. All the man wanted was the bird's trust, wanted just to see it up close. He would have to try to win its trust another day.

Eventually, I moved into Nello's apartment at 1306 Chisholm Street in the Bronx. It was on the fourth floor of a walk-up with granite stairs. The building was probably designed for the upper middle class when it was first built. It was in the shape of a U around what may have been a garden, but the courtyard had been neglected for so many years that there were only tufts of scrubby grass and a few ice plants drooping around the sidewalk. The apartments on the extensions of the U did not have neighbors on the same floor. Each apartment had neighbors only above or below. Since we were on the top floor there was only the roof above and neighbors beneath. Inside there were three rooms: a fairly large living room, a medium-sized bedroom, and a kitchen. The kitchen was long and narrow and had a window at one end. The window looked across to the other part of the U so that one could see into the kitchen on the other side. The window in the living room was unobstructed. The hardwood floors were in good condition and the bathroom was narrow, with a basin to the right of the entry, the bathtub along the same wall, and the toilet at the foot of the bathtub. There was no shower.

Since Nello had been living in dingy rooms on the west side of Harlem, he was inordinately proud of his home. He wrote a letter saying he was buying a mop, a broom, some cleaning powders and soap, which of course other people used to clean his place. The furnishings had been given to him or purchased at second-hand or Goodwill stores. There wasn't much. There was a white-painted wood table with three chairs in the kitchen, an old-fashioned gas stove that stood on four legs, and an old refrigerator. Fortunately, there was a built-in cabinet along one wall, because elsewhere in the apartment there was little storage space for clothes, linens, or other household necessities. Everything was very clean, even the shelves, where there were a few white dimestore plates, cups and saucers, one or two bowls, a frying pan, and two or three pots. In the drawers of the cabinet were towels and a couple of sheets. Entering the apartment there was a foyer as part of the living room and one end of the kitchen could be glimpsed from the front door.

In the living room was Nello's very large oak desk, placed next to the only window, and a wooden chair. There was one armchair of white plastic and a mattress on the floor covered by a spread, with pillows at the back resting against the wall, that served as a couch. Between the living room and bedroom was a small entryway leading into the bath and, to the left, into the bedroom. The bedroom had a double bed and one chest of drawers. The apartment had only two closets, one in the foyer and one in the small area outside the bedroom. The bedroom had only one window but the nearest buildings were at a lower level and a fair distance away so the sun lighted the room every day. Initially, the sparseness of the place did not bother me. We had a small electric phonograph with a stack of classical and a few calypso records, a large bookcase, an old, heavy typewriter—a bottle of rum, Angostura bitters, and ice cubes—the necessities of life. Nello had made friends with a local butcher and despite rationing we were always able to get prime steaks. He seemed to win over admirers without even trying. Once he went to Bonwit Teller to buy me a sweater. His belt had broken and he tied a piece of rope around his waist to hold up his trousers. His clothing consisted of hand-me-downs from Lyman Paine. Lyman, being rich and a New Englander, was parsimonious so the clothes had been well worn before they'd been passed on. Nello walked into Bonwit's as comfortable as if he were in his native Trinidad. Everyone stared at him, wondering whether he was a menial worker who had lost his way from the service entrance or a robber casing the place. The moment he approached a saleslady and spoke she was won over. He took a fair amount of time to select the color he wanted—he didn't want white, it was too virginal. The saleslady willingly took out almost every sweater, in different colors, and discussed with Nello the age and hair color of the recipient and I don't know what else.

At the time the neighborhood was mixed but Nello was the only black in the building. Across the street on the corner was a bar owned by a black man who allowed Nello to use his telephone since there wasn't one in the apartment. He did not want a phone, because people would have been calling him constantly. When he was in the Bronx he wanted to be away from everyone, especially members of his group, unless they were specifically invited to do some work.

I should have recognized warnings of what lay ahead as far as how the leaders of his group would respond to our union. Nello had asked one of the youngest members, Yonnie, to come up and put a lock on one of the closets. All Nello told him when he asked why it was being done was that it was going to be Constance's closet. Yonnie then told the others. When Nello showed me the closet I was surprised to see the lock, one of the ordinary type that opens with a combination of numbers. Nello explained that people were curious and he did not want anyone interfering with my things. He related two incidents that had happened to him since he had taken the apartment. One of the Trotskyists had come to visit, gone into his refrigerator and reported that Nello did not use oleomargarine but—horrors!—butter. Because of Nello's ulcer, the doctor suggested he drink eggnogs when he couldn't eat solid food. He didn't like the taste of raw egg. To make it possible to drink he put a few drops of rum or brandy in the mixture. One of Max Shachtman's followers observed preparation of the concoction and went back to report that Johnson was drinking himself to death up there in the Bronx. I didn't like the idea that his followers would pry into his personal and private affairs and wondered whether these were true stories or perhaps Nello had a suspicious nature.

On the day that I moved in, quite shaky and nervous about taking such a step, I was surprised to see Freddy Paine get off the subway train just after me. We then walked the two blocks from the Fremont Station to Nello's apartment. Her reason for visiting, she explained, was to give him a steak she had purchased from her butcher. I thought her timing was odd and wondered how she happened to plan a visit so precisely. When Nello opened his door he was obviously surprised at seeing Freddy alongside me, but he quickly suppressed his irritation. She handed him the package of steak but made no move to leave. Instead she asked with a rather falsely buoyant air whether he was going to offer her a cup of coffee. The three of us sat around the small white table in the kitchen for what seemed like hours but was probably much less before Nello said, "Well, Freddy?" It was quite clear he meant for her to leave and this time she got the message. After she had gone Nello said he had made it clear to the comrades that he would be unavailable for two weeks.

And we did have the two weeks. Nello occasionally called Raya to see if there was news but otherwise we spent the time alone. He played calypso music and taught me the dance. We listened to music for hours on end. We sat or laid on the mattress, holding hands and just being quietly content. He talked about cricket, said he had been a good bowler but not very good as a batsman. We went to the opera to see and hear Don Giovanni, and once to the New York Symphony. Nello would want to make a real evening of these events so we would have dinner out in a restaurant, almost always Chinese because other places would not serve blacks. Then sometimes we went to a place in the Bronx, within walking distance of his apartment, to eat juicy barbecued pork ribs. Other times he would cook dinner, usually steak, always rice and sometimes couscous, the dish of okra, cornmeal, and butter. Very often together we cooked porgies, red snapper, or kingfish sautéed in butter. We always started with his favorite drink, rum and bitters over crushed ice. I had to get used to his favorite breakfast—it made the whole house smell bad. He bought thick pieces of baccalau, cut off a chunk, and put it under the broiler until it had blackened, actually charred, on the outside. After carefully scraping off the charred part, he ate it with olive oil, butter, lemon, and rice. At first the odor was a little hard to endure so early in the morning, although we did not rise until around 9 A.M. Eventually I was able to cook his baccalau and serve it with a pan bread he liked consisting of Bisquick, milk, and butter and prepared in a frying pan on top of the stove, not in the oven.

Within a day my fears about intimacy with a black man vanished completely. I simply wasn't aware of any differences based on the color of our skins, only those because we came from different cultures. In London, among friends, he was often called *the last of the Victorians*. And because of my mother's strictures and behavior I felt at home. There was of course my intense belief in his political ideology. The only times that were difficult were when we were in public and people stared. As a model, I had learned how to protect myself by simply ignoring people. But those stares were different. The stares that Nello and I received were usually threatening or hostile—some people muttered to themselves or at us, others glared, got red in the face, and shook their heads. Nello was aware of my discomfiture and eased it somewhat by telling me that not everyone was hostile. He said some people were just curious and others were envious. It was obvious I was doing what I wanted to do with my life, while they had to live within social limits. I hoped he was right, and whether true or not the theory gave me something to think about while I examined individual faces and tried to analyze attitudes. This reaction took my mind off myself and I became slightly less self-conscious, although never entirely comfortable. A few years later when I was in Detroit I met the wife of the man who was the subject of a book I was writing—*Indignant Heart*. Effie Owens was a black woman who told me that she did not mind going about with white friends except that she did not like the way everyone stared at her. So it cut both ways—people were going to stare whenever there was a mixture they did not understand or were not used to seeing.

When the two weeks Nello had allotted to our being free from his political obligations ended, he went back to work. This meant he left around 10:30 or 11 A.M. every day and returned about 10 or 11 P.M. In addition to working out new approaches and ideas for his own followers, he was also writing two columns a week for the Trotskyist paper and magazine. Although I was studying and writing, the hours from 11 to 11 passed slowly, isolated and alone in the Bronx. Sometimes I took a break and walked to Crotona Park, which was not a particularly pretty one. Many evenings I would climb up to the roof and look out onto the street or up at the sky. During the day, after hours of reading and writing I'd listen to music.

Nello had moved the white armchair into the bedroom and placed it near the window. He said it was my room and I'd have a place of my own whenever he and his leaders had to meet at our place. Most of the time he met with Raya at her apartment on Sutton Place, and with Grace when she was not working. Lyman, I think, was working in a shipyard and sometimes joined them in the early evening.

A few times Nello sent a telegram asking me to meet him at Lyman and Freddy Paine's apartment on Hudson Street to have dinner. For people with money they lived simply. Their apartment had only one small bedroom, a kitchen too small for more than one person, and a living room. To save space, Lyman, using his architectural skill, built a table extending from the center of a wall of books that could be raised when not in use, much like a wall bed. Their couch was most uncomfortable and I wondered how Nello could sleep on it when after late meetings the Paines insisted he stay the night. It was also a contrivance of Lyman's and was made of wooden slats. There weren't any springs, just cushions that Freddy had covered with gay colored materials as seats and backs. It was difficult to get comfortable because the cushions kept sliding, forcing the sitter up against the wood slats. They did have a fireplace that worked and was welcome on cold snowy days in the winter. Despite this description the apartment was attractive in a bohemian style, which I liked, having seen so little of such arrangements as a child. Freddy was creative in flower arrangement and there were always attractive plants and flowers in all the rooms. They had one armchair and folding chairs, the latter kept in a corner of the room for times they had meetings. Freddy was an excellent cook and a good hostess but she resented always being in the tiny kitchen out of earshot while Raya, Nello, Lyman, and Grace sat at the table in the front room holding lengthy political discussions.

Freddy and Lyman's house in Northport, Long Island, was larger than the apartment at 629 Hudson Street. It was a marvelous place. When the tide was in, the front of the house, built on stilts, was in the water. A large deck ran across the entire front of the house where when the sun was setting guests were served cocktails and fresh clams or mussels. Lyman had a small sailboat, called a cat, and we sometimes took it or the rowboat out to catch crabs or pry mussels off the pier supports. They were a strange couple, for here again luxury was combined with penny pinching. Rather than purchase a refrigerator they made use of a spring that ran under the house by leaving some floorboards out of the kitchen. Here one would see a lettuce or tomatoes or butter in Tupperware bobbing about at one's feet with Freddy stooping down to pick up something needed for the dinner she was preparing. At least the lettuce never needed to be washed and was always icy cold.

Gradually I got to know Freddy, and I was intrigued by her marriage to Lyman in that she had been an orphan, brought up by her Aunt Mims, and he was heir to a fortune. Freddy's Aunt Mims earned a living making hats and Freddy, at eight years of age, was her helper. She hadn't had an education but learned all she could through books and watching other people. Later Freddy became active in organizing women in the garment trade. Although she was very young when it happened, she was haunted by the fire in March of 1911 when a sweatshop, the Triangle Waist Company, burned in New York City. About 850 employees were trapped in the inferno, mostly young women. The building was full of inflammable materials and the fire began only minutes before the Saturday workday was to end. There was only one fire escape and exit doors in the building were locked. About 146 people were burned alive. It took that terrible tragedy, Freddy told me, to make it easier to recruit members for the International Ladies Garment Workers Union. Freddy had also worked as a model for Diego Rivera and Jackson Pollock, a waitress, and a nursery school teacher. She never bragged about anything she had accomplished and, in fact, one had to know her very well to discover her extraordinary qualities. Freddy was an acute observer, but she was self-conscious when being observed. Her facial expressions changed the minute she knew someone was watching her. If it was in a meeting, she would purse her lips and draw her brows slightly down into an intense listening expression. Lyman did not help his wife's feelings of inferiority; he was probably the cause. His pet name for her was *Pussums* and in use it could be affectionate or a putdown. Almost every time Freddy spoke when people were present he would interrupt her in the middle of a sentence with *Pussums!,* a note of disapproval in his voice, and make a sort of clicking sound, not exactly a *tsk,* but similar. Freddy would lose her train of thought, flounder a moment, and then fall silent. When he wasn't around she was perfectly capable of expressing herself clearly. Freddy's weakness, when relating an event, was constant digression—going round and round with extraneous details until a listener was lost. But she had a real capacity for listening that invited others to confide secrets because of her interest. As a result she had many friends. Freddy also had a sense of style. She was an expert with the needle, made her own clothes as well as the designs, which were unique. In only one area was Freddy confident. She had modeled for a few well-known painters and knew she had a beautiful body, so when Lyman wasn't around she moved with grace and freedom.

Dick and Ellen were getting ready to move permanently to France and put the house on Charles Street up for sale. Before leaving for Paris, they took a house for two months during the summer of 1947 in Wading River, Long Island. They rented the house from Dr. Frank Safford, who owned nine acres of land on the sound. The Saffords' house was a large, brown, wood structure right on the beach. The Wrights' house was on a hillside, in a clump of trees that hid the beach. Dick was working on *The Outsider,* although it had not yet been given a name. Very often Dick and Ellen scanned the Bible and Shakespeare's works for title ideas, but this search only took place after a novel had been completed. I was invited to stay for two weeks and was happy to leave the hot, stifling humidity of the bleak Bronx and be with my friends once again. I was not happy about their move to France, or, rather, I was happy for them but hated the loss in my life. I took a Long Island train and debarked at a station that hardly looked like one. I don't remember whether it had a building where one could buy tickets or get information but I don't think there were such amenities. All I remember is a wooden deck, all splintered and weatherworn. Dick was waiting for the train and when he saw me his face brightened as it always did when greeting people he cared about. He grabbed my bag and led the way down some rough stairs to his new, shiny black Oldsmobile. It was a recent purchase of which he was proud. Dick had taken driving lessons before leaving New York and this was the first car he had owned or driven. I promised to teach Ellen to drive during my stay because he was too nervous to make the attempt. When we reached the house, Ellen, Julia, and Knobby the cat were waiting to welcome me. Dick wanted to get back to work, so Ellen, Julia, and I got into our swim suits and I drove down the hill to the beach. We spread towels in the sand outside the house of Dr. and Mrs. Safford. There were quite a few people either in the water or lying on the sand. I learned later that the Saffords had planned their cottages for artists and left-wing intellectuals, although, of course, they made quite a bit of money from their rentals.

The next few mornings Ellen, Julia, and I went out for the driving lessons. Ellen was a good student, although a little nervous, as most novices are, and she tended to be extra careful. She may also have been thinking of Dick's pride in this big new car and fearful of anything happening to it. After a few days Dick decided he wanted to join us in the daily lessons, which didn't make me happy because I could see that Ellen was dissimulating when she said she was glad to have him with us. Dick got in the back seat with Julia and we set off on the same roads Ellen and I had been using, off the main drag where there was little traffic. We had only driven a few minutes when Dick sat on the edge of his seat, clutching the back of Ellen's with some force. He soon began calling out, "Look out for that car!" or "There's a car about to pass us, watch out!" Ellen became visibly nervous and her hands began to tremble on the steering wheel. On our way home Dick again shouted out, "The next road is where we have to turn!" By this time, Ellen was completely upset, and just before reaching the road she turned into the sidewalk. Fortunately, on the other side of the pavement was only a vacant lot, and she pulled on the brake. She was so unnerved that I took over the wheel, waiting until we reached the house to scold Dick. I told him he was never, ever, to come out with us again when Ellen was trying to learn to drive. He looked sheepish and mumbled that he was only trying to help, but he accepted my ultimatum. After that we did not have problems and Ellen learned to drive.

Although we all enjoyed the beach and swimming every day, the best part for me were the nights. After dinner Dick and I did the dishes while Ellen got Julia ready for bed. Then came the bedtime stories and after that we sat around a fire on the cool nights and talked. Ellen soon went to bed but Dick and I stayed up half the night, always until midnight and many times still later, talking and talking. Dick did most of the talking while I made notes. We sometimes discussed the lengthy outline of the biography I planned to write. Because of the planned biography and a natural tendency to keep notes on anything that might be useful or important, I always had a steno pad and pencil at hand. We never discussed any of his work in progress but I could ask questions on any other subject and he would elaborate. What was thrilling to me was he often spoke as he wrote— wonderfully graphic, sometimes beautiful sentences, and always vivid imagery. Maybe because I was a fledgling writer the moods of creativity were especially interesting. Many times I asked Dick what his feelings were when he felt a work of fiction beginning to build itself in his mind. In the biography of Dick that I eventually wrote, the context of those evening discussions in Wading River was described, leaving me out as a participant. He had written pretty much the same information in *Black Boy*.

He told me that preceding the writing of all his fictional work he was overcome by a particular mood every time. It was a vague sense of estrangement from his surroundings, a baffled unrest, a slow stirring of myriad emotions that gradually possessed him. He was absolutely ignorant of what set such moods in motion. This state of mind did not follow any apparent logic: it did not require silence or solitude, and he had no power to order or time the condition, but when it came he could not dislodge it until writing drained it from his consciousness.

It often seemed to him that in the swelling out of the moods they took on flesh and blood, sucked into themselves events, long past and forgotten, telescoped alien and disparate images into organic wholes. A random phrase might recall a story told by a friend years before; a face seen through smoke in a restaurant, or a mannerism or gesture, revealed meanings and submeanings of episodes in his youth. Two unrelated events might occur and fuse into still another pattern entirely. A newspaper story evoked excitement far beyond the meaning of a banal crime described, a meaning that in turn conjured up its emotional equivalent in a different setting and possessed of a contrary meaning.

His own psyche would become so enmeshed with a fictional character that when he completed a sequence he had lived the same experience: if the person had killed, then he had killed. Dick had actually talked to his friend, the psychiatrist Dr. Frederick Wertham, about a dream that he had killed someone after writing about a character in one of his novels. Dick said he hated the slightest intimation of anything mystic, and yet in trying to understand the writing process—when the reality encountered receded and hid itself in another reality, which when hunted openly altered its whole aspect, thereby escaping introspective observation—there were elements of magic in the process.

I asked Dick, "How do you feel after you've finished a book?"

"Exhausted, completely drained mentally and physically, as if I'd just finished a marathon," he answered first. Then he added: "Emptied out, as if there is a deep void or like an old battery that needs recharging." During these incubation periods he read constantly, book after book, reports on trials, murders, suicides, scientific discoveries, social studies—even the information on a cereal box while eating breakfast. He would sometimes be filled with fears, and a creeping dread that he'd never find in himself the impulse or resources to ever write again. At the same time, after brooding for some months, the fears would lessen and what took their place was amazement and a quiet joy when the shadowy outlines of a new book began to break through his unconscious and start shaping itself in his mind.

I was always pleased that Wright shared so much of what seemed like his inner self with me. Not too many writers will discuss their motivations or work habits. But he was a generous man. He was generous in many ways, reading the rough draft of James Baldwin's *Go Tell It on the Mountain* and being instrumental in getting him a grant of five hundred dollars from the Eugene F. Saxton Trust Fund, established by Harper & Brothers to aid promising young writers. Occasionally Wright would grow exasperated and one evening opened up a fairly large closet filled from top to bottom with manuscripts from would-be authors. He said, "If I took time to read all this, I'd never get my own writing done." Whether from natural inclination or because people distracted him, Wright did not have many close friends. He was always writing or working out what to write in his mind. At one point he bought a camera and worked at photography. He claimed it was vital that he distract himself after finishing the morning's work writing. Otherwise his brain continued without letting up. And although he was affable, people were sometimes aware that his mind was far away—there'd be in his eyes an effect of looking inward, and a stillness. Sometimes I thought it was a way of recharging his energies, or protecting himself. He had some people resenting him without actually knowing why they felt as they did. I believe it was an awareness, not necessarily conscious, that this was a man who was utterly free. Wright freed himself from the stultifying and brutal south; he broke with religion; he left the Communist Party, without losing a determination to fight against society's destruction of individual personality; he showed he was not racist by marrying a white woman who was Jewish as well; and he left America to sink or swim in her inhuman bigotry. How many people have the courage to live without compromise, as Wright did?

17

There were different reactions from the Johnsonites toward our liaison. The young members tended to be friendly, somewhat in awe at first because I was an actress and a photographer's model, but soon at ease with me. They saw I was more interested in politics, particularly the Negro question, than in my appearance or the work I was doing. The problem was that I did not get to see them very often. Nello did not want me to *socialize*—the word he used—with any of the members. He said whatever I had to say or any opinion I might express would be interpreted as coming from him, as *his* point of view, which could cause problems. He explained, "Caesar's wife must be above suspicion," which I thought meant she must not have affairs. As far as his leadership—Raya (Rae, or Freddie Forest), Lyman Paine, Grace Lee (Ria Stone), and, peripherally, Freddy Paine—there could be no close friendship. At least Raya was able to hide her disapproval because she was essentially a warm, passionate woman. I think she was also somewhat like a Jewish mother, and loving Nello as she did, she wanted him to be happy. Sometimes she would give me a spontaneous hug. Whatever antagonism she might have felt was disguised by enthusiastic greetings whenever I came into sight. "Hello, beautiful!" she would call out, much to my discomfiture. It didn't matter whether there were a few or dozens of people in a room. Until Nello put an end to it, she bought me Claire McCardle dresses—one was the famous wrap dress, rather like a robe but short, and mine was of heavy white pique. I loved it. Nello said that it was wrong for the leader's wife to accept gifts of such magnitude. It made me wonder a bit since he was accepting seventy-five-dollar monthly donations from Lyman, which enabled us to live, although somewhat poorly. He said Raya was jealous of me and giving gifts made her feel less guilty. This type of analysis from Nello, who shied away from anything Freudian, was perplexing. And it was not until the end of our marriage that I understood why she might have been jealous.

Grace Lee hated me and having to hide her feelings must have been a torment. Years later, in the 1960s in Trinidad, Nello and Grace's husband, James Boggs, tried to curb her fury against me. But she was unable to control herself and had to give expression to what she herself must have known was indiscreet if not actually stupid. Nello wrote me that her rage was all-embracing. Of the three she was the one most intent on being a leader, desperate to be thought of as someone important. Lyman would rather redesign his house in Northport than attend political committee meetings; Raya was totally preoccupied with political questions involving the revolutionary possibilities in the U.S. and its failure in Russia.

Then under Nello's leadership and direction Raya saw an opportunity to develop her personal talents and instincts. Cannon did not give her that possibility. What working with Nello meant for Raya was that she could develop her own theoretical ideas about Marxism. She had a passion for theory for its own sake and was not much interested in organizational matters. One of Nello's few complaints about both Raya and Grace was that they would spend weeks pouring over a section of Hegel or a chapter of Marx, sometimes a single paragraph. But what he could never get them to do was pay the same attention to the problems of the organization as an organization. He said he must have told them at least twenty times that what they were doing was a form of literary escapism. His admonishments had no effect. One of the tasks Raya took upon herself was to teach young members a class in Marx's *Capital,* all three volumes, once a week. As far as organizational matters she could chastise comrades whom she thought got out of line, and she could complain about the Cannonite's treatment of women, but by and large her mind was always examining new ideas. I really liked Raya, although her enthusiasm was sometimes overwhelming to one who had been brought up never to show any feelings, particularly in public. In appearance and behavior she and Grace were absolute opposites. Raya was all soft curves and messy soft brown hair—apparently sexually attractive to men, although she was plain looking. Her first husband had been a fairly well-known stage actor, her second, Bernard Adams, a handsome, brilliant, distinguished, very nonassuming man who was named head of the World Bank and died in a plane crash. Her third husband was an attractive Irishman, John Dwyer, whom she wooed away from his wife.

Grace was muscular, square in body with broad shoulders, a moon-shaped face, straight, rather coarse black hair, and clumsy feet. Probably the reason her walk was clumsy was her heavy tread, and she used to wear oxford-like shoes until Nello suggested a more feminine pair. She was self-

deluded and egotistical and desperate to imprint herself on history. Grace's
father owned two restaurants in New York, Chin Lee's and Chin's, each
seating about one thousand people. Although she was not particularly attractive, when she courted male members in the radical left, they generally
responded. One of her lovers, Bobby Lenihan, said she almost scared him
off the first time they went to bed. She had taken off all of her clothes except for a black satin slip, and she hammered on her breasts, telling him to
feel how firm and hard she was. One time at Nello's, when I had dinner
with him in his apartment, there was a similar vaunting of her appeal.
Grace and a comrade from Philadelphia, Nettie Kravitz, were staying there
for a few days. They were not invited to dinner and arrived sometime later
in the evening. Both women were introduced and then went into the bedroom. Nettie did not come out again, but Grace came out in a black satin
slip like the one described by Bobby Lenihan. She was not wearing a
brassiere. There was little to support but she paraded herself in front of us.
Nello had been stretched out on the mattress while I sat facing him in the
white armchair. Grace plopped down next to him and proceeded to ask me
questions—in manner and tone similar to a prosecuting attorney—about
photographic modeling. Nello got up from the mattress and walked over
to the window. After a few minutes I said goodnight to Grace, and then
Nello and I walked down to the Fremont subway station. During the two
blocks we walked Nello didn't speak. When we reached the station and before I entered the turnstile, he shook his head. "That woman has no sense
of decorum." Nello said Grace had arrived one day when the three were
to have a formal meeting with Jim Cannon in a dress with a bare midriff.
He was shocked, but fortunately Raya came to save the day with a scarf
that she wound around Grace's waist.

Nello seldom said anything derogatory about any member of his group
but did not restrain himself that evening. I think he was embarrassed by
her behavior in front of me. Grace borrowed some books of his and when
they were returned she had made neat notes in her distinctive handwriting
alongside many of his. He shook his head and laughed. "Grace wants to
make sure that she goes down in history. These notes are for posterity. She
has a habit of saving every scrap of paper, filing it away neatly for proof of
her role in the coming revolution."

Lyman, a tall, thin New Englander, was cordial in a distant Bostonian,
gentlemanly way, but there was no warmth and I never trusted him enough
to try to become a friend. Freddy was torn between her natural proclivity
to make friends—she had a genuine liking for people—and Lyman's atti-

tude toward me, which made her cautious. She was always back and forth in her approach toward friendship with this woman C. L. R. had brought into their midst.

On a surface level, Grace and Raya appeared friendly and kept their rivalry from showing. Raya generally took the lead, and it was Raya with whom C. L. R. worked more closely, partly because Grace had not joined the group until 1940 and he had worked with Raya for almost two years. Raya was also more mature. She claimed to be the "first Johnsonite." Nello knew there wasn't empathy between the two women and worried that if anything happened to him they would tear each other, themselves, and the organization to pieces. Some years later, he wrote:

> The thing I have to do is to do what I can to adjust them, and the first thing is to make G[race] respect R[aya], in every way. . . . R's letter only brought home most sharply her strength and her weakness, and what I have been writing in the letters, trying to get G to do is to stop throwing out ideas. It seems that Ike [Sol Blackman] encourages her and tells her they are wonderful and she is wonderful and R isn't up to much, and probably that R is jealous. And that dumb G probably believes it. . . . Much of the trouble between G and R is the stupid way G refuses to recognise R's ability. I am writing a letter to G; you will see it and what she wrote to me. N. B. Get some of my type Scotch tape and always close up the letters as if they came from me.

Raya and Grace were Nello's handmaidens. He liked to be waited on, lying on his back on the couch, propped by pillows. They brought his slippers, took off his shoes, made him eggnogs, and cleaned the apartment, including the toilet. Nello was used to having people wait on him. He grew up in Trinidad, where he had a mother, sister, and aunts who served the men and boys in the family. He also suffered from an ulcer and had shaky hands from Parkinson's disease. Sometimes his hands shook with such tremors he could not hold a cup to his lips. With such ailments he needed to conserve his strength. One evening Ike, who hoped to be nominated to the political committee, accompanied him home, an unexpected guest. Nello always had a bath before dinner and I ran the water in the tub. Ike followed me into the bathroom and I left when Nello came in. Ike stayed, sat talking to Nello, and then scrubbed his back with a brush. I was resentful and probably shocked and sometime later told Zeb, Ike's brother, about the incident. Zeb laughed and said: "C. L. R. *let* him scrub his back, didn't he?"

I attended the Workers Party meetings with Nello. There were also Johnsonite meetings, but not held as regularly as this branch of the Trotskyists held meetings. The group had serious differences with the politics of the Workers Party leadership and members began to treat us with disdain and petty slander. At one meeting I wore a black silk dress with a high neck and long sleeves—a simple yet classic design—with a wide silver bracelet and a heavy silver chain, which caused a stir. After that we were labeled the "diamond-studded caucus." We were told Max Shachtman had remarked that C. L. R.'s "mistress supported him in luxury in the Bronx." The juxtaposition of *luxury* and *Bronx* was amusing to both of us; if he had said Riverdale, a posh area, the description might have been more appropriate. I completed a lengthy article on Wright, which was published in *Phylon* Magazine in 1946, and was continuing a study of black history and literature.

As the war was coming to an end there were wildcat strikes in the plants, possibly in reaction to having been forced to sign "no-strike" pledges during the war, but also because there was a fear of coming layoffs and massive unemployment. The unions had gotten behind the no-strike pledge and had actually joined the War Production Board, which left the workers at the mercy of their employers. While the war was being waged, they were fully behind the effort and production was at a peak that no one had seen or ever would again. Because the government was the client of the plants, producing ammunition and planes, supervision was not strict. Workers would sometimes fill in for each other, doing each other's work while some took care of personal needs or went fishing or on picnics with their families. They completed their daily company work rapidly and made what were called "government jobs." These consisted of bracelets, rings, small gift boxes, or parts for their cars made of scrap metal. There has never been such a time in the U.S. when workers actually enjoyed going to work.

At first the Workers Party took a stand against the no-strike pledge and agitated through *Labor Action* and in leaflets about the enormous profits being made by corporations. We handed out hundreds and hundreds of such leaflets intended to educate the workers. Gradually Shachtman began to pull back from support of nonauthorized strikes and eventually produced a pamphlet outlining what would happen postwar. The pamphlet was called *Plenty for All*. The Johnsonite position was that the workers should and could take over the means of production through sit-ins and wildcat strikes. We learned that while our group was concerned with meeting with workers and discussing how to reorganize production under their control, members of the Workers Party who had become union leaders were meeting with management to discuss how to control the workers. The Johnsonites believed that the workers were nearing revolutionary fervor and would take over the plants and form small self-chosen groups to run production. The Shachtmanites began to call us "stratospherists" and "petty-bourgeois dreamers," among other things. Nello and Raya began to discuss the future of the group, since both felt that trying to accommodate ourselves much longer to the Shachtmanite positions was not possible and led to demoralization of the members. It was decided that the Johnsonites would split from the Workers Party. Cannon on behalf of the SWP's position published a pamphlet that opened the door to a possible realignment. The pamphlet was called "The Coming American Revolution." Although the Johnsonites did not agree with all of the SWP's political positions, they could certainly agree on the notion that there would be a revolution in the U.S. Raya and Nello made an appointment to meet with Cannon to discuss the return. The agreement was that the Johnsonites could retain their identity as a caucus but must and would be disciplined Party members in support of the SWP.

The meeting was successful and a date was set when we would return to the Party. First we needed to break with the Shachtmanites and both leaders had to prepare their members, in our case for entering the SWP, and in Cannon's case for accepting us. While these negotiations were being made our group was busy writing and publishing documents that made clear where we stood politically. After the break with the Workers Party we had about three months on our own. This period as an independent group was probably the most stimulating for all the comrades. We were typing, meeting, hardly taking time to sleep or eat, buoyed up by our escape from six years of living within the Workers Party, where we had never felt completely welcome. The first document Nello wrote was "The Balance Sheet," which summed up our experiences and differences with the Workers Party. Others produced were "The Invading Socialist Society," "The American Worker," "State Capitalism and World Revolution," and "Dialectic Materialism and the Fate of Humanity." Nello was also working on an essay based on ideas he had discussed with Trotsky in 1938. It was eventually completed and published under the pseudonym of J. Meyer. The essay proposed that blacks needed to organize themselves independently, without being subordinate to any radical party or trade union. The title of the essay was "The Revolutionary Answer to the Negro Problem in the USA." Almost all of us were involved in producing a small newspaper. It didn't look much like a newspaper; rather more a pamphlet on 8½ by 11-inch paper, but everyone enthusiastically took part in writing articles or drawing cartoons. Finances were met by contributions from the members as well as some people sympathetic to Johnsonite ideas. Nello conceived of a newspaper to destroy in his own group the theory of the vanguard party. It was a practical and theoretical move in that members would be engaged with the outside world, not sitting around arguing the finer points of Marxism and their role in the coming revolution. Inactivity in any organization is like dry rot—destructive.

Toward the end of 1947, after our brief flurry of independence, we were welcomed into the SWP, where many of us had begun. There was some relief in that we were treated with friendliness, not the hostility we had suffered during our last years in the Workers Party. Although our position on the "Negro question" was different from theirs, Cannon agreed to setting up what was called the African Bureau and Nello was to be given his own office at the SWP headquarters on University Place. The SWP had few black members and had made little inroads in the community even with a branch located in Harlem. In the Workers Party, the idea of such concentration on the Negro question had engendered hostility from Ernest McKinney, whose party name was David Coolidge. Coolidge was also the man who mocked C. L. R. by holding little seances and trying to mimic him. He cheapened himself with such antics. He, was after all, a paid functionary of the Workers Party, a status shared only by the leadership. A small salary was taken from the contributions to the Party by its membership. There wasn't any pressure on comrades or any sum set, and no one ever complained about giving money to an organization he/she believed in. Coolidge had been active in trade union activities for generations and had full backing ideologically from the Party. He was hostile to ideas that struggles for civil rights by blacks had any value and, in fact, believed they would never become anticapitalist unless led by the revolutionary Workers Party. Since the Johnsonites believed that the autonomous black struggle had validity and was a direct part of the struggle for Socialism, Coolidge could not control his antagonism. I'm not sure, but there is also the possibility that his unbridled dislike had something to do with C. L. R. being a West Indian. Most American blacks did not like West Indians. These feelings may have been engendered by a sense of inferiority. West Indians were, for the most part, particularly those who came to the U.S., highly educated. And not having suffered virulent hatred and exclusion, West Indians moved about with much greater ease and self confidence than did American blacks. Another factor that may have played a part was that Coolidge was not an attractive man, having become bald rather early and being lighter in color than Nello. Nello, with a full head of hair, prided himself on what he called "good hair." When I asked what he meant, he said it was curly but not kinky. It was easy to comb, that's what constituted good hair. Coolidge was also short, while Nello was six foot three, and because of the difference in height, he tried not to stand where he had to look up at Nello. I don't know whether he complained to Shachtman, but if he did, nothing changed.

The WP and SWP positions were essentially the same, summed up by the slogan "Black and White Unite and Fight." According to their line, the struggle for equality was linked to that of white workers who would lead the way by their rejection of the dehumanizing effects of their work in production. The Johnson position was that given their position in society black people would be in the forefront of any struggle and act as catalysts that would carry white workers along with them. We insisted that demonstrations in the black communities, called riots by the media and others, were protests against the near-slavery conditions of their lives. The Communist Party's position was to support both Marcus Garvey's Back to Africa movement and the self-determination proposal that would divide the south into separate black and white areas.

About a month after I moved in with Nello, our doorbell rang at 2 A.M. Since we had been together such a short time Nello got up to answer. I heard the voice of a woman and expected her to have made a mistake in ringing our bell. Instead Nello took her into the kitchen, and the scrape of a chair told me they were sitting at the table. I got out of bed and stood in the doorway of the bedroom, trying to hear what was being said. Eavesdropping wasn't easy; I was afraid to cross through the front room and foyer because the boards would creak and I'd be discovered and disgraced. So all I could hear was the low murmuring of voices. I finally got back into bed but couldn't fall asleep without finding out what was happening. After about an hour I heard Nello and the woman walking to the front door as he ushered her out. By this time I was really curious as well as somewhat put out that he had not called for me to join them in this nighttime conference. When I asked him who it was, he at first said, "Oh, just an old friend." I persisted and learned that it was one of the two sisters with whom he had been sleeping before we moved in together. One sister was married to a well-known Harlem doctor and the other to a musician who traveled a great deal. I don't know and Nello never said whether the women knew that he was making love to each of them at the same time. But this night, when I learned who it was, I was furious. Mostly pure jealousy but also anger that a woman would visit *my* lover at 2 A.M. and that he would allow her to do so and not introduce me and include me in their conversation. All that Nello would say was that she was having problems with her husband that she needed to discuss. My hurt feelings and anger did not seem to make any impression on him. He simply wouldn't talk about her visit and went back to sleep.

It was my first experience with Nello's method of dealing with anything troublesome. He simply ignored whatever he did not want to deal with. There was no way that one could get him to talk; he became a stone wall. This episode was a blow to my ego. Here was a man who had spent eight years espousing love and finally persuading me to live with him the rest of my life, and now he would not share with me this strange woman's preoccupations or even think it peculiar that she should arrive at such an hour in the morning. Although my immediate feeling was both jealousy and hurt, I didn't spend much time thinking about Nello's odd behavior and very soon made excuses for it. His attitude toward me didn't change; he was as devoted as ever and the next day returned home with the usual dozen gladioli. The imitation orchid blossoms were open all along the spiky stems, which meant that they would not last very long, for which I was grateful. But I didn't tell Nello they were not going to last. He bestowed them with such grace and pleasure that I did not want to dampen his feelings. Nello and I did not reach that state of indifference in which we would be bored by lovemaking, possibly because he traveled so much and each homecoming was like a honeymoon. There was joy when we made love to each other and I cannot say what part of this joy was the body's and what was the mind's. Sometimes the senses responded; sometimes the spirit. He was utterly satisfying in every way, but when we weren't getting along there was no physical contact, not even the touch of a hand. Early on, in a letter written before our marriage, he claimed he would never go to bed with a woman who lived in the same city or even the same state as I. He would feel it was "sacrilege." And for a long time such an avowal was true. Great affection there was between us, but there were reservations and I knew them. He liked me as a companion and was passionately attracted to me as a woman. During the good times we were immensely happy. There were lovely moments of tenderness, of good interesting talk that was often so free there seemed no difficulty in crossing the space of individuality; it was as if our minds fused or were welded.

After Nello's eleven- and twelve-hour days he came home exhausted. While he undressed and drew his bath water, I prepared a tray with Italian or Jewish salami in thin slices, Italian or French bread, a bottle of Guinness Stout, and a glass. I would then sit on the lid of the toilet and hand him, in turn, a slice of bread and salami and then the stout. After a few bites and sips of stout he would tell me what he had accomplished during the day. For a time, probably because of the novelty—I had never seen anyone eat and drink in a bathtub before—and the intimacy with which he discussed the work he was doing, I was content. And almost always after his bath he wanted to make love before going to sleep. Preliminaries were physical and vocal and his admiration and descriptions of my body were unstinting. The long, deadly, lonely hours were forgotten.

But there were times when I tried to talk to him about the group's attitude toward me and he would freeze, just as he had done when the woman visited at that early hour. And there was no way I could break through the icy barrier. My first reaction was rebellion; I had come from the theater and was still earning money in modeling assignments, which gave me some self-confidence. It was when a decision was made by the leadership that I should stay at home and not work at all that real difficulties began. The leadership decided that the Immigration Department, prodded by Senator McCarthy, would step up deportation proceedings, especially against liberals and radicals. The wisest course then would be to prove that Nello had an American wife to support. The decision was not forced on me; I was ready to do everything possible to thwart both the immigration people and McCarthy. But my isolation was compounded by the bleakness of my surroundings. During one of Nello's self-questioning periods he called our Bronx apartment "the barracks." For a Californian the whole area was forbidding, all steel and concrete, no greenery anywhere in sight. Yes, there was Crotona Park about six blocks from the apartment, but it was an arid place when contrasted to the burgeoning trees in Laurel Canyon, Echo Park, or Beverly Hills. I sometimes rode the subway down to Central Park, just to sit and absorb the greenery. Then there was the apartment—there were no curtains at the windows, and fifty years ago watching a mixed-race couple was better than seeing a foreign movie. Just seeing us eating together in the kitchen fascinated our neighbors. Nello left every day around 10:30 A.M. and returned about 11:00 or 11:30 P.M. I studied or wrote for four hours every morning and then had to fill in the rest of the day. The silence surrounding me began to preclude creative thought. There were few household chores—and Nello only had breakfast at home and some salami at night—so shopping and cooking did not use up time. I tried sitting in Crotona Park but gave it up after fending off men who tried to pick me up, as they always do when a woman is alone. There was a bookstore down near the subway exit on Fremont that I visited every day, and then I walked and walked for miles.

My isolation soon became unbearable, particularly when Nello went into his withdrawal stages. After several months of silent treatment my frustration grew so strong I had to get away, just to regain my sense of proportion. Freddy and Lyman had given us a key to their Northport house and they were there only on weekends, so occasionally I would spend a few days looking at the sea and swimming if it was warm enough. Once I went to the Beekman Towers hotel and spent a weekend alone. It was not much fun sitting in the cocktail lounge before dinner drinking a lonely rum and bitters. Another time I took a train to Providence, Rhode Island, and then a boat to Martha's Vineyard, where I rented a room for a week. Restlessly I walked the beach until by the end of the week I felt that I should return home to my silent husband. Always the optimist, I planned new ways to approach him, to break the shell he lived in. He could write the most loving, intimate letters, but he could not seem to transfer the feelings they expressed into his day-to-day relations with me. It felt sometimes as if I was living on a surface, skating on ice. The difference was that I wanted to break through the ice even if it meant floundering in cold water. Anything was better than this exclusion. There was no one I could talk to either, which did not help matters at all. I didn't want anyone to think we were not getting along because we were in fact in every other way. Also, I did not want anyone to find fault with Nello, not simply because he was the leader of the group but because people were still prejudiced toward intermarriage. He could write, "I just wander around missing you. I have discovered why I went to the movies so often the last two or three years. Somewhere, somehow I found in them some substitute for you. I would like to see what goes on in a man's mind, really. . . . But the moment you came along I didn't want to go again. The moment you leave I am wandering towards them again."

Such a letter would send up flares of false hope and I would reassure myself he would change and all I needed to do was be patient and loving.

One Saturday morning around 11:30, Richard Wright arrived at our apartment with a big package under his arm. On his face was his special look, something between joy and conspiracy. The package when unwrapped disclosed the galleys of the last third of his autobiography, *Black Boy*.

Harper, his publisher, had refused to publish the section and Wright felt that the Communists were responsible because it described the way the Party operated and its suppression of self-expression and individuality. He placed the long, narrow pages across my arms with the sheets hanging down on either side, which felt much like holding a baby in its Christening clothes. "I want you to publish this with a critique of the section," Wright informed me. I looked at Nello and saw that he was smiling, his mouth curled around his pipe. He was pleased that Dick not only wanted the chapters published but had chosen me to write an essay. Nello had listened to the interminable discussions Dick and I carried on almost every time we were together.

My first task was to read and reread Dick's manuscript. This took several weeks and I made copious notes, filling up steno pads on both sides of the pages. When that was finished I went back to read the novels of Jean-Paul Sartre and other existentialists. I had given Sartre's *Nausea* to Dick after a first reading of *Black Boy*. Nello also became interested when I told him that without knowing the existentialists Dick was already examining the same types of emotions, as far as the feelings engendered by life as a black man in the U.S. The characters in Sartre's novels were filled with anxiety, psychic pain, tension, and dread, the same emotions revealed in *Black Boy* and *Native Son*. What was very different was that the existentialists were convinced that hurt, dread, nausea, and tension were the *only* manifestations of human personality, that man's condition in degradation is fixed and unchanging. Life is an unvarying torture, and since man is helpless, all that remains for him is to accommodate himself to anguish. But Wright still had hope and a social outlook. He was already familiar with the philosophy of Martin Heidegger, who questioned the meaning of human existence by probing into the existentials of its inner context. Dick felt Heidegger's theories were forerunners of the work of the existentialists. We discussed the statement by Sartre that the intellectuals in France were never happier than when they were under occupation by the Germans and fighting underground. When that activity came to an end they were left suspended—the belief in Russia under Stalin was tenuous, and what else was there to believe in? Thus they turned inward, promoting the notion that the state of man was to live in dread, nausea, and anxiety. Dick's analysis was that existentialism is a manifestation of a lack of effectiveness of political action among the intellectuals and the petty-bourgeois world and the inability of the proletariat to express its conceptions. Sartre and friends were restricted to the personal expression of what they wanted as human beings. This turning inward resulted in depression, anxiety, and a sense of worthlessness. Wright, as a black American suffering from the same spiritual and emotional maladies, knew quite well the cause of such angst—the world he lived in, that is, the intransigent mistreatment and abuse of black American citizens. This was reality, not an unchanging, philosophic state of being in mankind.

Nello got one of the members of his group, Cecelia Deitch, to type Dick's manuscript and she came up every day to use our old typewriter. The poor typewriter, which Nello called a *typing machine,* was as heavy as lead, weighed half a ton, and took strength to shove the return bar back and forth, but Ceil was devoted to Nello and eager to please. I stayed in the bedroom with my books and notes until it was time to prepare lunch. Nello was usually in meetings, either on University Place, at the SWP head-quarters, or at Raya's on Sutton Place. During this time I did not think of anything except the writing to be done—ideas, sentences, phrases woke me in the night and filled my head during the day. Gone were the lonely hours, as if they had never existed. A few times I went downtown to talk to Dick and he came up to the Bronx to see how things were going. He had to return the galleys to Harper's and they wanted to know when they would receive them. Legally, that part of the book and thus the galleys be-longed to Harper's. I asked Dick how he was going to explain a publica-tion that it owned appearing elsewhere. He put on his sly smile and said he would tell them he hadn't the faintest idea how someone could have got-ten the manuscript, that he certainly had not been guilty of breaching his contract. And, he added, it's not as if we are going to have a bestseller or even any real publicity with our little booklet.

After correcting all the typos—our typist was not a professional—Nello and I found a place to set in type Dick's part of the booklet. While this was being done I was completing the writing of my essay. Dick and I discussed only one idea that I had offered, leaving me free to write exactly what I wanted to say. I felt that some of my observations about the harmful effect of bigoted treatment on personality should be in the book and he agreed. I wrote the following in the 1940s and at that time the term "African American," could not have been used without causing hostility because of the connotation that black people were not true Americans. Such termi-nology also leaves out people from the Caribbean and South America.

> It is not oppression as such which is so devastating to the Negro person-
> ality but that he torments himself with self-doubt, dread, guilt, and confu-

sion. In Memphis Wright had been disgusted and horrified when Shorty offered himself to be kicked by the white men for a quarter. Now in Chicago he is learning that even a kick is perhaps better than uncertainty. He can now sympathize with "those tortured blacks who had given up and had gone to their white tormentors and had said: 'Kick me, if that's all there is for me; kick me and let me feel at home, let me have peace!'"

To live normally is abnormal because to live normally for a Negro is to live subnormal as a human being. "He must defend himself against, or adapt himself to the total natural world in which he lives." He must learn that he is Negro, separate and different from man. He must accept his circumscribed area of human action and limit his demands, not to his native talent but to what is established as his norm in America. What America thinks he is defines his position in life even to himself. He is Negro and must reassure himself of his worth or become aggressive in defense of his personality. He is never free. At home he is excessively tired and has no rest. He must always separate the real self from the defensive self, the hostile from the normal.

. . . There is a battle fought each time he meets the white world. He must arm himself psychologically each time he leaves his house. There is no anonymity; there is never the relaxation of a simple walk, instead there must be a constant adjustment to the reactions of every individual. White society never lets him alone. It intrudes on his personality, forces him always to consider its actions and his own reactions. Hate and fear are woven by American civilization into the very structure of his consciousness, into his blood and bones. They paralyze and cripple the growth and functioning of his personality, they become the justification of his existence.

The book was bound in gray and untitled; we named it *the little gray book,* was printed. Dick was pleased and the four of us celebrated with dinner at the Wrights, which Ellen prepared. The next step, Nello said, was to send it to every major library in the U.S. and Europe. He made a list and we sat together and wrote a transmittal letter and addressed envelopes. A few days later when I was putting books in boxes, ready to give out to our comrades, those of our own and those in the SWP, Nello returned from a meeting with Lyman, Raya, and Grace looking solemn. "Precious," he said, "let's have a little swizzle and talk." While mixing the rum, cracked ice, and bitters I wondered what could be happening that suddenly we were not just talking as usual, but we were to have a talk. I assumed that something must have happened either in our group or the SWP and hoped that we were not going to split again. Despite all the splits I had been in,

I had not gotten used to the fact that in the left there are always splits. Documents are written and there are arguments on the floor, sometimes heated, sometimes just too erudite to listen to, and sometimes foolish.

Such was not the case this time. The "talk" was actually the news that we would not distribute the little gray book to either our people or members of the SWP. Nello's leadership and a few friends could be given copies but must be told that they should not discuss the contents or let anyone know such a publication existed. My first reaction was that Harper's had discovered the booklet's existence and it was a legal matter. But it had nothing to do with Harper's; Nello's leadership felt the book would be viewed as propaganda by the SWP and might cause friction. We had promised to be good, loyal members and the book might upset the tenuous balance. The decision hurt because I had foolishly believed that the comrades would find me more acceptable, that I could really be one with the rest, doing my part to aid in changing the way people were treated, that the book would be considered as part of our belief that all people are creative and simply need freedom to exercise their individual powers. It was to be my revolutionary contribution and I had looked forward to their acceptance and to being able to make others see I was a serious revolutionary. Nello's own leaders had made the decision—the SWP leadership had not been consulted and, of course, had nothing to do with banishing the booklet. At that time I did not realize that the antagonism they all felt about me had found an outlet on the basis of politics. Some years later Nello confessed that it had been wrong not to distribute the book but he had to go along with the majority opinion and he, too, had accepted the premise that the book might antagonize the Cannonites.

I was not completely devastated, just very sad. I was a good comrade and if it was felt that the book would harm us, I of course gritted my teeth and accepted their judgment. Discipline was paramount, as I had learned early on in the Socialist Party. A good comrade accepted such; whatever the leadership decided, we went along. Such an attitude was not limited to the U.S. When Nello arrived in London one of the many things he looked forward to was horseback riding. For years he had sent me pictures of equestrian statues from many parts of Europe—postcards, pictures torn from magazines and newspapers—with notes exclaiming at the strength and beauty of the horses. He had often ridden in the West Indies and loved horses. One morning Nello took himself off to Hyde Park and had a fine time on a spirited horse. A few days later he was admonished by his comrades. Some comrade had seen him riding in the park and reported it back to headquarters. At the office Nello was given a lecture; revolutionaries did not ride horseback, and especially not in Hyde Park, where the aristocracy sometimes rode. Nello immediately gave up one of his pleasures, but he said later that he regretted doing so.

Although I settled down to send the little booklet on Wright to libraries and did not complain, Nello knew how disappointed I was and spent more time writing at home and having brief meetings instead of disappearing twelve hours a day. One week we were invited to dinner at the home of Grace's brother, Harry, and his Japanese wife, Julie. Nello did not usually accept invitations from the rank and file but when he saw that I wanted to go he agreed. Julie and Harry lived at 158 Orchard Street in a somewhat ramshackle building. Their apartment, however was a surprise. Julie had an artistic flare and had fixed up the railroad flat with paintings and flowers. The bathtub was in the kitchen, but she had disguised it with a cover that hung to the floor. Unlike many of the flats, this one had its own toilet indoors, off the kitchen. It wasn't much larger than a broom closet and when one sat on the toilet the small basin loomed over one's feet. Harry painted the floors in the other two rooms black and then waxed them. With white walls and colorful touches the place seemed almost luxurious in contrast to this European street filled with pushcarts. During the evening it turned out that Julie and Harry wanted a larger apartment and asked if we knew of anything in the Bronx. To my surprise they thought our apartment was wonderful, our poor, barren place. Of course it did have good hardwood floors and was spacious and airy. In fact we had so little furniture that any place would have been spacious.

When Nello and I reached home I suggested that we exchange apartments with Harry and Julie. I was very tired of being so isolated. I also thought that if I were closer to the comrades physically we might arrive at a closer relationship. It would also spare Nello the hour it took to reach the Bronx by subway. There was very little Nello would refuse me and he agreed that if it would make me happy then he was willing to make the move. On the surface, he was a man of peace, and he would do anything to avoid friction. He knew I was still hurting about the gray book and its lack of distribution. I also pointed out that I needed to be downtown, nearer to the New York Public Library, because I was going to continue to write about Dick. The Wrights had moved to Charles Street on the East Side and they were among my closest friends. The Raskins, too, lived on Sixteenth and were within walking distance of the Orchard Street apartment.

So we moved. But what a mistake. Orchard Street had seemed a picturesque area when I had visited it when living on Lexington and Sixty-second Street. The strange foreign bustle, the noise, the speech, the sidewalk displays and pushcart merchandise were all exotic to a Californian. Living two stories above it, though, was something else. In summer fish smells came in the window from the market just under the building and other decaying odors wafted up from refuse thrown from the pushcarts. We did not have the furniture and I did not have Julie's talent in home design so the place was unattractive, to say the least. Our secondhand bedstead had broken in the move and we slept on a mattress on the floor of the front room. There was one other tiny room between the front and the kitchen. This was to be Nello's study, such as it was. There was a drapery he could pull and it would give him a little privacy so we put bookshelves on the back wall and managed to fit his desk in the rest of the space. I did not find a bathtub in the kitchen romantic when I had to live there. It did not please me either to eat on top of a bathtub. That was the only table we had.

Orchard Street now filled with coffeehouses and boutiques, was at that time almost a slum, a bedraggled street filled with pushcarts selling everything from fruits and vegetables to shoes and clothing. It also contained a raucous crowd from early morning until night. The building in which we lived sheltered gypsies on the top floor and one had to pass a gauntlet when entering or exiting. They smelled bad and were constantly asking for money. Even worse than gypsies, in the building behind us, a drunken man began to bawl out and break glasses every night about 7 P.M. I was often alone and would stand at the back window of the kitchen and listen to him singing. For some reason he seemed to hypnotize and frighten at the same time. I'd be sitting in the front room reading or listening to music but there would be a feeling of waiting, an unconscious attunement to his footsteps as he returned from the street. As soon as he went into his apartment he began to smash the glasses and throw furniture around before starting to sing. When I heard him go into his apartment I would turn off all the lights and go silently along the narrow hall of our apartment to the kitchen. There I'd look out the window and see the man's shadow passing back and forth across the blind and listen to his painful tunes. The songs were never lyrical; they sounded of such rage that even when soft or hummed the anger was apparent. He would sing for hours and all the while I was glued to the window listening. When I told Nello about my nightly activities, he said, "Lord have mercy!" My preoccupation with the man "meant something." It was important to discover its significance.

Nello believed that any idea I had, almost the breath that I drew, was vital and significant politically. He told me to write about the drunken man and I tried to take his advice but gave it up after about one page, single spaced. I couldn't see anything "politically significant" in either the man or my fixation. In fact, he and his caterwauling became another factor in my dislike of Orchard Street. At least in the Bronx I could stand on the roof and the air was fresh and no one was yelling.

But that wasn't all—Grace and her lover, Ike Blackman, moved in across the hall from us. Ike was like an octopus, all tentacles reaching out to feel and pinch. Then, since we were next door to one of his leaders, Nello did a lot of writing at home. Most of the work was on deadlines, with Grace and other comrades waiting to pick up pages and proofread. People were in and out all morning. We had no privacy, especially because of Grace, who was always barging in, sometimes without knocking if our door was not locked. I usually kept the chain lock on because of all the strange men visiting the gypsies who lived on the top floor—not necessarily to have their fortunes told. Grace would knock in a peremptory fashion and every time I took off the chain lock she'd say: "Constance, really, there is no need to lock the door. Just leave it open so I can come in and out without disturbing you." Instead of telling her why I locked the door I'd smile apologetically as though I'd forgotten again. One reason I didn't tell her I was afraid of the gypsies and strangers was because we, as Socialists, were supposed to love all human beings, make excuses for their lapses by blaming them on social conditions, and generally maintain objectivity but never fear. I do not preclude the possibility that part of the reason I put the chain in place was spiteful, an attempt to let Grace know she was not welcome. I don't think she got the message and if she did it made no difference in her behavior.

After a morning of work, at about one o'clock, Nello would put down his pen, light a cigarette—he smoked both cigarettes and a pipe—and say, "Well, sweetie-pie, how about a little lunch? I have achieved mightily today." Many times we prepared lunch together and shared our usual drink of white rum and bitters while rice, red beans, porgies, red snapper, kingfish, or a meat dish heated and I made a salad. Those were good days. Bad days were when Grace joined us, bringing giant cartons of Chinese food from one of her father's restaurants. One time in addition to food she brought a quart carton of peeled, roasted almonds. Because of these sumptuous gifts we had to be courteous and invite her to eat with us. Or she would knock on the door and say, "Constance, what are you cooking? It smells delicious!" Grace insisted on discussions even when she had no response from Nello. He did not like to discuss politics when he was eating—it upset his stomach. In fact, we rarely discussed internal politics when he was at home, although I typed, read, and edited most of his speeches and articles. He had neither the slightest egotism nor writer's pride, and he was eager to hear criticism as much as praise. Nello was perpetually interested in comments or criticisms and waited anxiously for me to finish a book or a poem or listen to a new recording so we could discuss its merits. We listened to many hours of music or talked about Shakespeare, Aeschylus and Sophocles, Michelangelo, Picasso's *Guernica,* Becky Sharp in *Vanity Fair,* characters we had seen in movies, the grace of certain baseball players, the comics/cartoons, and music. The breadth of Nello's interests was awesome. We were never dull, and the range of our topics was always expanding.

Visits at dinner time were difficult, but after awhile Grace began coming early in the morning. Mornings were the very worst time for Nello. His ulcers required food as soon as he awoke to forestall acid accumulation. While he washed up, I always hurried to prepare breakfast, usually his favorite, baccalau; he would get back into bed, and we would sit quietly to eat. Grace would arrive before Nello could take a bite of food, plop herself down at the foot of the bed, sometimes with pen and notepad, and begin to talk about the organization or some plan she had, or whether the SWP was going to do one thing or another. Nello always suffered after these meetings. He asked me why I answered the door when she came knocking and I said she knew we couldn't be out so early in the day and would continue to pound away. She was nothing but persistent, like a juggernaut. Then Nello said, why didn't I just tell her to come back later? When I tried to do so it made no difference at all. She simply pushed past me as if I were a child. Her energy was frightening.

On one such morning, Nello was propped up in bed with his breakfast tray on his knees, and Grace came in, eager to make plans for his upcoming trip. He was to catch a plane that morning to begin a lecture tour, starting in Philadelphia and moving on to Cleveland, Chicago, Boulder, Detroit, San Francisco, and Los Angeles. He would be gone for about a month. I had also discovered a lump on his neck and he had promised to have Dr. Gogol examine him when he reached Los Angeles. We had said our farewells the night before and I knew there would be phone calls and letters all along the way so I was reconciled to it. Besides, being a good comrade, I knew that hearing him lecture would probably bring in more members. All the comrades were preparing for his meetings, bringing their friends and relatives to hear this great speaker. Grace launched into his schedule and then quickly switched to what she thought most important. She began by saying she knew nothing would happen to him, but in case something did, he must dictate his will to her, leaving everything to the Johnson-Forest group. Although outraged, I kept a straight face and looked to Nello to put her in her place. He said nothing, just continued to eat his breakfast and changed the subject. Perhaps that was the best way to handle Grace, because after looking at him expectantly for a few minutes, she dropped it. But I was furious. After she left I asked Nello, in not too pleasant a tone of voice, why he had not told her to mind her own business. He sighed and then explained that there wasn't any point in doing so, since he was not going to leave anything to the group and that in case of a disaster everything quite naturally would come to me. "But why didn't you tell Grace that's what you would do?" I demanded. As far as being left Nello's effects, this had nothing to do with my feelings—I couldn't have cared less about papers and used clothing and books. My persistence was fueled by anger and a feeling of humiliation initiated by Grace. I felt that Nello had failed to defend me. It seemed I always had to be Caesar's wife or a saint and never respond to slights by his colleagues. I just swallowed my pride every time.

While Nello was away there were two unpleasant episodes, both of which frightened me. Grace and Ike had a party one evening and although I was invited, I decided not to go. Around ten o'clock I heard screams and a lot of noise and my curiosity was aroused. I stepped across the hall and found Grace's door ajar and walked in. There was broken glass all over the kitchen floor and Ike was holding Grace in his arms and threatening to lower her bottom into the shards of glass. She was shrieking, half in laughter and half in terror, and the others were standing around trying to get Ike to stop. He finally put Grace down and people began to sweep up the debris.

Another day I was sitting behind my locked door, keeping very quiet and hoping no one would know I was home because Ike had made it obvious that with Nello away he was going to make a move, never considering that he was supposed to be a faithful follower of Johnson-Forest. In the afternoon Frank Monico, a comrade, came to visit and when he entered I forgot to lock the door. In a very short time Ike walked in, sat at Nello's desk, and began to read his and my correspondence. Frank mimed to me, "What's he doing?" I walked over to the desk and took the letters out of Ike's hands and asked him what he thought he was doing. He grabbed the upper part of my thigh and when I pulled away, taking refuge behind Frank, he strode out of the apartment. He was red in the face and breathing hard. The walls next door were thin and we could hear Ike pacing back and forth like some tiger in a zoo, only heavy-footed. Frank was upset and concerned and said, "Ike has lost control. I don't think you are safe here with Jimmy away." I didn't know what to do and was, in fact, frightened. There was brutality in Ike, even the way he treated his wife by flaunting his affair with Grace. He went home once in a while to see his children but made no mystery about where and with whom he was staying. And his habit of putting his hands on women without consideration for their feelings revealed not only a coarseness of character but cruelty as well. Frank walked back and forth for a minute or two and then said, "I'm going to call Raya." When she answered the phone, he told her what had happened and what he feared. She responded immediately and told Frank not to leave me alone but to bring me to her place, where I should plan to stay until Nello returned. So that's what I did. I slept on her studio couch for a week and nothing was said to Grace or anyone else. Nello, whom I called from Raya's apartment, was upset and didn't seem to take in that I was safely out of the Orchard Street place. He wrote a special delivery letter: "I got up this a.m. suddenly frightened. I find that my reactions are delayed very often. But I was frightened for half an hour and off and on all day. Darling, get away from it, go to Freddie's, go to Frank's, go anywhere, but get away and send to tell me that you have. Otherwise I shall be without peace."

Nello did not lose his temper; in fact, I never ever saw him lose control or show rage. But he called every day and insisted I stay close to Raya and not return to the Orchard Street apartment until his return. When he came back to New York, nothing was said or done and we all continued as if Ike's crazy outbreak had never occurred. About a year later I was told that Grace made a laughing comment to a member of the group: "Constance thinks she's so beautiful that every man is about to rape her." It was obvious then that Ike had made up some cover story in case Grace or anyone else found out about the episode.

$$\begin{array}{ccc} & \sim & 18 & \sim \end{array}$$

When we met, Nello was about thirty-eight and I was nineteen or twenty years old. Our backgrounds were both similar and different, yet we were alike in the way our minds functioned. Not that I was the slightest match for his intellect or education, but we were attuned in personality, or our brains were genetically similar. He was born in Caroni, Trinidad, but spent most of his youth in Tunapuna, a village approximately nine miles outside the bustling city of Port of Spain. I was born in Fresno, a small city in the heart of the great San Joaquin Valley, a few hundred miles from two major cities, San Francisco and Los Angeles. Nello's mother had been educated in a Wesleyan convent and my mother only finished high school in Savannah, Georgia. His father was a schoolteacher and my father sold shoes in a store. Both of us inherited an appreciation of literature from our parents and were widely read. He had been a celebrated cricket player and had been listed as Queen's Royal College's best bowler for 1917 and 1918. I had won some awards for athletics, and had held the record for the sixty-five-yard dash for several years. I was the only woman at the time allowed to run the high hurdles. Nello graduated from Queen's Royal College about a year before I was born. I had only one year at Fresno State College. He became a professor and I went to the Highland School of Nursing and then married at eighteen.

Nello's life in Trinidad was richer than mine in Fresno in that he attended plays and concerts, contributed essays and reports to small magazines, and was something of an authority on literature in Port of Spain. He was still in his twenties when two of his short stories, "La Divina Pastora" and "Triumph," were published. Then in 1928, "to purely amuse myself," he said, he wrote a novel, *Minty Alley*. After that Nello began the biography of Captain Arthur Andrew Cipriani, who led the island's first mass-populist movement. Cipriani had served as Commander of the British West India Regiment in World War I and Nello was drawn to the man's agitation for the "unwashed and unsoaped barefooted man," the people he had written about in his two short stories. I was writing poetry, but nothing had been published. While teaching at the Queen's Royal College in 1918 he staged a complete version of Shakespeare's *Othello* to make certain his students would be able to pass their preparatory examinations. I didn't read Shakespeare until high school and never went to concerts or saw professional plays until I was in my teens.

Both of us became restless in our small communities; while he went to England in 1932, I went to Fresno State College in 1934 to study medicine, preparing to leave for San Francisco. My dream was to end up in New York City. In Manchester Nello became a cricket correspondent for the *Guardian* and then for the *Glasgow Herald*. Both of us became involved in politics and considered ourselves anti-Stalinist Marxists. A striking similarity between us is that we believed in good and evil and both of us wanted to change the state of the world for the better and unleash the creativity that we felt lay in ordinary people. We hoped to bring forth a society in which people would be free to express their unique, individual personalities. Both of us held the view that there should be a redistribution of wealth. Everyone should be provided with shelter—a house or apartment—food, medical care and medicines, and clothing. Such necessities should be rights due to all people. If luxuries are desired then people should work for them, but the mainstays of life should be free. That millions of people are homeless and children go to bed hungry in the U.S., the richest country in the world, is scandalous. Worse—it is criminal. And if some people choose a life of wandering and not working they should be permitted to do so.

As far as our personalities, Nello and I were not fixated on our psyches. The world did not owe us a living; we owed one to the world. These were days long before the eruption of the "me generation," so disastrous to the community at large.

By the time I met Nello, he had written numerous books, among them a classic, *The Black Jacobins: Toussaint L'Ouverture and the San Domingo Revolution*. He had attended a founding conference of the Trotskyist Fourth International early in 1938, where he met James Cannon, one of the founders of the American Communist Party who split from the Communists to launch the Trotskyist opposition to Stalinism in the U.S. I had joined the Trotskyists when I was fifteen. When Nello and I met and I heard him speak I knew we were one intellectually, particularly with our outlook and appreciation of black Americans. And last but not least, he was black and I white. I had been dismayed by some of the ignorance and subliminal racism among my comrades. So when Nello voiced what I felt, it was like a fresh breeze flowing and I no longer felt alone in what before had been an emotional reaction that I had not been able to present in words to my comrades or anyone else. Here is an excerpt of what he said then:

> We say that the Negro struggle, the independent Negro struggle, has a vitality and a validity of its own. This independent Negro movement is able to intervene with terrific force upon the general social and political life of the nation, despite the fact that it is waged under the banner of democratic rights, and is not led necessarily either by the organized labor movement or the Marxist party. This means, and this is most important, that it is able to exercise a powerful influence upon the revolutionary proletariat in the United States and that it is in itself a constituent part of the struggle for socialism. The Negro will be in the vanguard of any revolutionary change in the United States.

The radical's slogan "Black and White Unite and Fight," had been unsatisfying to me, but I didn't know why. The Communists' and Trotskyists' conviction that it would be white workers who would lead the way to Socialism—blacks would simply tag along behind—to me left blacks in the position they were already in, being acted upon and taken advantage of rather than being full participants in their own futures. And both the Trotskyists and the Stalinists urged blacks to subordinate racial issues to class issues. In other words, "keep on suffering, there'll be pie in the sky, by and by." And at one point the SWP even frowned on mixed marriages or couples because whites might not join an organization that permitted interracial bonding.

In the church where C. L. R. spoke, there and then, I became the first Johnsonite. But what I actually became was not a Johnsonite, but a "Jamesite," which I did not realize until a few years later. Although his political outlook made me feel at one with him almost immediately, I thought of Nello as a friend and confidante. And I was married and would have a second husband before we ever became intimate. Nello was aware of our age difference and when he returned to New York he confided to close friends that he had met the girl he would marry. When asked why I was not with him he said, "I have to wait until she grows up." As soon as he left Los Angeles on his way to meet with Leon Trotsky in Mexico he wrote me a fifty-page letter, and there followed many years of letters ranging from single sheets to fifty or sixty, all written in longhand. These letters were my education—a sort of correspondence course in *everything*. What was refreshing after my years with singularly one-track-minded comrades was his multi-faceted, diverse, complex, and always questing intellect and enthusiasms. As the years passed, the letters became personal, in that Nello poured out ideas, thoughts, and experiences he said he had never told anyone in his life. We had both read all the volumes of Havelock Ellis's *The Psychology of Sex,* as well as the Bible from cover to cover. Although we had read Freud and were aware of his genius, neither of us believed that people were irretrievably marked, and thus doomed, by the treatment they received as children. In certain ways, although we were not religious, we believed in an aspect of Catholic ideology: the perfectibility of man.

Nello had gotten a Mexican divorce from his first wife, Juanita Samuel Young, who lived in Trinidad. Juanita was of Spanish and Chinese descent, from Venezuela. He had married her in 1929. Eric, Nello's brother, told me she was beautiful, but Nello had not been passionately in love; theirs was a traditional West Indian marriage. She was to keep the house in order, cook, and be his bedmate when he desired. She was not interested in politics. She worked as a secretary and must have been enterprising, because in those days Nello said that there were only three roles permitted women in the Caribbean. One could marry, be a mistress, or be a prostitute. Apparently it was only after the massive oil strike in the thirties that jobs opened for women. He described his life with Juanita as "pleasant." She, on the other hand, told Nello that the only time he paid her any attention was when he was on top of her. On weekends he would gather up the gramophone, records, and books and they would take themselves to Tunapuna to stay with his mother and father. Juanita became pregnant, but nearing term the baby died as a result of the umbilical cord twisted around its neck. Nello did not seem particularly saddened, only described the infant as a fine looking baby boy. Even then he was hoping to leave Trinidad for England when the opportunity arose. They had been separated since 1932, when he sailed for England. After living in London for about a year he wrote to Juanita and asked if she wanted to join him. She declined to do so. Nello said she was a proud woman and knew he did not really want her and that was why she refused.

Nello and I lived together for about a year before we decided to marry. Dick and Ellen Wright were pleased about our decision. Although they were open minded about people living together unwed, Dick rather than Ellen thought only marriage could be considered permanent. His attitude was contradictory, since he had been married once before to a dancer, Dhimah Meidman, which lasted less than a year. Nello and I did not tell anyone in the group about our plans and in May 1946 took ourselves by bus to Fort Lee, New Jersey. I don't know why we chose Fort Lee, whether there wasn't a waiting period or whether New York didn't allow intermarriage. Probably the former. Our witnesses were two policemen who could barely control their rage and consternation at this black and white union. They swelled at the neck of their uniforms and their faces were red throughout the short ceremony. At the end of the brief rite we kissed hurriedly— on my part, in defiance—and left the ominous atmosphere as fast as we could. Dick and Ellen asked us to join them on Charles Street for a celebration with champagne. Ellen had baked a wedding cake so we spent a few hours together.

Before returning to our Orchard Street apartment we decided to eat dinner in a restaurant. There were not many Chinese restaurants in the Village so we chose one with French cuisine. I knew that Nello was nervous when he saw there weren't any black, Asian, or Mexican faces in the place. I wasn't happy about it either but we were seated before we could change our minds and leave. At the table, Nello withdrew completely into his frequent and impenetrable shell. I tried to talk to him to establish normal behavior, especially since people were either watching us outright or pretending to ignore us. He would not respond; what I felt was conveyed to the people around us was that I was some strange person he had picked up. I became extremely upset; after all, this was my wedding day and Nello appeared to have forgotten that a few hours before we had taken a giant step—marriage. When I could not bear it any longer tears began to drip down my cheeks and I could not stop them. Since I did not cry unless I was angry Nello would not look at me, just gazed down at the table and its settings, completely stoic. I knew when he went into his shell of ice nothing would change, so I put down my napkin and left the restaurant. To calm down I walked a couple of blocks and then waited for a downtown bus. Nello followed me and was seated on the bus watching out the window to be sure that I got on. We sat together as if nothing had happened, not speaking, not touching, just recovering from a traumatic day. But the day hadn't ended—we were about a block or two from our place when two cops began to follow us. The streets were deserted and we were vulnerable. Nello whispered, "Don't look back, walk slowly and look straight ahead." The cruelty of it all—in addition to the fear we felt, we dared not touch each other or hold hands, which might have given comfort. Fortunately, we were not stopped, but the two police followed us to our doorstep. On the stairway, out of sight, Nello put his arms around me while I hugged his waist, both of us trembling. Normally, he was oblivious to the reactions of people who were hostile toward blacks, whether alone or with me, but cops late at night were another story. In bed we didn't talk about the incident, just held on to each other, tighter than usual, until we were tired enough to assume our usual position, which Nello called sleeping "spoon shape."

Our first months together, except for the hostility of Nello's leaders, were essentially romantic and loving. In bed, Nello did not like a lot of activity and once described someone he had slept with as "too busy, all over the place." We connected quietly and slowly and lay very still. The only movements would be in our internal muscles, squeezing and releasing. Our mouths and lips, whether kissing or whispering, moved slowly as well. The build-up to orgasm would be so intense that when it occurred he cried my name and sometimes I wept.

Nello especially liked falling asleep still inside me; it was not exactly comfortable but pleasant nonetheless. Dancing together alone at home was often part of the sexual act, moving our bodies in unison. Sometimes we put on a calypso record and he taught me to dance to its rhythm. He was a marvelous dancer, very graceful in every movement. He would never dance at Party socials, though. When I asked him why he wouldn't, he said if he danced with one woman he would have to dance with each and every one. On my part, I loved to dance and he encouraged me, saying he liked watching me move around the floor, doing the lindy. However, he never lacked for attention. He had the art of pleasing women without troubling himself at all. I think every woman he met wanted to get into bed with him. One could see it in their avid glances. Women and sometimes men would sit on either side of him and at his feet, on the floor when there weren't chairs at hand. He had a wonderful way of getting people to talk to him, even the most shy. And it wasn't a tactic or something planned in advance; it was a genuine interest in everyone to whom he spoke. He would ask questions that fell into a pattern. He would begin with, Where were you born? Did you go to school in the same town? What were you interested in? Where do you work now? What is it you have to do every day? Do you like the job? What time do you start and finish work? What time do you get up in the morning? Do you take lunch or eat in a cafe? What do you have for breakfast, lunch, dinner? People answered his questions and became so convinced of his interest that they poured out their most private thoughts and longings. He made people feel special, that what they thought or did was important. They were also left with a feeling that they could accomplish anything they set out to do. He did not talk very much but would sometimes say, "Is that so?" or "Lord have mercy!" The inflexion would be different, depending on what had been said. Most of the time I was absurdly pleased by the way people reacted to him, and it had nothing to do with wanting the acceptance of a black man. Except when we were harassed by the general public, questions of color never entered our minds.

Nello had endearing qualities, not the least of which was an absurd sense of humor. He described his amusements as approaching insanity. Sometimes he invented a person to whom he would tell jokes, other times he made speeches, on anything—to blacks on Fascism; to a Party convention calling for a new spirit in the leadership; to workers just before an assault against Capitalism; on the Nazi-Soviet pact—anything that came to his mind. Throughout the speechmaking he strode about the room, pausing occasionally and gesticulating at times to emphasize a point. He could take a very serious subject and by manipulating his vocal tones and making inappropriate faces make me shriek with laughter. Then he would recover sooner than I and admonish me, "Now, now, sister, control yourself." And off I would go, laughing again. After what he called *speechifying,* he would sit down and make notes of the things he said and they often formed the basis of future articles and speeches.

When we were alone way up in the Bronx, we possessed each other, and Nello was absurdly romantic, which gave to sex a transcendent joy that both of us felt. There were times when it seemed as if there was osmosis between us. Most married couples signal each other with glances that others do not decipher. But Nello and I did not even have to look at each other to exchange the same thoughts with or about events or other people. He was always watching me, but with such subtlety that I only realized it from the letters he continued to write, even during our marriage. He described my expressions or lack of them, the color changes in my face, my hairstyle at the time, the shape of my legs. There wasn't anything that he missed—it seemed he focused the powers of his intellect on my appearance and personality. There wasn't a lot of talk about love except through written words, but he surrounded me and coddled me as if wrapping me in swaddling clothes. But he kept me separate from the group as much as he could.

I was still hoping that Nello's leaders would accept me and went through periods of frantic assistance—typing documents by the hour on an old half-broken-down typewriter, handing out thousands of leaflets, proofreading, and serving lunch or tea to his leaders. For some time Nello looked on these activities without comment, but eventually he let me know that he did not approve. He wanted me to concentrate on my own writing. Grace, he said, had approached and reproached Wright, telling him he should join the Johnsonites because he was taking up too much of Nello's valuable time. Wright immediately went to Nello with the story. Nello was emphatic in his reply. He told Dick his job was to write books, not join political organizations. He had a very dim view of artists trying to become politicos. Their work was as important as those involved in politics.

The romantic idyll did not last very long—Nello was caught up in the break with the WP, which was to come out with its theory that Russia's government was a form of bureaucratic collectivism, while the Johnsonites' theory was that it was State Capitalism. As a result of this political schism and the poor treatment the group had been receiving, the Johnsonites were in transition to rejoin the SWP. But not his entire group wanted to leave the WP. Nello toured the country to win over the opposition—Philadelphia, Denver, Chicago, Detroit, Los Angeles, and San Francisco—which took over a month. Among the Johnsonites who did not want to split from the WP and enter the SWP were the leaders of the Detroit branch, Martin Glaberman, who worked in an auto factory, and Johnny Zupan, a shop steward and a member of the United Auto Workers Union. There were also a few comrades who took the side of Artie Fox, who had prepared his own documents in opposition to Johnson-Forest. I don't remember what Fox's political statements were and no one else I've spoken to remembers either. Convincing some of the comrades was for Nello a strenuous activity, taking hours in some cases and requiring all of his patience. At one such meeting he began talking to Marty and his wife, Jessie, at 2 P.M. on a Sunday and by dinnertime they had not been won over. They then had dinner and Marty and Johnny left and Nello talked to Jessie for three hours. She was finally won over. Then about 11 P.M. Marty and Johnny returned and they talked again until 2 A.M. Marty was at last won over. Nello said Marty's reluctance had not been on political grounds—Marty never disagreed with Nello politically. The reason he did not want to leave was that there were members he felt could be won over to the Johnsonite position on State Capitalism.

At the same time, because of the cold war climate, Senator Joseph McCarthy, the House Un-American Activities Committee, the FBI, and the Immigration Department stepped up their activities and began to appear on our doorstep every two weeks. We lived in fear that Nello might be deported or jailed. Along with visits from the immigration authorities, we were under constant surveillance by the FBI. The agents usually arrived early in the morning, around 5 A.M. I think it was a deliberate ploy to waken people and thus make them more vulnerable. On one particular day I answered the ring of the doorbell at 5 A.M. and there was only one man standing in the hallway. It was obvious that he was FBI, because they all have a certain look. They do not have beards or mustaches, their hair is short and well barbered, they wear suits and ties, and they do not have any outstanding characteristics. One would find it difficult to pick them out of a crowd. However, on this particular morning the man had reddish-blonde, curly hair, cut very short. He asked to see Mr. James and I asked him to wait for a few minutes and closed the door, leaving him in the hallway. I went into the bedroom, where Nello was just awakening, and whispered, "FBI." He got out of bed and said let them in and went into the bathroom to wash up. When I opened the door again a second man had joined the first. I invited them in and after asking them to be seated I sat on a hassock and said nothing. After a few minutes of silence, one of the men asked me if I was an artist. He had looked at our paintings that Gali Malaquais had given us. My answer was simply "No." Another silence and he tried again: "Are you English? From the U.K.?" My answer again was "No." I knew immediately what prompted the questions. If I was an artist, or English, then he could find a reason for my marriage to a black man. Obviously a white, presentable American woman would do no such thing.

Nello came into the room, looking imposing even in his bathrobe. Both men stood and he motioned them to their seats. Nello and I had worked out a system based on FBI tactics. Two men always visit and one asks questions while the other watches facial expressions and body language. So Nello became the speaker and I the watcher. Neither of us ever volunteered information or made any explanations, but Nello did answer their questions. The line was drawn, of course, at naming any names at all. A direct question one time was: "Is Richard Wright a Communist?" Nello said, "No, he is a famous author." The same question was asked about Chester Himes and Ralph Ellison, and the agents received the same answer. I always sat quiet and stared at the agent who was the watcher. The watcher then grew uneasy and was distracted from his usual role. He would glance at me from time to time and then look around the room, but he was unable to concentrate on Nello.

Nello and I tried to take these encounters in stride but the persistent visits of men from the various organizations were a strain, particularly these early morning sessions. However, Nello cautioned members of the group not to develop an "FBI mentality." He said it would result in distracting them and cause them to believe there was someone hiding behind every tree. During a conference in Detroit where members came in from all the branches in the country, someone reported to Raya that there were FBI men parked in front of the hall. She became more excited than usual and hustled Nello and me out the back entrance and into a car, where we were told to lie down in the back seat. We drove away. After about an hour at the home of a local comrade Raya called and said it was safe to return. I always felt Raya somewhat enjoyed such episodes. They may have reminded her of her days as a child having to escape the Cossacks when they rode through her village beating and killing people. She always became pink-cheeked, her eyes shining, as she arranged for our safety. The FBI was relentless, even visiting clients with whom I worked and volunteering information about me. The men showed their badges and after a few questions about how well they knew me they asked whether the person knew I was married to a Negro who was a dangerous subversive, a Communist? Fortunately, most of the people with whom I worked were not particularly sympathetic toward the FBI organization. They would often call to tell me they had been visited and what had been said.

It seemed ridiculous to me that so much attention would be paid to us and to our little group—at most, perhaps eighty Johnsonites and less than a thousand Trotskyists, with WP and SWP combined. The Communist Party had hundreds of thousands of members and sympathizers. It could hold a conference or propaganda meeting in Madison Square Garden and fill the place, leaving only standing room. The Party had an immense membership because of its support of the revolution in Russia as well as its vision for the U.S. appealed to people from all walks of life, who were fervent in defense of its activities. And many of the Communist Party actions were admirable, which I did not learn until many years later.

It was not the strain of being under constant harassment by the immigration authorities and the FBI, or the hostility from people who could not control their anger when they saw us together, or even the determination by the Johnsonite leaders and a few of the members to exclude me from serious activities that eventually broke my spirit. It was Nello's inability to give of himself except through letters. He was always protecting himself, something I did not realize at the time. A prime example was an evening with our friends Gene and Francesca Raskin. After dinner one evening we sat in their front room discussing music. They were both musicians and

Nello enjoyed talking and listening to them. They performed publicly and he loved actors and the stage. In London, he had played a role with Paul Robeson in an adaptation of *The Black Jacobins*. Nello was sitting in one armchair and I was sitting in another a few feet distant. He was being particularly brilliant and I had an intense feeling of love and pride in this man who was my husband. When he looked toward me I smiled, and my feelings of love flooded toward him. In an instant, less perhaps, he withdrew. Up came the shield or wall behind which he lived. I couldn't understand what had happened to him so suddenly. Some time later when I managed to get him to explain, which was rare, he told me that my personality had hit him like a ball of fire so intense that he could not take it. He thought I wanted something from him. He had to protect himself. Any expectancy from others rang alarm bells, and he drew into his shell as rapidly as a turtle. In 1947, I wrote:

> Rather than have any disagreement, Nello's method was to simply retreat behind an impenetrable wall. He could not express his emotions. Instead, he walked about the Bronx carrying on lengthy, furious arguments with me and with himself—all inside his own head. Then he would come home and discuss politics, literature, anything but what was troubling both of us. If asked a personal question, he changed the subject . . . And I was spoiled, not only because of the attention that actresses receive but because the eight years of letters from Nello had made me feel like a princess. Suddenly, I was Cinderella; the ball was over and I was relegated to cleaning the kitchen for cruel stepsisters.

One time he did not speak to me an entire weekend, not even during breakfasts, lunches, and dinners. I hit upon a tactic that I hoped would break through his icy wall. Spite and anger probably fomented the action. Taking our little record player to the dinner table, I put it on the chair next to mine. Then I put on Billie Holiday, singing "Love me or leave me—let me be lonely—I want your love, but for me only—I'd rather *be* lonely than happy with somebody new." Nothing happened. I began to sing along with Holiday. There was still no reaction. Nello simply ate his meal as if no one was in the room. There wasn't any expression on his face. When he finished eating he wiped his lips carefully with a napkin and rose from the table without saying excuse me.

Later that night I felt guilty and ashamed and wondered how much I had damaged his ulcer. Was acid flowing over the raw spots in his duodenum? When we went to bed I wanted to say I was sorry and make amends but I didn't know how to begin. Instead of talking, which probably wouldn't help matters, I put my hand on his thigh. Nothing happened. Usually at my touch on thigh, stomach, or even his back there was an immediate response. His physical reaction was like a Jack in the Box and we made jokes about his readiness whenever I touched him. He was very proud of his virility. So this night, shocked and faced with a flaccid penis, I raised myself on an elbow and kissed his mouth. His thin lips did not respond, just grew thinner and firmer. Nello then pushed me away and got out of bed. He grabbed his robe and went into his little cubicle, drew the curtain, and sat at the desk. I followed him in acute distress. Having had no experience with male impotency I blamed myself. I did not appeal to him anymore. He did not love me in a physical way. I felt crushed. I sat on his lap and put my arms around his neck. He stayed stiff and rigid, keeping his arms at his sides, and if I had not held onto his neck I would have fallen off of his knees. I cried almost hysterically, something so rare for me that when it happened the sobs and tears were impossible to stop. There was such pain I felt I might choke. He must speak to me, we must talk, I insisted that he listen to me but he did not respond. Nello's version of it appeared later in one of his letters:

> I remembered with remarkable vividness how that night of the great quarrel how uncontrollably you cried. And after a time I said: "She likes an audience—she knows Grace will hear and she cries loud and talks loud." I didn't think that only. But I thought that too. Then I went inside and you followed. I remembered how you fought—insisted that I listen and speak to you; I knew at the time that I was not responding—wooden and obstinate and stubborn. But I knew too that my saying you wanted an audience was spiteful and mean. Then you sat on my knee and were very tired and wanted so much or rather needed so much for me to take you close and love you. I remained distant and made only a few gestures.

At times there was about Nello's appearance something not of this world. Our friends, Dr. Paul and Sylvia Nesson, met him one day on the street and saw him before he recognized them. Paul said, "He looked like a saint." But Nello was not saintly; his world was one of suspicion, he did not trust people, and many times he mistook the slightest happening or reaction of someone as revealing ulterior motives. And at the same time, he looked at people in general as being remarkable humans and especially enjoyed listening to them describe their work and their lives. His was a conflicted personality.

When my little trips away from him accomplished nothing except letters saying how he longed for me, I declared that we were to separate. I would still live as his wife, in name only, however. This was necessary because he and the group believed he had a better chance of staying in the U.S. if he had an American wife. But I told him he could consider himself not married and I would do the same. He was free to come and go as he pleased, which he always did anyway, but now I demanded the same privilege. I would take over the bedroom and he could sleep in the front room. I did continue to cook his breakfast, knowing that mornings were difficult for him and his ulcer, but I took my tea and toast on a tray into my room.

But this living arrangement became impossible, at least for me, and I decided to move out for a while. Nello did not protest; he may even have been glad to go back to his old ways without living with someone who demanded more than he could give. I called an old boyfriend, who picked me up in his convertible, to the excitement of the neighborhood, and took me to the apartment of two comrades, Hank and Cuppy, who were about to move to Detroit. The move to Detroit was part of an exodus designed to get the comrades closer to the workers. This political move was called "proletarianization." The move was to rid the organization of any remnants of vanguard Party politics. It was intended to promote the self-creativity of the working class. The leadership also believed the comrades needed the experience of work in factories to rid themselves of their petty bourgeois upbringing.

Along with this effort was the idea of what was called the "third layer." The first layer was leaders. The second layer was the petty bourgeois intellectuals, and the third layer, the workers. The only one actually affected was the second layer. These comrades were not to lead, were to give way in meetings to the third layer if those members wanted to speak, and were in fact told to be "full fountain pens." We were commanded to listen to what the third layer had to say and write it down. It was part of the attempt to wean members away from thinking of themselves as leaders of the workers; however, it did not work. The idea also caused some upsets and one or two of the "third layer" people were actually angry. One was a secretary who came from the working class and had laboriously taken classes and studied to be middle class. She eventually gained a position as a secretary and was very proud of her achievement. She did not consider herself a worker any longer and was outraged at what she felt was herself being forced down. There were a number of workers who did not think that there was anything praiseworthy in being a worker. It was usually the middle- and upper-middle-class members who felt excited and proud when working in menial jobs in factories. With this silencing of the more educated or intellectual members, sometimes discussions in meetings were so foolish it was difficult to sit through them without falling asleep.

Hank and Cuppy were to leave for Detroit in about a week and I would take over their apartment. In the meantime I slept in their second, tiny bedroom, not much larger than a closet. Hank left before his wife, and I was moved to the larger bedroom when I came down with the flu. One afternoon Cuppy got a telephone call from either Raya or Grace telling her that Nello needed some typing assistance and could she please meet him at the Paines' apartment on Hudson Street. She was delighted to be singled out and left in a joyous mood. She did not return until about eight in the evening, when she bounced into my room and said she had been in bed with Nello. Cuppy then proceeded to tell me the details. I'll never forget her first words: "I threw my panties in his face to tease him!" I think my numbed first thought was, I hope they were clean. Nello was so fastidious and sensitive to aromas that he insisted I prepare onions and garlic wearing rubber gloves. He said that in the heat of the bed the odor of these bulbs became more potent and overwhelming. My second thought or reaction was that Cuppy was supposed to be my friend. I was not so much hurt as enraged, but I said nothing. In fact, I pretended indifference, as if I were totally disinterested. What also went through my mind was that Nello must have been striking back at me—but why did he have to choose a friend, especially one who couldn't wait to give me the news of their coupling?

A few days later Cuppy left to join her husband in Detroit and I stayed for a short time in the apartment, tending a cat they had abandoned. In a day or two I began to be more sympathetic toward Nello and tried to believe that his impotency the time we were together made him need to prove it was only temporary. But the episode hurt terribly, and I turned to my friends Gene and Francesca Raskin. They invited me to stay with them for awhile so I moved to Sixteenth Street, where they lived. I lost a lot of weight and found it difficult to sleep. One afternoon I received a phone call from Lionel Steinberg, with whom I had been a friend for years, ever since high school. We had stayed in touch and he generally called me once a month just to see how I was doing. I poured out my heart to him and he responded immediately, saying he was sending me an airline ticket to join him in Delano, California. He said I needed time to recover and rest and he wanted my companionship. Lionel owned vast acreage planted in grapes, having inherited the land and business from his stepfather, David Freedman. Lionel's father died when he was only six. The company farmed over one thousand acres of grapes in Delano and Arvin, as well as two thousand acres of cotton, melons, and wheat in the Mendota area west of Fresno. When the grapes were ready for picking he took lodging in the same area to oversee the work. At that time he still lived in Fresno, where he had grown up. In 1959, Lionel was appointed to the California State Board of Agriculture by Governor Edmund G. Brown and served on the board under three governors: Brown, Ronald Reagan, and Jerry Brown. He was national treasurer of Farmers for Kennedy and Johnson and state chairman of Farmers under President Johnson. He negotiated the first labor contract with Cesar Chavez's United Farm Workers' Union, thus earning the animosity of the Associated Farmers organization.

The airline tickets arrived by special delivery a day or so later and I began to pack my bags. I didn't know whether I would return to New York or what my future would be, so I called some of the women comrades and gave away my winter clothes. Francesca wasn't too happy about my proposed trip; she felt that Nello and I should get back together. She was also afraid that I would drift back into the days as a model and after the breakup with Gilford. She accused me of making men fall in love and then leaving them shattered when I so pleased, and said it was not fair behavior.

Lionel rented a bungalow for me next door to his own in a court built around a swimming pool. It had a front room, tiny kitchen, and bath. Everything was fresh and clean and Lionel had filled two bowls with grapes and vases with flowers. After picking me up at the airport, he dropped me off at the bungalow and went back to work, saying he would be back to take me to dinner after sundown. The weather was hot, around 100 degrees, so the first thing that interested me after unpacking my bags was the pool. Lionel didn't arrive until about 6:30 so I had time for a nap and was dressed when he arrived. We had dinner and then drove around the countryside.

The next morning Lionel took me to the vineyards and we walked what seemed to be miles. Each variety of grapes had its own area and was picked at different times. The grapes were in different colors, all beautiful, and even their names were intriguing: Almerias, spoken softly with a rolled r, grow on frames, making a canopy of green to walk under, with the large grapes dangling overhead; Alicantes, round, deep purple wine grapes with flat, pointed, dark green leaves. Then there are all the common but lovely names of the table grapes: Tokays, Ladyfingers, Malagas, Emperors. The leaves were beginning to turn yellow because irrigating stops when picking begins. There were Jeeps that seemed to dart down the rows, dropping boxes for the pickers. The pickers were Mexican, Filipino, Slav, Oklahoman, Texan, and Indian. They seemed dressed more or less alike, in blue or brown with here and there a splash of red from someone's bandanna. There were only a few black pickers, and their dark skin was soft looking and blurred because of the clay dust. Lionel loved the vines and the ground they grew in. He reached down and picked up some sandy soil and sifted it through his fingers. "Look," he said, "see these tiny shells? This land was once under water." Lionel was a rare soul, extremely intelligent, very modest, an authority on grape growing and other crops, a lover and collector of the impressionists, and a voracious reader. He was liberal, not radical but open-minded enough to listen to my extremist views without argument. He was interested in what I had to say.

The next morning he decided I'd had enough walking around the day before and took me to an area not far from one of the vineyards for a surprise. He had purchased and set up for me a target, knowing I liked archery. He had even gotten a bow with a forty-five-pound pull and I couldn't remember how he knew I was strong enough for that type. Then another surprise—he had borrowed a kitten from somewhere, only a few weeks old and affectionate. "So you will have company that won't bother you while I'm away."

After a few days of such pampering I began to feel full of energy again, so when a telegram came from Nello I did not cringe. As soon as I had arrived I called Francesca and gave her my address and phone number. She, in turn, gave them to Nello. The telegram was roughly three hundred words. It said, in part:

> After a hard year I understand myself and so can understand you. You are wrong in thinking that I purposely put it aside for something else. A pattern which had moulded my whole life and not ineffectively fought against the new experiences I sought for personal reasons. My greatest discovery is that I need them in all aspects of my life. Both the violence of the last letters and the subsequent silence were the results of a primitive jealousy and the old reserve fighting a last battle for self-preservation. These things had never happened to me before.

The telegram ended in reference to my intended divorce actions: "The information you ask for I shall send soon as I put my hand on it. But my lawyers say that if you take the step immediately you will hit my public life as hard a blow as I have hit my personal self."

Nello said he was flying out to Los Angeles and would be staying with the Gogols. He had been frantically calling and writing them to find out where I was, until he thought of the Raskins. I don't know why he thought I would turn to a member of the organization for solace or peace of mind in such a crisis, particularly Raya's sister. At any rate Nello called as soon as his plane touched down, not waiting a moment longer, and we arranged to meet the next day.

Lionel insisted on taking time off to drive me to Los Angeles for the meeting. During the week, I had talked to him about my marriage and the problems I faced with a man who was incommunicative. Lionel had not offered any suggestions or solutions but eventually predicted that I'd be back with Nello in two years. And he was right, only it was sooner than that. We arrived at the home of the Gogols, but Lionel refused to go in with me. I told him I didn't know how long I would be and he said he would take care of some business and return in a few hours. If I was not outside, he would simply wait until I came out.

Nello answered the chime of the bell instead of Bessie, which seemed odd, because she was always curious about callers, especially when Nello was in the house. And if he had been telling her about me then she would certainly want to be present, if only to see that we did not reunite. "I sent her away," Nello told me solemnly. We went into the front room, with its windowed wall stretching the whole length. Raphael Soriano, a protégé of Richard Neutra, designed the Gogols' home; he was a famous architect noted for extremely modernistic designs. Soriano's first house was in Silver Lake and the Gogols' followed soon after. It was built on a hillside and had two decks overlooking Los Angeles. Built in the shape of an L, one could look across to the foot of the L and into the bedrooms. On the second level there was another deck leading from a large study. The basement was partially underground and was designed to hold a two-car garage and a large laundry room. There was a built-in seven- or eight-foot sofa on one wall of the living room, placed so visitors could look out through the floor to ceiling windows onto the deck and into the trees beyond. The dining area was at one end of the large front room. One entered on the ground floor into a hallway and to the right was a huge, narrow kitchen. The kitchen was a sterile room, all sharp lines, and had a Monel metal sink, something very new at the time. Bessie was a fanatic about cleanliness, always cleaning up after her housekeeper. I think she scrubbed the floor almost every day. It was gray and as tough as the linoleum used on battleships. At dinner, at least whenever I was there, as soon as we had finished eating and were talking over coffee and cognac, she jumped up from her seat and left the room. Back she came with a vacuum cleaner and proceeded to sweep the floor under our feet and around our chairs. Of course it was impossible to talk over the whirr of the vacuum cleaner.

Bessie did not resemble her sister Raya in any way, except for possessing enormous energy. When she spoke the words came out in a rush, and she was talkative. She was fiercely attached to her sister but they did not get along too well when they were together, probably because both were very strong-willed women. Bessie tried to organize everyone's life, including her husband's. He complained privately that he had only one afternoon off from seeing patients, surgery, and autopsy duties. He had made the mistake of letting his wife know that he did not work on Wednesday afternoons. She then began to organize all his free time—picnics and meetings with comrades, drives to the seashore, every activity she could dream up. As a result Lou, who was a goodlooking man, always seemed tired. He was quiet when Bessie was around, but then most people were because she took charge. Even in meetings she was prone to interrupt the chairman or speaker if an idea occurred to her. But she was a diligent worker for the group and a fierce supporter of Marxism. Some comrades were critical of Bessie because she lived in a luxurious home and had charge accounts at Bullock's Wilshire and Sak's. But the criticism was muted because the leaders always stayed in her home when they visited Los Angeles.

Bessie did not like me and told the comrades, "Constance left the movement and went out and had a fine time as an actress and model and then came back and stole our leader." But then, I don't think she would have liked anyone whom Nello favored. Lou Gogol explained to Nello, "Since you came and this interest of yours in Constance began, B[Bessie] has changed. Her nervousness, tension and the way she shouts at the children and makes an issue of everything are worse than before. . . . You see, you are a man who exercises a considerable fascination over women and along with politics and what you represent there is also mixed up sexual desires and jealousy of which the women themselves are not aware." Nello said he almost froze. He had known that Raya had been in love with him for years but did everything she could to hide it. She could not hide her feelings entirely, though, because any time he sat and talked to someone she immediately found something urgent he should do.

Nello and I did not embrace and were formal with each other as we walked into the living area. We sat on the couch where a sheaf of papers and notes was lying. He placed the whole batch in my lap and asked me to read them later. Among them was his lengthy article on dialectical materialism, on the back of which was a dedication he had written to me. He said it was for us—it told me who he was—but I very much doubted that dialectical materialism or its analysis could clue me in about this complex man who was my husband.

Nello said he'd been writing half the night and day and that Bessie had been angry, storming about, knowing he was writing to me. He thought it best to send her away before I arrived. This admission was a new one to me. Normally, Nello would not allow criticism of leading members. He might sometimes mimic their behavior, but it was always with good will, never mean or cruel, and always in private, just when we were alone. That he sent Bessie away, and away from her own home, was a new departure. But I was still on my guard, probably extra defensive.

Nello began a plea for reconciliation by saying he had read and reread all my letters. One he meant to frame and keep on his desk, the others he would bind into a booklet. Instead of feeling delighted at having my ego stroked, I was dismayed. My first thought was here we go again, everything in writing but no talking to solve problems. He continued by saying he could not live without me, that if I left him he would never recover, there would be a deep pit in his soul. He admitted he had known about the group's hostility toward me, but instead of taking my side he had made excuses that would put the blame upon me. He said his friends had spoiled him and in return he felt a terrible need to justify it, to be the one to symbolize the sacrificial aspect of the movement. He had made it a fetish at my expense. Just when I was beginning to warm toward him he said he would probably become a world leader and needed me at his side. If there was anything I did not want, it was that he be a world leader. I did not have any desire to be at the side of any leader, no matter how great. I had suffered enough through his local leadership and by nature had no desire to lead or help lead anyone. I found it difficult enough to know what I should do, without telling someone else the path to take through life. When I didn't respond, Nello spoke again about how much he needed me and how he would change, he would "roust out the devil in [himself]." We, or he, talked for a few hours, and it ended when I said I had to leave, but I would think about what he said. He had to be satisfied with those words and, looking wistfully at me, had to be content. He asked whether he could see me again soon, perhaps tomorrow? I said yes and asked if he would like to go for a drive, if I could get a car. We agreed I would call later and make arrangements for the next day if possible.

Lionel was waiting just down the block, reading some legal-looking documents. He did not question me but was obviously interested in what had been said. I gave him a brief outline of the conversation and asked if I could borrow his car the next day. Lionel agreed immediately. All I had to do was drive him to the vineyards early in the morning. Lionel was an angel and I almost kissed him, but knowing how he felt about me I restrained myself. Lionel and I remained friends all his life.

𝓍𝓎 *19* 𝓎𝓍

There wasn't smog in California in October 1947, or if there was it was invisible. The air was fresh and the sky bright, especially in Los Feliz Hills, where Neutra- and Soriano-designed homes were prevalent. When I drove up the hill to the Gogols' modern tiered house I could see Nello waiting in the doorway. Bessie was glaring out the kitchen window, which faced on the front driveway. First I drove us via San Vicente toward its end at the sea, then along that beautiful coastline out to Santa Monica and Malibu, and then inland. In the 1940s there was beautiful unpopulated country around Los Angeles, filled with orange trees, groves and groves of the fruit. During some parts of the year the air would be redolent with the sweet aroma of orange blossoms. Now the blossoms had been replaced by the golden globes and dark shiny leaves of the trees.

I don't remember what we talked about; probably I did most of the talking because Nello seemed reluctant to speak. Here was this great orator who could hold the attention of small or massive audiences and he couldn't speak about intensely personal subjects. It seemed weird that he could not talk to me. But then when he was on stage he was speaking about politics. In fact, he never discussed anything personal or said how he felt about someone—only with me and mostly in letters. He, of course, wrote a letter about our drive:

> But as we drove on Wednesday and you talked so calmly and serenely (once you burnt with desire to write a pamphlet on the Negro question. I resented it. Thrust you aside. Instead of being happy and helping you) you sat driving and talking to me, so calm, so serene, so sure, and so splendid. All I could do was to thank my lucky stars that you existed and I knew you.
>
> I am asking you to stay. Don't go back. Stay with me.

If it appeared I was serene and untroubled, then it was out of character. I must have been acting. But I do know that he was trying as hard as he knew how to change his ways and that he wanted to keep our marriage. And how can one not respect a person for, and help in every way, an effort so momentous? How many people can admit they are wrong and go about mending the errors, large or small? And to change one's life at the age of forty or more is like climbing Mount Everest—just Nello's desire and determination to do so affected my outlook. Probably I was influenced by thinking something was wrong with me, especially if I could not make a go of this, my third marriage. I'm sure this fear entered into it, but most of all, I was ready to give Nello every chance. That must be why he thought I was serene. Calm, yes. When one makes up one's mind, then a calm descends, at least for me. I did not tell Nello my decision to return. I wanted to keep it to myself awhile, not to keep him in suspense but so I could be sure of my own mind and also read the pile of material he had given me.

That evening Lionel took me to dinner and we had our customary drive but returned to our cottages a little earlier. Although I didn't tell him what I planned he was a sensitive person and had seen me carrying the large envelope containing the letters. At the door he put his arms around me, kissed me on each cheek, and said goodnight without comment. After showering and turning up the air conditioning I hopped into bed and spread out the letters, putting them in the order of their dates. After reading the one on the covers of his article on dialectical materialism, I put the pamphlet aside. Dialectical materialism was not as important as Nello's personal letters.

The letters spoke of him as having been a jailer, not a husband. Over and over he said how much he loved me and how I had been wronged. In the past his relations with women had been simply to relax, never doing anything else. He had been terrified that he was too old for me. A very sad line that almost made me cry was "The old me, the one who was destroyed at a stroke. . . . And the new one couldn't make it." He admitted the hostility of his group and said he had not done anything about it, had, in fact, put the blame on me. He described our Bronx apartment as a barracks and now realized how harsh an environment it had been as my introduction. He said Orchard Street was even worse, its "narrowness and all the callers." I had not cared about the bleakness of the Bronx apartment; it was the bleakness of our relations that had been daunting. He pleaded with me to stay with him, promising to take three months off and remain in Los Angeles. He said he had three hundred dollars and could expect thirty-five dollars a week for the next few months. By the end of December he would be on the SWP payroll again. There wouldn't be anything luxurious but it would not be grinding poverty. Bessie would let us stay in her home or we could get a place of our own. I was ghostwriting a book for the Barbizon

School of Modeling, being paid three cents a word, which would bring in a little more to help out. Nello said that if Mr. Krassner, who had hired me, did not like my remaining in Los Angeles then "let him go to hell."

Nello even promised to split the housework fifty-fifty, which I'd never complained of. We had so little furniture it was not hard work to sweep, dust, and mop. Both of us were tidy people so there wasn't a lot of picking up and putting away to be done. From time to time, Nello occasionally approached two or three youngsters in the neighborhood and gave them twenty-five cents to sweep and mop the kitchen and bath. The children were in awe of him and thrilled to earn twenty-five cents, a lot of money in those days, when our apartment rent was probably thirty dollars a month. The Orchard Street place was about half that. Nello was well-liked in the area around our apartment; the butcher even saved steaks for him and he did not have to use ration tickets.

It took several days for me to decide to return to Nello and he wrote every one of those days. He described a musical evening put on by Bessie for comrades and sympathizers that he refused to attend. Yes, they would play some music, but Nello knew that he was the reason the musical had been so quickly arranged. He would be on display, expected to meet and talk to about fifty people. Bessie may also have hoped that the gathering would take his mind off the possible reunion with me. At any rate, he would have none of it and wrote:

> Now all during the week B [Bessie] has been telling me about this musicale, some branch. I said "*No,* I shall have nothing to do with it. I am going out." B said "The c'des [comrades] will be glad to see you!" I said "*No.* I'll go to bed." She said "No, go upstairs and read." I said "No. They will come." She said: "A few c'des would like to say hello."

Nello was lying upstairs, covered by a blanket, while the party went on. Bessie kept coming up and trying to get him to change his mind.

> Here she comes again. No, it is Everett [Washburn]. This ends it. (hour later) Bessie has come up and we have quarreled in front of Everett. I will not go down. She wants me to. I have refused. She is mad and I have told her off. She had gone down, come back for Everett and we didn't speak. We shall have it out finally. I'll leave here if necessary.

Everyone finally left about midnight.

> Now I am downstairs, everybody is gone, and I am writing to you, most ostentatiously at the table in the dining room while Bessie cleans up. The at-

mosphere is freezing—I am contributing my share of the freezing. There were 60 people downstairs and I was to come down and relax with them! This was N.Y. all over again.

I was to relax with them! How in the name of heaven was I to do that? 70 strange people. The request was not only unreasonable, but it was subconsciously but very powerfully motivated. It was a protest against my preoccupation with you. I knew it as such and fought it as such.

Nello's actions astounded me. He had never taken a stand against the wishes of members of his group, particularly not where I was concerned. My reaction was that he was really trying to change and had begun the arduous task. I was thrilled and secretly delighted that Bessie had been put in her place. In fact, I think my reaction was to gloat, not that I would show my feelings to anyone, not even Nello. That would be revealing as well as gauche and I was not going to let hostile people know that they could hurt me to the extent that I would preen myself at their discomfiture when they were put in their place.

When Nello and I reunited Bessie pretended to be pleased and at first I shared Nello's room, the den at the top of the stairs. It was a pleasant place with its own private deck looking out over the trees and houses lower down the hill. We had decided to accept the Gogols' hospitality until we could decide what to do if we stayed in L.A. Nello had a speaking engagement in Oakland or San Francisco and wanted me to go with him. Bessie's hospitality did not last long. She made up some reason to change our living space and put us in the basement with the washing and drying equipment. Windowless, with a cement floor, it was pretty bleak and a radical change from the breezy, sunny upstairs den. Neither Nello nor I complained. In fact we had some amusing times at Bessie's expense. She had a habit of creeping to the door leading to the basement and trying to eavesdrop. We could hear her tiptoeing and then see the shadow of her feet where the door did not quite meet the flooring. When she was there we kept absolutely quiet until she went away. Using my imagination, I drew a picture of Bessie hovering at the top of the stairs, much to Nello's delight. We were so glad to be back together nothing seemed to upset us.

We flew to San Francisco and stayed in the apartment of Filomena Daddario and William Gorman. It was a ramshackle place built of wooden slats, and in the kitchen there was an alarming deep hole. Something was wrong with the pipes underground and work to fix them was underway but taking a long time to complete. Both of us were afraid of that deep pit, especially at night. We were told not to keep the blinds open because the neighborhood was all white and unfriendly as well. But with all our care someone must have seen us because cans or rocks were thrown at our window in the middle of the second night we were there. For an hour or so we sat up in bed, huddling together, wondering what to do if someone broke in. The police would not be of much help because zoning was such that there were areas where blacks could not live or stay. We were in such an area. Fortunately no one broke in and we left for L.A. the next day.

In our absence Bessie had arranged a party to welcome us back and presumably celebrate the continuation of our marriage. In this case we felt we should attend, especially since she assured us that only comrades had been invited. The party was on the following Saturday night and Bessie prepared a buffet of a variety of deli foods, everything one could wish for. She also had a full bar, but as with most left-wing parties, a number of people also brought wines and liquor. Nello and I had our usual white rum on crushed ice with a dash of bitters. The first hour was pleasant; in fact I was filled with joy. Nello sat beside me most of the time and even held my hand, something he had never done before in front of the comrades. He appeared so happy that just looking at him made me feel that all the pain we had both suffered had been worth it and our marriage was going to survive. Is it wise to be extremely happy? Is happiness inevitably followed by its opposite? Two comrades came in late, having arrived from New York. One was and had been my closest friend within the group. She was about five years younger than I and we had liked each other from our first meeting. She was a bright youngster then but ignorant, and I had enjoyed reading to her from the works of Shakespeare, among others, as well as the criticisms of D. H. Lawrence. We both particularly liked his essay on Walt Whitman and Lawrence's bombast.

This friend greeted me with great warmth and hugs but almost at once whispered that she had to talk to me. We went out on the deck and found a corner to ourselves. She was bursting with news, her eyes intense with excitement. "I saved your marriage," she announced. That was a surprise, since I thought Nello had actually saved our marriage by reviewing the past and determining to change the future. So I simply kept quiet while she burst out confidently, but without embarrassment. She had slept with Nello while I was away. She then gave me all the details. After the act, she said they lay next to each other nude and she argued my case—telling him he should spend more time with me and that the leaders were hostile and not treating me right. I don't know what else she said because something simply closed off—my ears? My brain? Whatever. This was my friend and she was giving me a blow-by-blow account of an affair with my husband. At least Cuppy, in the affair in New York, had not been a close friend, and she had made no excuses about pleading my case or trying to save my marriage. We went back inside to the party and the rest of the evening was dim, as if I was under an anaesthetic. Reaction had not yet set in. Later when everyone had gone and Nello and I were down in our basement I told him what my friend had said. His response was: "She's a trouble-maker." "But is it true?" I insisted. Nello said it was nothing, meant nothing. He added, "She's too busy in bed." That was some excuse, a bewildering one, but I dropped the subject, still dazed from what I'd been told.

In the days that followed I locked away the hurt and once again made excuses for Nello's behavior. After all, I had gone to Los Angeles intending to get a divorce. Ergo, he had every right to sleep with someone else. I did not feel the same about my friend; even though we continued to see each other for many years, I never again had respect for her, and certainly not trust. I will never understand how a friend can sleep with another friend's lover or husband. Despite my mind finding extenuating circumstances for Nello's behavior with my friend, my heart had not accepted or forgiven. Otherwise I can't find a reason for what happened a week or so later. On Lou's afternoon off Bessie decided we should have a picnic in Griffith Park. She had discovered a secluded rocky area with a center of grass. We had a delicious luncheon—Bessie never stinted on food and was an excellent cook. After eating we set out to climb a hill. About halfway up the slope I lagged behind and sat on the very edge of a small cliff. My whole body seemed flooded by weakness and nausea, and life seemed utterly purposeless. Nello, who had gone on ahead with the Gogols, returned and when I saw him, a giant outline against the sky, another sensation choked me. I stared away down the dry hill with its stumpy bits of gray green groundcover, hoping that he would not touch me. Squatting beside me, he asked: "Well, my precious, what is it?" I blurted out that the idea of our marriage and of him made me sick and gave me a feeling of hopelessness, even of revulsion. Nello's thin mouth became thinner; he looked up and away, toward the trees on the opposite hill, finally forcing himself to look at my face. His face was rigid, so stiff it was difficult for him to speak. "There is nothing, nothing I can answer to those feelings. They are something I cannot fight—helpless, I am simply helpless, if you cannot bear the sight of me, then I cannot help you." He stood and looked at me; his eyes showed such pain and his face was so terrible; his whole body appeared broken, as if it had been pieced together. He lifted me to my feet, dropped my hand, and started off blindly. I caught up with him and pulled him down on the cliff. Whatever happened, I think it was the terrible pain he was suffering that banished the feelings of hopelessness I'd been having. Something gave me a feeling that there were good reasons to be alive and I was able to talk, to reassure, to blame myself, fatigue, the strain from the past months. I went on and on until at last his face relaxed and he said, "You've been twisted and turned in every direction and your nervous system is feeling it. We will be alone and I'll devote all my time to seeing that you are put right. You need a lot of attention and I intend to devote myself to you. Sugar pie, you will be radiant again. We need to see that you gain some weight and have some peace. I will see to it, just leave it to me."

Nello and I decided to find somewhere to stay by ourselves. We did not mind sleeping in the basement but we were growing irritated at never being alone. Bessie was always intruding. I was writing the book on modeling and Nello was reading and thinking about articles he would be doing when we returned to New York. Constant interruptions annoyed us, but since we were guests we had to control our displeasure. One of the comrades found us a room in the home of sympathizers who had a large house. They were very willing to let us stay with them until we were ready to return to the East Coast. The problem, however, which we did not find out until later, was that it was in a restricted area—that is, no blacks allowed. The room was spacious and we had our own bath. They were a nice couple and after showing us our space in the refrigerator and where everything was located, they left us to ourselves. They did ask us to keep the draperies closed all the time and that's when we learned that, seeing a black person in the house, neighbors might call the police. Since we did not want to return to the Gogols' home we had to adjust ourselves to these new restricted living quarters. We ate, slept, and worked in the one room. We felt closed off from the world, because if we went out it had to be at night and with great care taken so that no one would see us. After a few weeks of living in this confined space both Nello and I grew irritable, even while trying to control our feelings. I could have gone out but didn't think it was fair to leave Nello imprisoned while I was free. So I fretted and was not as patient as he was. I also hated the feeling that I had to be careful all the time not to use the kitchen when the homeowners might want to prepare drinks or food. And, of course, Nello could not have his favorite breakfast, charred cod, because of its horrific odor while cooking.

As the weeks passed Nello once again became silent. He was probably afraid I would make a scene or lose my temper over something or other. The Immigration Department finally interrupted our isolation. We had been tracked to Los Angeles and there was a warrant for Nello's arrest. Myra Tanner Weiss, a leading member of the Los Angeles branch of the SWP, got in touch with Bessie to give her the news. Both women came to where we were staying to discuss what should be done. After talking over the problem Nello decided it would be wise to give himself up, that is, submit to arrest rather than try to hide. Phone calls were made to members of our group as well as to those of the SWP and a strategy was developed, guided by Nello's preferences. For some reason it was decided that Myra and Bessie would accompany Nello to the main police station, but I was not to go with them. When I protested they claimed the police would be more hostile if they knew Nello had a white wife. They said the L.A. police were violent bigots and Nello could be harmed. I had to do as they said, but I felt a wife should be with her husband when he was in trouble. Myra and Bessie picked up Nello early the next morning, promising to let me know what happened as soon as they could. I waited all day without hearing from anyone, afraid to go outside or take a walk because someone might call. Finally around 6 P.M. Bessie drove up and said Nello was going to be let out of jail, where he had spent the day. He had asked that she pick me up so he could see me as soon as he was released. Bessie parked outside the jail and we had to wait about half an hour. Nello came out at last, bubbling with enthusiasm about the wonderful day he had spent. He had notes and phone numbers from prisoners who asked him to make calls for them to their families. According to him he had met some remarkable people and heard their fascinating stories.

Bessie and Louis Gogol mortgaged their house to raise the bail needed to get Nello out of jail. They also managed to get permission for him to return to New York, the place of his residence. We had been advised that Los Angeles was notorious for its animosity toward blacks and immigrants and we'd have a better chance in New York, a more liberal state. We flew back to New York and went to the apartment at 1306 Chisholm. After consulting with his own leaders and those of the SWP, Nello retained a lawyer, fortunately one who was sympathetic and unbiased. I don't remember many of the details but we had a breather and went on with our lives once again. We decided to have a baby now that we felt our marriage was solid, so one night we set about to make this happen. Afterward, Nello said, there you are, we're going to have a child. Both of us were so naive we assumed I was automatically pregnant after that first night. For a month we went around in a rosy glow, keeping our secret to ourselves. At the end of the month, to our consternation I had my period. I eventually did become pregnant, though, and then once more we received bad news. The Immigration Department had refused to accept Nello's Mexican divorce and had declared we weren't legally married. Another divorce would have to be obtained and a second marriage ceremony take place. Again, after consultations with comrades, it was decided that we should go to Reno, because a divorce would take only six weeks and we needed to remarry as soon as possible, not only for the child to be born but to thwart the Immigration Department. Fortunately, I had come into some money—a few thousand dollars—and we made plans to go to Reno. We could not live together, because Nevada did not allow intermarriage. But we were determined not to be separated again and made plans to live apart and meet surreptitiously. I would get a job to fill up the time. I don't remember who made the decision that Nello should go to Nevada ahead of me, find a lawyer, and see how we could meet while living in separate quarters.

On the first part of the trip, enroute to Chicago on the New York Central train, Nello wrote: "As soon as I leave N.Y. for a few hours I begin to see it in perspective. And you stick it, fighting to help me. Believe me I am very conscious of it, always. I know you are good and solid and faithful and true. I love you, now more than ever. And I now have a third addition—Nob. Already I think of us always as three. I am full of love for you, darling. Take care of yourself for the sake of the three of us.

In Reno, Nello found a room in the home of a parson with a bath and shower upstairs but no hot water. A woman in the house told him to buy food and she would cook his meals. He hoped she would continue so he would not have to eat in restaurants. The Jim Crow in Reno restaurants was powerful, with only two or three places set aside for blacks—one joint, a Chinese restaurant, and a place owned by a black. Nello found a lawyer by going to the Greyhound station and asking one of the porters to recommend someone. The man sent him to the YMCA, where a young man, Mayfield, was to take his finals on the Monday for a graduate degree. Mayfield recommended a friend of his from law school in Oakland. He said she was a good lawyer and would not overcharge. Nello was nervous and asked if her sex and his race would prejudice matters. Mayfield said not at all. He called her and made an appointment for Nello, who preferred a man but did not want to offend Mayfield, who had been helpful and friendly.

Nello found that the lawyer, Charlotte Hunter, knew all the black members of the Reno community. She was in her thirties, active and friendly.

She said there should not be a problem with the divorce since Nello had been separated from Juanita for over sixteen years. It would take about ten weeks, instead of six, because Juanita would have to be served and given time to respond. During a dinner with other clients at the home of Hunter, she mentioned that she had entertained Paul Robeson at one time, which startled Nello. He immediately let her know that he was a radical but not friendly toward the Communist Party. Hunter was liberal, sympathetic to radicals and blacks. She told Nello she did not *practice* law; for her it was a form of service. She handled immigration cases of Mexicans and problems with the FBI or cases involving blacks living in Reno. She was obviously a perfect choice as our attorney. Hunter was also thoughtful of Nello's financial status and did not know what to charge. She wanted to be reasonable and finally asked if three hundred dollars, all told, would be acceptable. Nello told her he was a writer and Hunter asked if he would like to give lectures while in Reno, which she could arrange. When Nello told her he did not want to give lectures but would like to work outdoors, Hunter called a rancher friend who owned a place thirty-five miles out of Reno at Lake Pyramid. It was in the middle of the desert on an Indian reservation, rather isolated and ideal because Nello hoped we could both find work on the place without attracting too much attention. He was translating and I was to type Daniel Guerin's book on the French Revolution, which would bring in some money. We were paying rent on the Chisholm apartment although we'd be away. Hunter thought we'd be paid room and board plus a hundred dollars a month if we both worked, but lived separately, of course, at the Pyramid ranch. While waiting to hear whether he'd get the job, Nello relaxed by reading *True Romance* and other movie magazines. He thought they published more interesting stories than those in *Collier's* and the *Saturday Evening Post*. He wrote me that he was tired and feared he had a mental sickness. He said he could barely walk outside one morning. Nello was struggling with the problems we had when he was unable to talk to me except through letters. This was wearing him out, he wrote, "But somehow there is a barrier. I am going at it. Ideas are beginning to shoot up. But I love you. There is nobody else and I do not even imagine life without you. *We* go ahead, some way somehow, we'll come through we, you, Nob and I."

Nello called on a Sunday night in August 1948 to tell me how much he longed for me to join him in Reno. He was only waiting to see whether he would have a job or not. I was to take my typewriter and his *History of Philosophy* by Hegel, all the volumes of Sainte Beuves that had anything to

do with Corneille, Racine, and Moliere, and also the *Age of Corneille.*
Then he wanted the *Cambridge Ancient History,* and the books we had on
Greek and French tragedy. He ended by telling me not to lift anything
heavy. I was also to bring my driver's license, social security card, and marriage certificate.

The job came through from the owner of the Pyramid ranch, a Mr.
Harry Drackert. In one of his letters Nello described him as "50 odd, small,
fit, still competes in rodeos, wrestling cows and riding bucking horses, a
good shot, busy with the ranch, but busy with the girls. There is always one
around from Reno—Harry this and Harry that. And he takes them over
to his private quarters at one end of the ranch, and the women who work
here are mad."

Nello was hired as the handyman and paid fifty dollars a month plus
room and board. For the first time in his life he would do physical labor
and was delighted at the prospect. This was a surprise because he had always been protective of his hands—he always wrote with a pen, preferably
a Waterman, and believed manual work would stiffen his fingers. As a
handyman his job was to rake leaves, pick up debris such as papers, see after
water jets for irrigation, water the plants and wash the walks, mow the
lawns, and help put baggage onto the station wagon, wash dishes in emer-
gencies, and dry them twice a day. He was to eat in the kitchen with the
cook, the cowboy Bud, two waitresses, the pantry man, and the house-
maid. He lived in one of the cabins but when there were many guests he
would be moved to different ones, depending on the newcomer's preference. Bud slept on a cot in the stable and Nello wrote that he would do
the same if necessary. Drackert, an old rodeo man, was a gentleman and
Nello said he did not hover over his employees. The transition from seden-
tary living was a drastic change, but Nello stood it very well—in fact he enjoyed the work and the atmosphere. He was especially intrigued by the
other employees and wrote long letters about their appearances and actions that read like novels. Although Nello was intensely loyal and fiercely
defensive of his group, he was happiest when away from them. His mind
seemed to blossom, unfettered by the rigidity of politics. Most of the time
in the midst of his adherents he viewed everything—people, movies, plays,
operas, sports, literature—through the lens of his ideology. The difference
was that there seemed to be a wider range, a greater freedom, to his thinking when he was away by himself.

On a Monday morning, August 18, 1948, I began to hemorrhage. I was
alone in our fourth floor apartment without a telephone. The one neigh-

bor, who lived across the street and with whom I was friendly, was at work. I couldn't think of what to do and was afraid to go downstairs to the bar and call a doctor. All I could think of was that our child might be lost. Not knowing whether it would help to stop the bleeding, I put a pile of ice cubes in a towel, put the lot on my stomach, and lay down on the bed. By early afternoon the bleeding stopped and I ventured downstairs and used the telephone in the bar to call my doctor. This obstetrician was German, with an office on Park Avenue. I don't remember who recommended him, but he was expensive for those days—three hundred dollars for the delivery. He was rather pompous, but friendly until he discovered that we were an interracial couple. Then he became rude and abrupt. At this stage, however, he had not met Nello. He prescribed some new pill and told me to stay off my feet. When I asked if I could fly to Reno he said absolutely not, unless I wanted to miscarry. I then called Nello and gave him the sad news. Although he was bitterly disappointed, his main concern was for me, that I would be all right. He said he would call Freddy Paine, whom he was sure would see to getting food for me and whatever else was needed. Apparently Freddy told Grace and she and Grace came up every few days to bring food, newspapers, and magazines. I was well looked after by these two people, who seemed genuinely concerned. After about six weeks the doctor let me resume normal activities and I began typing the Guerin manuscript as quickly as Nello sent the translations. Because he wanted to include me in what he had to say to his leadership, he sent his letters to Raya, Grace, and Lyman to me, cautioning that they should be sealed up with the special tape he always used so they would not know I knew anything about some of the problems.

While he was away I learned that Freddy had talked to Raya about raising money and purchasing everything needed for our unborn child. When Nello heard this news he was furious. He said it was an attempt to take us in charge by the "tendency" and he would have none of it. It was *our* child and only we were to be responsible for everything. Again, this was a new Nello and he was trying hard to change the way we had been living before, where I had to adjust, not the members of his leadership.

There was a growing conflict between Raya and Grace that he was trying to deal with from long distance. He wrote a long letter to Lyman mentioning our personal affairs, which was also a change from the past. As far as I knew, Nello had never spoken, and of course never written, about our marriage to anyone except our friends Francesca and Gene Raskin. And that was when he was trying to persuade me not to get a divorce. Otherwise, he was extremely reserved and kept his own counsel. In Lyman's letter he spoke openly about the group's hostility toward me, evidenced, he felt, in the malicious gossip spread about him. He pointed out the antagonism between Grace and Raya. Raya was put out when Nello relied on Grace's grasp of philosophy and asked for her comments on the dialectical materialism document. Grace felt she would make a better leader than Raya. Both women hid their hostility under the cover of comradeship, but Nello always knew it was there. He said Grace threw out ideas willy-nilly, often without thinking them through. Raya had to be held in check because of her inability to conceal her bitterness and anger as a result of having been unable to express her creativity in the SWP. In Detroit the comrades were acting up, attacking SWP members of the local for not taking a more aggressive position on recruiting black people. Everyone had been warned that the tendency was to blend in and not make waves, which had been part of the agreement with the SWP political committee. Then Grace and Ike wanted to raise money to bring Nello back from Reno for a visit; Grace wanted to move to Pittsburgh, where Raya and John were now living. Everything appeared to be falling apart in his absence. Nello appealed to Lyman and tried to make him understand the behavior of Raya and Grace, and that the lack of control by the Detroit comrades posed dangers for the group. He also explained that although he appreciated Lyman's years of financial assistance, he intended to earn our living. His first step had been taking on the translation for Guerin. Nello felt that if he were financially on his own there would be less intrusion in our personal affairs. Another reason for doing work for Guerin was to relieve the SWP from paying him his weekly salary, especially if it meant taking one of their own people off the payroll. Then there was always the Immigration Department and the FBI, who would be interested in how we managed to live. If those organizations learned we were being supported, their case for deportation would be strengthened. Everything had to be on the up and up. Lyman did not answer Nello's letter.

Despite group problems and his work as a handyman, Nello was enthusiastic about the amount of writing and reading he was doing every night. He was determined to complete a study of the dialectics of Hegel. When he went into town once a week he bought a small bottle of cognac. After dinner he would smoke his pipe, have some cognac, and settle down to work. His hands were stiff from all the yard work, but he was able to overcome the problem. The translation of Guerin's book was going well. He had met Guerin in Paris, when he was writing *Black Jacobins*. Guerin admired Nello, but more than that he liked him very much. When Guerin visited New York he spent a lot of time with us. He was never, as far as I know, a member of any of the groups, but he sometimes attended meetings. Daniel was a pleasant and generous man. His home was in Paris and he had a large estate in the country where he invited artists to live when he was absent. He did not charge them anything at all. Chester Himes stayed there, as well as Richard Wright. Many of the Johnsonites did not like Guerin, who, although married, never hid the fact that he was gay. In our small group there was a new recruit, an attractive young man, well built, blonde, with a sweet smile. Daniel took a liking to him and when he left to tour the U.S. he took the young man along. There were some raised eyebrows by comrades as well as a buzz of unpleasant gossip. Nello saw nothing wrong in the liaison and I always thought the arrangement was fine, although I kept this to myself. The youngster, who was, after all, about eighteen years old, would receive an intellectual and physical education. It was not a case of seduction per se, because we had all pretty much known that the young man was also gay.

Living mostly out of doors gave Nello a different perspective. He said after work when he took a shower before dinner he felt like a new man. We did not have a shower in the apartment in the Bronx and he had always soaked in warm bath water. Now he was encouraged by the Reno experience to suggest we take some weeks off from time to time and go somewhere by ourselves to walk on beaches, climb mountains, and generally have more of an outdoor life. He also suggested that we see more friends who were not involved in the group's politics. We knew many people besides Wright, Himes, Ellison, Cayton, Reddick, and the Raskins, some better than others. There were James T. Farrell, Dwight and Nancy MacDonald, Saul Bellow, Irving Howe, and a wonderfully generous and brilliant man who was an art critic, Meyer Schapiro. I was more than willing, of course, and was not at that time skeptical of his being able to follow out these good intentions. He seemed to be changing as well as struggling to understand and fight against what he called the demons in himself:

> In many ways I think I have passed a great milestone in my own life down here. I knew for years that something was wrong somewhere. The evil spirit, the demon, fought to hold me in the old groove. I know now exactly what the writers in Scripture wrote about, they and their demons. But I am sure now that that is over. But there are a lot of pieces to be picked up and patched together. I shall make it, I'll do the best I can. You loved me in a

way that I used to wonder at. I couldn't understand it for I underestimated you. If you put half the tenacity into your work that you gave to me, you will be a wonderful writer.

Nello did not excuse my weaknesses and failings, and I had plenty. Among them was a desperate need for constant reassurance that I was loved and worth loving. Living with someone who has such a need can be disastrous. I was used to being the center of attention at all times. I was also exceedingly jealous and could feel denigrated if the person I loved even looked at another woman. The fact that Nello was always surrounded by women who were eager to get into bed with him is not an excuse. If there hadn't been women so handily around, I would have been jealous of strangers. If I believed in astrology, then my birth sign, Gemini, would be accurate in that I seem to be twins, or to have a split personality. At home I am unsure of myself, almost craven in seeking approval. In public, outside the home, I wear a mask and people believe I am self-assured, calm, and always happy. Actually I am moody and withdrawn, with extreme highs and lows. Now that I am older I can step back and say, this is an up week, this is a down week, and I don't fall into such despair when depressed. I went through a bad period of anxiety taking the form of agoraphobia and was nearly paralyzed at leaving the house and being out of doors. At a bus stop during such periods I walked up and down, back and forth, trying to control the waves of terror washing over me.

In one respect I seem to take after my mother in that when angry or hurt I close up into a stony silence—no one can break through during such times. It isn't pouting or sulking, it is a complete retreat. To handle problems during our marriage I simply ran off somewhere just to be alone. Another peculiarity is that although I want to save everyone in the world and have this seemingly widespread love of people, I don't really like people at all. That, of course, excludes friends and relatives—for them I have a lot of love as long as I don't see them too often. Space is a necessity, not just spiritually but physically as well. When writing I want to walk around in my home and the rooms must be large. Spiritually, for lack of a better word, I want to be left alone, not even talked to very much—unless it is to hear something new or something I know nothing about. I am a worrier, worrying before, during, and after an event. If there is nothing to worry about, I can make something up. I don't like gossip, it bores me, yet I always read the *Dear Abby* and *Dear Ann* columns and have a passion for *Judge Judy*. I was always enthralled by films in which a large raucous family surrounded

Anna Magnani, envying such a lifestyle. But when I am being honest and thinking about what it would mean in loss of privacy to be in the midst of such wrangling and loving, I realize I could not ever live that way—it would drive me mad. I detest people who whine and complain all the time. But I also don't like people who take the stance that everything is perfect. They are the ones who can be standing in a hailstorm and if one says anything gloomy they respond with something positive and cheerful. I'm sure during my marriage to Nello I had other faults that may have contributed to his habit of closing me out.

There was some mix-up over the serving of papers on Juanita in Trinidad and the weeks dragged into months. Toward the middle of November, Nello wrote that he would be coming home and for me to make the wedding arrangements, our second one. I didn't want to return to Fort Lee, where the antagonism was so fierce, so I looked for a justice of the peace on Long Island. By this time my pregnancy was beginning to show, but not too much since I had lost thirty pounds during the early months. Nevertheless I felt somewhat embarrassed. Not only would we be presenting ourselves to the minister as a black and white couple, but a pregnant one as well. They might think we were being forced into marriage. There I was worrying again before anything happened. Nello's attitude, a sane one, was not to worry until something bad happens and very often nothing does happen. Nello arrived and the next evening we took a train out to Long Island, found a cab, and arrived at the home of a justice of the peace. He was a thin, white-haired man who showed no surprise or animosity when we came in. He called his wife and she acted as our witness. She too showed no hostility, in fact was quite friendly. We went directly home, again via train, and had our own private dinner celebration, Nello cooking the steak and rice while I set the table and made and tossed the salad. We had planned to take a week's vacation at Big Bear, a resort, but couldn't find accommodations that would accept black people.

On April 4, 1949, our son, C. L. R. James Jr., was born. Eric (Bill) Williams came down from Washington, D.C., a few days before the baby was due to be of help if we needed him. When I went into labor he held one of my hands while Nello held the other. Unfortunately, labor pains lasted two days, and added to that particular torment was a taxi driver strike. Bill suggested that we call the police and get them to take us to the hospital, but Nello would have none of that. He said, "Lord have mercy, and let my child be born in a police car? Never!" We were finally able to get an ambulance to take us to Sydenham Hospital in Harlem. I was in labor all day and Nello waited patiently. About 8 P.M. he finally left to get some dinner and the doctor was annoyed. He wanted to do a Caesarian section because the baby was upside down, a breech birth, presenting buttocks first. To perform surgery, the doctor needed Nello's consent. But after the two days of labor, the baby was not going to wait any longer, and as a result I tore through the vagina into the rectum and had to have surgery to repair it. Nello was standing outside the operating room when I was wheeled out, with our baby boy lying next to my shoulder. Nello said Nobbie appeared exhausted but looked up at him with bright intelligent eyes.

I was released from the hospital not only in pain from the surgery but with breast abscesses. When I tried to tell the doctor about them, he shut me up by saying he would tell me all I needed to know. By the time we arrived home I was in so much pain that Nello called the doctor, who refused to make a house call despite the fact that by then I was running a high fever. Nello was outraged: "You do not intend to see after my wife in this emergency?" The doctor told him no, get another doctor. Nello then informed him that we would not pay the balance on our account, which was to take care of after-birth recovery. We found another doctor who practiced in the Bronx and he came to our home immediately. When he looked at my wounds he shook his head and said, "That is criminal treatment." Fortunately, Nello had arranged for a nurse to come in and see after Nobbie until I was well, and she arrived in a few hours to take charge. She was a wonderful person and fell in love with the three of us, especially with our baby son, Cyril Lionel Robert James Jr. She stayed for six weeks, until I could take over the household again. Nello called the baby Nobbie because while pregnant I lost thirty pounds and through the surface of my stomach could be seen and felt little knobs from his hands and feet when he moved around.

Every evening Nello held Nobbie in his arms and talked to him in baby talk, cooing at him. When Nobbie was ten days old he cooed back at his father and Nello declared we had a genius on our hands. He said, "Remember: Nob is not to be made a B/K [Bolshevik] by force. *He* must decide."

Unfortunately, this pleasant interlude did not last. Nello went back to work and was away most of the time. He also became his old, quiet self. During winter, unless it was snowing too heavily, I always took Nobbie out in his carriage. This meant struggling to put him in a snowsuit. In those days they opened only down the front and one had to force the babies into a small space without hurting them. Then there were the stairs to get down and up with a heavy carriage and a heavy child. Nobbie weighed nine pounds at birth and gained steadily. Until he began to walk, I could spend the time in the park reading while he slept. When I looked around at all the mothers sitting on benches, each watching one child, it seemed a waste of time and energy. Here were all these women unable to read or even think, just wasting away. Some, of course, chatted with their neighbors, but many just sat idly by like sentinels.

When he was a few months old, Nello decided I must have part of a day off each week. He would take care of the baby while I could see friends or whatever. The way this worked out was that before leaving I prepared formula, sterilized bottles, put out a change of clothing and diapers, and all that goes with looking after an infant. It was a lot of work that I normally took care of automatically and without the preparation of formula because I was breastfeeding. When I'd return after my short sojourn, Nello would announce that it was no problem at all, not at all difficult to see after our baby. He declared that I had an easy job of it. Much later I learned that either or both Grace and Raya came in my absence and looked after Nobbie, while Nello did his usual writing.

Nobbie, a beautiful child and extraordinarily intelligent, developed rapidly—walking, for example, just before he was eight months old. Unlike most infants and young children he could amuse himself for hours, playing alone with his toys or, later, reading books. Nello and I were not aware of any problems until some years later when he would be diagnosed as exhibiting signs of schizophrenia. Even if we had known, it is unlikely that we would have sought psychiatric help. Nello was opposed to psychoanalysis, believing only self-centered intellectuals sought such explanations. It absolved them of any consideration of the social relations and their impact on individuals. Willie Gorman, a member of the Johnson-Forest group, suffered from dementia to a degree that he was institutionalized for a time. He laughingly told me that Nello's belief was that "a good political line is the cure for all ills."

When Nobbie reached fourteen he had a breakdown, suffering from hallucinations and hearing voices, and it was then that a number of psychiatrists made the fateful diagnosis. After writing the music and lyrics for an album produced by Motown Records, he walked away from the group he had formed and became a street person. Nello never accepted that anything was actually wrong with his son, despite all evidence to the contrary.

ᨕ᨞ 20 ᨞ᨕ

It had been with great hope that both of us, I believe, imagined that our separation, while painful, would lead to a deeper intimacy. Nello struggled to merge the political and personal sides of his personality. Each was important, but it often seemed that his politics stemmed the flow of his creativity. Why else was he so happy and able to turn out thousands of words seemingly without effort when he was away from his group? Of course, Nello could turn out thousands of words dealing with politics as well, but his artist side was held in abeyance. He knew the radical left, including his own people, were suspicious of art; they felt it distracted them from the serious business of creating the revolution. Comrades often quoted Lenin's refusal to listen to Beethoven because he claimed it weakened him. Nello, privately, was appalled by the ignorance of these American comrades. He was always handing out reading lists to the youngest members and was pleased that Grace had her Ph.D. and Lyman was a Harvard graduate. He also reveled in Raya's expertise in the field of political economy, especially Soviet political economy, and the ease with which she translated from the Russian. Nello felt that important questions of human subjectivity and individuality were not on the agenda of radicals. He set out to change that attitude. Most comrades lacked a sense of humor and felt guilty when they enjoyed themselves overmuch, a repetition of the atmosphere in which I grew up. Our tiny group had noble and grand ideas of creating a better life for people worldwide, but as individuals they led narrow, circumscribed lives. They made every sacrifice—financial, physical, and personal—and there wasn't much energy left to simply enjoy themselves. Even our parties were political. They were to raise money or gain new members. Some people enjoyed themselves by getting a little drunk, but of course never the leading members. If the few who drank too much were working class, comrades were tolerant, because in our political view a worker could do no wrong.

Nello began work on his book *American Civilization,* to which he later added a subtitle, *The Struggle for Happiness.* The book was to be our own, that is, not part of the Johnson-Forest output. It was to be published commercially as a way for us to be independent financially. He wanted very much to be happy with me but felt guilty about our relationship the moment he was back in the maelstrom of factional politics. And soon after his return from Nevada he was forced again into the confines of his political life. He put aside the book as well as the translation of Guerin's *French Revolution.* We were back to depending on Lyman's monthly contribution. In Reno, Nello became addicted to the slot machines, something that had never happened to him before. He simply couldn't resist their lure. He lost the money I had given him as well as the advance from Daniel Guerin. Lyman sent Nello money to pay off his gambling debts.

In letters, Nello told me that I was the most important person in his life, that he could not face life without me. But these needs and emotions were forgotten or lost when in the presence of his political associates. Tensions between us grew once again. Because of the daily care of Nobbie, I was not writing, which made me brood all the more. If I had been able to lose myself in important work, we might have worked out our problems. Our sexual life suffered as well. Whether from fatigue or fear of possible impotence such as had occurred briefly on Orchard Street, Nello's approach was now once every month or so. Earlier in our relationship, when I complained that every two weeks seemed a long time to wait, he wished out loud that I were an older woman. Why? Because, he said, they know there are long periods when people do not have sex and it was nothing to worry about. He did not understand that a woman cannot be ignored for days or weeks and then be ready to hop into bed in a passionate embrace. There are many ways of wooing a woman and touching or caressing is only one—talking and listening and kindness all lead to bed, if men only knew this.

A bright spot for me was when Dick Wright arrived for a short visit in September 1949. He was on his way to Buenos Aires to make a film of *Native Son.* He had been in Chicago to arrange for some of the scenes to be shot in the slums of that city. Rachel, his second daughter, had been born on January 17, 1949, and Dick showed us pictures of the baby and asked, "Isn't she a living doll?" When I asked about Ellen he said she was just fine, but I remembered that Dick had taken off for Rome to recuperate after Rachel's birth and wondered how she really felt. Although I loved and admired my friend and even was overly protective of him in writing or talking to others, I knew his weaknesses. Everyone has good and bad sides, and Dick seemed to have a split personality. His good side was his creativity, his warmth, his generosity, and openness to new ideas. His bad side could be encompassed in one word—selfishness. He liked to tease but his teasing was actually needling. Dick could stick needles in people more expertly than an acupuncturist. Chester Himes told me that one time Dick teased Ralph Ellison to the point where it became unbearable. Ralph grabbed a kitchen knife and only Chester's intervention kept him from stabbing Dick. But there are two versions of the story. Dick claimed it was Himes who did the teasing and that Ellison pulled out a switchblade knife and was about to attack him. Dick said that he stepped between the two and prevented the mayhem. I have no idea which story to believe but I do know that in my presence it was always Dick who did the teasing, not Chester. When I visited the Wrights in Wading River, before they left for Paris, he pretended he was teaching his kitten tricks but was, in fact, torturing it until the poor thing hid under the bed whenever he came near. Every time he approached the bed it would hiss. The kitten's behavior only seemed to spur him on, and he was relentless in pursuit.

Dick was to play the lead role in the film, that of Bigger Thomas. After he left, sailing to Argentina on September 22, Nello and I wondered how our friend, who weighed about 175 pounds, could possibly fit the role of a poor, skinny, ragged boy. Nello had arranged for Dick to meet our friend Eric Williams, who was now in Trinidad working for the independence of the island. Dick's ship would make a stop in Trinidad and Eric was arranging for him to make a speech to the organization he had founded: The Peoples' National Movement. Every meeting, held in an open square in Port of Spain, drew thousands of people. Eric called these regularly held meetings a university, because the main thrust was to educate the workers, which he believed would lead to the independence of Trinidad and Tobago—the end of colonialist rule. Eric, backed by the oil and bauxite workers, was successful and eventually became prime minister of the two independent islands.

Almost a year passed before we saw Dick again, after he had completed the film and was on his way back to France. He came again to our place in the Bronx, accompanied by a young woman, Madelyn Jackson. She was a Latin-American dancer with dark hair and eyes, quite attractive though she became less so through her behavior. She was wearing a white, starched dress, almost as short as a mini and years before this style was worn in the U.S. Dick paid no attention to her, because as was his way he was pouring out to Nello and me all his adventures since we had last met. Madelyn kept moving in her chair, deliberately arranging that her skirt would crawl high up her thigh. Then she would make a sort of wriggling motion, meant to be sexy, and pull the skirt down slightly. At the same time, she would purse her lips in a little pout. I saw Nello glance at her once and then with lifted eyebrow look at me. Madelyn's efforts were wasted on Dick—he was too busy talking about the difficulties in making the film. In August 1950, Dick and Madelyn sailed from New York—he to go to France and she to stay in Haiti, where she had been born. I learned later that Dick contemplated moving to Haiti to make a film about Toussaint-Louverture and had talked to Nello about collaborating on a script that would rely heavily on Nello's classic about the successful revolt. Apparently he also planned to continue his romance with Madelyn Jackson. Where this left Ellen and his two children I didn't know, but I voiced my concerns to Nello. In fact, I was indignant not only for Ellen's sake but because I detested a woman so desperate for attention that she needed to exhibit her thighs. Nello was fond of Ellen and wondered aloud what she would do if Dick left his family. But, he cautioned me, it was not our affair. About my attitude toward Madelyn he laughed and said: "To some it comes naturally, but if you don't have it you do the best you can." I made him explain. "With genuine sex appeal it does not have to be shown off, or paraded. It simply exists. That poor woman doesn't have the real goods." He made me laugh, particularly when he used the expression, "real goods." I was, of course, secretly pleased by his criticism of Miss Madelyn Jackson. Later we learned that she wrote Dick that she was having an affair with a Haitian politician while at the same time considering going to Argentina to live with a wealthy landowner. Nello's warning about staying out of the lives of Ellen and Dick did not keep me from brooding about it. I was angry about the affair. He and Ellen had been so much in love that it seemed to create an aura in a room. They rarely touched in public, but their awareness of each other was palpable and very pleasant to see and feel. What pain Ellen must be feeling, one who had such a passionate and loyal love for her husband and was now displaced by such a tart, were some of my emotional reactions.

After the brief visits from Dick, Nello became attentive again, as if stimulated by and brought back to a world in which he had made me the center of his life, if only in fits and starts. He forgot having wished I was thirty and was more than pleased by my sexual appetite. We went to dinner in a Chinese restaurant and then to an opera, *The Magic Flute*. I was beginning to feel happy and hopeful again, but it didn't last more than a few days; then Nello called Raya and again buried himself in work and meetings.

I was still awarded my one afternoon and evening out to break the monotony and respite from motherhood, so after a few weeks I began lunching with my modeling friends, Stu Hoover and Madeline Patterson, and visiting the Raskins. Much as I enjoyed being with my friends, they could not substitute for a consistent relationship with Nello. I began to feel a desperate loneliness and an uncertainty about what my life was going to be in the future. One night after Nobbie was in bed I went up the short flight of stairs to the roof and stood looking down at the miserable street and then up at the sky. Such a wave of hopelessness came over me that I felt overwhelmed. Is this all I'm to know, or to be? Is this going to be my life? Since I was a passionate supporter of Nello's politics, condemning him wasn't possible. Yet there was a rage burning in me I did not fully recognize. There weren't any answers and I did not see any way out of the dilemma. Fortunately the feeling did not last too long—I had to get back to my young son and make sure he was sleeping soundly. I loved him more than I had loved anything or anyone in my life. He was such an intelligent happy baby, loving and affectionate and with a particular look of delight on his face when I picked him up.

During the summer Nello accepted an invitation to teach at the SWP's summer camp in New Jersey. We would be given free room and board at their resort and be away from the terrible heat and humidity of New York. We were given a large room just off the kitchen because they thought it would be convenient for preparing food for Nobbie and Nello. There was a building set up as a restaurant or mess hall where everyone could eat, but we had particular needs. We only stayed in that room for a few days before we asked to be moved. Comrades came and went at all hours, making coffee, getting cold drinks, preparing lemonade, having snacks, and talking politics interminably. We were moved upstairs into another large room with an alcove in which to put Nobbie's crib. After preparing meals for Nello and Nobbie I sometimes ate in the dining hall with the other comrades and found the change from isolation in the Bronx pleasant. Nello's leaders were not at the camp and, in fact, very few Johnsonites visited. My friend, the one who told me she had pleaded my case while screwing Nello, came to stay for a week with her husband. She got along with everyone so there wasn't any feeling of factionalism and the SWP people who had accepted me were friendly to her as well.

As part of the entertainment the comrades decided to put on an original play, based on Al Capp's comic strip. I was asked to play Daisy Mae and accepted. Nello was not at all pleased and wanted me to decline the offer.

He said he did not think it dignified for his wife to appear on stage in such a play, particularly since I'd be wearing a very short skirt as in the cartoon: "It was unseemly," he said. Nello had never objected to my appearing in bathing suit advertisements when modeling, but we were not married during those days. It still surprised me that he would assume such an attitude. But I was stubborn and perhaps a little vain. They had chosen me over everyone else to play the part and my excuse to Nello was that I could not let the comrades down. He was displeased but I paid no attention. We rehearsed every night for about a week before the performance. The play was a big success and the cast was elated at the audience response. Nello did not attend but remained in our room, as he did most of our stay when he was not teaching.

During this time my friend and I met two young men, one of whom was the son of a political committee member. The two young men were full of energy, having just returned from serving in the armed forces. The camp became too boring for them and they suggested we drive into the nearest town and go dancing. So every night after I put Nobbie to sleep, my friend, who had slept with Nello, and I went out with these two men and danced the night away. We felt somewhat daring, drinking beers and sneaking away from the resort each night. Nello did not ask what I was doing and I did not tell him. But there soon began to be rumors about our behavior, which placed him in a difficult position. In our relationship this is the only act on my part that I'm ashamed of—he was helpless and I paid no attention to what he might be feeling. He never said a word, but he wrote a letter to Lyman saying he might need some money in an emergency, in case he had to leave the resort in a hurry. He did not go into details as far as I know, simply saying that a situation had arisen that could become ugly. It was not decent behavior on my part and I was haunted for many years by my cruelty. My friend from California had all kinds of excuses for me—I needed the outlet after having been tied down with Nobbie; I was much younger than Nello and had to have some fun in my life; and he had had his affairs, so why shouldn't I? Those were her excuses for me, but I couldn't accept one of them. I wondered whether she had similar excuses for betraying her husband and was surprised that he did not question her whereabouts every night. I think he was probably sleeping, which he did a lot of, probably to escape his wife's nagging and domination. That escapade and one other remain with me today.

Back in the Bronx after our weeks away Nello went back to his old habits of working all day and sometimes into the evening with Raya and

Grace. And once again he became silent when at home. The atmosphere became intolerable. Nothing worked; even when I did my best to please him, he did not respond. What was painful was that he had written me from Reno with so much understanding.

> And the night we quarreled and I said "I'll leave now" and you said "O.K. I accept. I am sorry I'll do the best I can." Again, I hit low. I couldn't say anything. I didn't know what to say. But I knew that it was terrible, that your spirit should be beaten down. And sometimes when we quarreled and I remained glum; and you would make the effort and say something and take the blame so to speak. Those were my worst moments. I should have said something. I felt them. They must never happen again.

Those moments were happening again and the old feeling of hopelessness began to set in. I finally decided that I would go back to work and find my own apartment. Nello was scheduled for another speaking tour so before he left I informed him of my plans. I assured him that I would remain married to him to aid in his struggle for citizenship and against deportation. He was not happy, even with such assurances, but pride would not allow him to ask me to change my mind. After he left I found a two-bedroom apartment up four flights of stairs on Thirteenth Street in the Village. Just around the corner was my friend Mary Sarin Covan's shop, and Washington Square was just a few blocks away where I could take Nobbie for outings. I soon found modeling work and a babysitter. The SWP headquarters was also nearby on University Place. Also in the neighborhood was my friend Walter Goldwater, who opened the first bookstore specializing in African and African-American literature and history. I was still a gung-ho revolutionary and attended the meetings of the SWP along with some of my young Johnsonite friends. They assumed that my stay on Thirteenth Street was temporary, just while Nello was on tour, and I did not enlighten them.

Evelyn Novak, the wife of George Novak, one of Cannon's leaders, and a member of the political committee, took a great interest in me and at the time I did not know why she did so. We were supposed to be good members, friendly and amenable, so I hadn't any reason not to welcome her friendship. Evelyn told me that a comrade was coming in from Akron, Ohio, to become the new editor of the newspaper. She sang his praises, saying that he was an intellectual who had gone into a tire-making factory and been a success. By that, she meant he had made friends with the other workers and, I guess, had not collapsed from the arduous task of building tires of all sizes and shapes. He had been married but was divorced and had a young son, about twelve or thirteen, whom he adored. Evelyn added that he was also sexy. I didn't pay a whole lot of attention to what she said because she had been having a few drinks. Other comrades said she was a lush, although they were careful to whom they said this because of her husband's position. The new editor's name was Jules Geller, and he was introduced at a meeting in the headquarters of the SWP. It was a sizeable gathering, with all the branch members attending. Afterward, while standing toward the back talking to someone, I looked across the room and saw Jules staring at me. Evelyn probably had spent time coaching him about my attributes. That rather trite song with the line "across a crowded room" is probably popular because such emotions really do happen to people. A wave of feeling passed between us, probably sexual but something more too, as if we knew each other without even having said hello. We stared at each other for what seemed an interminable amount of time, until I turned away. But I knew we would see each other again and investigate this sense of mutuality. It did not take long, because Evelyn, the matchmaker, called a few days later and invited me for cocktails and to meet Jules. I don't know whether it was in Jules's apartment or a borrowed one, but it was on the West Side not far from St. Vincent's Hospital. I remember it well, not only because of our romance but because there was a White Tower hamburger place where delicious hamburgers were served for five cents. They were quite small, so one had to eat two or three, but they were very good, with minced onion and a slice of pickle cooked into the meat. The juxtaposition of two appetites is weird, but that's the memory.

Evelyn had prepared drinks and appetizers and we had a pleasant hour. After that she put on a record and suggested that we dance. She and Jules took the floor and I could see that he was a good and graceful dancer. I could also see that Evelyn was a bit tipsy—she sort of leaned all over Jules and was not entirely steady on her feet. Very soon she said she needed to get some fresh air and left us alone. Jules and I then danced for about an hour, without talking, just moving together as one as if we had known each other for centuries. Finally, I decided it was getting late and said I had to get home, my babysitter would want to leave. Jules walked me across town and down to Thirteenth Street. We said good night with a handshake, and I remember that he held my hand longer than was usual. There was something electric about Jules, a type of magnetism. He was handsome, but not an Adonis: not very tall and slim; his head just slightly larger than one would expect from the framework of his body; his skin pale in contrast to medium to dark brown hair and eyes. He had a warm smile and nice even teeth. He also smelled good, an important factor in sexual arousal.

Jules did not call during the week but we went out for coffee after the party meeting. We talked about politics but without mentioning any of the theoretical differences between our two groups. He told me about working in the tire plant, how the workers sometimes fell asleep on their buses home from fatigue after a day of assemblyline motions. Within a few weeks we became lovers and he was either very experienced or had a natural talent. Soon after our first couplings, Jules said he had fallen in love with me the first night he saw me across the room. So much for that song—it does happen. I was at least half in love, but by this time I felt battered by two divorces and a possible failed third marriage, so I held back, keeping from unleashing my emotions completely. I had also promised Nello that I would maintain our marriage because of the Immigration Department's persecution. My second husband, Edward, had curbed my spirit by telling me that if I couldn't make a go of our marriage something was seriously wrong with me. Nello's approach was to warn me that if I left him it meant I was abandoning the revolution and turning back to the bourgeoisie. Both warnings had the anticipated effect—I felt guilty at wanting to stretch my wings and be free.

Fortunately, Jules was a gentle person, very quiet, but with a golden tongue, in more ways than one. He helped me through difficult times of depression by talking logically, not acting as if my fears were foolish. I told him that he could talk a woman into bed; he knew just what to say and I don't mean by sexual innuendo. It was just his understanding and sympathy that drew out at first a desire just to have his arms around me and after a time a feeling that life was not as bad as it had seemed. He had the quality of not being judgmental, even though he had strong opinions. Jules made me feel that I was something wonderful that had happened to him. Nello, I believe, wanted me to become famous. In one of his letters he wrote he dreamed of me on a stage after a brilliant performance and then I turned to him before anyone else. And he was secretly judgmental, essentially about himself. He could listen to others for hours and inspire them and make them feel that they could accomplish miracles, and during our courtship he had the same effect on me. But afterward he felt guilty and became judgmental about his love for me. He wanted me to become famous so he could find an outlet, at least say to himself, you see, I was not wrong about her, it is my associates who are wrong. Jules didn't care what I did as long as I was happy and he did his best to make me forget problems. He never criticized or spoke against Nello, and he loved Nobbie. In fact, he never pushed me in any direction, just reassured me when I took a step that was unsteady. I probably would have married him, but politics intervened, as it always did.

One afternoon there was a knock at my door, and when I opened it, there was James Cannon on the doorstep. He was carrying a cane and out of breath from the four flights of stairs. I was certainly surprised to see the SWP leader, but I invited him in and sat him at the table. I gave him a glass of water and then put the kettle on for some tea. He probably would have preferred an alcoholic drink, but I didn't offer any. With his ulcer problems, drinking did not help. Cannon came to plead the case for Jules, although Jules did not know anything about the visit or even that Cannon was aware of our romance. It had been Evelyn who had made the appeal. Cannon urged me to leave C. L. R., saying that marriage to a black man was too difficult and no one would hold anything against me if I could not stand the strain. I stayed away from that argument, being too stunned to answer. I told Cannon that Jules and I had different political positions. He then told me about the fights in the early days where comrades became so heated over an issue that they threw chairs at each other during meetings. He stayed for about an hour. When he left I, being a disciplined comrade as well as shocked that the leader of the Trotskyists would visit a lowly rank and file member to persuade her to break up her marriage, and reveal a shocking indifference to racial bias, picked up the phone to report to Nello. Raya answered the phone and refused to listen. She shouted, "You traitor!" and slammed down the receiver. Two of my friends, also members of our group, Madeline and Phil Romano, came that evening and I told them about Cannon's visit and conversation. I also told them about Raya's refusal to listen to me and said Nello should be informed. I don't know whether they told Nello or another member but Nello chastised Raya and made her apologize by paying a visit and listening to what I had to say. She came but listened with an abstracted look on her face and finally left, still hostile. Next, friends told me that Nello made a speech on a tape played to all the comrades saying that my loyalty was unquestioned, in that my first reaction was to report what had happened. A few days later Nello called and asked to see me. He turned up early one evening laden with gifts. First there were the gladioli, a huge bundle of them. There was also a robe, which he called a dressing gown, in apricot bound in pale green satin, with a Bergdorf Goodman label. There was also a prime steak about the size of a large platter and a bottle of rum. The steak was a special treat because meat was rationed. During and for a while after the war, almost everything was rationed—gasoline, meat, butter, shoes, stockings, and even canned goods.

Nello began by saying he had been upset at my choice of apartment location, because the Communist Party had members living on the block and perhaps in this same building. Nello had to be careful after the murder of Trotsky. Once, a West Indian, whom we discovered was a Stalinist, joined the Johnsonites. It turned out he had been instructed to disable or "remove" Nello. I have no idea how we found out about the man, but Nello and I left in the middle of the night and stayed in the Paines' Northport home for several days. After Nello's admonishment about the location and danger level of my apartment, he quickly changed the subject. The purpose of his visit was to ask for yet another chance, and to say that we needed each other. He argued again, as he had in Los Angeles, that we belonged together, and that no one else had a right to intervene. He offered me work for our group— something supposedly only I could do— that would, as he phrased it, "strike a blow for the revolution." I was to go to Detroit and take notes about a black comrade's life. Then I was to write a book based on this man's experiences. The man, Si Owens, worked in an auto plant and had been born in Mississippi. Nello promised I would be in charge and only Si and I would be responsible. No one else was to interfere. What about Nobbie? I asked. He said he would take care of him. He would stay with Raya and John, who were in Pittsburgh, and would look after him while I did the interviewing. This was a surprise, especially that no one would intervene, but there was more to come. He said after I finished interviewing Si, he would take a year off and we would go to California, where he would write a book he'd been planning for years, about *Moby Dick*, the great white whale. Beginning in 1946 Nello had studied the writings of Herman Melville and Walt Whitman. During this time or a little afterward, Nello had set Raya, Grace, and me the task of reading and analyzing Melville's fiction. For some reason, since he did not think *Pierre* was anywhere up to the tale of *Moby Dick*, he assigned the novel to me for study. He planned to submit a book about Melville to a commercial publisher because it might sell and make it possible for us to be financially independent. He also continued to make notes on the *American Civilization* book.

Nello promised that we would rent a small house and purchase a second-hand car, and that he would not have anything to do with his group during that time. We would have a chance on our own. He said he had finished a document called "The Balance Sheet Completed." It was to be handed out to SWP members, and then the Johnsonites were going to split from the Trotskyists. He asked me to be part of the group, all walking out together at the next meeting. Absolutely no one was to be told. It was to be a surprise to the Trotskyists. I had to mention Jules. How could I keep such a break from a man who had been so kind and loving? Nello said Jules was a loyal and disciplined party member, and, whatever he might feel personally, he would have to inform his own leadership. Therefore, I must not let him know what was planned. This part I did not like and I felt like a traitor, but my own organization had to come first. I was loyal to the Johnson-Forest tendency. I was also the wife of the leader and my comrades would never forgive me if I betrayed them. But another split! And I was being asked to break with Jules in such a cruel manner, a good man who loved me, who had treated me with such tenderness, and who loved my child. Although I gave no sign, my world was crumbling around me. And could I believe that my husband would really change, that the icy edifice he had assumed so many times would finally melt?

Before our exodus, Nello gave me "The Balance Sheet Completed." There was a reiteration of our political differences, but what was striking about it was its human quality. One section spoke of SWP members who felt they had sacrificed so much for the good of humanity. This was a particularly telling point of criticism. We had noticed that at major events sometimes even leaders wept when making speeches about their trials as revolutionaries. I had been astonished when Rose Karsner, Jim Cannon's wife, put her arm around me and told members she was proud of me, that I had sacrificed a career as a model and film star for the good of the cause. It had never occurred to me that I had sacrificed anything; I had *added* to my life. I felt the same way about marrying Nello. The whole world changed, or rather I saw it differently. Despite the invasion of our privacy by group members and aggressive bigots, there were many advantages. Whenever we took a train and entered the depot, wherever there was a red cap, no matter how busy, he dropped everything to assist us. In the dining car to Washington, with passengers hostile and making it obvious, we had better service than anyone. Waiters competed with each other to give us anything we needed. When I traveled alone with Nobbie, I was looked after as if part of a vast family or army. Most importantly, I gained a deeper understanding of the world around me. A view of the world is very different from the bottom up rather than the top down. As an outcast my vision cleared and I saw everything as it really is, not hidden behind my own perceptions or how I would like things to be. Marriage to Nello, then, opened vistas; no sacrifice was involved. My mother could never understand this feeling of enlightenment. She thought I married a black man because of my *big heart,* which made me sympathetic to everyone the world mistreated.

Everything went according to plan and we walked out of headquarters in unison before the stunned gaze of the SWP membership. Nello had arranged for Nobbie and I to stay with friends. He, and his leaders, believed Jules and other members would pay a visit to my apartment to dissuade me from leaving. And this did happen; neighbors told us people pounded on my door for hours.

My trip to Detroit had been arranged and a few days later Nello took me in a cab to the airport. We had not gotten together as yet, but it was unspoken that after my assignment in Detroit we would meet and move to California. Arriving in Detroit, I was met by Cecelia and Peter Lang, who took me to their home. Although the apartment had only one bedroom, they had prepared their front room, including a typewriter and space for me to work. I called Si Owns, whom I'd met several times during conferences, and arranged that we would work at the Langs' every morning for about three to four hours. Cecelia and Peter worked in factories and would be gone most of the day. It took two weeks of steady work to complete the first stage of the book. I prepared an outline of each chapter, choosing the subject of each after conferring with Si. When I sent my outline to Nello he showed it to Raya, who immediately tried to intervene. Without his knowledge, she called me and insisted I add a chapter on the Congress of Industrial Organizations (CIO). Since Si had never had any experiences with the formation of the CIO, I refused. She said it did not matter whether he had been involved in its formation, it was an important development in the lives of workers and should be in the book. She couldn't convince me; it would have been a lie to write about something that did not happen. Fortunately, when I phoned Nello he agreed and may have told Raya to back off and not interfere. So far, and for the first time, I was getting his support, and against one of his leaders. It did not make me feel victorious but it strengthened my confidence in my approach to the story and, of course, in Nello.

At the end of two weeks of hard work, I had half a dozen steno notebooks filled with the story of Si's life. Some of his experiences were similar to those of Wright's. Tennessee, when Si had been growing up, was not too different from Mississippi, Wright's birthplace. Si was not a writer, but he was a good storyteller and could describe events in vivid detail. He had lived through the Detroit riots in 1943 and gave me a first-person account of what happened from day to day. At the onset of war, recruiters went south to solicit workers, black and white, for work in the factories producing munitions. They promised high wages in the northern factories. The response was so great that by 1943 approximately 100,000 blacks had moved to Detroit, and about that many whites. Black people felt they would no longer suffer the racism of the south, but the white southerners took their history-old bigotry with them to Detroit. To make the situation more tense, housing was in short supply and blacks were excluded from all public housing except one called the Brewster project. Many lived in homes that had no indoor bathrooms but still paid rent three times higher than families in white districts. The army and navy were still segregated and black people faced public discrimination in all parts of the city. In the factories whites were resentful because they had to work beside blacks and disrupted assembly lines by slowdowns and stoppages.

By 1943, after several years of minor, but sometimes violent, skirmishes, Detroit erupted. Mobs of whites spilled onto Woodward and began beating black people who were getting off the streetcars after work. Six policemen were shot and another seventy-five injured. Whites began overturning and burning cars, and looting stores belonging to blacks. It was like a war, Si explained. The riot could not be contained by two thousand city policemen and over one hundred state troopers. Whites beat blacks while the police stood by and did nothing to prevent it. The rioting lasted thirty-six hours, with thirty-four dead, twenty-five of them black. Si witnessed several deaths and the machinegunning of a building by state troopers. He said white people living in the black area were never harmed. Some of them sat in front of their houses and watched what was happening. The mayhem did not end until Mayor Edward Jeffries Jr. and Governor Harry Kelly appealed to President Franklin Roosevelt for help. Federal troops came in armored cars and jeeps with machine guns and patrolled the area, and finally the mobs of black and white faded away.

In my outline there had not been a mention of the 1943 Detroit riot, and at this point I was not sure where in the book it would fit. Si was eager to include the story, and I felt this firsthand account had to be written. Our intuition was justified and the Detroit riots became chapter 8 in the book eventually named *Indignant Heart*. I was now ready to move to California to renew my marriage once again and write a book on the life of Si Owens, a black auto worker.

⤐ 27 ⤏

In Los Angeles we found a small, woodframe, two-bedroom house in Compton, next door to Watts. Our block was occupied on one side by white families, mostly from the south, and on the other by black families. Our house, as if fated, was in the middle and was the dividing line. The house was similar to the one in which I grew up. Almost the only difference was that there were no dividing doors between the front and dining rooms, which made that part of the house appear more spacious. The bedrooms were small, just enough room for the bed and a chest of drawers. The kitchen stretched across the back of the house, with a breakfast area midway in front of a window that overlooked a small, fenced-in garden. Nello and I decided at once to make the dining area our work station, he at one end and I at the other end of the table. That would mean having our meals in the kitchen, but we needed a workspace where we did not have to lay out or put away our work every day. We took the front bedroom and put Nobbie's crib in the back bedroom because we could keep an eye on him from the dining area where we would be working. The place was furnished adequately, if not in the style that I would have chosen. But it was more comfortable than either of the apartments we had in New York. I was also happy to be able to walk outside into my own yard and not have to climb up and down steps to see some greenery.

On one side was a white family and on the other a black couple who did not have children. The white family pretended we were not there, but the black couple on the other side became friends. We also became friendly with a family who lived across the street just in front of our house. We bought an ancient car for a hundred dollars, almost a vintage model Chevrolet, pretty beat up but it ran. I found a nursery school where Nobbie could be cared for from eight to twelve every morning except on Saturday and Sunday.

Nello and I enjoyed taking drives, often to the seashore, where Nobbie could run in the sand. We were often stopped by police and never knew what would happen. Two friends drove us to Palm Springs one weekend and on our return a police siren sounded close behind. Nello, Nobbie, and I were sitting in the back seat of the convertible and the driver told us not to say anything, to let him do all the talking. We were happy to obey. One of the police officers got out of the black-and-white car with one hand held at the side, hovering over but not touching his gun, walked toward us. There wasn't much traffic at that time, particularly on the route we had taken, and I was frightened—whatever happened, there might not be witnesses or anyone to whom we could appeal. The policeman did not speak to the driver but asked Nello abruptly, "What's your name and let me see some identification." He was decidedly unfriendly. Our friend asked, "What is the problem, officer?" The cop said, "We've had a report on a robbery and this man fits the description." If I had not been so scared, I would have laughed in his face—Nello, of all people, resembling anyone else. Nello appeared calm and handed over not only his identification but also his wallet. He was a good actor. The cop glanced through it and instead of giving it to Nello, tossed it in my lap and sneered at me. Without another word he turned and went back to his police car. We went on our way but the cops followed us for several miles. Our friends, who were white, were quite shaken and wanted to know if this sort of thing happened very often. And was it because we were in California? This type of harassment never ended. Even when I was driving without Nello and Nobbie was in the car I would be pulled over. One cop, after stopping me one day and then following me for a week or two, even asked for a date. He probably assumed I was either foreign or a prostitute. After all, the laws against interracial marriage did not end until 1967, and this was in the 1940s. Even when the law changed, black and white couples were not safe.

Nello was true to his promise and did not become involved with the California Johnsonites. He also discouraged Raya, Grace, and Lyman from writing or phoning. He settled down quite happily, surrounded by books and papers, and worked away at writing his book on *Moby Dick*. He alternated the work with notes on *The American Civilization*. I sat writing the Si Owen book every morning as soon as I drove Nobbie to nursery school. As I completed a chapter I would send it to Si in Detroit. He would read and make suggestions for additions or approve what was written and return the material. I shudder today that I sent originals and kept just the carbon-stained copies. There were no computers and we did not have access to a copy machine. Nello wrote in longhand without carbon paper, but he at least had his originals after I typed his first draft. Nello did not like me to work in the garden because he said it would make my fingers stiff for typing. I think he wanted me to write all day but there were other chores that he sometimes forgot. The little house had to be kept clean, as did Nobbie, and shopping and cooking took up time. Nello often helped with the cooking, which we enjoyed doing together. I think I insisted on pursuing work in the garden not only because I liked growing plants but also because I could be alone for some time during a day.

Life is not what we would like it to be, and seldom what we've planned. Nello and I had our year apart from the group, but not together; we were soon forcibly separated. After several months of relaxation and adjusting to the new routine, Nello was arrested by the U.S. Immigration Department and sent to Ellis Island. The leadership of the group ordered me to stay in California. I never learned whether Nello had anything to do with the decision. The theory was that our separation could be used in the case because the Immigration Department had separated a man from his wife and child. Whatever the reasoning, I was not happy about it. Foolishly—as far as the group was concerned—I always believed that a wife or husband should be with her or his mate in times of crises. But, as usual, I acceded to these dictates despite feeling angry. Added to my worries about Nello were other problems. I was very lonely and am also a coward, frightened at being alone in a house with so many windows and doors. I took hammer and nails and went around nailing the windows, leaving just enough space for air circulation. Fortunately, there was a spotlight in the garden that I kept lighted all night. But even with such precautions I was awake most of every night, going from room to room and looking out windows to be sure no one was sneaking up or getting ready to break in a door. Many nights I hovered over Nobbie's crib, watching his calm breathing and hoping that nothing would happen to him or to me.

Once a week I attended the local Johnson-Forest group meetings and during the days I worked steadily at the life story of Si Owens. My next door neighbor and I had coffee in the garden early every morning and she was a big help in keeping up my morale. One week I invited my mother for a visit and she agreed to spend a night with us in Compton. We had not been on good terms, because I had offered to meet her at the Farmers' Market for lunch and she had refused. She probably thought Nello would accompany me and did not want her friends, Bess and Nell Reagan, to see her with us. Nello chided me about my attitude and urged me to call my mother, but I was stubborn. He explained that mother's feelings were natural and logical. If I had been living permanently in Los Angeles, she could have adjusted to our relationship. But I would be leaving and if she lost her friends, she would not have anyone. Be that as it may, I drove into Beverly Hills and picked her up while Nello was on Ellis Island. She had not known I had a child, because she had been so opposed to my marriage that I did not write to her about the birth of a grandchild. When I picked up mother, Nobbie was standing in the back of the car. She simply glanced at him as she got in the front seat, and then looked away. After driving a block or two Nobbie put his hand on her shoulder and said: "Are you my Grammy?" Tears came into her eyes and she put her hand over his and said, "Yes, I guess I am." Back at our house in Compton, Nobbie captivated mother entirely. Without meaning to offend and not even knowing that she was doing so, she kept saying "But he's so bright! But he's so intelligent! But he's so handsome!" Always that preface *but*. For a change I kept from losing my temper and didn't reply. She meant no harm, but bigotry is so deep rooted that some people do not recognize it when it appears in the simplest remarks. However, I learned something important about mother and the thinking of some southerners as well. During the evening, after dark, when Nobbie was asleep, mother said she was worried about me, about my living in such a neighborhood. My immediate response was to lash back, saying that the black neighbors were friends and would not harm me. Mother replied, "No, dear. I wasn't talking about the black people. It is the whites I'm afraid of. You don't know how mean and vicious these crackers can be."

On Ellis Island, Nello was placed with political prisoners: five Communists. The Communists knew he was an open enemy. He had written or translated books against them, published in the U.S., England, and France. He had publicly condemned the British Communist Party fifteen years earlier when they did not support a revolutionary campaign against imperialist aggression in Abyssinia, Ethiopia, the West Indies, and Africa. He had often made speeches in Hyde Park and lectured against Communism in the U.S. He remembered a friend of his in France during the Vichy tyranny. As soon as the Vichy government fell, the Communists murdered him. He knew their long record of murder of political enemies, including Leon Trotsky. He didn't think they would actually kill him, but they could make his life miserable. Nello would have to sleep in the same room with these men and he did not feel comfortable about their proximity. He did not dare protest and ask to be moved because if they found out it would make matters worse. For a few days the Communists seemed not to know how to act toward Nello. He thought at first they believed he was a spy but after a few days accepted him as a fellow prisoner. Just as the situation seemed to be tenable, Nello was told by one of the men that his friend, William Patterson, was coming to see the man. This was a shock. Nello knew Patterson and Patterson knew him and had, in fact, slandered him in Communist circles and in the black community. Fortunately, Patterson ignored him and nothing untoward happened.

Nello settled down to complete the work on his Melville study, *Mariners, Renegades and Castaways,* jailed, he was then, in the very midst of renegades and castaways on Ellis Island. After a very short time he learned that a man, Nello called him "M," was the leader of the group of jailed Communists. M wrote a series of articles published in the Communist press about Ellis Island and its cruel and inhuman treatment of prisoners. The articles were circulated worldwide and came to the attention of the Department of Justice. The FBI visited M and asked him to report on the prisoners and the island's conditions. Nello did not want M in any way to be his spokesman, because it would mean he was being linked with the Communist Party. He was pretty certain that placing him with Communists was deliberate on the part of the government, which was well aware of his attitude toward the Communists. By putting him with the Communist prisoners, it could then claim that Nello's political activities were essentially the same as the Party's. He would have no chance of remaining in the U.S. If a claim was made that Nello was an illegal alien, a foreign subversive, it meant that he could never appear before a congressional committee to defend himself. He would be denied all legal rights and liberties.

Nello spoke with respect about the security officers on the island. He said for the most part they were pleasant and sympathetic, just trying to do a decent job under difficult, intolerable circumstances.

In New York, Ike Blackman acted as the go-between Nello and the lawyer we had hired. No one from the group was to speak to Nello at all while he was on the island. But one day, in an excess of emotion, Raya grabbed the phone to talk to him. She could not bear the separation. Nello promptly hung up the receiver. Ike talked to Nello almost every day and reported to the lawyer and Raya and Grace. He never called or wrote to me, and I was told that I could not phone Nello. Nello wrote and once or twice was allowed to speak to me on the telephone. He told me about the food, that it was certainly the worst thing for his ulcer but that he was determined to keep up his strength and was forcing himself to eat. After three weeks he couldn't eat at all. He became afraid that the ulcer would perforate because of the food, but he did not want to complain. He did ask that he be allowed to have some of the food from the cart that passed his room on its way to the infirmary. He also asked for milk, but he could not live on milk alone and became very weak. The Communists smuggled some breakfast to him one morning and later threatened to go on a hunger strike if he was not given the diet he needed. Nello asked our attorney to take some action so he could stave off another perforated ulcer, but the attorney was told, let him see the doctor. They put Nello in the infirmary and the doctor examined him and afterward explained that they did not have the facilities on Ellis Island to take care of a case such as his. He then asked Nello what food he could tolerate. Nello told him specifically—lean meat, crisp bacon, plain steamed rice, chopped vegetables, and milk.

But after the doctor's visit, nothing happened. The same miserable diet served in the dining hall—essentially poor quality meat spiced up to make it edible and greasy fried fish that made him sick—was served to the patients in the infirmary. Nello's inability to eat resulted in a flow of acids perpetually bathing the lining of his stomach. For many hours at a time he had excruciating stomach pains. Appeals by his attorney went unanswered by either the Immigration Department or the Ellis Island officials, and they refused to give him special food. Our lawyer then talked to a Mr. Shaughnessy, the district director of Immigration and Naturalization of the Port of New York. Shaughnessy's response was that if he did not like it here in the U.S., he was not forced to stay; he could leave and go back to Trinidad and drink his papaya juice. It was obvious from his comment that as far as he was concerned, Nello could die. Louis Gogol called and wrote to the administrators of Ellis Island, warning that Nello's life was in danger if he did not receive immediate care. By this time our attorney decided to request bail. Nello had not wanted to make such a request but had to agree because he was so ill. The case came up before a Judge Knox, but unfortunately he could do nothing because of a rule in the Second District Court that bail could not be granted where a decision was pending. But Knox advised our attorney to fly to Washington and put the matter before Attorney General McGranery, who he said was a humane man and had the authority to grant bail. The day before the case was to be heard in Washington, Nello was hospitalized in Stapleton Hospital on Staten Island. McGranery denied bail because he said that since Nello was in the hospital there was no need to take the matter further.

Nello stayed in the hospital for two months. During that time, he was guarded twenty-four hours a day by three guards in eight-hour shifts. At night the guards sat right outside the door or actually in his room. He had committed no crime, and the government itself had admitted he was a man of good moral character. Yet in a hospital he was treated like a prisoner. The Department of Justice's actions toward Nello were those imposed on dangerous people, murderers and insane criminals. In a sense it was ludicrous because he was fighting to stay in the country and was certainly not going to run away.

After two months Nello's ulcer improved and he was returned to the island. Two days later, on October 7, he was let out on bail and called with the good news. When I asked him why he had been silent for two months, he told me what had happened. If they knew, the Johsonite leaders had not told me how seriously ill Nello was. If I had known, no matter the party strictures, I would have bundled up Nobbie and taken a plane to New York. Even if the authorities had not let me see him, he would have known I was nearby and whenever he had been ill in the past he did not want me out of his sight. He said he felt safer when I was with him.

Nello urged me to pack up everything and return to him in New York as soon as I could. He would find us a place to stay, even if temporary. Before leaving Los Angeles I learned that the leaders had decided Nello should give a class to a few of the young members of the "third layer." My first reaction was positive; he would enjoy a job that he liked, teaching eager young people. About a week after Bessie Gogol told me about the class, the husband of one of the chosen participants called and asked if Nobbie and I wanted to drive to the beach. He had something important to tell me. At the beach, he told me that Nello and his wife were having an affair. He was upset and angry and felt betrayed not only by his wife but by the man whom he admired as the leader of his organization. He kept saying, "My God, the man is almost old enough to be her grandfather." The couple had a small child a few months older than Nobbie. If my friend was upset, I think the word did not express my feelings. The next time I saw Bessie I told her what was happening and to my outrage and astonishment learned that she had recommended the names of some of the attendees. She stated proudly, "And with what Jimmy has been through I would line up every woman in the group and let him take his pick or take all of them."

After Nello had been released on bail, I had been getting ready to leave Los Angeles for New York when during my monthly period I began to hemorrhage. Lou Gogol came to the house and after an examination put me in the hospital. He arranged for a neighbor to look after Nobbie. Gogol discovered fibroid tumors of the uterus that required surgery. Nello, contacted in New York, did not want me to travel, feeling that my life might be jeopardized. This wasn't the case, but since we knew and had confidence in Gogol, it was decided that my trip should be delayed for surgery and recovery. The only question I had to answer was whether to remove the uterus. Since Nello and I had discussed having another child I said no, it had to be kept intact if possible. The surgery went off without any problems and recuperation was fairly rapid. I left for New York around the end of November. Nello met us at the airport, thinner but looking happy to have his family back in his arms. We moved into a one-bedroom apartment in the Chelsea Hotel on West Twenty-third Street. The apartment had a tiny kitchen, a spacious living room, and a comfortable bedroom. No mention was made of his presumed affair.

The American Civil Liberties Union joined our attorney to fight for Nello's request to remain in the U.S. The case attacked the constitutionality of the proceedings against Nello as violating the First and Fifth Amendments. We now had to wait to appear before the Court of Appeals. As a result we lived from day to day but without the constant visits from FBI and immigration agents. The only bright side of this waiting period was that Nello could now speak openly from public platforms. In the fall of 1952, the Columbia University Institute of Arts and Sciences proposed that Nello give a series of lectures. There were to be six talks devoted to "The Idea of Personality in Great Literature." The lectures developed the theme in the work of six great writers: Aeschylus, Shakespeare, Milton, Rousseau, Melville, and Dostoevsky. Very early in our relationship, Nello had talked about the relationship of individual personality juxtaposed with society. The subject fascinated him and he believed that in the U.S. the strictures of society were limiting the creativity of its citizens. All of the lectures were extraordinary, and people who attended the first one came back for all that followed.

One very memorable meeting at Columbia was when he spoke on Melville. The auditorium was large, but it was not large enough; people eager to hear him speak stood along the sides of the hall and at the back wall. Nello explained that *Moby Dick*, which he felt was Melville's finest novel, had confirmed his longheld point of view about the creativity inherent in individuals and its frustration by the society in which they lived. Unlike members of the left, including some in his own group, he looked at personality before placing people in a historical context. It was something like the arguments between those who believe solely in environment and those who believe who we are and how we behave depends on genes. It is neither one nor the other, but both. Nello's main premise was that the Pequod was a factory and the crew, its workers—a whale had to be captured, then its blubber cut into chunks and rendered into oil. The harpooners in the whaling industry, who were masters of what today we would call technology, did not need overseers or managers; they knew what they were doing. The crew was a symbol of personality or humanity, up against the unbridled, solitary individualism of Ahab, as captain. For me, and perhaps for some members of the audience, Ahab was not unfamiliar—we had just been through a war with Germany. When Nello finished speaking there was a standing ovation. The president and owner of a major toy company came backstage to shake his hand. A week later several huge cartons of toys arrived for Nobbie. There were so many packed in the boxes that we hid all but one or two of the toys. Every week we put away the toys that had grown familiar and presented Nobbie with a few new ones. There were enough toys to last over a year.

Nello's stay on Ellis Island gave him an understanding of *Moby Dick* that nothing else could have done, and he had in mind a final chapter about his experiences. He decided to write in the first person and use the chapter as an appeal to remain in the U.S. The chapter, titled *A Natural But Necessary Conclusion,* revealed the humanity yet mixed motives of the Communist prisoners. Before his internment Nello would have dismissed them as dangerous opponents because they were Stalinists. But on Ellis Island they had treated him with kindness. He dedicated the book to our son: "For my son Nob, who will be 21 years old in 1970 by which time I hope he and his generation will have left behind them forever all the problems of nationality."

The dedication was beyond race or color—it was Nello's desire to see a world free of tribes, nationalism, or religiosity. He read to me from Melville's *Redburn:*

[The U.S.] Settled by the people of all nations, all nations may claim her for their own. You can not spill a drop of American blood without spilling the blood of the whole world. Be he Englishman, Frenchman, German, Dane, or Scott, the European who scoffs at an American, calls his own brother Raca, and stands in danger of the judgment. We are not a narrow tribe of men . . . No: our blood is as the flood of the Amazon, made up of a thousand noble currents all pouring into one. We are not a nation, so much as a world.

Nello said Melville portrayed a world of human personalities, living as the vast majority of humans live, not by ideas but by emotions, seeking to avoid pain and misery and struggling for happiness. This concern, the struggle for happiness, was the main theme in his book on American civilization. Although I was always happy during our discussions—which ranged so wide—nevertheless my own struggle for happiness was never on the agenda. How was I to avoid pain and misery? He was again immersed in politics with his leaders, meetings with his lawyer, and writing until late at night. In addition to preparing lectures, then polishing them for a future book, he wrote voluminous letters to Jay Leyda, who was a Melville scholar and writer; Meyer Schapiro, a friend and art critic; and Quentin Bell, artist, writer, critic, and nephew of Virginia Woolf. This schedule was compounded by meetings with the other leaders of the Johnson-Forest group. His silent mode took over, and once again we became estranged. During the day I took Nobbie to Washington Square, walking and pushing his go-cart from Twenty-third Street to Eighth Street and then across to the park itself.

As Christmas approached we stopped talking to each other entirely, except for ordinary everyday civilities. I did not feel much like a celebration, but for Nobbie's sake I decided to buy a tree and decorations, and presents, and then I would cook a turkey dinner. Thinking to please Nello, I invited Ike and Grace to join in the festivities. On Christmas morning I made Nello's favorite breakfast, charred salt cod, then fed Nobbie and gave him his gifts. Nello had not shopped so I told Nobbie the presents were from his daddy and mommy. I gave Nello his favorite pen, a Waterman, and waited in anticipation for a gift from him. After Nello had opened his gift and Nobbie was happily playing with his toys, Nello settled down at the desk and began to work. My hurt at not receiving anything at all was overwhelming, but I was too proud to show it or to ask Nello why he hadn't bothered to get me a present. A few weeks later I learned that he had bought a present, for one of the young women he slept with while I was in California. It is not possible to keep a secret in small towns or radical organizations. Someone tells one person in confidence and the news spreads everywhere. Grace had helped pick out a skirt, I think it was, and apparently did the gift wrapping and mailing to hide it from me.

During our Christmas dinner an incident occurred, seemingly insignificant, but under the circumstances more important than it would have been another time. Nello complained that his back hurt and I remembered that a few years earlier he had had such a pain. The reason I remembered was that we tried something called Ben Gay, which I massaged into the skin. Nello said he had never had a back pain before and Grace agreed. I told him about the earlier pain and Grace piped up again, saying that she knew "for a fact" that Nello had never been troubled with backaches. Nello supported her claim so I fell silent. I was beginning to wonder how many more of these sly insults I could stand.

After about a month we moved to Apartment 4A on 417 West Twenty-first, in a building owned by Mrs. Rena Slaughter. She was a widow who had the entire third floor of the four-story building and lived with her sister, Lucy, and young son, Malcolm. Rena and Lucy were petite women, both with gray hair cut short. Rena's face was more round than Lucy's, and she wore an intent expression when someone was speaking. She did not miss anything; she was shrewd, intelligent, and open-hearted. Rena and Lucy accepted us without hesitation, when almost all other landlords would have turned us away. They were Jewish and understood about prejudice. At any rate, these women were perfectly comfortable with Nello and came to admire him. Rena and he especially shared a similar, rather ironic sense of humor and often laughed at things no one else understood. Many times, and particularly in the 1940s, whites were uneasy when meeting blacks, even those whites who believed themselves unbiased. They made an effort to please, to indicate that they, at least, did not agree with uncivilized people who scorned blacks. Sometimes they would tell us that they had a black friend or friends, totally unsolicited remarks intended to place them on "our side." Such remarks and behavior simply made us uncomfortable. But Rena was perfectly at ease with us, a mixed couple and son.

We were given a front, fourth-floor apartment. It had a fireplace, a tiny bedroom, a small living room, and a kitchen. The kitchen had been constructed from what must have been a small closet. When I knelt to open the door of the oven my rear was in the living room. It had advantages because I could always be part of the conversations in the front room and yet prepare food. We often waited until the coals died into red embers and used the fireplace in which to cook steaks. The two large windows had wide sills, so they served as seats where one could look out onto the street and see the tiny garden in front. I spent many hours sitting in the window, listening to music. Malcolm was only a few years older than Nobbie and the two children developed a close friendship. Malcolm was a model child, intelligent, sensitive, and polite. He suffered from asthma and was rather delicate but never seemed to dwell on his illness. Most important, of course, was the wonderful rapport the two children had almost at their first meeting. They never disagreed or fought over toys or anything else. When Nello was away and with Nobbie playing downstairs I worked again on an outline for the biography of Richard Wright, who was now living in Paris. How I missed our visits and walks in the Village, especially since I was alone so much of the time. We had been living for some months in the apartment when I noticed that Nello was receiving airmail letters from Los Angeles that he folded and put in his wallet. Before, he had always showed me his mail, so this was really strange behavior. My curiosity grew to a point that was almost unbearable, but I didn't ask any questions. He probably wouldn't have answered, as was his custom.

On an evening when Nello was soaking in the bath, I opened his wallet and found two letters, each from a different woman. Both professed great and undying love, written in a trite, juvenile style, but a sentence in one letter was a blow: "If there's a divorce, can we get Nobbie? He's only in her way." I am surprised that I did not confront Nello; my rage was nearly uncontrollable. Take my husband, but how dare she even mention my son? She neglects her own child and has the gall to ask for mine. That slut, I said to myself. Nello came out of the bath feeling amorous. I was far from feeling the same way, but I subdued my fury, knowing that an attack would arouse anger and drive him into himself once again. There was also my experience that all the men I had known became hurt or hostile if refused sex, a double standard, of course. Men can say no, but women must not. I think it has something to do with their sense of manhood. Under other circumstances I might have refused Nello's preliminaries, but I responded almost cold bloodedly, thinking we could talk during the afterglow of the act. It would be a good time to find out about these women whose letters I'd read. Nello seldom went to sleep immediately after coitus. Unless he was extremely tired he was affectionate, cuddling me in his arms and murmuring endearments.

After awhile, my mind pondered how to bring up the subject; I couldn't let him know I had ransacked his wallet. I began by asking: "Do you want a divorce?" He said, "No, of course not." I tried again, "Are you interested in someone else or having an affair?" "No," he said. I wasn't getting anywhere. I tried once again. "Let's leave out the fact we are man and wife, what if we were just good friends? If something changes in a relationship between friends, don't you think they should be told?" Nello said he didn't know why I was asking such foolish questions, but yes, if anything changed there should be honesty between friends. With those words, he turned on his side, pulled me close against his curled body, and fell asleep. My dear Victorian husband had lied to me—a crushing fact, as we had always been open and honest with each other. This discovery was almost too much to accept. Nello never lied; as he said, "it wasn't cricket." In fact, he once said that the two parts of his inheritance were Puritanism and cricket. His father had loved and played cricket and was apparently a superior batsman; and his mother was a moral, straitlaced Anglican who would not let Nello play cricket on Sunday or even listen to band music. Another source of self-discipline had been his immersion in English literature from the age of eight. Integrity and loyalty were as ingrained in him as his color was permanent. Nello believed that cricket had helped form his character. One did not cheat or lie, injure or mock others, all summed up in the phrase "it isn't cricket." He also thought these qualities formed the character of the British people. In the 1950s Nello was horrified when the press reported that U.S. university basketball teams had sold out games in exchange for money from bookmakers. He was even more shocked to find that his own political associates shrugged their shoulders and couldn't understand why he was upset. Time and again he brought up the subject when we were alone. Nello was so honest that when I bought him a pair of loafers one Christmas he said he didn't like them. Hiding my disappointment, I said I'd return them for his usual, laced-type shoes. Nello said, "No, leave them for a bit." Months later he tried them on and found he liked them very much. But on Christmas morning, there was no dissimulation, even when he knew my feelings might be hurt.

But this night, lying in bed with him sleeping beside me, I marveled: what an actor! I had watched him often enough preparing his speeches, walking back and forth, timing every gesture, and shaping every tone of his voice. Most painful was that he had been acting when he responded to my questions, saying he was not interested in anyone else and nothing had changed between us. Whatever our past problems were, I thought we had been honest with each other and did not think he had lied before that night. Or had he? Had I lived all these years blithely unaware, feeling secure at the worst of times because he loved me? But for a woman to write "if there's a divorce," was serious. How could the question have been raised unless divorce had been discussed with my husband? Something felt broken or smashed within me. My mind skittered back and forth, suggesting first one course of action and then another but discarding each one until I fell asleep at last with Nello's body curled against me, holding me in his arms.

The next day after Nello left to meet with our attorney I couldn't concentrate on writing. I was still horribly and bitterly upset about the letters and Nello's lies in response to my questions. Nobbie and Malcolm came up from downstairs and we went walking to one of the piers on the West

Side. Looking at the water usually soothed me, but this time even the swells and the lapping of waves against the pilings had no effect on my mood. Walking home, we stopped at a soda fountain where the boys had a "perch up," as Nello called sitting at a counter. Later in the day, a feeling of revulsion followed by despair at the life we were living—but principally at Nello's lies—overwhelmed me. I decided I would not go to England if he was deported. This time the separation would be final. Lord knows we had tried to make our marriage work, but it continued to fall apart. I wouldn't tell Nello until the case was decided, but enough was enough. The next day a letter arrived for him, and after reading it he tore it up and threw it in the fireplace. After that letter no others arrived at our address. I wondered whether my questioning had made him cautious. Always suspicious, he may have arranged to have letters delivered elsewhere.

By 1953 we had been interviewed together and then separately by the Immigration Department. Eventually, every avenue closed. Nello decided he would leave voluntarily rather than be deported. If he left of his own accord, he would be able to return in the future. Deportation would mean permanent exile from the United States. After I was certain Nello was leaving, I told him I would not go with him. Off and on, but it seemed to me halfheartedly, he urged me to change my mind. One of his arguments was how difficult it would be to raise Nobbie, a black and white child, without a father. He couldn't change my mind. Eventually Nello gave up trying to persuade me and left to stay with the Paines. I did not see him again, not even to see him off on the ship. But I cried for days after he was gone. In an attempt to escape pain I wrote out my feelings:

> My arms are empty before I leave you
> And nausea weaves baskets of my flesh.
> What will I do when I am gone
> and no longer see your mouth turn
> sideways, pin-pricked with love.
>
> When you are with me, I can ignore you
> because of warm osmotic changes
> as we talk and laugh with people.
> You are close, my flesh feels your warmth across a room
> and I turn my back feeling your knees in the hollow of my knees,
> your breathing on my nape, your mouth in my hair.
>
> What cold will ascend me and hold me strangled
> when I have left you.

Three failed marriages, and this one we had believed would last forever. That he had lied haunted me. Looking at my son, I often wondered whether I had made the right decision—separating him from his father. Well, I would be mother and father and see that Nobbie never lacked for warmth and affection. As for me—it turned out I could not live without steady warmth and a faithful lover.

I completed the book on Si Owens and we agreed on a title that both of us felt reflected his character and accomplishments. But Raya intervened. She wanted to call the book *Indignant Heart,* after a quotation by Wendell Phillips. Si and I did not agree. He did not feel "indignant," that word in no way described his feelings. Although there had been serious difficulties in his life he had been astute enough to overcome them. Working for a time as a chauffeur, he saw beneath the southern gentleman façade, and it had amused him to appeal to their white vanities and thus get favors and better treatment. Then he had gone north, found work in an auto plant, and become a respected member in the United Auto Workers Union (UAW). If anything, the title needed to express the character of a strong man, confident of himself and beyond a feeling of indignation. Si and I lost, of course, and Raya had her way. The book was published under the title she chose. Si and I were to use fictitious names, he for the reason that he could lose his job and lose the support of the UAW if that occurred, and I because of my relationship with Nello. The surprise and disappointment for me was that only the name Si chose, Matthew Ward, appeared on the book, as if he had been the writer instead of the storyteller. I should not have been disappointed or surprised. A similar burial had happened with my booklet on Richard Wright. The leaders had taken over and I accepted their decision, because I was still under the sway of the organization despite the blows to my ego and freedom.

Soon after Nello sailed for England, I consulted a friend and lawyer, Conrad Lynn, about a divorce. Lynn said I could have the marriage annulled on the basis of nonsupport. Nello hit the ceiling when he heard the news. He would not have the world think he had not supported his wife and child. While I was considering his point of view, he took his problem to the group without my knowledge. A few weeks after he had spoken to me, a special meeting was called of the New York and Philadelphia Johnsonites. The subject was not announced, simply that the meeting would be held in the apartment below mine, where a comrade, Priscilla Barb, was living with her daughter, Natalia. When I went downstairs only a few comrades had arrived and we waited for the others to show up. Nettie Kravitz, a member of the Philadelphia branch, seemed to be in charge of the meeting and my curiosity was aroused. I wondered whether something had happened to the group in her city that would involve New York. Other comrades began to arrive and each one was taken into the bedroom and the door was closed. This had not been my introduction upon entering and I became uneasily suspicious. There was also a refusal to meet my eyes when a comrade would come out of the bedroom. The meeting was finally called to order and I raised my hand. "Comrade Nettie," I asked, "does this meeting have anything to do with my personal life?" The answer was yes. I got up from where I was sitting and said, "I refuse to take part in this meeting. My personal life is not the business of my comrades." I walked out, leaving silence behind me until I was halfway up the stairs. Then I could hear the meeting continue but did not bother to eavesdrop. It was sickening and reminded me of the Trotskyists long ago on a river bank, when the comrades discussed my should- or would-be sex life. The trial, for that's what it was, also reminded me of the one held by the Communist Party that Dick wrote about in the last third of *Black Boy*.

I continued to attend weekly meetings but no one would speak to me. Even the chairperson would not recognize my raised hand when I wanted to comment on a political question. Eventually, antagonism from the comrades lessened. We were a small group and everyone was important if we were to carry out the work of the local. Quite a bit later I was elected co-organizer of the New York Johnsonite group. It consisted of approximately ten people, most of the New Yorkers having moved to Detroit and Los Angeles. The leadership was now centered in Detroit, where Raya, Grace, and Glaberman shared the title. Lyman and Freddy had moved to Los Angeles, where Lyman was group leader along with Bessie Gogol. Essentially the group relied on directives from Nello in London but was finding it difficult to keep going. We were producing a printed version of what had begun as a mimeographed sheet prior to our rejoining the SWP. It was still named *Correspondence,* but it was not selling well even though we were attempting to write—with our full fountain pens—what the workers, women, and youth had to say. There was a tinge of exaggeration, creating an aura of unreality. Most of us would talk to one teenager, for example, and then write an article declaiming "Teenagers say" or "Young people are critical of the school system." The word "they" was used most of the time, which eventually made me feel uncomfortable. How could *one* speak for *all*? One day a friend asked me, "Who are 'they'?" When I was unable to give more than a feeble answer I determined at once that from then on I would be specific and utterly objective in everything I wrote.

In New York an opportunity for a major story presented itself when an independent union of subway workers burgeoned and set itself against the Transport Workers Union (TWU). Zeb Blackman, whom I had known since he was sixteen or seventeen, and I decided to seek an interview with one of the new union's leaders, Frank Zelano. Zeb was a good friend who was always ready to cheer me up during bad days. For a man so young, he had a down-to-earth outlook, very objective and honest and not given to a lot of doubletalk as were some of the leaders and rank-and-file members. Zeb also had a very appealing personality; he laughed easily, had a subtle sense of humor, and was always full of energy. He was better looking than his brother, Saul (Ike), and had blondish brown hair, one lock of which kept falling onto his forehead. Where Saul was fat, Zeb was solid and well-built. I think when Nello left the country Zeb determined to become my protector. He was very intuitive and was aware—without my mentioning it—of the difficulties I had with the leadership. I don't remember whether Zeb or I called Zelano, but he agreed to meet us for an interview and promised information about why there was a need for an independent union. Zeb and I met Zelano in a small coffee shop in the Village. Zelano was older than we expected, his hair showing strands of white and gray and his hands displaying the lines, wrinkles, and discolorations of age. He was slim, not very tall, wore glasses with wire frames, and looked more like a grandfather than a leader of a union. Zelano was, however, a live wire, filled with energy and enthusiasm. He talked to us for two hours. The main premise of his argument and the reason for the subway workers' dissatisfaction was that the TWU, supposedly their union, did not support their aims. As happens quite often when a union becomes powerful, its leadership had taken on the trappings of corporate management. With such huge salaries and luxurious offices, chauffeurs, and fraternization with corporate management, these leaders had more in common with industry CEOs.

We spent several days writing the story and notified Detroit that we would require sizeable space, almost the entire issue of the paper. We received approval and sent in the article. Over a thousand papers were sold, with copies pasted up by the transit workers in all the rest stops of the subway system. The New York members were ecstatic at our success, but where we expected jubilance from the Detroit leadership we received the opposite. Letters were sent off to Nello accusing the New York group of running wild and trying to take over the organization. Basing his reply on their information and without writing to us in New York, he wrote a strong letter to Detroit that we did not see. They sent in Martin (Marty) Glaberman to bring us into line. Glaberman, who was generally easygoing and seemed open minded, was in actuality a stern and rigid Marxist. He was utterly loyal to Nello and defensive of what I felt was a one-sided view. Any discussion of Nello in a wider context than his Marxist views aroused antagonism. As if receptive, Glaberman listened to our enthusiastic ideas for follow-up articles on the struggle of the transport workers. When we finished he gave us a stern lecture about losing our heads and forbade us to proceed any further without approval from the leadership. Zeb and I were crestfallen but had to obey. No one in New York understood what we had done to cause such a furor.

Some months later, Conrad Lynn called to say that two children, Hanover Thompson, ten, and David Simpson, eight, were being held in the adult jail in Monroe, North Carolina. They had been arrested because a little white child, Betty Lou Sutton, seven years old, had kissed David on the cheek. Lynn wanted me to go to Monroe and interview everyone concerned and write a series of articles for *Correspondence*. The major newspapers were not giving the story much play. An English journalist, Joyce Egginton of the *London News Chronicle*, had covered the story and now reporters were no longer welcome in Monroe. Lynn, as the children's lawyer, wanted publicity, which might arouse enough public opinion to free the boys.

Having been burned for our story on the transit workers, we requested permission from the leaders in Detroit for me to go to Monroe. That having been given, Lynn and I met so he could brief me on how I should make my approach. It was during this briefing that I had my first sense of what living in a southern state might mean in one's daily life. I had never been in the south and reading about inequity and brutality is different from going into the lion's den. Lynn and I had been friends for several years and he was also an admirer of Nello. He was a short, dark, rather homely man, with small eyes and thick lips that seemed to be slightly open even when he was not talking. He was thin, wiry, and physically fit, keeping his body conditioned by playing tennis every day. I think one of his brothers was a tennis pro. When Conrad Lynn began to speak, any preliminary judgment that he was unattractive, even ugly, disappeared. His intensity and personality were such that one left feeling he was actually a handsome man.

This day when we met he was at peak form, passionately angry about the treatment of the two little boys. In the jail, he said, the adult prisoners were frightening the children, telling them that they would be taken out to a farm where there were cows. Cows, they claimed, had horns and would probably attack them. Lynn said the children were in tears, near hysteria with fright. He controlled his anger and gave me a short history of the events leading up to the arrests in Monroe. Robert Williams, an ex-Marine and president of the local National Association for the Advancement of Colored People (NAACP), had antagonized the white leadership in Monroe. After putting away the medals that he had won serving in the war, he worked as a skilled machinist, but he was fired when his employer discovered he was president of that hated organization. Williams then decided to enlist everyone he could in the NAACP. He went around soliciting people who had not been approached before, talking to women who cleaned for the white community at seven dollars per week, to the unemployed men hanging out in the pool halls; to the street sweepers and toilet cleaners and cooks. Soon there was a gigantic branch—almost the entire community joined except for a few middle-class Uncle Toms who wanted to "cool it." Dr. Albert Perry, a popular medical doctor who was so respected he actually had white patients, joined Williams, and they became co-leaders. Perry was already a member of the NAACP but had grown disgusted because of its inactivity and refusal to face the serious issues in the community.

Williams's and Perry's work in Monroe came to the attention of the central leadership in New York and they were called in and admonished. The NAACP relied on a lot of white people for donations and was essentially a middle-class organization. Roy Wilkins, who was then head of the central leadership, chastised Williams and Perry, saying their actions would antagonize people who might be sympathetic and give money for the good of the organization and its work throughout the U.S. According to Williams, what Wilkins was objecting to was the recruitment of a poor class of people, laborers, not middle class. Instead of bowing to Wilkins's wishes, Williams told me, "I began to fuss." He went downtown and told Mayor Wilson he was tired of having black kids drown every year in irrigation ditches and wanted the use of the city swimming pool. There was only one pool and it was just for white kids. The mayor refused to even set aside one day a week when black kids could use the pool. Williams and Perry then rounded up all the children and their parents and escorted them to the pool. When the black children got into the pool all the white kids ran out and went home to tell their mothers and fathers. After receiving complaints, the mayor instructed Chief of Police Mauney to take care of the situation. Mauney strapped on his guns, filled his car with deputies, and led a parade of KKK members into the black neighborhood. Later, when questioned by federal agents, Mauney claimed he had "just been along for the ride to protect all the citizens." In the black community the Klan members began throwing bottles at women and kids and shooting at random. Two men were wounded before the Klan set off for the home of Dr. Perry.

The cavalcade was destined for a surprise. Williams, Perry, and members of the community put up a strong metal chain at the entrance to his drive and surrounded the perimeter of the hill with sandbags. After everything was prepared they all put on the helmets they had worn in the war and armed themselves with rifles and other small arms, including a machine gun. Perry told me the Klan's and Mauney's initial visit was on a very black night; there wasn't a moon, and from the top of his hill he could see lights flashing from all these cars as they rolled along. Soon they were near enough for him to hear singing and shouting. "Southern white men are very cheerful when they have a job to do," Perry said. From a distance Perry heard shots and yells and the cars increased their speed. In the lead car was Chief Mauney and he apparently stepped on the gas and came on faster than the rest, right up the road and onto the doctor's property. There was a crash and both headlights broke and the car seemed to ricochet as if snapped backward on a rubber band. All the other cars scattered like a bunch of ants. Mauney had run into the heavy chain that Perry and his neighbors had stretched across his driveway. This first night was such a surprise to the chief of police and his brother Klansmen that no one had to shoot at the Klan. The following weekend the Klan gathered again and attacked Perry's house on the hill, but received such a fusillade in return they had to retreat. After several more attempts, but without succeeding in injuring a single black person, the Klan gave up the fight. Chief Mauney built a barbecue and shooting area for the Klan eight miles out from Monroe. Here the Klan held wiener roasts and practiced shooting. Their target on the range was a cut-out figure of a black man with a rope around his neck. Lynn laughed and said, "In Monroe, even a cardboard figure of a black has to have a rope around its neck for those crackers to feel safe."

These were the events that led up to the incarceration of the children. Chief Mauney brooded after a dressing-down from Mayor Wilson for having failed to silence Williams and Perry and for attracting the attention of the federal government. He wanted revenge. Mauney waited for his chance, cruising around and watching some very young children playing together— white and black. Finally, he singled out two boys, Hanover Thompson and David Simpson, because he didn't like them. He liked their mothers and had approached both women sexually and been turned down, so he especially didn't like their children. One day he hid in some bushes overlooking a little ditch where the children were playing. David and Hanover were looking for daddy longlegs. They were joined by Betty Lou Sutton, a little white girl who knew the boys because their mothers cleaned her house. The three children always played together, which the chief knew from past experience. Betty Lou slid down the side of the ditch and looked for spiders but soon got bored with the game. She sneaked up to Hanover when he was stooped over, looking in the grass, and kissed him on the cheek. He pushed her away and told her to go away and leave him alone. Betty Lou left and went home. She told her mother she had kissed Hanover. Mrs. Sutton was horrified, scrubbed Betty Lou's mouth with soap, then put her in the bathtub for a real cleansing. She was scolding her daughter so loudly that they did not hear the screen door open and Chief Mauney walk into their front room. Mauney told Mrs. Sutton that her daughter had been raped. The child denied that anything had happened except her kiss on Hanover's cheek, and her mother believed her. Mauney persisted and then left, telling Mrs. Sutton to take her daughter to the doctor for an examination because "niggers lust after our white women." She did not take Betty Lou to the doctor; she believed it had only been a kiss, and she did not have the money for doctor visits. She was frightened of Chief Mauney—he could lose her husband his job as a truck driver. She told her daughter to stay in the yard and not go anywhere. Then she called Mrs. Thompson and Mrs. Simpson and told them, "You black bitches, don't you bring your boys anywhere near my little girl. They immoral. Kissing a pure little white girl."

Chief Mauney picked up the two boys, put them into the local jail, and told everyone who would listen that the boys had raped a little white girl. I don't know how an eight- and ten-year-old could accomplish such an act, but some southerners will believe anything. Williams and Perry tried to intervene but Mauney told them and the mothers of the boys that he had locked them up for their own protection and he could not let them out until some decision was made—to put them in a reform school or keep them in jail. Williams had then gone to see the local United Press reporter stationed in the town, but he did not want to get involved. That was why

Williams had then called Conrad Lynn, not only to act on behalf of the children but to get some publicity about the case.

From the time my plane, the *Golden Hawk,* landed in Charlotte until I returned to New York an unusual feeling took over—as if the current of my blood flow was slowing. My hands, although not icy, were cold and I had a physical sensation of internal trembling, as if all my organs were shivering. I felt unprotected for the first time in my life. At the hotel where I registered in Charlotte the desk people were, to me it seemed, overly pleasant. There was an excess of good will. If they knew the purpose of my visit, I believed their outward charm would turn into rage. I would be in danger. After leaving my bag in the room I left the hotel, following instructions to use an outside telephone for a call to Monroe. I reached Williams and was so relieved I felt like crying. He asked whether I had talked to anyone and, of course, I said no. Then he said to rent a car. "We don't want you at the mercy of bus drivers or passengers. When you reach Monroe call me again from a phone booth at the corner of Main and Magnolia. Okay, you got that?"

Early the next morning I purred into town in my rented gray Plymouth and stepped out into the dust on Magnolia Street to make my phone call. Looking about, I couldn't understand why anyone would want to live in such a place. There were some men standing around; their skin was pale and to me they seemed to have mean facial expressions, particularly around the eyes. They stared openly, without any attempt to hide their interest. Men looked at me in New York but these southerners were different—they knew I was a stranger, someone suspect, especially since I wore big city clothing. Looking down the street I saw there was not one black face in sight. When Williams answered the phone he gave me instructions. I was to interview Mayor Wilson; Chief Mauney; Ashcroft, the editor of the local paper, the *Inquirer;* Judge Price; and District Attorney Richardson, who was also head of the state Democratic Party. For my own safety, we were not to meet until I had completed all the interviews with these white representatives. When I finished I was to go to the home of Dr. Perry, meet the mothers of the children, walk around in the black community, and then spend the night.

My first attempt at an interview was with Mayor Wilson, also the local dentist. He would not see me. Instead, through his nurse, he requested that I submit questions in writing. Then he decided he would only talk before his city council. Finally, he ran out of the office, his nurse confided, leaving a room full of patients and one in the chair. Judge Price broke down enough to show a report from the reform school where Hanover Thompson and David Simpson were being held after a week in the city jail. The report claimed the children's mothers and their homes constituted an unfit environment for the boys. Every time I went to the *Inquirer,* Ashcroft was not in and the clerk did not know how soon he would return. Mrs. Sutton, the mother of the white child, was understandably hysterical because of all the publicity and refused to see anyone. My worst interview was with Chief Mauney, purported to be a member of the Klan and certainly a staunch supporter. He had a round, rather moon face with very white skin and black hair. His hands were strong looking but pudgy and there were black stiff hairs sprouting on his knuckles. He perspired freely and kept wiping his forehead with a grayish handkerchief. I showed him my press pass and asked, "Is it true you have two youngsters in jail here?" The chief didn't answer; instead he said: "Your jus 'bout the purties' little gal that's come tuh our town fur many a moon." I don't know whether he was drooling, but it sounded like it. I looked down, determined not to make eye contact if I could help it. Then came an inspiration. I said: "Would you say that the situation here is inspired by the Communists?" The floodgates opened. Mauney called Williams that "buck nigger Bob," saying he was a Communist, an actual member of the Party. He claimed the "niggers" were happy until Williams came along and stirred them up. There had never been a bit of trouble until he got back from being in the Marines and started acting uppity. He went on in this vein until I was eager to leave the jail. He wasn't drooling. He was spitting all over my pale green suit. I thanked him for the information and he walked me out to my car. For a moment I was afraid he was going to join me but instead he patted my hand and said: "Come back soon, yuh heah? Iffen there's anything ah can do fur you, you jus' holler, heah now?"

At last, tiring of the runaround and carrying my tape recorder, I went to the real boss of the city, the chairman of the Democratic Party, District Attorney Richardson. The DA had his office in a big old white house right near the center of town. The clapboard house was well kept and stood two stories with little green gables at the attic level. Two cement steps led to the porch, which, unlike the rest of the house, was worn and losing its paint. Through a screen door I could look into a varnished hallway that had a spindly-legged plant stand holding a carefully tended fern. I rapped on the door, but no one answered. The house had an empty feeling and I grew uneasy. But in another minute a door opened near the front of the hallway and a tall man with graying hair walked toward me. His face was ruddy and he was wearing a smile that did not seem genuine. The face was smiling but the eyes were watching. I asked if he was District Attorney Richardson and he said yes, he was, and opened the door for me. "Well, little lady," he said. "What can I do for you?" Before I could answer I heard faint sounds coming from the next room. Richardson suggested that we go down the hallway to the back of the building where, he said, his main office was situated. We settled into a large office that looked out onto a sparse garden where the sun was shining on the plants. Again there was noise from the next room and I was sure that someone was tiptoeing across the hall to listen to our conversation. I pretended not to hear anything. If he wanted a witness, let him have one. I knew that in a town so small, Richardson must have heard of my presence, but I showed him my credentials and asked if I could tape record the interview. He said no: "Those infernal machines make me nervous and I can't think straight." "Well, may I take notes?" "Certainly, little lady." Richardson nodded his head majestically. Before we could begin he wanted to know about my family, where they were born, where they lived now, who their mommies and daddies were. He nodded with seeming pleasure when I told him that my father's family owned some cotton factories in Georgia and my mother's cousin was mayor of Palm Beach, Florida. Still another ancestor published a newspaper in South Carolina. I had never met even one of these relatives and had no intention of ever doing so. Roy had visited one branch in Georgia when he was in the air corps. He told me they were "typical southerners." That was our shorthand description for bigots. Richardson was really warming up with this litany of southern heritage and when I brought in a few people from mother's side of the family he determined I was practically a southern belle. I thought it was safe to begin the interview. "As democratic chairman of this state, could you give me a little background on the area and its relationships before talking about the boys in jail?" I asked.

Putting the tips of his fingers together and resting his chin on their points, he began smoothly. "Our Nigras have the best conditions of life in the whole south. Naturally, almost all of them are illiterate and it will take some time to integrate them into the schools as the government has stipulated. Now, I personally have a woman who works for me out at my place and she has about twelve children. They spawn like fish, you know." He chuckled indulgently. "But I can't get them to go to school. They're just naturally lazy. Their school is only five miles from my place and you know they act as if they are too good to walk there and back. They keep wanting what white children have, buses and all that. But they have to earn it."

This conversation was not going anywhere; at least the information was not welcome or accurate. I took a silent breath and jumped in. "What about holding two children in an adult jail?" I tried to make my voice soft and inoffensive but I'm not sure the attempt was successful. My voice was rather deep to begin with, something in the range of Tallulah Bankhead's alto. Fortunately, Richardson was not offended—my southern ancestry still held sway. He removed his chin from the ends of his fingers and clasped them loosely in front of him, across the surface of the desk. He seemed proud of his hands, gazing down at long fingers tapering to well-manicured nails, and he took his time answering my question. "You have to know their history. Hanover has been a problem to the city for quite awhile. He once stole a ham from the back of a restaurant—claimed he was hungry, an obvious lie. Our chief of police has had his eye on him for some time. And the other boy, David, he's just as bad. These boys are potential rapists and we have to stop them right now."

Richardson was getting wound up and this was just what I wanted. I leaned forward in my chair, hiding my real feelings, and appeared to hang on his every word by an alert silence.

"This Nigra organization, the NAACP—I call them the 'nappies'—are all a bunch of Communists." Richardson stopped to laugh at his joke and I think if he had been close enough he would have jabbed an elbow in my ribs to emphasize the word "nappies." "They come down here and stir up our Nigras. And we don't intend to let them get away with it. We're going to run them out of town right along with that leader of theirs who is too smart for his breeches. Now, I'll let you in on a little secret, but don't take notes." Obedient, I put down my pen.

"We don't ever intend to have integration in our sweet little city, not in schools nor anywhere else. I'm only telling you this because you're southern and you understand the situation. So, even though *officially* I go along with the government's ruling, just between us, we in this city will fight to the last man to keep our city clean and pure and free from contamination by culluds."

Richardson continued in this vein, occasionally raising his voice to make a point, but for the most part speaking in a monotone. Where he had started more or less politely with the supposed less hateful expression *Nigra*, he lapsed into *niggers, mongrels, pickaninnies, black bucks, rapists,* and *black bastards*. Richardson denied any knowledge of the Ku Klux Klan despite his police chief's reputed affiliation.

As soon as I could interrupt without showing antagonism, I excused

myself, saying other appointments were waiting. Richardson carried my
tape recorder to the front door and kept his other hand on my elbow, ever
the gallant southern gentleman. Through the screen, just as I reached the
front steps, he said: "Little lady, perhaps we might meet later tonight and
over some drinks and dinner get into this subject a little deeper."

Free of my obligations to interview white officials, I went into the black
community, to the home of Dr. and Mrs. Perry, and the deep, internal
shaking in my body began to ease. The house, sitting on a small hill, had
sandbags all around it and a heavy metal chain guarded the drive. As I
neared the house I resisted a desire to zoom up the hill, remembering the
fortifications. At the top, however, the chain was down and I was able to
park close to the house in the driveway. Dr. Perry opened the door and invited me in, where I was surrounded by what appeared to be the whole
community, all holding guns. The room was almost packed. Perry introduced me to his wife, who greeted me warmly, and Williams introduced
me to Mrs. Thompson and Mrs. Simpson, the mothers of the children. He
explained that walking through the neighborhood might not be safe for
me, so everyone decided to meet at the Perrys'. They would take turns so
everyone would have a chance to speak. We listened to the tape recordings
made during my morning interviews and Lynn remarked that Richardson's vow to retain segregated schools could be used in the defense during
the trial of the two children. Before beginning the interviews Mrs. Perry
took me into the bedroom where I would sleep and gave me a chance to
wash my hands and face. It had been a strenuous day and when she offered
to make me a martini I was delighted. My first recording was with the
mothers of the children, who were, of course, upset and worried. They had
not been allowed in the jail to see the boys and were able to visit only once
at the reform school. Both women cried a little, not for themselves but
imagining the fear and terror their children were experiencing. When the
mothers finished talking, others in the room were eager to have their stories recorded. After several hours, one of the outside guards, a thin, tall
dark man, came into the front room. Silently, he pulled open a bit of the
drapery at the window and pointed out front. At the very edge of the doctor's property was a police car. The guard explained: "Those are two of the
chief's men. They've been there for 'bout an hour."

Conrad Lynn laughed. "In a few more hours they will know you betrayed them, Constance." While we watched, another police car joined the
first and we could see Chief Mauney's moon-shaped face when he leaned
out the car window to talk to one of the other officers. I did not feel happy

or calm; in fact, I was pretty frightened. But no one else showed any fear; in fact there was some merriment, so I hid my feelings. We went on with the interviews and then, about one A.M., another guard came in and said the Klan had gathered nearby and announced that they were going to "fix that Yankee reporter." I was surprised to see Williams signal to two other men, who picked up their rifles and followed him out the door. The three men returned in about half an hour and I asked what had happened. Williams said they had persuaded the Klan leaders to go on out to their barbecue place. He told them: "I'll be real mad if you do anything to my friend, the reporter. And just about the whole neighborhood's in the doc's house right now or around it and they'll be real mad too." What especially amazed me was the bravery and audacity of not just Williams but all of the people I met. They did not show any fear; they joked about the situation and laughed. There was some tension, though, of people under fire. We heard nothing else from the Klan that night. They were apparently intimidated by a community ready to go forth and meet war with war.

Another interruption was a call Dr. Perry received from a patient who was in labor. Again two armed men left with the doctor and were gone for about three hours. Perry came back whistling, in the best of spirits, and announced: "It's a fine baby girl." Everyone began to leave after deciding who would guard the house during the night. I was given a gun and told to keep the blinds drawn in my room. Then Perry took me to the kitchen, where he opened two cans of tomato soup, dumped the contents into a shiny, Revereware pot, added water, put it on the stove, and then ground black pepper into the liquid—so much I thought he would never stop. He assured me it would be good for the nerves and help me sleep. If I didn't cough myself to death first, was my thought, but I kept it to myself. Finally in bed I thought I'd never sleep, imagining Klan members eluding the guards and sneaking up to get me. The gun next to my bed wasn't a comfort but I finally fell asleep from complete exhaustion.

The next morning after breakfast Perry, Williams, and Mr. Rochelle Thomas, in one car, and four men in another car followed me to Charlotte, where I was to catch my plane. One car led and the other followed, sandwiching me in between. All the men were armed and holding the rifles up in clear view through the car windows. I was told it was legal to carry arms in North Carolina, if they were openly displayed. What a strange part of the country is the south. A few miles out of Monroe I sensed a shadow pulling alongside on the left. It was a Monroe police car carrying four cops. They pulled alongside, keeping abreast and glaring at me. It was an icy cold morning and my hands were almost numb, even with the gloves I was wearing. The cops did not make me feel warmer. Were they going to run me off the road? It was with great relief that one of the cars carrying my friends pulled up, almost to the police car's bumper, and forced it to speed ahead. The lead car did not leave enough space for the cops to pull in front. My friends in the other car then dropped back and again I was safely sandwiched front and back. The cops pulled off the road and apparently returned to Monroe.

I trembled all the way to Charlotte, where there might be partial integration and perhaps safety. I checked out of the hotel, returned my rented car, and started for the airport. However, when I got in a cab, the state patrol followed. Nearing the field, a second state patrol car joined the procession. At the terminal two patrolmen followed me in and stood at the exit. I hoped they were there to see that I left the south. After a final phone call to my friends in Monroe, the last precaution, should there be any trouble, was a note in my pocket: "Call Dr. Perry in Monroe, Atlantic 3–3783. Tell him the reporter is in trouble." The note was to be handed to any black person in the airport.

Dr. Perry and Robert Williams suffered for their refusal to accept the dictums of white authorities in Monroe. Perry was accused of performing an abortion on a white girl named Lily Mae. She had visited his office and requested that he perform such surgery, which he refused to do. Perry was a practicing, believing Catholic and followed the teaching of his church. He was convicted nonetheless and sentenced to the chain gang. The only frivolity surrounding this catastrophe was a joke that swept through the black community when they heard the accusations. It was said that the spelling of her name, "Lily Mae," should simply be changed to "May." People who knew her said she would, could, and did as often as possible. It turned out that she was a friend of Police Chief Mauney. The mayor had coveted Perry's house and choice land and was able to purchase it for about one-quarter of its value. The only reason anything was paid was to prevent suspicion in case the Federal government was roused to investigate. Perry served several months but was forever banished from Monroe. He was told, "Don't you even fly over this town in an airplane."

Robert Williams was forced to leave Monroe or face life on a chain gang. Sometime after my visit there was a skirmish against the Klan by members of the black community. The community was victorious but a riot continued to punctuate their action and act as a warning—the Klan should never return. During the riot an unsuspecting elderly white couple drove through the neighborhood and their car was surrounded and stopped by a gang of youngsters in front of Williams's home. Williams intervened and took the couple into his home to keep them from possible harm. The couple eventually went on their way but were interviewed by the local press. Although they made no accusations and, in fact, told the reporter about Williams's support, the police chief would not accept their version. He and some men went to arrest Williams, but fortunately news had reached him of Mauney's intentions soon enough for him to escape. He hid out in New York, where I met him in Harlem, at the home of Mae Mallory, a formidable fighter for equality and justice. Williams was smuggled out of the U.S. and eventually reached Cuba, where he was greeted and welcomed by friends. Many Cubans had read of the "Kissing Case" and the role played by Williams and Perry in the community. Williams was saluted as a hero and eventually honored by a meeting with Fidel Castro.

The jailing of Hanover Thompson and David Simpson I named the "Kissing Case." Other papers, the *New York Post,* for one, then published a series of articles under the same title and the mistreatment of the children became known worldwide. A series was published in *Correspondence* titled "I Went Behind the Iron Curtain—in USA." The editor added an announcement: "Coming! The Inside Story from Monroe, N.C., as recorded on tapes. Exclusive!"

❧ 23 ❧

Nello left the country in 1953, the year that the election of Dwight D. Eisenhower signaled the continued reign of Wisconsin Senator Joseph McCarthy. It was the first time in twenty-four years that the Republicans controlled administration of the government. For a brief time we hoped McCarthy might be discredited and removed because a report on his actions was issued by a Senate privileges and election subcommittee claiming that he was activated by personal interests. The only pleasant remembrance of 1953 is that Ralph Ellison won the National Book Award for *Invisible Man*. When I called to congratulate him he was his usual reserved, slightly austere self, but quietly pleased—he said it was unexpected, although his agent had felt there was a good chance he would receive this recognition. It was also a year of the continued war in Korea. I don't remember that we spent much time discussing the war; earlier the Johnsonites had taken a stand against all wars. Although we felt that members of the Communist Party were enemies, we were dismayed when thirteen Communist leaders were convicted by a federal grand jury in New York of conspiracy and advocating forcible overthrow of the U.S. Government. Would the government act against us next? That was our main concern. The climate in the U.S. did not improve. Later in the year Julius and Ethel Rosenberg were executed in Sing Sing Prison. This was a terrible and historic event. They were the first civilians ever executed in the U.S. for espionage. It was claimed they had given secrets about the atomic bomb to Russia. None of us believed they were guilty of anything more than membership in a radical organization. There were protests throughout the world against the execution.

We were not surprised when 1954 began with the same witch-hunt mentality against anything or anyone liberal. President Eisenhower announced that his policy was to regain the initiative in the world fight against Communism. He also revealed that over two thousand government employees had been fired under the administration's new security system.

281

Senator McCarthy was so fanatical and egotistical that he decided to take on the army. In April, hearings were conducted by the Senate Permanent Subcommittee on Investigations, of which he was chairman. McCarthy accused Secretary of the Army Robert T. Stevens and Army Counsel John G. Adams of standing in the way of rooting out Communists in the military. According to Stevens and Adams, McCarthy was miffed because preferential treatment for one of his staff members, G. David Schine, was refused. Taking on the military proved to be a big mistake and signaled the eventual end of McCarthy. Some of us believed that when the American public saw McCarthy's crude and vicious behavior on television they turned against him. At the end of July a Senate select committee voted to censure McCarthy for conduct unbecoming a senator. And in December he was condemned in a vote of a special session of the U.S. Senate for his conduct in Senate committees. We all breathed a sign of relief but were still concerned about actions taken in January 1955 by President Eisenhower—approximately three thousand people were discharged from federal employment within a five-month period, May to September, because they were considered security risks.

During these difficult times we did not gain new members and even lost a few. We also had problems selling *Correspondence* or getting subscriptions. The newspaper had been placed on the subversive publications list by the U.S. Attorney General and readers were afraid to add their names to our mailing list. *Correspondence* was also denied second-class mailing rights and one issue in July 1954 was termed unmailable because it expressed sympathy with shop-floor workers rebelling against inhuman assemblyline work. We were accused of trying to incite murder and assassination. Lyman was giving more and more money to bail us out of debt because for some reason we kept printing thousands of copies when we could sell only a few hundred.

Nello's letters came every week, sometimes more often, pointing out what was wrong with the group, that we needed to get out into the world and forgo so much introspection. He was still convinced of a coming mass upheaval in the U.S. and urged us to circulate *Correspondence* and talk to people, especially in factories. Although the rank and file were never privy to the internal machinations of the leadership, I was fortunate in that Nello still confided in me. I in turn was able to let him know about the conflicts and tensions in our small group. Raya was the first to indicate dissatisfaction, usually the first sign when members began to break away. Grace joined Nello in London, where she collaborated in writing a pamphlet,

"Facing Reality." It was motivated by the Hungarian revolution, when in October of 1956 that entire society erupted against the Communists. Workers in the largest factories selected their own leaders and formed rank-and-file committees. These committees then met with those in other factories and formed a network of resistance. Their demands were an abolishment of quotas, a raise in salaries, and control over health and safety issues. Soviet tanks responded and although there were sporadic strikes for weeks, sometimes paralyzing some industrial areas, the uprising was crushed. But then in June there was an uprising in Poland and the formation of workers' groups demanding control over production. The formation or actualization of such committees and groups of workers had been predicted years earlier by the Johnsonites as the future in America. We had said and preached there would emerge against Capitalism these self-organized groups of workers who would choose their own leaders and reorganize the production processes. For such political theory, the Trotskyists called us the "stratospherists." In addition to lauding and describing the revolutionary actions in Hungary and Poland, the pamphlet "Facing Reality" asserted that Nkrumah's nationalist movement, struggling for independence of the African nation, was inspiring revolutionary change elsewhere. It elaborated on Nello's theories about the black struggle in the U.S., claiming that Africans fighting for their own freedom would stimulate and inspire workers in industrialized nations. Nkrumah eventually became prime minister of Ghana.

Raya was sharply critical of the pamphlet on the basis that its conclusions deviated from Marxism. My first reaction was that she was resentful because Grace had been chosen to work on the pamphlet with Nello—envy, I thought, and the old, never quite hidden antagonism between the two women was still in bloom. I also remembered how she cried and pleaded to accompany Nello to England. It is possible that in some subterranean part of her mind envy and love and jealousy played a part, but if so, these were superficial reactions. I smothered these petty suspicions, admitting to myself that Raya was a serious person whose politics ruled her life. I don't remember all of her arguments against the pamphlet except for something to do with statism as opposed to State Capitalism. Here I was lost completely because I didn't know the difference between the two. Raya also disagreed with the section on Nkrumah's national movement triggering rebellion in other nations. My attitude was thoroughly partisan—she disagreed with Nello; ergo, she was wrong. On the local level, Raya spoke about making *Correspondence* more explicitly political. That was another area I could not understand—what more need we do? It seemed political enough to me. But having made up my mind, I did not pay much attention to the arguments. Some of the comrades said that what Raya really wanted was an intellectual magazine. Within a fairly short time, she split with the organization and she and her followers took with them all of the desks, file cabinets, refrigerator, chairs, display boards, and books. Our Detroit headquarters was left with only a pile of back issues of *Correspondence*. Si Owens, for whom I had written *Indignant Heart,* followed Raya. She started a newspaper called *News and Letters* and proclaimed herself leader of a "Marxist-humanism" organization.

Raya's abandonment so shocked the remaining members that their anger gave rise to renewed enthusiasm. Nello suggested that James Boggs, a black auto worker and long-time activist in Johnson-Forest, become editor of our newspaper. All of us increased our monthly dues and determined to succeed although we were now down to about twenty people. We wrote and published pamphlets, Nello sent articles, and then he wrote *Every Cook Can Govern: A Study of Democracy in Ancient Greece.*

Group enthusiasm did not last long and as a result my tendency toward too much introspection burgeoned. I began to feel tired of living a life in two worlds, one at work and the other in a clandestine organization. FBI surveillance continued, even after Nello was forced to leave the country. The agents visited my friends and employers, not asking for information but giving information—marriage to a black man, a dangerous Communist, and untrustworthy. During the Hungarian Revolution there was a twenty-four-hour watch on my apartment for several weeks. The agents did not attempt to hide. On the contrary, they stayed in plain sight and followed me openly when I left the apartment. They also followed any person with whom I went out. One friend, John Hayes, whom I had dated when I was first modeling, was a gung ho American who had enlisted in the army and served in the war. One evening when he left my home in Long Island he was approached by two FBI agents. They displayed their badges and asked him to get into their car. When he demurred they said they just wanted to talk to him privately. If he refused, they would take him down to their offices. John of course agreed and they sat him between them in their car. One of the agents said that they had investigated his past and saw that he was a loyal, true American. They wondered whether he knew he was mixed up with a dangerous Communist, Constance James, who was married to a black man. The black man was even more dangerous and had been arrested and deported. These were people, the agents asserted, who planned to destroy democracy by tearing down the government. John's only comment to the agents was that he had not seen or heard me say anything about destroying democracy. The two men eventually let John out of their car, but they followed him home. On another day, Nobbie and his friend, Malcolm, were given ice cream sodas at our local drug store by two agents and then questioned. Neither child responded; these were strangers and they had been taught not to talk to such people. But they did drink up their sodas before running home.

Again I was wearied by what seemed to be endless splits, which I'd survived, beginning on the West Coast with the Socialist Party. Added to what was actually the beginning of a disillusionment was concern about supporting Nobbie financially and emotionally. I was forced to work, but he needed attention. My current job was with Jason Phillips, a television producer of the *Quentin Reynolds Show.* I wrote story boards, went out as assistant on shoots, appeared in some of the films as a bit player, called stations to request time on the air, and was consulted by the show's editor when cutting film. A less pleasant task was to see that Quentin did not get too drunk before the morning's shoot. Sometimes I did not reach home until it was bedtime for Nobbie. One evening his babysitter said he had been in tears when she picked him up at nursery school. After she left I bathed him and got him ready for bed. Then I sat with him until he began to explain what had happened. Trying not to cry, he said at nursery school the children had to line up and each pair was to hold hands. One little girl had pulled her hand out of his and said she would not walk with a *nigger.* Nobbie did not even know what the child was talking about; it was the first time he had heard such a word. He only knew it meant something bad, something that separated him from the other children. My heart hurt. Quite suddenly, and apparently without volition, my own experiences when around Nobbie's age almost overwhelmed me. Here we were in the liberal northern city of New York and my child was experiencing the pain of bigotry and discrimination that my parents brought on others by their southern attitudes. What had changed in almost thirty years? Nothing.

The next day I went to Nobbie's school and tried to convince the administrator that something was seriously wrong and needed correction. The white woman met my recounting of the incident with a blank stare and then told me I was exaggerating the incident and not to worry about such minor problems. Too infuriated to be coherent over "such minor problems" as the wellbeing of my child, I left her office. I didn't trust myself to answer or speak to her any further. The next week I found a mixed-race nursery not far from our Ravenswood apartment. After a few days Nobbie seemed to have settled into the new place quite happily. For about a month, that particular problem seemed to have been solved, although travel time for me was difficult to arrange and I was always racing, always out of breath. Then suddenly one morning while I was combing Nobbie's hair and getting him ready for school, he looked at himself and said, "I wish I was white." My breath stopped, but I didn't reply, just waited to see what would come next. He continued: "Or I wish I was black." During work that day I made an appointment with Nobbie's teacher and met him just before school let out. I told him what Nobbie had said that morning and was surprised when he smiled. He asked me to walk to the door that led to the play area. "What do you see?" he asked. At first I didn't know what to look for and then said, "Black and white children." The teacher said Nobbie's reaction was perfectly normal. He was the only brown child in the place, and that was why he wanted to be either black or white.

For a month or two everything appeared normal, but one night I got home late and found two shelves of my books shredded. Nobbie had a toy axe that he had used against the books. He stood at my side, watching and waiting. I turned to him, broke into tears, and said, "Why? Why?" He began to cry and said: "Mommy, I wish you were home." I wiped away his tears, hugged him, and promised to stay home for awhile. The next day I quit my job and hoped we could get by on unemployment insurance. Nobbie needed me and nothing was more important than his wellbeing.

I resigned as co-organizer of the group and settled down to being a fulltime mother. Although most of the New York Johnsonites remained friends, I began pulling away from group activities. Nello had arranged with Lyman that the money he had been receiving for many years should now go to me for child support. Lyman and Freddy must have heard of my apparent disaffection. It did not take long for news to reach me that they were questioning whether I was spending the seventy-five dollars per month on myself, on personal items. Since Nobbie needed dental work, straightening his teeth at a cost of one thousand dollars, I didn't bother to defend myself, just tried to put such pettiness out of my mind.

I'd been through so many splits in radical organizations that I'm surprised I did not anticipate the next one until Filomena Daddario paid a visit, presumably to recruit me. I liked Fil even though she too had gone to bed with Nello. At least she waited until I was off the scene and he was in England. She used to sing for us privately at home, when we had small groups together. Fil's voice was not strong but it was pure and sweet and she had a charming way of performing without self-consciousness. During Fil's visit she did not mention the word, "split" but talked about her admiration for James and Grace Lee Boggs. She hinted at differences and some estrangement with Glaberman. Fil declared that it was not possible for Nello to run the group long-distance, from London.

Soon after Fil's visit, I heard that Lyman and Freddy and Grace and James had ganged up against Glaberman and the rest of the Detroit group and left the organization. Lyman immediately wrote and declared he would no longer send seventy-five dollars a month for Nobbie's support. I don't know how it was managed, perhaps Lyman owned the title, but they took the name *Correspondence* with them. In their talks and publications, they agitated for a revival of virtue and morality in the U.S. And their ideas for a policy of Americanization of Marxism were to approach people in the American vernacular and integrate Socialist themes with traditions familiar to the people of the U.S. Instead of an earlier vision of releasing the creativity of workers through revolution, they substituted a rather amorphous conception of the development of the "whole person." Social and human ties, and a more human way to live, could be built within Capitalism. It was obvious that they had lost confidence in the possibility of any substantial change in the U.S. The group met regularly every summer at the Paines' summer home on Sutton Island and tape recorded their discussions. Eventually they published *Conversations in Maine: Exploring Our Nation's Future,* a book based on the Sutton Island recordings. They abandoned Marxism and instead of class struggle their publications sprouted with abstractions such as "freedom, justice, and community." What they aimed to do was advance toward a new society by individually developing the whole person. Part of this was supposed to be achieved by developing one's place, meaning a particular neighborhood or block or city. With my Johnsonite training such ideas sounded like nonsense. Raya at least remained serious about her belief in Marx's theories and continued to write serious books. Among these were "The Marxist-Humanist Theory of State Capitalism: Selected Writings," and "Marxism and Freedom: From 1776 until Today." Whether one agreed with Raya's point of view and conclusions or not, she was not someone who could be easily dismissed.

The remnants of our organization took the name "Facing Reality," which was the name of the pamphlet on the Hungarian uprising. Glaberman went to teach at Wayne State University and had a small success in interesting students to the extent of agreement, but they did not join the organization. In 1962, reviewing the two splits, Nello wrote to say, "The movement which we started has been broken up almost to bits."

At a distance, Nello and I became close again, and letters began arriving as well as stories for Nobbie. In one letter he sounded quite melancholy, and because of his continued need to write and keep me in his life, I felt his remarks referred to what we had lost in our personal relationship. He said he was distressed when he thought of the work he used to do for the group. Nello did not feel bitter; the feeling was more of regret—that he had wasted his strength, his time, and his health on something absolutely useless. As the months went by, the bond between us returned to what it had been when Nello had shown his love mainly through writing. Over the years, he sent me each of his books, all inscribed in shaky handwriting. On the flyleaf of *The Future in the Present* he wrote, "For Constance, Past, Present & Future, Nello"; on *Spheres of Existence*, "For Constance, We Have Shared, Nello." Sometime later I sent him some Mozart, Beethoven, and Bach recordings, which he said he missed hearing. By return mail he wrote, "Dearest Constance, Your parcel of music was very welcome. It brought back to me some of the happiest times of the old days. I expect that was why you sent it. Also because it had done that to you and you were certain it would do the same to me." The letter was signed: "As ever."

Nello had always invented bed-time stories for Nobbie, making them up as he went along and telling them to him while we sat on his bed. The stories were the adventures of two children, Bad Boo-boo-loo and Good Boongko. The boys belonged to a club with characters named Lizzie the Lizard, Flibbert the Flea, Storky the Stork, Moby Dick, General Sharkenhower, Big Bruno, Peter the Painter, and Nicholas the Worker. Nobbie was included in the club under the name of Choongko. Some of the stories told of ancient mythology, such as the Trojan horse, and there were a few about Michelangelo. He did not omit William Tell and his arrow. The Tell story ended on a political note with Bad Boo Boo Loo saying that William Tell was "one of those who helped Switzerland to gain its independence."

It was not easy to leave the shelter of the Johnson group and the ideology that had been the core of my life for so many years. There is emotional safety in agreement with others and I was unused to thinking for myself except when dreaming. For the first time in over fifteen years there wasn't the umbrella of an organization and no one to tell me what to think. I was frightened at being out in the open on my own, feeling unprotected. I felt I was holding onto a rope over an abyss, never knowing whether my hands would slip or if I could climb up to safety. But what was safety? A Catholic priest leaving his orders must feel as I did—is he betraying his God, his people? My ideas had always been grandiose and now my thoughts were that I was betraying humanity, particularly minorities. Something terrible was happening; there had been my life, every day with assumptions of purpose, usefulness, meaning. Around me had been people whom I believed to be important, sure of themselves, so sure that history was theirs and they were necessary to history. I had never felt insignificant or that my feelings were in any way insignificant, yet I had been held in a vise, unable to exercise even ordinary, normal actions and reactions. The "tendency" had made all the decisions: twice they had interfered with essays and books I had written. When Nello was taken to Ellis Island it was they who decided that I and our baby should remain on the West Coast and prove to the government that they had separated a family. It was the tendency that prevented me from exercising my normal instinctive reactions to be with my husband, an ill husband—having ulcer attacks so terrible that we had a surgeon standing by. Though rebellious, I behaved. What the leadership decided, I carried out. But I knew if I voiced my protestations they would think I was peculiar to raise such ordinary questions. They were indifferent to the products of feelings.

My acceptance, except for quite unspoken anger, was almost nihilist. I became isolated from everything and everyone, even from myself. At times a kind of apathy overtook me—anything that could be done easily or naturally lost its value. Had I accepted meanings where I unconsciously recognized there were none? Was it only my physical body trapped in my surroundings that overwhelmed me or was it ideas that I held for twenty years? I began to understand Sartre's existentialism, particularly *La Nausée* and his character Roquentin. Standing on a beach, Roquentin picks up a stone to skim and then is overcome: "I saw something which disgusted me; I no longer know whether it was the stone or the sea." Anxiety that had overtaken me off and on over the years returned and decided to sit at my elbow instead of flitting back and forth. It would be years before I could recover from the fright of being free.

Thus ends the first half of my life. As painful and sometimes disorienting as those years were, I would not make substantial changes if I could. To have been loved unendingly by a man such as Nello makes it impossible to harbor even a whiff of bitterness. We were never strangers. We were linked inexorably from our first meeting until the day he died, blood relatives, just as in families. Whatever our quarrels, kinship remained. And when I married again years later, Nello called us his family and stayed in our home whenever he came to the United States.

And I do not regret my years in leftwing organizations. Most of those whom I knew were good people, seriously intent on changing society so there would be equality—in treatment, in housing, in food, clothing, and the nurturing of personality, if only in the abstract. The experiences I had in these leftist organizations reinforced my natural opposition to fanatical monism, stereotypes, aggressive nationalism, bigotry, bias, smallmindness, and limits of thoughts and expression. When I was a member I was as righteous and all-knowing as any member of a sect. Never again will I believe that I or anyone else is in *sole* possession of the truth: about what to think; how to live; what to do or be. It is dangerous to think that only you are right, that you know the truth and all whom you know must agree or something is wrong with them.

Literature, history, anthropology, and art make clear that differences of cultures and personalities are as deep as the similarities (which make us human). We are enlarged by the rich variety in the world if we open our minds to differences. We become more civilized. If we cannot or do not open ourselves to the infinite differences among peoples in the world, we become irrationally prejudiced, filled with hate, and, at the extreme, we wish to murder those who are different. If Hitler's death camps haven't changed our thinking about racism there is not much hope for humankind. There is only one way to rid ourselves of bigotry and hate and that is through knowledge. By itself education will not rid the world of aggressiveness or dislike for the *stranger* (in religion, color of skin or culture). But studying the history, anthropology, culture, and laws of other countries may break down the bias that comes from fear of the other, or unknown. If we can appreciate what is in another person's heart and mind, we enrich our own lives a millionfold.